Also by Greg Dinner

A Murmuration of Starlings
Narcissus In Utero

A
REQUIEM
FOR
HANIA

Greg Dinncr

Dinner, Greg.
A Requiem For Hania / Greg Dinner

For further information contact
Ogham & Dabar Books
Kilrateera
Mountshannon
Country Clare
Republic of Ireland
V94 H9YN
Visit: **www.gregdinner.com**

Printed by Ingram Spark

ISBN: 978-1-7377743-0-3

This is a work of fiction. Names, characters, places and incidents either are the product of the author's imagination or are used fictitiously, and any resemblance to actual persons living or dead, businesses, companies, events or locales is entirely coincidental.

Excerpts of this novel have appeared in 'The Galway Review'

For my Parents,
And for Deborah
All deeply missed

And as always
For Annie
Who holds me up and
Stands alongside

The following is a work of fiction.
It was largely inspired by true events.

And a story that was told....

We leave something of ourselves behind when we leave a place, we stay there, even though we go away. And there are things in us that we can find again only by going back there.

Pascal Mercier
"Night Train To Lisbon"

When I discover who I am, I'll be free.

Ralph Ellison
"Invisible Man"

Prelude

Trisagion:

Hymn of Prayer and Remembrance

She shouts out in anger. In memory. She shouts louder still, this young woman. She cries out, all she is, was, might be. No harmony here. Only dissonance. Moments not passed, rather living and reliving as she was and is and will be.

There was a story she had been told, but she no longer remembers. She no longer hears the words. She no longer hears the music. There once was music. Now there is silence. And in the silence, resonating emptiness, whispers once shared, fear once exhaled, prayers once uttered, she, you, we...exist.

She does not know where she is. She walks along a forest path. Light peeks in, out, like a shy child, trickling in here and there, light through pine reaching high above her, witnessing too. She cannot remember the name of the forest, only that she feels she has been here before. The path has been well trod. Footprints turned to dust, long ago perhaps, or not so long ago. She simply cannot remember, just as she cannot recall why she has come here. She tries to find answers, but none are found.

Silence surrounds her, envelops her. Not even birdsong, and she listens carefully. Not an insect buzzing. Perhaps she is deaf? But she knows she is not deaf, any more than she is blind. Blinded, perhaps, but not blind.

She bends down on the path, picks up a handful of dirt and stone and pine needles. The smell of the forest explodes into her nose, her mouth, her lungs. So she is alive. She was afraid she might not be, but she is. She stands again and as she does the forest all around bursts into the smell of the forest that she somehow remembers: the pine, the primrose, the ivy and moss. The wind. She can't hear it, but she feels it against her brow, her face, feels it pass. Noiselessly pass. How strange that it should speak to her not with a song through trees, but gently placing its whispering fingers on her cheek as if to say I am the wind, you are here, we are here, we take this walk together. You will not hear me but you heard me once, and will hear me again.

As if to say: you are alive. This is not death. You will know death, but this is not it.

She smiles, just slightly, and lets the forest wrap around her, the bluebells, the horsetail, blackthorn and bramble, hogweed, nightshade. Musical canon, each

3

flower, each plant and shrub contributing its own contrapuntal melody, one following the other, variation on a theme, the same theme reflecting one to the next, repeating one to the next, singular but a part of the whole, the place, the notes still in silence, the music in silence.

And repetition. There is repetition, with the slightest, still silent variation.

Void of sound, she imagines the music plays. It plays for her. The notes. The canon. She imagines and it is so.

Walking then further along, the darkness, this place, the path narrowing, the forest drawing her in, further in. Protecting her in its way, but not protecting. Others it could not protect. Solace perhaps, but unable to prevent what was, what happened here.

She does not know what happened here.

She continues through the high grass. She feels the blades and seeded tops brush against her thighs. She sees patterns of the breeze paint brushstrokes over the canvas that is this clearing, a work of art at once life affirming but also life destroying. A canvas painted by whispers murmured long ago, here in this place, whispering her name if she could but hear it, whispering her, body and soul.

She walks to the edge of the clearing where the grasses comes to an immediate end and where she comes to a sharp stop. The clearing breaks here and drops over some four or five meters, below which is a quiet lake, a pond really, no more. This silent place. Fluid graveyard of the dead, the void of their voices and cries buried below, imagined, reimagined, but not heard.

The water does not move. Still, reflecting like a looking glass. She above looking below and she sees herself. Her image. She recognizes who she is, or who she must be. Only then does she realize, below, on the far side of the water, stands another, a woman also, somehow like her yet not like her. Older, much older with hair now white and lines of time upon her face and an expression that speaks as much of the past as it does of the present. And this place.

She, the older one, looks around, at the water reflecting her white hair, her tired eyes, the lines in her face. How did I get here, she wonders? Why am I here? I am here because of her, the older woman thinks. Or she because of me. My memories, my dreams. My nightmares. Here there are nightmares, but I fear to

4

remember. I would run but I am old and I am tired and I can run no longer.

She sighs, this older woman. It is the sigh of one who has seen too much, and suffered, and would choose to see no longer. It is so.

Funny, she thinks, I can see the water just beyond me, there, here, reflecting. In it I can see the younger woman, watching me. Around me I see the trees of forest ahead, behind. But I cannot hear them. I cannot hear the music. I wonder if that is because I no longer care to hear the music.

The forest has its secrets. The forest keeps her safe and makes her fearful. Do not speak here. Remain always quiet, alert. Hide beneath ground cover. They might come. Who are they? You know who they are and they might come. The older woman is afraid. They might come.

They came.

She knows there is something she must remember. A journey. An experience. A silent scream. A life. A life extinguished. A death. Or many. She must remember, but she cannot remember, try though she might.

She looks away, this older woman, and sees at the edge of the trees, emerging slowly, walking cautiously with a stick leading and supporting and steadying, walking towards the small lake's edge, a pond's edge really, she sees him.

No, she does not know his name either. But knows him. And knows him not at all. Does not recognize him.

He stares at the older woman, near but not near. He sees, across from her, on the other side of the water, standing above the water where the land continues, higher, a younger woman too.

He looks at them, the old woman, the young woman. He does not know their names. He does not know why this place. Why he walks in this forest. He only knows that he belongs here. That here reflected there are notes that play out his life, his name, which he cannot remember, who he is, which he cannot remember. He can see the notes as he sees the trees behind and before him, as he sees the blue sky above him. He knows he belongs here. He knows the notes he sees before his own eyes dictate the song of a heart and a memory and a dream and a nightmare too. A symphony of the soul. His soul. He knows he has created these notes this music this language where first one instrument then another then a third follows the first then the second then the third and they are the same but not the same, counterpoint, repeat, you must repeat because in repetition and imitation and deviation there is meaning, finally, there is meaning. There is life. His life.

It is at that moment that the older man who has come here creaking with his stick pointing out a path that will lead to revelation and redemption, that moment when he has seen at the water's edge, on the other side, an older woman turn her head as if frightened or in shock, and the younger woman standing higher, above, react as if confused and quizzical and he himself not knowing them but somehow knowing them and hearing nothing but seeing the notes before his eyes, it is at that moment that he drops this stick that has led him to this place, this place he knows but does not know, raises his arms, his hands, raises them, then as if waiting, he will stop, wait, and finally, raises them further, sharply, slightly, only to let them drop slightly as well.

Then as his hands drop sharply, slightly, his palms raised as if holding up the sky, holding perhaps time itself, he now hears the primal cry of a single musical note, a note he recognizes, calling out to him in pain and remembrance and the moment past and the moment future and that same note that the older woman suddenly hears too the cry of exaltation and invocation and atonement and the younger woman too acknowledges that the silence is broken by a single sound, child's cry, mother's cry, human cry, life cry and death cry of a single note that she hears playing on the wind there, here, now.

And they begin to hear the story. And the story will be retold. The truth told, retold, diverts, becomes lost, becomes found, following an inevitable path, an inevitable journey. They will listen. They will hear.

They hear the first scream of life bursting forth.

They hear themselves, one and together.

They each separately, and together, finally hear the song.

They each separately, and together, finally hear the music. And their journey can begin. But only just the beginning. Only the first step. Thus listen. Witness. Hear.

Kyrie. Kyrie Eleison.

It begins.

Warsaw

Summer, 2006

"Oh God! Oh!"

Muttered quietly, a head turning on a pillow, somewhere between fear and gentleness, between dream and nightmare, her eyes burst open, startled, unexpected. Agnieszka Janiec, Aga, awakens with a start. Shakes her head, dispelling the confusion and chaos of her sleep. Her loose cotton t-shirt clings to her neck and shoulders. Sweat drenched. Dreams do that to her sometimes. So too do the Warsaw summer nights already hot and humid, made worse by the Vistula River running through, wet and hot and close even as the dawn arrives.

Aga stares up at the bright white ceiling, with its wide gently whirling fan unsuccessfully attempting to push air around the large room, trying to hold onto the dream even as it fades from view. She feels as if she is trying to hold onto a lot these days, herself mostly. Sometimes she feels a bit at sea; now is such a time. A bit lost from herself. Rudderless. Such feelings come and go.

All the while the blades of the fan slowly turn, around, around, around…

She looks to the other side of the bed, where Stefan, her lover, lies snoring just slightly, oblivious to the world. In some ways oblivious to her. He seems at ease with himself, his own dreams. In control of such. That is the way he is. The urge to reach out to him, to run her fingers over his brow, push back his long graying hair, hold her hand against his gentle face, passes quickly. Her hand moves, then stops in check. At the moment, this moment, she prefers her own silence, not his embrace. Not right now.

So she watches him quietly, this man more than twice her age, who can be gentle and cruel and indifferent and concerned and funny and arrogant and forgiving all at once. And never once. Aga had met him some two or three years ago when he directed her at the Ateneum. The play was forgettable, her performance more so, but Stefan was not. He was daring, challenging, indifferent to audiences and enjoyed being a thorn in the side of the government of the day. He took risks and she liked that. She was a risk, just as he was. Being his lover came easily, came naturally. She found it easy to acquiesce to his demands as a director, just as easy to acquiesce to his demands as a man and a lover.

She knew what to expect from Stefan Marcin. She knew what to proffer. Others warned her. Actresses had come and gone. But Aga too chose to take risks.

Despite the age difference—he was over sixty, she barely thirty--Aga found him dynamic, challenging. Alive. That mattered. So she willed herself to take the challenge and she took it. The doubts remain, but never really take control; she simply keeps them to herself.

Her glance flits around the room: his minimal taste, his piece of art on the wall, his things. Here she is a shadow, not a mistress but a silent player on his imaginary stage; while others no doubt mutter about such things, for now she is happy enough with her choice. Let him think he is molding her into his creation. The truth is more complex and it is her truth.

Aga gets out of bed, throws off her t-shirt and walks quietly down the upstairs corridor to the shower room. She stares at her naked image in the mirror, her strawberry blond hair, tousled and uncombed, her blue eyes, her breasts small almost like a young girl's, challenging and insistent. Her image stares back at her, neither curious nor confused but thoughtful somehow: how did she get to this place? Where does she go from here?

She shakes her head, just slightly, frowns, just slightly, then turns and climbs into the shower. She turns on the water as hot as she can take it, letting it beat against her forehead and face, then the back of her head, her shoulders, the small of her back, washing away thoughts she prefers not to have. Eyes closed she stands motionless, solid, not statuesque because she is not a statue, is not beautiful, but rather as one gathering her surroundings until such are within her, making her strong, accepting, at ease rather than on edge with the world into which she must shortly emerge. She turns again, facing the water beating against her face and chest, waking her, enriching her, turns it to cold, as cold as she can take it, refusing to pull away until she can take it no longer.

She emerges, shivering, grabs a towel, draws it over her, quickly runs it through her hair, then throws on a bathrobe hanging on the door. She turns the collar up around her neck, leaves the bathroom and walks downstairs to the open plan kitchen and living room. Stefan had originally bought the ground floor below this as an office for his theatre and film company and continues to use the offices as such, although at the moment his work is quiet so there is little activity. He subsequently bought the second and third floors of the five story building and converted them into a large duplex apartment. He had once worked on a film in New York and had stayed in an artist's loft in Manhattan. He had said he wanted to recreate such in Warsaw and this was the closest he could come. Thus he kept open space, with brick or stone walls where possible, minimal rooms with as few belongings as he could manage, excepting for his few pieces of art and various posters of classic American films or those projects he himself had directed. The result was an apartment at once interesting and sterile, authentic as a director's space but not as a Warsaw business or home. Aga liked being here for the precise reason that she could leave if the time came. And she knew the time would come. She kept her own studio apartment in the north of Warsaw, in Nowolipki, for just that time. She could have rented it out if she had wanted. Used it as income in the quiet times. But somehow she just left things as they were. A bit of a safety net, she told herself.

Stefan's kitchen on the first floor of the apartment is important to him. He fancies himself an excellent cook and enjoys entertaining those whose talents he seeks and those whose talents made him what he is. Cooking was never of much interest to Aga, but a morning cup of coffee is. So she makes herself the mandatory cappuccino from his even more mandatory espresso machine, then lets herself out onto the balcony where she can gaze down at the street below and watch the day begin.

Stefan's apartment is on Mokotowska, just south of the old town, a narrow, mostly residential street. Aga stands on the balcony quietly sipping her coffee. From an apartment block across the road a man emerges in shorts and hurries away on his business. A delivery van races along and passes. Then there is silence.

Above she hears the screeches of some starlings that race across the sky then disappear. Several swifts soar down from buildings above, gliding around a street corner then quickly gain height, only to drop low again. Theirs is like an avian ballet, movement of beauty and abandon. A sense of possibility.

A slight noise behind breaks her reverie. She turns. Stefan stands watching her.

"You're up early," he says, his eyes piercing.

"Yes."

"Sleep okay?"

"Yes," she nods.

He looks at her, long and hard. Puts his hand up against her cheek. She does not take her eyes from him.

"You are beautiful, Aga," he says.

"Am I?"

He shrugs. "Yes. Yes, you are."

She takes him in, all of him: his just slightly receding but still thick hair, his piercing glance, his physique. His strength. His self-confidence. Enough and not enough. She smiles, turns and walks back into the apartment.

He follows.

"What is your plan for today?"

"Wednesday. Otwock."

"Ah yes. Your grandmother. Duty calls."

"Hannah isn't a duty."

"She depends on you."

"And I on her."

"If you say so." Stefan turns away, walks into the kitchen.

"What about you?"

"Me? Work. Mariana will be coming over to help."

"Mariana? No doubt…"

"Aga, she is my assistant."

"Um hm…"

"Don't. Just… don't."

Aga stares at him. She suspects, knows, does not know, tries to care. Sometimes it is difficult to care.

Perhaps luckily, perhaps as a warning, her cell phone rings. She reaches for it on the table as Stefan opens the refrigerator.

"Cześć? Yes, Grandma. Yes. Dzień dobry. Good morning."

Aga's Grandmother Hannah, somewhat deaf now, speaks loudly into the phone.

"Agnieszka, are you coming here today?"

Aga smiles. Her grandmother alone refuses to address her as Aga; she has always insisted on Agnieszka, her one-time school teacher's formality not to be

11

challenged.

"Yes, Grandma, I'm coming."

Hannah Kielar says nothing for a short moment, mulling it over.

"But are you sure you are coming today? I know you are a busy woman these days.

"I will be there, Grandma. You know it is Wednesday."

"I know it is Wednesday."

"I always come down to see you Wednesdays. I will be there later this morning."

"You will take the train?"

"Yes, I will take the train."

"Then I can expect you."

"Yes, Grandma, you can expect me."

"You are certain?"

"Yes, Grandma, I am certain."

"In life, nothing is certain. I know. But good, if you say you are certain, I will also be certain as much as I can be."

"I will see you later, Grandma."

"Yes, yes. My Agnieszka."

Her grandmother Hannah hangs up the phone. Aga smiles slightly, shakes her head. Looks over at Stefan.

"Wednesday," she says.

"Yes. It is." And he turns away.

*

Aga takes the commuter train south from Warsaw for the forty minute journey to the village of Otwock, where Hannah Kielar, her maternal grandmother, lives. The train at first follows the Vistula River before it cuts away and finally crosses the small Swider River near to its mouth at the Vistula. In the late morning the train is largely empty. As it creaks along Aga thinks about Stefan. She cannot be certain he is having an affair with his assistant Mariana. Something in a glance between them, however, a particular look, makes her suspect he is. Perhaps her own relationship with him is approaching its natural end. Does she want it to? She deeply admires him. Does she love him? Can mutual respect lead to love? Is there mutual respect? Questions without answers. She knows she should be worried, bothered, angry perhaps. Why then is she mostly indifferent?

Aga shrugs. Turns away, stares out the window, ignoring the questions that wish not to be ignored. She watches the scenery pass, the urban warehouses and low income apartments quickly replaced by forested suburbs and open countryside. The questions thus released, put aside. She sighs. A role she will play on a different stage.

Rooks grazing on an irrigated field burst into the air and begin to fly away as the train rumbles past. She watches their black wings rise and fall against the blue summer's morning sky. Higher, towards the horizon, then out of view. She wonders, then stops wondering.

Aga makes the journey to Otwock weekly. She is particularly close to her Grandmother, probably closer than are her Mother or Aunt, when push comes to shove. Aga and her Grandmother have always had that kind of special relationship that was never really shared with Katarzyna, Aga's mother and Hannah's oldest daughter. Such is the way of things.

Aga had been the one to decide that she would try to visit every Wednesday. Her mother of course drives down from Warsaw every few weeks, but Aga knows it is her own visit that Hannah prefers.

They had all tried to convince her Grandmother to sell the house in Otwock, to move closer to them in Warsaw, but Hannah would not begin to entertain the idea. She had lived in the two story wooden house since 1950, when she moved there with her husband Kazimierz a year before Katarzyna's birth. Kazimierz had died only a few years later, but Hannah had not wanted to leave, had never wanted to leave.

Aga shrugs. She knows her Grandmother can be stubborn when she wishes. She often wishes.

The train pulls into the small red brick Otwock station and Aga climbs down. She walks out of the station, takes the viaduct beneath the tracks and begins the twenty minute walk to her Grandmother's house. Once this had been a popular spa and sanatorium town, where Warsaw's genteel came to 'take the airs' and the waters. Its sanatoria became home to many a tuberculosis patient. And while several sanatoria remain open as hospitals, the heyday of the town has faded. Most people now simply pass through. A simple place with a difficult history, like so much of Poland, that has been papered over, grown tired, forgotten or forgetting.

The roads are quiet in the summer heat, none more so than Poznanska Street, still unpaved, stretching towards the waters of River Swider in the distance, with its swimming holes and play areas. Houses here are silent but for the summer insects and birds resting in the warmth, unpretentious structures where neighbors do not interfere, keeping their curiosities mostly to themselves. When Hannah moved here with Kazimierz more than fifty years ago, the two-story house was outside town and considered by the State appropriate for the doctor and his young wife. But over time the town came to meet the house, which became one of many along this back road suburban rather than rural street, showing signs of age and fatigue.

The house sits recessed behind a long front garden, hidden largely by large shrubs, all behind a low brown wooden fence. A few flower boxes with even fewer lonely flowers bowing rather than remaining upright adorn some of the window sills. Her grandmother once loved her flowers, but like the woman herself they are bending to the inevitability of time and forgotten care. Aga walks down the path to the house porch. As usual the front door is open and equally as usual she lets herself in.

"Grandma? Hello…," but there is no reply.

Aga walks down the hallway to the old fashioned kitchen at the back of the house. Through the thin, slight rear door she sees her Grandmother sitting out in the garden, a blanket over her lap despite the day's heat, gazing away from the house in a world of her own. In her eighties, Hannah has got terribly thin, Aga thinks. Birdlike. White hair. Fading. Her once strong forbearance has long since disappeared. She must have seemed a strict teacher to her young charges, but that would have been long ago. Now she seems frail, alone, taking her journey one step at a time. Alone at a time. Her mind, her voice remain strong. Age, however, demands its due, excepting neither protest nor hesitation.

Aga walks out into the back garden. Hannah hears the door close against the latch and looks around. Sees her granddaughter. Nods.

"I thought it was you."

"Yes, it's me, Grandma. As I promised."

"So you did."

"It is warm today. Are you not warm with that blanket?"

"It suits me. How was your journey?"

"As always. Just a little commute."

"It was not always that way you know. For me, Warsaw was always far. But never far enough. For me."

"You could come to Warsaw. We could find you a good place to live. You would be nearer to us."

"No. Warsaw… No."

She is silent. Aga knows not to press the issue. In this way they sit listening to the summer day drip slowly in its own time.

"I have lived in this house for a long time."

"Yes."

"My life began here. It will end here."

Aga smiles.

"Your life did not begin here, Grandma. You moved here with your husband in, what, 1950?"

"1951. You did not know him, your Grandfather. That is when my life began. When I began."

"But you were a girl before that."

Hannah looks at her granddaughter, then away.

"You never knew your Grandfather. He died long before you were born. Katarzyna, Maja, they were very young. They do not remember."

"Grandfather?"

"Sometimes…sometimes I do not remember. His face. He was gentle."

"How did you meet?"

"…It does not matter."

"I bet he was smitten with your beauty."

"No. No he… He was a doctor. I remember. He almost could not ask me to

15

marry him. He took me to hear music. In the forest. He… I almost could not say yes to him. But he was sad, and so I did say yes. I remember. Then the State allowed us live in this house. And my life could begin, you see?... My Agnieszka. Child."

Aga smiles. Hannah looks away, away from the house, gazing, dreamy.

"It is nice here in the garden. The birds. The quiet. But it is very warm. Would you like to go in, sit in the cool of the house? I could get you a drink."

"I am waiting."

"Waiting? For me?"

"Not for you. Why would I wait for you? You are here, are you not?"

"As promised."

"Of course, it is Wednesday."

"For the postman? He only comes to the front, Grandma. You know that."

"Not him. I do not need to wait for him. He comes this afternoon. There are others. I am waiting for her. Perhaps I will see her if she is here."

"Who?"

Hannah continues gazing away.

"Grandma? Who are you waiting for? Are you expecting someone?"

"There are ghosts, you know."

"Grandma?"

"They need me, I think. I can hear them playing in their yard. I watch them. Sometimes I hold their hands. I think they hold my hand as well, Agnieszka, while I wait for her. I cannot leave them."

Aga wonders if perhaps her Grandmother is growing confused with the heat, with age.

Hannah looks at her, sternly at first, then with a resigned nod.

"It is hot today. Maybe she will come. One day."

Aga nods, not understanding but sensing there is nothing here that needs understanding. Hannah gazes intently at her granddaughter, then away.

"Perhaps one day."

Later, when they have had lunch, as Aga wipes down the kitchen and puts things away, she hears her Grandmother put on some music in the sitting room.

"Would you like some tea?," Aga asks, walking in.

Hannah shakes her head no.

"What's that?"

"Mrs. Nowak, next door, she gave it to me."

"I thought you did not like Mrs. Nowak?"

"Busy body. But…"

Hannah shrugs. Aga listens to the music. It is like nothing she has heard before, classical, modern, part electronic, repetitive, grating yet rather haunting. It demands to be heard in a funny way.

"Who is that?"

Hannah shrugs, nods towards a CD case on the table. Hannah picks it up, glances at the notes. *The Warsaw Suite/ Pawel Weisz.*

"Do you know this man?," Hannah asks her granddaughter.

"No. But you know, me and music…"

"Polish. But he left Poland in 1968. He never returned until two years ago to write this music about Warsaw. Imagine."

"He must have been ready to return."

"To Warsaw? No one is ready to return."

"I like it."

"I do not. Or maybe I do, I cannot decide. He writes concertos. He writes for artists. He writes for movies. Who is he, this composer? I am not sure why Nowak gave it to me. Busy body."

"Well…it's not Chopin."

"I do not listen to Chopin."

"Everyone listens to Chopin."

"No! No…"

Aga stares at her grandmother, whose face has hardened a bit as she shakes her head. She glances up at Aga, then away, at the CD player.

"Kazimierz, your grandfather, he liked Chopin. Very much. It is why he almost could not marry me."

"Because of Chopin's music?", Aga asks slightly incredulously.

"I remember, a day like today, a spring day in 1949. I remember. He borrowed his supervisor's *Pobeda*. You know this car?"

Aga shakes her head, sits down opposite her grandmother.

"A GAZ-M20. Soviet. Imagine that; I still remember. There were not so many in those days. I remember. It was hot, like today. We had driven up from the South. He wanted to see his new office and then he said he had a surprise. I remember. We drove around the city and away. I did not know where we were. The forest. I did not know. We went for a walk. He was sweet. Handsome. He said he had a treat. We went to a white house. At the edge of the woods. He said do you know this place? He was so pleased with himself. His surprise. This is where Chopin was born. Our greatest musician. I tried to smile. I tried to make him think it pleased me because it pleased him, very much. A young man Kazimierz knew, a friend from his boyhood days, was giving a concert there. Chopin; *Second Piano Concerto*. I still remember. I tried to sit, to close my ears, not listen. But the music, I... I did not want this. I could not listen, I could not..."

"Grandma?"

Lost in her own reveries, her memory, Hannah does not look up.

"I had to get up, leave the room. I ran. It was a summer's evening, still hot. The forest. I hated it. I knew the forest but could not tell him. I knew where I was. I hated it, all of it. Kazimierz followed. I was sick. So sick. I vomited until I could vomit no more. Tears. No, I said to him. No, I..."

Hannah is silent for a moment. Aga stares at her, concerned, confused.

"He had intended to propose to me that night, under the stars. The music and the summer stars. He had a ring. And I vomited..."

"And he married you regardless, Grandma. Remember?"

"...Yes. He forgave me. And he still gave me the ring. A day later. He laughed. He did not understand and he laughed."

"And no more Chopin."

Grandmother looks at Granddaughter. She does not smile. She glances downwards, the recesses of her thoughts a place Aga neither understands nor reaches.

"We married. Your mother was born. He was offered this house. The Communists said he should live here, I should live here. So we came. Your mother was born. We stayed. He did not know she might be here, she…In Otwock, she…Yes, we came. And my life began. That's it."

Aga watches her grandmother turn away to listen to the music.

"One day, Agnieszka, aniołkuy, my angel, I will tell you. One day. When my life began here. He gave me a name and my life began. It was here. I began. That was how it was. It is how it is. I know…This music. The Composer. He writes about Warsaw."

"It says he did not return for forty years."

"Warsaw. What does he know? He writes after forty years. Forty years he is far away. Or maybe he did not leave. Maybe not."

*

Some ten days later, a mid-morning Sunday when a gentle breeze was finally cooling down Warsaw, after a Saturday night of too much drinking at the Oparach in the Praga district, talking with theatre friends over the quiet sound of the gravelly voiced musician on stage until the early hours, Aga groans with despair when Stefan appears on her side of the bed with a glass of fresh orange juice and the requisite coffee. He nudges and pokes. She throws a pillow over her head and tries to disappear without much success.

"Get up, it is almost midday. Come on."

"I want to die."

"There is something I want to show you. A surprise. Get dressed."

"Let me die."

He won't let her die. And he will not leave her alone, poking and prodding no matter how long she tries to hold her breath and pretend she has passed into the nether world.

Later, much against her will and with a good deal of grumbling and bad humor, she climbs scowling into his fifteen year old Mercedes saloon.

"I am not kidnapping you."

"Yes, you are."

"You are acting like a child."

"Compared to you, I am a child."

"Uh huh."

She refuses to speak to him as he drives through back streets, south, away from the river. Fifteen minutes later, Stefan turns off Żelazna Street in the Wola district onto the grounds where numerous dilapidated buildings of an old factory sit decaying and turns off the engine.

"You know this place?"

"No. Should I?"

"Used to be the Norblina Factory. They made silver plate here for almost two hundred years, until the War. Famous for it. There is a museum in one of the buildings. Museum of Industry, but it is closing."

"I see."

"Yes?"

"No."

Stefan chuckles, gets out of the car.

"Come."

Aga has no time to protest. She follows him down a side alley of buildings, then he leads her into a single story warehouse building off to one side. Within is a large open space, fallen bits of brick and timber and broken metal littering the floor.

"So, what do you think?"

"Wonderful. Want to tell me what this is about?"

"There... we will keep the set work there. Minimal. We will not need a lot of space. We will dig out up front to lower the stage slightly. Rows of seats there, there, rising on scaffolding. We will keep the atmosphere, the feel of the factory that was once here."

"You are putting a theatre in here."

"Of course. I have taken the lease. One year."

"You're kidding?"

"No. Why? It is perfect. Newest theatre in Warsaw. My theatre."

"For a year? You are mad!"

"Yes. And I have the production. Two in fact. In repertoire. You want to hear?"

"I'm listening."

"I have been working with Karol. You know Karol? Yes, you know. Of course.

He had an idea. I had a better idea. So we put his idea and my idea together. He wanted to do a version of the *Oresteia*. You know Aeschylus plays? Of course you do. Karol, he fell in love with Elektra. Her passion. Her anger. Her politics. But me, I am also interested in the sister who dies first. Iphigenia. The sacrifice. What is the relationship between these two sisters, I wonder? What does one sister feel about the other? The sacrifice, the murder. Two sisters, who are one separated by time and experience and reaction. Do you see? Between them the brother Orestes. I see their tragedy as a story of our Poland today. The sacrifice, Europe, Russia, the State. The ones caught between. The bastards who really rule our country. Elektra, Iphigenia. I think it can be something special. Karol, he and I we are doing something special. And provocative. We will make the government angry. It is a story about Greece, about Athens in ancient times, but it is a story of Warsaw, of our time, of what government can do, what the Conservative bastards in the shadows still do. We will be in their face."

"Which you like."

"Of course. Karol, he writes. Fast. Well. There will be two plays. One night, then the next. Two plays. Saturdays we will put on both together. One in the afternoon, the other in the evening. It will be a challenge. Elektra and Iphigenia. One Orestes. But the two women, sisters, night, day, antithesis, thesis, sisters who hate, love, need, reflect. Never together in the same play but never alone emotionally. So, one actress. You, Aga. One day Iphigenia, one day Elektra. One day the innocent, the victim. Passive. Accepting. But strong. And the other day, the sister. Angry. Forceful. Broken and breaking. Two sisters. One actress."

Aga stares at him, her mind racing, her thoughts racing.

"You want me to play both parts."

"Yes."

"It is crazy."

"Of course. And brilliant."

She turns away, walks around the cavernous space. Shakes her head at the gumption of it. Looks back at him.

"And brilliant."

"A bit like me. And as you will be. We will open in November. Four months

21

run, maybe five if the play is a success. A guaranteed scandal. It will succeed."

"Winter. You will need heaters in here. A lot of heaters."

"We will have a lot of heaters. Or you can play the roles naked. That will make them all warm up very fast."

Aga walks up to him, shaking her head. Looks straight at him. Sighs, smiles. Nods.

"Thank you."

"Don't thank me. You were always right for this idea. You should thank Mariana. When I told her the idea, she said you would be perfect. I had to agree."

Aga stares intensely at him with the slightest hint of a smirk keeping the irony at bay.

"I'll bet she did. I will thank her, Stefan."

She leans up to him, kisses him on the cheek.

"It is a wonderful idea. I am enthralled. Thank you."

Outside the building they hear a car pull up and a car door open.

"Adam. He is meeting us here. He will help me design the space. The sets will be minimal. The costumes. Everything will be story and acting."

Aga leaves Stefan with the designer Adam, discussing Stefan's plans. She goes outside, walks along the empty alleyways of factory buildings and debris. Stefan once specialized in guerrilla filmmaking and he liked to bring such ideas to the stage as well. He was known for it. It suited his temperament. It suited the rebellion against his age. And it suited Aga, or certainly did at the moment. Stefan loved to instigate, to get people talking. They would talk. And Aga likes the thought of being a part of the conversation, whatever the demands on her might be. Two roles, two plays, alternate nights. The demands will be great.

Her cell phone buzzes. Her mother.

"Yes, mother."

Katarzyna Janiec is a practicing family psychologist, which half amuses Aga, as she often feels it is her mother who could use counseling more than clients. Aga's father, Witold, is a communications business executive who had done well in the Communist state, but who now struggles with the office politics of the capitalist world. He is proud of his daughter, although finds her world confusing, if not outright chaotic. The parents' values are quiet rather than antagonistic towards the government of the day, however better than it was in the Communist era. They aren't practicing Catholics, but the values of a conservative Church sometimes continue to hold some sway over their lives.

"Are you free, Aga?"

"Sure. Free enough. How are you?"

"Good. You know. Fine. I want you to do something for me if you are free."

"I am with Stefan in south Warsaw. In Wola."

"Wola? There is nothing in Wola."

"Next job."

"Will it pay?"

"Not much."

"Then not much of a job. I want you to go down to your Grandmother this afternoon. Can you do that for me?"

"I am seeing her on Wednesday."

"I know, but I promised I would visit today, take her to the market. I can't go now."

"Mother…"

"Maja rang me. She has been ill. She asked me to help."

"What is the matter?"

"The new drugs. They are making her sick. I do not want your Grandmother to know."

Aga's Aunt Maja had had a relapse of her breast cancer and was on a new regime of chemotherapy. She and Aga's mother had always been close.

"I wouldn't ask you if I could go, but I promised her."

Aga hesitates. How often does she have to jump for her mother? This is not the first time. But she relents. She knows her Grandmother would be disappointed should no one come down, knows too that she allows the cupboards to go empty if Aga or her mother doesn't take Hannah to the market once or twice a month.

She thinks that Stefan will be annoyed but in fact he is too tied up with the discussions about his plans with Adam to care. He tells her to take the car; Adam can take him back to the apartment later. A kind if unusual gesture.

Aga thus drives the short journey to Otwock, promising to meet both director and designer for dinner later that evening. The Sunday afternoon traffic out of Warsaw is light. She is at her Grandmother's house less than an hour later, after stopping first to pick up some flowers that she knows Hannah will like.

Aga parks the car in front of the wooden gate, grabs the flowers and heads up the walk, smiling to herself at the thought of the coming months. The intensity will be good for her. She knows the two characters from classic Greek plays. She looks forward to what Stefan will do with them. She looks forward to the challenge of the two roles as one.

The front door is, as usual, open. She hears music coming from the sitting room, the same music she remembers from the previous fortnight's visit. Her grandmother must have decided she does likes the CD after all. Aga smiles at that.

"Grandma? It's Agnieszka. Mother could not make it. I will be right there."

Aga walks into the kitchen, finds a vase, puts the flowers in water.

"I have got some flowers. Would you like them in there?"

Her Grandmother does not answer. Aga finishes arranging the flowers and clearing away the cut stems, then walks into the sitting room. Her grandmother sits in her 'special' chair with her back to Aga.

"Mother could not make it so I volunteered. I have flowers... Were you waiting for her? Or maybe for someone else like you said, eh? Your secret friend."

Aga smiles, remembering what her grandmother had said the two weeks before, sitting in the garden. She walks over to the old woman and sits down in a chair opposite.

Aga's smile freezes, then dissipates into the ether.

She looks at the frail old woman.

She looks at Hannah's head tilted to one side, leaning down almost against her breast. Her eyes are open. Her mouth is partially closed.

She sees the mug of tea, fallen on the floor beside her.

She sees the quiet in her Grandmother's expression. The lack of fear, or pain.

She sees a gaze that, while focused downwards, is at once far away, but also empty in those still open eyes.

"Grandma?" She whispers, knowing there can be no response.

24

The music comes to an end. The music stops. The silence surrounds Aga even as it envelops her grandmother Hannah. The silence is suddenly louder than the music had been, louder than the room itself, the world itself.

Aga sees the silence.

Aga sees that Hannah does not breathe, that Hannah sits quietly in death, as if waiting still.

Aga does not move from the chair. She does not cry out. She is not afraid. She feels simply: empty. She knows she must call authorities. She must act. But not yet. There will be time to make the calls she will now have to make. But no, not yet. For these moments she wants to sit with this old, bird-like woman who had been so frail, now so silent, this Grandmother she had come to love so, she loves so. This moment Aga wants now for herself. Her own memory. Her grief.

Now her loss.

She looks at her Grandmother. She looks at Hannah Kielar, who lived here. Who said her life had started here. And through her life, so too Aga's.

She looks away, towards a window facing out to the back garden. No one is there. No one has come. Hannah had waited. Perhaps she had been looking out the window. Perhaps the ghosts had called to her. Now Aga, no, now Agnieszka, waits with her. In the silence.

The grief overwhelms in that silence.

Aga waits.

They wait together.

*

The burial takes place the following Saturday afternoon in the Otwock Cemetery, at a grave Hannah will share with her husband, Kazimierz Palinsky, who died in 1956, a year after the birth of his second daughter. Hannah had said after his death that she could no longer keep his name as it was not hers to keep and reverted to her birth name of Hannah Kielar. Over the next few years she had trained as a teacher and, with the approval and accreditation provided by the Communist government of Polish People's Republic, taught in the local primary school for almost thirty years.

The hot weather of the previous weeks has finally broken and a light if still warm rain falls on the day. After a requested short ceremony at the church, with a minimal funeral mass, Aga, accompanied by Stefan, her Mother and Father, her Aunt Maja and her Uncle and their three children, as well as a few older neighbors, accompany the remains to the gravesite. A few prayers are said. A few silent tears. And that's it. A life comes to an end.

They gather for a meal at a local restaurant. Witold, Aga's father, pours glasses of vodka as is tradition, but the mood is subdued. Hannah's friends, if there had been many, had long since disappeared with time and age. The few neighbors, although invited, had kindly declined to join them for the meal. The family were left to the quiet of their own thoughts and memories. There were many such: of daughters growing up, marrying, of their own children growing, but in an odd way few of Hannah herself. Certainly few of the Hannah who Aga had come to know, and respect, and love. It was almost as if in the rush not to remember there was a rush to forget.

Aga took a quiet moment to ask her mother about Kazimierz, her Grandfather, but was not surprised that Katarzyna offered little, indeed knew little. Kazimierz Palinsky had died just before his first born's fifth birthday, so Katarzyna barely remembered him. Hannah had always chosen to speak little of her husband. Little of the years before her daughters had grown. Little of loss. Katarzyna of course knew that her father was a doctor, but of what she had no clue. Aga related to her the story of the proposal that went awry, which in fact her Mother had never heard.

"Come to think of it," her Mother said, "you are right: I do not think I ever heard her listen to Chopin. She never mentioned him I suppose. Must be the only citizen of Poland who did not."

"A Sixties revolutionary."

"Your Grandmother? Hardly. She towed the party line. If she had not she would not have been allowed to teach. It was like that then."

"Did she ever talk about her own family?"

"No. Not really. I know her own mother lived on a farm somewhere not far from Krakow. She died when your Grandmother was still a young girl. That is all she ever said. She was a very private woman, my mother."

"Funny."

"No. It is how she was. The War did not touch her much she said, but these were still hard times I suppose. She made her choices and she chose not to remember, not to go back."

"I guess not."

"We have decided to sell the house, but not soon. Your Aunt needs several months of chemo and rest. It is difficult. There will be enough time to sort through my mother's affairs. There will not be much left. She lived on her pension. If there is anything you want, you should say. You can think about it. We will take our time."

"I can help when you wish."

"We will see. I know you have this play. It is good for you, Aga. You have your own life. Just as I have my patients. And I want to help with Maja. There will be time, but not now."

Later, as the meal comes to an end, Aga tells Stefan that she prefers to stay behind, pay a last visit to her Grandmother's house. She will take the train back that evening. When all have driven away in their respective cars, back to their respective lives, Aga quietly walks through the town towards Poznanska Street. The light rain has stopped. The clouds hide the late afternoon sky. The world seems a sadder place. She is glad she has the time to herself.

Aga opens the small wooden gate, walks up the walkway to the front door. She notices the few flowers that remain in the flower boxes. They will die soon. There will be no one to water them. It is as if they know their own fate, already fading. Silent.

The door is locked now. It will remain locked in the coming days, the coming weeks, or longer. Aga has a key and lets herself in.

She takes in the silence. It was often there and she was often aware of it while Hannah was alive. Now it shouts out its emptiness.

She walks into the kitchen. A glass on the counter. She washes it for no particular reason, dries it, puts it away. She checks the old refrigerator to make certain all food has been removed, that nothing can become spoiled with no one to clear it away, but her mother or aunt had remembered to empty everything. Or perhaps she had done that herself. She no longer recalls.

She looks around the room, knowing there will be no one to make a cup of tea again, or such will be another family's role sometime in the future. Her Grandmother will not be there to sip quietly.

The remainder of things. Their lack. Life taken. Life of a person. Life of a house. Life of a family now gone from here forever.

Aga looks out of the slight back door, at the garden. It will become overgrown. It already seems empty, sad.

She looks into the distance, towards the horizon at the back. She too could wait for someone, for her, whomever, but she knows no one will be coming, no one would ever come. She hears her own laughter playing hide and seek in this garden when she was little, hide and seek with her Grandmother Hannah who was never really as strict as she appeared.

No, no one would ever come.

Aga turns, goes into the sitting room, now empty. She looks around the space, struck by how the only photographs on display, indeed the only photographs in the house, are of her and her cousins, her mother and her aunt: their weddings, as younger women, but not as children. No photographs of Dr. Kazimierz Palinsky. No photographs of Hannah from her own youth. No past, barely beyond Aga's birth. She picks up one photograph of herself and her grandmother from a play Aga had performed in. Hannah had been pleased but quiet.

"It is your path," Aga remembers her saying. "To be someone else, someone you are not. To revel in it. To live it."

Now she is not there to walk the path alongside her granddaughter. To witness.

Aga sits in the easy chair that had been her Grandmother's. She sees the frail, old woman even now sitting there. And sees her with her head bowed, the life extinguished.

Aga notices, largely hidden beneath the frame of the chair but sticking out just slightly, a plastic CD cover. She pulls it out. It is the CD of the music that had been playing when Aga found her Grandmother. It must have got pushed under the chair when they were cleaning the room. The music Hannah said she hated and yet seemed to entrance her, music she wanted to listen to but did not understand. Aga smiles.

"Forty years he is far away. Or maybe he did not leave," she had said.

Aga remembers her Grandmother's words. She had not liked this music for Warsaw, this 'Warsaw Suite'. But she listened to it. Perhaps she listened often.

Aga takes the CD from the cover and puts it in the CD player still in the room. Turns it on. Sits back, taking in the music.

Repetitive. Grating yet haunting. Aga remembers.

It was likely the last thing her Grandmother heard before she passed away.

Aga sits quietly and listens to the entire musical suite. The music stops; still she sits as the room grows darker.

Finally the darkness takes over. Aga decides not to turn on the light in the room. There is nothing further she wishes to see, not in the light, not in the dusk.

She takes the CD and puts it back in the plastic case then places it into her bag. It is the one thing she decides she wants to keep. There is nothing further she wants. Not now.

She stands, walks from the room, opens the front door, closes it. Hesitates.

Then locks the door behind her.

The flowers in the window box are dying.

The memory will remain.

It is possible Aga, Agnieszka, will never return to this house.

She does not look behind as she walks up Poznanska Street and disappears into the evening light

*

Over the coming many weeks Stefan busies himself with the creation of his theatre. The project, as he calls it. Everyone pitches in to design, build, imagine, put up scaffolding, create lighting, create the atmosphere Stefan wants. For Aga it becomes the release she craves, still mourning her Grandmother's loss. For weeks she joins Stefan wearing the requisite hardhat, clearing, lifting, cleaning, painting, building, watching the theatre space take shape. It is a different kind of creative enterprise than Aga is used to, but its physicality gives her real pleasure.

After ten weeks or so the space itself is nearly ready, with the heaters finally and gratefully installed as the weather is already turning. Stefan and his company begin to work through to the two plays, two as one. The work proves as difficult as he had foretold to Aga. She not only has to learn the diametrically opposed roles of two plays simultaneously, but each requires a physicality that makes great demands on both her mind and her body.

As more cast become involved in rehearsals and the constant read-throughs, the plays begin to take shape, just like the theatre where they are to be performed. Once the three extra actors who take on the ensemble role of a chorus commenting on the characters, while in truth commenting on the church and Polish politics, become immersed in their roles and their own movement on stage, and the images of mixed media that flash behind them are used in rehearsal, Aga begins to get a real sense of just how provocative the plays are likely to become. Stefan has decided he wants the theatre, like the plays themselves, to feel claustrophobic, prison-like. Cell-like. He pushes Aga and the rest of the cast to use physical presence, movement, contortion in new ways, to push themselves into pain and through pain heightened expression.

Night after night Aga returns home in mental and physical agony. But by the same token she begins to grasp entirely the power of the story and the words, the characters and the gestures and movement creating within her a sort of quiet euphoria giving meaning and shape to her present life and work.

All this time her Grandmother Hannah's death remains in the background, a profound, quiet grief at a loss that pushes Aga forward, that makes the cries of anguish of both main characters she plays in alternate performances--the victim Iphigenia, the fury and revenge-driven Elektra, each a different kind of victim-- much more poignant, and personal, and real.

The opening approaches. The nerves force adrenalin through Aga's body, her brain. The fear. She does not usually feel such uncertainty when embarking on a new project, but these two particular plays, in concert with the loss of her Grandmother perhaps, or perhaps the uncertain knowledge of Stefan's infidelity of which she has nevertheless become quite certain, or perhaps even her own somewhat lacking self-confidence makes her quietly, physically sick. Such fears drive her on. Fears that she at once loathes and at once cherishes.

When all then is said and done, however, Stefan's vision pays off as the plays open. *Radio Maryja*, as well as the *Gazeta Wyborcza* and the *Nasz Dziennik* are

30

unsurprisingly hostile, but the majority of the press are at the least supportive and in some cases ecstatic. More importantly the audiences flock to the small space. All future performances after the opening week quickly sell out. Aga's own notices are particularly strong, with several reviewers noting how difficult the plays are to perform physically, particularly on Saturdays when the two plays stage in tandem.

Before long the plays become must see events for the Warsaw theatre-going public. Many of the most conservative voices that have yet remained in positions of influence do indeed find the work subversive. Stefan receives both official and unofficial threats. Because of such he unsurprisingly feels elated. That is his nature.

In the days that follow, as the routine finds its rhythm, the performances grow easier for Aga, both physically and mentally more manageable. While still demanding, still exhausting, and while the nervousness never truly disappears, she begins to find calm within herself, the power of the roles she plays on stage giving her an inner strength that she not only uses in her performance but in the quiet moments at home. Then she finally feels she can breathe, and reflect, and live again. There had been days when she was not sure she would survive from day to day. As things ease, however, she finds she is able at last to master her time rather than wanting to run away from it.

On a Sunday, a day off in early December, with Christmas approaching, Aga's mother Katarzyna rings to see if Aga might be free to join her for coffee that afternoon. They had not had time together for months, between Aga's work schedule and Katarzyna's patients, let alone her Mother's time spent with Aga's Aunt Maja.

Katarzyna is already seated when Aga arrives. Aga finds her mother looking a bit drawn and tired, slightly agitated.

"So your plays, they are going well I believe."

"Yes. Very well. Sold out until March."

"No Christmas this year?"

"We'll have a few days off."

"Will you come to us? Your father would be pleased, as would I."

31

"Of course. I always do."

"I know, Aga. I know."

"How is Aunt Maja?"

"She is doing better now, thank God. The chemo will end with the new year. The cancer is in remission. She is tired but improving. It is not easy."

"No. I will visit when I can."

"She would like that. We all know you are busy. She understands. And we are proud of your success. Your Grandmother would have been very proud."

"I miss her."

"I am sure."

"Do you?"

"Of course. She was my mother. But we must move on. She was a part of all of us. Is a part of all of us. But…life is still to be lived."

Aga nods.

"She would have like your plays. The passion. There is much passion."

"And the politics?"

"Phssst… Grandma Hannah had little time for politics or those who are afraid of change. She did what was required. But politics? No; never. I think she would have enjoyed the provocation, although would have pretended she did not approve. But she would have approved, my myszka."

Aga smiles. Her mother rarely calls her myszka any longer, but when she does the affection is clearly genuine.

"I am proud of you, Aga. Truly. And you can be proud of yourself."

"Thank you, Mother."

"I know you are busy with things right now, but there is something I need to give to you."

Katarzyna leans down to her bag and pulls out a thick, sealed, large manila folder.

"Your Aunt and I, we finally began to clear Grandma Hannah's house, and we met with the advocate in Otwock who handled her affairs. It turns out she had kept a box at the bank. There were some unexpected funds, through her husband. Not a lot, but Hannah had chosen to save these. She was never much of a spender. Maja and I will split the money and my share will go to you."

"Mother…"

"No, it will not be much, believe me, with costs and such. But that is not what I want to talk to you about."

Katarzyna pushes the sealed folder over to Aga.

"Also in the box was this, completely sealed. As you can see, your Grandmother wrote here on the envelope that this was to be given to you. I have had it at home for a few weeks but wanted to give it to you now."

"What is it?"

"To be honest, Aga, I do not know. Your grandmother declared all her material interests properly and there is nothing missing so I do not think this has material value, but clearly it had value to her and clearly she felt it important to leave for you."

Aga picks up the large envelope. She starts to open it but her mother reaches out and takes her hand.

"No. No, not now."

"Mother, if…"

"No. In your own time. And if in time you want to show it to us, to tell us, you will do so. But your Grandmother, she had a particular bond with you, Aga. I loved my mother, as did Maja. But there was always this distance, you see? Not a distance of—of anger, or disrespect, or indifference. She was a good mother, if a bit strict perhaps. But she did love us and supported us in hard times. And there were hard times. With you, however, it was different. I think she wanted you to have this for yourself, whatever it contains. So we are giving it to you. Both Maja and I agree. When you have time, you can see what it might contain. We are of course curious, but perhaps it may be something that should remain between you and Grandma Hannah. Perhaps its value is something you alone will grasp, I do not know. There will come a time. You can tell me, or not. Show us, or not. What I do know is that you were terribly special to her. Important to her. So, whatever this legacy is, it has to be yours and perhaps yours alone. Yes?"

Aga looks at her mother, down at the folder, back at her mother. She nods, slowly. Then leans over and kisses her mother on the cheek.

"I love you, my myszka. So did she."

Later, back at Stefan's, sitting downstairs, Aga begins to open the folder, but changes her mind. She needs to give this some space and right now she does not have space. Too consumed with the plays, with the roles she needs to play, she decides to leave opening the folder until another time. She puts it amongst some of her own belongings, to wait for another day. In doing so she notices the CD of Weisz's 'Warsaw Suite' that she had taken from her Grandmother's house the day of the funeral, some months prior. She had not listened to it since. Aga smiles and decides to put the CD into the player. She sits, listening to the music, particularly thoughtful during a quiet section after its more chaotic, challenging opening.

Stefan comes in while she is listening.

"What's this?"

Aga hands him the CD cover. She decides to say nothing of what her mother had given to her that afternoon.

"Hm. I knew Weisz, you know. I was at university, met him then."

"Really?"

"I only knew him vaguely. He was teaching at Staatliche Musikschule when I was at the University of Warsaw. Days of anger and protest. That is another story. He was a good few years older. We had friends in common. That was 1967, '68. Difficult times. I found his music interesting but distant. And I was in film then, not really music."

"I am not sure if I like the work or not."

Stefan stands listening for a couple minutes.

"He has done some film scoring since those days. I remember I told him film was the art form of our generation. Might be interesting to work with him sometime, you never know. We tried to find something once, believe it or not. Perhaps now... I will make some food. Tomorrow will be busy again. Mondays are always busy."

He disappears to the kitchen. Aga returns her attention back to the music. She lets the folder her Grandmother had left for her slip from her thoughts. And after a few more minutes, she turns off the CD player and heads upstairs to shower.

*

34

In the run-up to the Christmas holiday the theatre is particularly busy and the plays continue being well received. The last three days before Christmas Stefan runs the two plays together rather than alternating. By the time Christmas comes, Aga is overwhelmed with exhaustion.

As she had told her mother she would do she spends the holiday at her parents' home in the Warsaw suburbs, much of the time simply sleeping. Christmas itself proves to be, unsurprisingly, a quiet affair. It gives her a few days to rest and think, however, and to make some decisions.

She returns to the plays on Wednesday, December 27th as planned. The theatre remains open through an early performance on New Year's Eve, then as scheduled closes for a desperately needed break until January 8th.

Aga has decided during this time to move back to her small studio apartment in Nowolipki. She desperately needs space to herself, but she has also come to the realization that it is time to separate from Stefan. It is not done in anger and there is no angry confrontation when she tells him. It is, simply, time. His was a controlling personality. Aga in fact probably enjoyed such control on the stage; certainly he inspired her and pushed her limits well beyond her normal comfort zone. But all this had proved wearying in their private life. Stefan is not particularly surprised, nor indeed hurt or offended. Aga suspects that Mariana will soon take her place, or if not the rather oft hovering assistant, then another actress or stage designer or some other production girl or acquaintance or fan. Although saddened, Aga is hardly distraught by this conclusion. She plans to finish off the plays' runs, then look for something fresh—professionally, personally.

She and Stefan agree to spend New Year's Eve partying with the rest of the cast. On New Year's day she is up early and he kindly helps her move her things later in the day. She promises that she looks forward to the following two months at the theatre, possibly even three if extended and that their parting is as much from the sheer exhaustion of the previous months as it is that the relationship has run its course. They both know in truth that it has. Aga hopes in the future, once the plays have closed, the theatre has closed, they will find other projects to work on together. It has been a successful collaboration she agrees, creatively fulfilling if emotionally lacking, at least at times.

The next two or three days she spends sleeping. Exhaustion has now completely taken over. She does not tell her parents of the break. They would likely be as happy as not. They had neither particularly liked nor disliked Stefan. Certainly they admired his talents as a director and a creative force. But the age difference between their daughter and the older director had always made them uncomfortable.

While putting her clothes, books, various things away in the studio apartment, making it livable once again, Aga picks up the manila folder that she had yet to open. Knowing that now she has time to peruse her Grandmother's things, her 'gift', she sits down in the quiet of the winter's evenings and opens the package, allowing all the contents to spill out onto the floor.

Before her are a small pile of papers and records. Some pages of a diary. Reports of some sort. Various notes. Pages of scribbling and invoices and stories. Hannah's birth certificate and identity papers from the 1940s. The history of a life. Amongst these is an envelope with her name on it, and within a letter, addressed to her. Aga knows that these are in essence her Grandmother Hannah's final words to her, her final wishes perhaps. Aga's hands shake slightly as she turns on a lamp that throws shadows against the winter light in the apartment, the only light that she has on. In the semi-darkness, in the quiet, despite fatigue and with the memory of the last few visits to her Grandmother and the last time she saw her, alone, silent, forever then silent in her chair, Aga closes her eyes then opens them, takes a deep breath and begins to read:

My darling Agnieszka. Moja droga, moja skarbie, because you truly were a treasure to me from the moment you were born.

I suppose I see in you a bit of myself, or the self I once dreamed about before this was extinguished. I had planned to destroy all these bits and pieces I had collected or held onto for many years and often wanted to destroy, but I hesitated to do so. I did not know why. I know now.

I am in the final weeks I think of this life. Perhaps even days, who can say. I do not know why I think this is so, but I think it is so. And rather than now destroy these items that tell a story, I have decided instead to leave them for you. You can destroy them if you wish. Share them if you wish. Bring order and sense to them, write them with coherence and grace, reveal them. Because by bringing order and a story, you might remember for me. I have spent much of my life afraid to. I have spent much of my life terrified of reliving. But you, my Agnieszka, you might understand. So much I had forgotten. Had hidden. So much I chose to forget. And I had forgotten. But in your lovely face, your smile, your warmth, I have come to accept that what lay dormant was not forgotten, not really. It was all there, all here, in these scribbles and fragments of memories that I managed to retain, now so faded and yellowed, but which once came to define me, was once a story. My story, hidden.

I have decided that it is best that you be in receipt of these things, not your Mother, not your Aunt. This is not because I do not love them. Indeed I do love them, dearly. As I do your younger cousins.

But in you, moja skarbie, I have seen something I understand, in truth I always understood. I see that life is a journey and that which you are following resonates with my own. Because within you there is longing and a search and a need to know even when you do not want to know, do not want to see. Sometimes you have to see the unimaginable. I have seen in your profession and in what you bring to it, this desire, no, this need for truth. I have seen something unique. I have seen your heart revealed and what I have seen is good. A gift. That is why I have decided to leave these fragments and papers to you. To find the truth that we all ultimately seek.

Amongst the papers I retain here, you will find my birth certificate. It tells you that Hannah Kielar was born 1924 in Nowy Wiśnicz, on a small farm. My mother you will read was Helena Kielar, married to Kacper Kielar. I never knew him, although I know he died. Helena chose to speak little of him and what she told me I have decided should rest with her. It is not a part of my own story.

You will also find some doctor's notes that I came upon, notes written confidentially by Dr. Kazimierz Palinsky, which I only discovered many years later. I should have destroyed these, but I did not. You will see that Kazimierz Palinsky was my doctor, first my doctor. And later he became my husband. My beloved Kazimierz, who loved me, and indeed I loved him, gently, in my own way. There were things Kazimierz thought he understood, but he did not understand. He did not know. A history I could never reveal to him.

When I married Kazimierz, in 1950, I became Hannah Palinsky. That was my name then. It allowed me to escape much. But not all.

And when my Kazimierz died, so unexpectedly, so painfully with that awful illness of his, I realized I had no right to his name. No right to him. I was not deserving.

So then I became Hannah Kielar once again. I raised my daughters. I became a teacher. I told authorities what they needed and wanted to hear. I was known, and accepted, and I lived out my life this way.

Except that my life was a falsehood that had become the truth, that even I believed was real.

Mostly you will find various musings I had as a girl, for I was a girl once. Some diary entries I must have made, oh, so many years ago, so many. Some fragments of memories. And some stories and recollections about what happened. About what guilt I carry. I have always carried. About the great loss. About the horror. And there was.

Many pages have been lost, but there is enough in all these papers to form a picture, a memory. A brief glance into my time. My memory. My bequest to you, perhaps.

I am sorry. I will tell you that. I am sorry for so much. I hope, truly hope that if *you are able to make some sense of this story, these events, to offer clarity, to understand, then you will help me find some sort of redemption in the next life. That, my Agnieszka, my Granddaughter, is all I can wish to hope.*

You need to know another truth. That is my final bequest to you. The boundaries of this map need be redrawn; perhaps that is the task I leave with you.

Hannah Kielar, my life, my map, my name, but not my name. Hannah Palinsky once, but not my name. My husband lived to hold me. But I could not let him know me. Any more than I could ever let the authorities know what they did not know. Any more than I could let my own daughters know.

No one has ever known the truth, my past. No one. But you must. Now, it is time. The right time. Necessary. And so you must.

There was despair. My despair. And there were secrets. My secrets. Unspoken. Remembered. Forgotten and in the forgetting, known and remembered. Those secrets almost disappeared. Almost. Until now. Secrets about this Hannah Kielar, your grandmother, who was and was not, who lived and lived not. I not her, not her not I.

Because there was another.

In these papers, in your thoughts and on the road you will take, like a shadow on a cloudy day I might thus reappear only momentarily into the light, before I will once again disappear. And thus never was. I never was. But only but for the briefest of moments, my Agnieszka. I was here and need to be here but one more moment. Here for you to see and witness.

There were so many clouds. So many.

My name was Hania Stern then. Once. A lifetime ago. Then. I was she, was I. Long ago. Shadow of a self, of a story.

As you go through these few papers, some reminisces I have decided to write down, my gift to you, I hope you will understand. And forgive. And bear witness to a past that is yours and not yours not your Mother's but mine, except in mine it is yours too. Moja skarbie. I am yours.

My name was. Mmiałem na imię. My name was. Once. Long ago. My name was Hania Stern. This name has not been uttered in more than sixty years. Hania Stern. I have never told anyone this. Not your mother. Not your Grandfather. No one I worked with nor taught nor ever knew. Ever.

The name disappeared. Hania Stern. I disappeared. Shadow not of this earth, on this earth. Until this moment as I write. You need to hear the story, what I now choose to tell of it, because I am old, because I am within you and of you, because soon I will die. You must know the story, or some of it that I am able to tell. While there remains time ahead, the days or the hours, I cannot be certain.

Hania Stern.

And there is one further thing too that I must tell you here, now, moja droga, my beautiful Agnieska, Granddaughter, child. One thing you must know. One thing to hear singing in your ears, the notes of a sad piano playing. The memory I have that I give to you. In this. This story. This song. One thing to know. And remember.

Hania Stern once lived. I was Hania Stern. Once. A memory ago. Once. Hania Stern was my name.

And Hania Stern was once a Jew in Warsaw.

First Movement

Lachrymosa:

Hania's Lament

Warsaw, 1938-43 /
Kobierzyn, 1947-49

Joseph Babinski Specialist Hospital/ Institute of
  Neuropsychiatric Disorder, Kobierzyn (Krakow)
Patient Identification: 46-10/276
Patient Name: *Kielar, Hannah*
Patient Birthdate/Locale   *04Apr1924/Nowy Wiśnicz*
Consulting Psychologist: *Dr. (hab) K.Palinsky, D.N.,PhD.*

<u>*Monthly Patient Report*</u>
17 June 1947

This is my first requested report submission regarding the patient, H.Kielar, since taking over her case as her consulting psychologist on 15 May 1947.

<u>Physician's and Treatment Background</u>: It will be helpful to set out for our supervisory committee the circumstances of my involvement with the patient from mid-May of this year. I joined the staff of the Institute in March, 1947. My initial training in clinical observation and psychotherapeutic analysis began at the University of Vienna in 1937-38 under the tutelage of Rudolf Dreikurs and Charlotte Bühler, with emphasis on what is referred to as the Vienna Psychological Society 'School'. From the end of the War until January 1947 I completed further research and training at Jagiellonian University, Krakow, prior to retaining this position at Kobierzyn.

I am thirty-one years old. I was born in Wroclaw. I spent the War years with the Polish Free Forces in Britain as a translator in the British War Office. During this period I attended lectures in psychotherapy at King's College in London, England, as time permitted, as well as occasional lectures and discussions at the British Psychoanalytical Society, where I attended talks by Melitta Schmideberg and Michael Balint.

The committee will recall that in the patient evaluation meetings during the first week of May, 1947, the case of H.Kielar came under some heated scrutiny. The early conclusions as to her mental stability and behavior, detailed in the notes of previous psychological evaluations and in several medical reports here at the Institute, suggested deep-rooted unconditioned psychosis with a likely propensity to schizophrenic behavior. Doctors' notes further suggested possible early or mid-childhood trauma leading to severe bouts of depression that had resulted in H.Kielar no longer being able to speak, or more to the point 'choosing' not to

41

speak, as it was determined that there was no noticeable damage to vocal tract or larynx, no sign of partial or total hearing loss, and indeed the patient did not demonstrate any lack of intellectual capability.

Summarizing part of the discussion during the committee's evaluation of the patient in question, Dr. Nowak, you will recall, was steadfastly of the opinion that the best treatment for H.Kielar given her presumed personality disorder would be to proceed with trepanation. Dr. Nowak considered his work utilizing bi-lateral frontal leucotomy, following along the lines of Dr. Walter Freeman in the United States, demonstrated proven results in patients with both depressive and schizophrenic affinity and with a prevalent tendency to socialization breakdown.

Other analysts present, including Dr. Szymański, were strongly in favor instead of progressing treatment with the introduction of certain psychosomatics as might be physiologically appropriate given this patient's age and obvious malnutrition, and given the patient's circumstances as best as the Institute has been made aware of such. Dr. Szymański was quick to emphasize medical advancements of such treatment; amongst the committee and in the psychology community at large there are currently many proponents for medicinal therapies, particularly supported in the current climate of my own Jagiellonian University thanks to the work there of Professor Władysław Heinrich. This method of treatment, however, I personally do not agree with Dr. Heinrich is appropriate for all patients suffering mental and emotional disorders, nor concur that such is entirely acceptable and indeed ethical in all cases of mental illness, despite our commonality of academic institution. In the case of this particular patient, it remains my opinion that pursuing such medicinal course of action at this time would likely be counter-productive or even result in a negative prognosis.

Indeed the committee will recall I forcefully argued that it was far too early in the patient's treatment to consider either the recommendations of Dr. Nowak or Dr. Szymański. Passionately believing in the benefit of dialogue and subsequent analysis particularly espoused in the work of Dr. Alfred Adler when president of the Vienna Psychoanalytical Society, I argued strongly in the case of H.Kielar for primary psychotherapeutic exploration within the parameters and concepts of individual psychology, given its potential for pragmatic socialization, interpretation and the management of individual mental health disorder.

At this point supervising senior Dr. Łados suggested that the patient, H.Kielar, might perhaps be allowed to continue analytic treatment with myself as consulting psychotherapeutic analyst, to see if the stages of treatment I suggested might prove beneficial, rather than more radical treatments others had suggested, at least over a relatively short term at the Institute. This was ultimately agreed unanimously by all in attendance. I was therefore directed to take H.Kielar under my auspice. It was requested also that I issue to the committee monthly evaluation reports for a period of approximately one year, to see if there were common benefits in continued behavioral analysis and social encouragement, as well as to outline any and all symptomatic mitigations to the patient's apparent mental illness. Should no apparent improvement become discernible after this time, the committee agreed to re-review the recommendations of others, including both Drs. Nowak and Szymański, should it be determined that more radical treatments might therefore be of greater benefit to the patient.

<u>Patient History</u>: H.Kielar was committed into the care of the Institute here at Kobierzyn in November, 1946. She exhibited elemental signs of basic malnutrition and vitamin deficiency, deemed unexceptional given what we know about her, and indeed given the difficulties throughout Poland during the War years. She remains underweight, although her physical condition has improved somewhat in the months she has resided here at the Institute. Despite this suggested malnutrition, H.Kielar was deemed to be in relative good health with no invasive physical procedure recommended. It was noted and commented, however, from her physical examination upon her admittance to Kobierzyn, that H.Kielar's hymen was no longer intact and that sexual intercourse had occurred sometime prior to her committal, although there is little from what was known of her history to suggest that any sexual intercourse was involuntary or the subject of rape. Nevertheless, this cannot be ruled out, particularly given the circumstances in Poland during the occupation and War years. This may or may not prove a pivotal point to explore in the patient's analysis, particularly in line with Dr. Freud's teachings on trauma and his reflections on cathexis that can find itself in conflict with instinctive compulsivity.

As is on record, H.Kielar was introduced and committed to the Institute by the Parish Priest in Nowy Wiśnicz, Fr. Jan Daněk. Daněk explained to the admitting psychiatrist that there was not much he knew about the patient, who he believed had been living 'feral' on the family's largely destroyed farm some 13 km from the town of Nowy Wiśnicz. Daněk himself had only become Parish Priest at the end of the War, following the natural death of the then Parish Priest, Fr. Wladyslaw Zieliński; thus he was understandably vague about the previous and formative years in H.Kielar's life. Only after installing himself comfortably in the previous priest's parish duties and living quarters had Daněk found in Zieliński's papers remarks that the old priest had been occasionally looking in on and taking food to the daughter of one Helena Kielar, the patient in question's mother. Zieliński had apparently written that the girl was living a 'wild unstructured' life subsequent to the mother's death in late 1944. Having been unaware that the mother was deceased, and not having been attendant at that woman's internment, which indeed had been unknown in the parish, Fr. Zieliński asked the girl what had happened to her mother. H.Kielar would only indicate that her mother had been killed by some retreating German soldiers. Fr. Zieliński recorded that he chose not to press the girl further, given her seemingly fragile temperament. For her part, H.Kielar provided no further information on the matter, and indeed kept her distance from the older priest in the few visits he subsequently made prior to his own demise.

When Fr. Daněk went to see the girl after coming to the parish, he found no trace of her at the largely burned out farmhouse and assumed she had gone. He made a repeat visit several months later, again finding the farm in a state of abandonment and ruin. He thought no more of the business until almost a year after his arrival at the parish, when a local parishioner informed him that there was a girl 'living feral' on the Kielar property. Fr. Daněk returned to the farm once more, this time finding the girl 'half starving and witless', having been living largely unseen and unknown in a small animal barn some three hundred meters from the destroyed farmhouse. He also indicated at this and all subsequent meetings that the girl was mute, while seeming to understand all he said. As Fr. Zieliński made no previous comment to this fact, indeed just the opposite in

44

relating what he understood of the girl's mother's demise, we can presume that such behavior coincided with the long period without social contact following Zieliński's death. Whether primary trauma occurred during this period resulting in either an inability or conscious choice not to speak is an area that must be explored in analysis.

Fr. Daněk, with the help of two local parishioners, was able to find papers relating to the young girl in the ruins of the farmhouse, which were presented to the Institute for safekeeping. These indicate that the girl was born on 4th of April, 1924; she is thus twenty-three years of age, although she looks younger, in part due to her malnourishment. The located birth and identity papers dated years prior to the outbreak of the War, along with the identity papers provided by the German Nazi occupiers, confirmed identity. This was substantiated by an identifying scar-like birthmark under her arm just to the side of her left breast, having been noted in the other paperwork. Of the girl's father, little was known, although according to local parishioners the father had 'run off' shortly prior to the outbreak the War and was rumored to have died in Krakow during the Nazi occupation. Again this should be an area of exploratory analysis in relation to the girl's emotional state, as discussed at length in the work of Dr. Freud as to the importance of the father-child dynamic particularly in relation to the Oedipal period of a child's emotional development; this too may offer clues to the trauma-resultant illness of the patient.

It is finally noted herewith that H.Kielar has been assigned a small room in one of the cottages on the property in order to maintain the patient under observation as necessary, and that upon my own suggested involvement in her case and subsequent to my primary evaluations I arranged for an initial period of consultation and analysis initially consisting of three weekly sessions of ninety minutes each.

Dr. Kazimierz Palinsky, D.N.,PhD
  (Consultant Psychoanalyst, Babinsky Institute/ Kobierzyn)
  Personal Case History: The case of Hannah K.

30 June 1947

Upon meeting I found Hannah K. to be an attractive but thin young woman of medium stature. She is somewhat younger than I, but the age difference is not substantial. This may prove helpful later in her therapy; we will see. Her hair, cut very short and boy-like, starting to grow out, is of a light-brown or perhaps dark blond color. Her short hair and thin stature makes her look even more waif-like. Vulnerable. Perhaps even a bit lost. Her eyes are unusually and quite vibrantly green. While some have remarked that these seem vacant, I prefer to describe such as withdrawn, taking in light but not reflecting such.

This and the following weeks of consultations proved to be meetings of often painful silence. My objective was, indeed is, to create a bond of trust between us. In line with Austrian psychoanalyst Dr. Alfred Adler's phased principles espoused in his writings and therapeutic studies, principles which I steadfastly support and choose to emulate, such a relationship is essential to progress any hope of successful analysis, and it was clear that this process needed to take time and be handled sensitively. I would seek to develop a warm, empathetic bond with the patient in order to understand her experience over time. I knew most of all that I could not rush matters; patience is essential.

Hannah K. appeared at each appointment on schedule, and whilst I detected minute breakthroughs by sometimes having the consultation door open upon her arrival, at other times closed, forcing her to acknowledge a desire to gain entry, or at least acceptance of such, little more was accomplished.

Although I had accepted this initial period would be difficult, and whilst I detected certain levels of intelligence behind the withdrawn gaze of this troubled young woman, I had quietly hoped nevertheless I could move through the first phase as prescribed through Dr. Adler's research more rapidly, if for no other reason than to make it easier to stand up to the likes of Dr. Nowak, a strong proponent of trepanation, or equally Dr. Szymański, who has pushed very hard to experiment on this patient with the latest psychotic medicinal treatments. I continue to find such proposals questionably ethical. Unfortunately, however, the patient gave very little in the way of any preliminary bond of trust needed to push any treatment forward, and I have to say I began to lose the necessary confidence I had maintained, namely that analysis and dialogue alone could help bring about some sense of normalization to this attractive and, I feel, gentle young woman's life. I found myself as a psychologist stuck in the first stage of the first phase of Adler's therapeutic processes and had no definite pathway with which to move forward. I was simply locked.

Towards the end of the first month I came upon the idea that perhaps, should Hannah K. be sufficiently literate enough—knowing such would be questionable given her rural, quite isolated upbringing only exacerbated by the War—she might write thoughts in a small notebook should she choose to do so, or if not to write, then perhaps to draw elemental pictures. These might in turn serve as the basis for beginning assessment leading to some sort of therapeutic dialogue. Even one-sided dialogue.

The patient did return over each of several sessions with the said notebook in hand; however it showed no sign of having been opened in the confines of her quarters.

My own despair began only to increase.

Last week that despair emerged and I allowed my own feelings to be known in consultation. As usual Hannah K. entered the consultation room and sat down, still showing no intention on lying on the sofa. And as usual she glanced only briefly at me, then turned away, staring outside at the warm sunshine and quiet of the rear gardens.

Rather than sit in silence as I normally did, however, I began to talk, and to express the concern I truly felt on her behalf. I explained that I sought more than a doctor-patient relationship, I sought to help someone I thought needed, no, wanted, help, and to do so before more extreme measures might be suggested by others whose primary goals were to reintroduce patients into society without addressing underlying problems, without caring. I told her that I, too, had known difficult times and that I was desperate to find ways to move forward, not only for her as my patient, but for myself. I explained I wanted to find a way to make her trust me for her sake, but for me to trust her for mine, for the benefit of us both. I told her I had known fear in the dark days, and knew it still—and that now I found I knew fear for her sake as well. I told her I had to believe that there was life, could be life, could be something for the future, could even find belief in God, when so many said this was no longer possible given what Poland had experienced and become, given what Europe had witnessed. I told her that I was indeed a witness now to her life, almost like the chorus in one of those ancient Greek plays, commenting to others. But I did not seek simply to act as chorus. I needed for both our sakes to engage and understand. I needed to find a way forward for both of us, doctor and patient. That is the nature of who I am. So who was she? What was inside of her? How could I help her understand, engage with me as her therapist, find a goal that had to mean life itself was the goal? Was such not possible? I needed something. And I was afraid I would be granted nothing, for I argued aloud and alone that it was in her ability to so grant.

Not once in this outburst did the patient respond. Not once did she look at me. And when I dismissed her with some emotion and obvious frustration until the next consultation, she glanced at me only long enough to take the notebook from my hand; she then turned and left the room.

My despair at this point was indeed great. I feared I might have to see her succumb to the suggested treatments of Dr. Nowak, or Dr. Szymański, and I knew of no way I could easily stop such if it came to it.

And then.... And then....

The breakthrough came at the next session. The next truncated but meaningful session that lasted only for a minute.

I had the door to the consultation room shut this time, when Hannah K. was scheduled. I heard, as I had heard on earlier such meetings, her quiet footsteps approach the room and stop. She had taken to knocking if the door was closed, had even recently simply entered, as I had encouraged her. This time, however, there was no knock and no movement. I waited, indeed remained determined to wait. Two, three minutes passed. Then five. Still I did not stand to open the door. Then more time.

Finally I had had enough of this game and opened the door. Hannah K. stood looking at me. For the first time she did not avert her eyes, but stared at me, taking everything in. I told her she should enter and stood aside, but she did not do so. I looked back at her again and still she held her ground.

"Hannah?," I said; "You can enter."

But she did not move. Finally she held out her hand that grasped the notebook and handed it to me. I took it. She stared at me for another moment or two, then turned and walked away, neither with haste, nor slowly. I watched her go, saying nothing, then closed the door behind her. I returned to my desk. Looked over at the empty sofa where she neither sat nor lay down. She was not there. She had chosen not to engage at all. Then I opened the notebook.

Hannah K. had blackened the first page entirely with the ink of her pen. The entire white sheet in the small notebook was colored black. That was all. And that was enough.

She was telling me there was darkness within her. This was what was meant in her 'drawing'.

And I knew that, while it would well take months, years perhaps to reach her, to touch upon that darkness and lighten her world, even a little, I would one day reach her.

I would one day, I think, understand.

Warsaw, 1938-39

Hania yearned for her mother's cheese and strawberry cake. She had never known her Babka, her mother's name for her grandmother, but her mother said she had in fact learned the secret recipe from her own mother before she had died a long time ago, so it should truthfully be known as Babka's cake, not hers. Hania's mother swore this was the most famous of all cakes in Poland, so much so that others named their cakes after Hania's grandmother; thus Babka cake was now served in households everywhere. Hania knew this to be a made-up story but giggled at the thought nonetheless. And then of course there was the cake.

Her mother used to make the treat only on Fridays to greet the Sabbath eve. When the weather was good, while the strawberries were deep red and ripe for picking, they would take a cart and horse, or sometimes even the train from the train station on Chmielna Street, up to Łomianki and there walk into Kampinos Forest before the sun of the long summer days became too hot. They would walk for forty minutes or so through farmland filled with the finest Polish cows to a particular farm, where they would buy the fresh, rich cheese that they both knew Hania's father adored. No matter how busy the farmer might be, he always had time to cut some cheese for them, making certain Hania had a slice for herself to eat on their return. Then they would take the long way back so they could fill her mother's basket with only the reddest of wild wood strawberries picked in the forest near Palmiry.

Sometimes, if she was free, Hania's Aunt Lea, her mother's sister, might join them as well. Lea would jump on the bike she kept in the cellar of her apartment building on Twarda Street in the centre of Warsaw and ride up to her sister's in the northern suburb of Zoliborz. Hania's mother would borrow the neighbor's bike with its rickety child's seat on the back. Hania would install herself there with her arms around her mother's waist; her mother and Aunt Lea would then pedal up to Kampinos, waving to shopkeepers and people rushing right and left all along the way.

Once back home, Hania's mother would roll out the extra dough she had left from making her Sabbath bread, fill it with fresh strawberries and cheese, using

50

only the best butter she could find. That was the secret, she would say to Hania. The butter had to be just so; only the best would do.

Hania loved to see her father's face when the cake appeared after the Sabbath meal.

"Not bad, Zivia," he would say, "you have made better I think, but not bad." Then he would wink at Hania and her little brother Shaul, as her mother punched his arm and pretended to glare at him, trying to hide her smile.

"I will kill you, Marek." But she never did.

Those were happy memories for Hania. But it had been some time since her mother had made her Babka's secret recipe cake. Summer days were turning to early autumn, and even over the summer past such ventures to Kampinos proved rare. Her mother and father had to work very hard now; times were not easy. Now too Fridays would be school days for both Hania, who would soon turn thirteen, as well as her brother, almost four years younger.

Hania enjoyed her school work. She wished she could attend every day. She had hopes of one day teaching school herself, or becoming a famous scientist, or perhaps a doctor working in the secret jungles of Africa. She dreamed she might go to America.

But for now she had to contend with school limited somewhat because of the cost, greater for her mother and father as they had to pay for Shaul as well. Hania lived in dread that she might have to attend one of the poor free Polish public schools near to her home, where the best she might hope for would be vocational training rather than working towards the matura certificate she desperately wanted so that she might one day go on to university. A Yeshivat or Beth Jacob school was out of the question as her parents, while observant, were hardly Orthodox believers. As were her parents' dreams for their two children, Hania dreamed of a life beyond, a life better. Dreams cost money, but she refused to believe they were not possible one day.

Hania's mother was an actress and singer who sometimes had work on the radio, or sometimes performed in local theatre. In previous years she had acted with the Warsaw Yiddish Arts Theater, the VYKT, small roles that nonetheless gave her real joy. The theatre group had only recently started performing again.

51

Zivia hoped to be a part of the company that would perform *Shulamis* at the Nowości Theater when the VYKT returned to Warsaw, once they had finished in Krakow at the end of the year. When so much of Zivia Stern's time these days was taken up with seamstressing work, seeing her mother flushed with excitement at the possibility of acting with the theatre company again gave Hania great pleasure. Surely there was nothing like watching her mother practicing her lines over and over for a role on the radio or the stage, or watching her experiment with makeup or putting on costumes that she would wear in the theatre.

Hania's father always said he was the luckiest person in the world to have married her mother, that he could not understand what Zivia saw in him, such a lowly workman. But Hania understood his teasing. Marek Stern worked across the river in the south of Warsaw at PZT, the technical state radio works, as a foreman engineer. Hania knew her father was not a lowly workman as he claimed, but in fact had many responsibilities in overseeing the building of the newest kinds of radios, not only for individuals but for the government as well. It was through this work when a young man that he had met her mother, when Polskie Radio was first being built in Warsaw. Zivia had been with a group of young actors who came to review plans for recording dramas while Marek was installing equipment in the new building. According to her father, he was instantly smitten with the beautiful actress who glanced at him as she walked past, but was terrified of approaching her. Zivia sniffed at this story, saying Marek had not been as shy as he suggested, but that he was shy enough. Had she not therefore been forward enough, who can say what fate may have allowed. Whatever the truth, Hania knew her parents had been very much in love, and to this day still were.

Hania adored her father, only wishing he did not have to work as hard as he did. He explained that as a foreman, and a Jew, he had to work twice as hard as others. He said his bosses kept an eye on every step he took, that he had to prove his worth over and over. Hania was certain no one worked harder than her father, nor as well. And despite the long hours away at the factory he always had time for her and for Shaul when he returned home, no matter how tired he was from the long day and from the long walk it took him to travel to and from the factory gates on Grochowska Street in Praga-Południe on the far side of the river. He particularly enjoyed the early morning journey, crossing over the Vistula on Kierbedz Bridge, gazing down at the river and the city sometimes just emerging from the dawn mist, jumping out of the way when two old horses each pulling a droshky tram from one side of Warsaw to the other would pass, the drivers ringing their bells and shouting at the horses: "Come on stara dziewczyna, move along my old girl! Move along!"

Hania remembered one morning, very early, her father woke her so she could join him on the walk over the bridge as he journeyed to work. They stood for a while above the great Vistula, watching the terns and seagulls swooping low over the rolling waters, fishing for their breakfast even as the sun just began to rise.

"Beautiful, Hania. Isn't it beautiful. This is what I want for you. You and Shaul. Always such beauty. Such possibility. It should be so."

She remembered he pressed his palm gently against her cheek, smiled, turned and continued on his way over the river to work. Hania watched him disappear, then stood for ages staring at the birds racing over the waters, at the city, at life beginning to bustle in Warsaw. He was right, she thought. It was beautiful, and as her father and her mother said, their lives together here made the hardships worthwhile.

Now that Hania was almost thirteen both her mother and father felt it would soon be time for her to help support the family needs. Her mother thought perhaps Hania could take some work as a seamstress after her classes, for the girl had a decent enough hand with a needle and thread and a good eye for design. Work might be hard to come by but the community helped its own and an apprenticeship was not out of the question. Hania of course had dreams, and so she should; but dreams did not put food on the table. Her mother took extra work, sometimes sewing late into the night so that she could take a role in the upcoming play which would pay next to nothing. Hania too might have to make sacrifices. The nature of things for all.

It was her Aunt Lea who came to the rescue that autumn.

Hania thought her mother's younger sister, Aunt Lea, and her husband, Michael Elster, were quite simply the most wonderful people she knew. Aunt Lea played the piano like no one Hania had ever heard. She often gave music lessons on her beautiful piano in the front room of their large apartment on Twarda Street or in the houses of many rich and famous people who called on her to teach their children. The Elster apartment was spread over two floors of the building and had space not only for her piano but for her uncle to have an office as well. Her Uncle Michael was a very talented architect; his services were always in demand and he had done well. Thus their large apartment in the centre of Warsaw was, in Hania's eyes, a most wondrous place, making her own family's small rooms in Zoliborz seem slightly down at heel, albeit full of the love of her own family. But even if such had been true, neither Lea nor Michael ever had attitudes suggesting they felt this way. They treated Hania and her family as their own. Although Lea was a good bit younger than her sister Zivia, the two women remained inseparable. And almost every Friday the Elsters looked forward to joining in for Sabbath dinner at the Sterns' apartment.

These dinners inevitably ended in some argument between her father and Uncle Michael, sometimes about politics, which Hania did not really understand, or often about religious matters. Her father was much more religious and less international than her worldly uncle, thus was far more prepared to take the Rabbi's words to heart when they came from the synagogue. Still, neither man was conservative and Orthodox in the way of so many others, especially those from the poorer communities, often those who had come to Warsaw from the East or indeed beyond the Russian frontier. Any argument quickly died down, particularly given the warmth of both their wives, each quick to embrace her husband with a kiss and a smile and a remark that the husbands were not so far apart really, and how lucky each sister was to have married such men of talent and principles--at which point Hania and Shaul would giggle and pretend to kiss one another loudly with big wet smacking lips, causing the adults to laugh and to pour the vodka that Uncle Michael inevitably brought for all.

It was perhaps unsurprising therefore that Aunt Lea might come to Hania's rescue when it came time to discuss how the girl might help her own family.

To the great joy of not only the Elsters, but indeed the Stern family as well, Lea had given birth in March to a boy, Jakub, her first born son. To say that Lea and Michael were ecstatic was, of course, an understatement. For several months Hania walked into the centre of the city for the hour it took her to get from

Zoliborz to Twarda Street to visit her aunt and the infant Jakub, a walk she thoroughly enjoyed as she usually strolled through Powązki Cemetery on her way there. Hania loved exploring amongst the beautiful old tombstones and haunting statuary, or staring at the graves of the famous along the Avenue of the Distinguished. She loved visiting the grave of Chopin's younger sister Emilia, which always made her think of her Aunt Lea, who could play Chopin's music like no one Hania had ever heard. Or she would pass by the grave of the artist Stanisław Maslowski, whose watercolors she remembered seeing in a museum and thought particularly beautiful. She would wander too through the Jewish cemetery just across from Powązki, with its rows and rows of nearly hidden graves, where she would stare at names that still sounded familiar in the Warsaw she knew, or Hebrew letters on gravestones that she could neither read nor sound, as she had yet to study this strange language.

Later she would arrive at Aunt Lea's, often hearing all the way down the street her aunt playing such beautiful music well before Hania knocked at their front door. And while her aunt would practice in the front room, Hania might sit quietly upstairs in the nursery playing with the baby Jakub, tickling him or making faces, telling stories or holding the baby's small fingers while he in turn looked back at her with wide open loving eyes.

So when it was time to discuss Hania's future in the year ahead, Aunt Lea pushed aside the notion that Hania might spend the majority of her days sewing clothes for Zoliborz neighbors or, even worse, taking an apprenticeship at a workshop in the community. Lea sat back in her chair, looked at Michael, then proceeded to suggest to Hania's parents that Hania be allowed to help with Jakub. Michael was terribly busy just then with his work. Lea wanted to return to teaching and, hopefully, performing once the baby had been weaned. There was a school for girls down the street from them, at 27 Twarda, run by Fanny Pozner, whom Lea was friendly with. Hania might school there in the mornings, then come to the Elsters in the afternoons to work on her studies while looking after Jakub, freeing Lea and Michael to pursue their own professional responsibilities. Lea and Michael would pay Hania a small wage. If Hania's mother still wished, Hania would continue to have one day of her weekend free to take on small seamstress repairs, at least until the girl learned if she wanted to follow such a vocation or continue to study for higher level secondary school if finances allowed in future years.

Zivia and Marek looked at one another. They hated the thought of taking advantage of their sister and brother-in-law. Lea assured them, however, it would be a gift not for Hania, but for her and for Michael, that they could afford to do this and that they needed the help. The young girl clearly loved little Jakub. They in turn trusted Hania implicitly. She was no longer a girl but already a young woman and they had no doubt that she would take her responsibility with the infant conscientiously, with the kind of maturity they had come to recognize in her.

Thus it was settled.

Hania's face lit up, knowing the strolls through Powązki that she so enjoyed might continue on the way to Twarda Street and her waiting charge before the days became too short, and on the walk home. Even with winter quickly approaching and the snows that would inevitably fall, she was greatly pleased. Mostly it would mean the beginning of a love affair with this perfect little child, no infant more perfect in all of Warsaw she was absolutely certain.

*

Although the leaves had started falling from the trees and cool autumn winds blew around the corners of the Warsaw streets, the weather continued to be warm enough to take Jakub out in his baby's carriage in the afternoons after her class at Miss Pozner's school. Sometimes her Aunt would be giving a music lesson in the house, or practicing for a recital she was due to give with other musicians or a singer. Sometimes too her Uncle would be at the house working on drawings or plans he needed to update for this building or that scheme.

These were also the hours that Hania enjoyed best, pushing the baby up to Krasinski Park to sit amongst all the mothers with their new baby carriages, all seated along the rows of benches in the manicured gardens, each mother comparing her infant to the one next to her. Hania had no doubt that Jakub was the most beautiful of them all, the smartest and one day would be the most talented. She had only to look at his thoughtful green eyes, the same shade as her own, and the unusually long fingers on his tiny hands, to know that he would become a most special child. Nothing pleased her more than showing off her own charge to the other mothers, and indeed letting them believe, as no doubt some probably did, that the infant was her own.

The other reason that gave Hania so much to look forward to each morning as she began her walk to Twarda Street was that she had made a best friend at Miss Pozner's school, a girl who Hania enjoyed seeing almost as much as she did her baby cousin.

The teachers at the school used to say that Alicja Leder was a wild, uncontrollable tearaway who would land herself in Serbia Prison if she was not careful. Certainly Alicja's brown eyes always seemed to be dancing with mischief that burned brightest during religious studies. No one could act out a girl turning to a pillar of salt better, and she seemed to like nothing more than to push the teacher as to the meanings of beget, begat and begetting when this came up in Bible readings, as it often did, or what exactly could be made of all this lying around naked and drunk that Noah apparently relished when he should have been out checking on the weather.

Alicja Leder, a year older than Hania, lived up on Nowolipki Street, not far from Krasinski Park, with her uncle. Her mother had died when Alicja was born; Alicja never spoke of her. Her father was an engineer working in the Caucuses somewhere, or so Alicja said. He would send money to her uncle so that his daughter could attend Miss Pozner's school, writing to her that he hoped she would one day make someone a good, obedient wife. Alicja laughed at this; perhaps it was the reason she rebelled as often as she did. Certainly, she said, the zlotys he sent to Miss Pozner's school were the reason that 'wild Alicja' would not be asked to leave. So more the reason to push them to think of doing so.

Most of the girls were nervous of Alicja and she rather loved terrorizing them, but with Hania things were different. For reasons neither of them quite understood, Alicja took immediately to this new girl who walked her way daily down from Zoliborz and who in many ways was the exact opposite of the spirited mad girl, or so some of the others said of her.

If many of the girls at the school, and most certainly their mothers, had little time for Alicja and her antics, Aunt Lea found the girl's spirit just the antidote for her niece's obvious shyness, and was happy enough when the two girls took Jakub out in the baby carriage in the afternoons. Sometimes, however, if Aunt Lea was practicing at home, Alicja asked if she might sit quietly in the house with Hania, just so she could listen to the music. Once or twice she even asked if she might remain there alone while Hania took Jakub out walking. The music calmed her in a way nothing else could, particularly some of Chopin's *Nocturnes*, which Lea was rehearsing for a winter concert. Hania did not mind if Alicja asked to remain behind. She saw beneath the bravura so usually on display from the spirited girl a yearning for something, perhaps for the mother she had never had, the sister she had never had. That may have been why Alicja was so attracted to Hania: while appearances suggested that the relationship was the result of Hania's need, that she looked up in wonder and some confusion at the older girl's antics, the truth was in some ways slightly more complex and perhaps just the opposite. In the quiet of the evening, sitting with Michael and talking about the two girls, Lea put it that if Hania needed Alicja, Alicja needed Hania—and in a way they both cried out for the absolute need of Jakub: the responsibility of looking after a child, the changes within both from girlhood to womanhood almost somehow reaching out for this little infant's hand and smile and warmth. Adulthood was never easy, she remarked, and Michael agreed.

Sometimes Alicja would join Hania part way towards Zoliborz in the late autumn afternoons so the two might wander through Powązki together, before the evening gathered round as the sun began to set ever more quickly on the day. They would kick crisp brown dying leaves between the crypts, or pretend to be statues amongst the statuary in the cemetery, or hide behind gravestones trying to creep up on one another when gazing in the wrong direction. They rarely saw mourners or other people on these afternoons so they could be themselves, tell frightening stories to make them both scream with mock fear or real delight, or sing a song, or fantasize about boys who might one day become husbands. Alicja insisted she never wanted a husband, that no man could be trusted and men were just donkeys when all was said and done. Hania tried to argue with her, saying that neither her father nor Uncle Michael nor Shaul, who Alicja had yet to meet, was a donkey.

"Well, maybe there are exceptions," Alicja said. "Maybe. But almost all men are donkeys and all donkeys are asses and almost all men are therefore asses, good for one thing and one thing only."

"What's that?"

Alicja looked over at her younger friend, whose sincerity was obvious. She cupped her hands and held them high against her thighs, then grunted and started to laugh with delight. It took a moment for Hania to understand what her friend suggested, then she too burst into laughter. Both girls fell to the ground on some old graves, rolling in the dead leaves, laughing like crazy people.

The sort of memories neither would hopefully forget.

One cold afternoon, Alicja joined Hania for a walk up to Krasinski Park, pushing Jakub in the carriage. They sat on a bench surrounded by mothers and their children, listening to the gossip. Alicja poked Hania to notice one mother or another, one baby or another, then make a funny face or gesture about the offending parent or child, causing Hania to giggle and turn away from more than one glaring adult.

Finally growing weary of this game, Alicja dragged Hania away from the crowded benches.

"Come," she said. "That way. Let's take that path, look."

An overgrown path through trees and bushes led away from the manicured gardens where most of the mothers sat enjoying the autumn sunshine. Alicja skipped ahead, leaving Hania to struggle as she pushed the carriage through the undergrowth. After catching up with her friend, Alicja grinned mischievously.

"We are the brave, wise queens of the ancient Nile, preparing for battle against the Polish invaders. We'll frighten them away from our villages or make them slaves to build our temples."

Alicja pulled Hania and the carriage behind a bush, hiding from the main path. As someone passed, she would shake branches, startling the unsuspecting victim who would look around in surprise. The two girls broke into giggles after the confused person could no longer hear them. Later Alicja tiptoed back onto the path to imitate someone's walk or follow along behind most comically; when her prey turned around, Alicja feigned innocence, or bent down to tie her shoe.

At one point a mother with her infant turned and raised her voice in annoyance. Alicja ran off through the bushes, laughing, with Hania lagging behind, pushing the carriage. As Hania emerged through some trees, the wheels of the baby's chair became stuck against some raised tree roots. The buggy nearly tipped over as Hania pushed ever harder.

"Careful!" she heard a voice say. Hania looked up to see a well dressed young woman staring at her, a rather stiff, formally dressed but equally handsome man at her side. "Do you need help?," the woman asked her, her voice accented.

Without waiting for an answer, the man walked over to Hania and lifted the carriage over the roots and onto the path.

"Thank you," said Hania, as Alicja appeared, joining them.

The woman, quite pretty, looked down at Jakub. Smiled.

"A beautiful child. Is he yours?"

"Ours," Alicja quickly responded. "We are both his mothers."

The man looked at her, nodded slightly.

"An interesting trick. Your sort have babies when very young it would seem."

"Don't listen to my husband," said the woman. "He tries to learn what it will mean to be a father and he still has some way to go."

"She is pretending," said Hania. "He is my little cousin. We look after him."

"Ah," said the man with the accent. "Then you should be careful where you are walking, so no one gets hurt."

The woman gave her husband a warning glance.

"He is a lucky baby," she said. "I'm sure he is lucky to have you. His eyes are beautiful, like yours," nodding towards Hania. "You could almost be his mother. I am sure his real mother would be pleased with his care."

"No doubt," said the man. "So: good afternoon."

He nodded, and the well dressed couple strolled away. Hania and Alicja watched them continue along the walkway.

"She's beautiful," said Hania.

"Do you think so? I don't. He on the other hand…but I do not think he is my type."

"They weren't Polish."

"German. I heard them talking earlier. Germany. Awful."

"Why?"

"They want to eat us up."

"Not all Germans are awful."

"Of course they are. Especially the pretty ones."

"You mean her?"

"I mean him. The German and his Wife: they were especially jealous of us I think. Come on!"

And Alicja ran off again down the main pathway, with Hania pushing the baby carriage and hurrying after.

A couple weeks later Hania was on her own with Jakub and again had taken him to Krasinski for fresh air. She stopped at a bench to sit, taking the baby from his chair and putting him on her lap, bouncing him as he smiled and cooed.

"He is happy," said a figure on the far side of the bench.

"Yes, I think so. Are you happy, eh?," Hania asked her charge, then looking up at the woman bundled against the cold wind, watching her.

"Your cousin, if I remember."

Hania realized this was the German Woman she had previously seen.

"May I?"

The woman pointed to Jakub, stood up to move closer to Hania, then sat down again. Hania hesitated, then handed Jakub to the woman, who placed him on her lap. The woman stared into Jakub's face and took his small hands in hers, turning them over in her palm.

"His hands are so small, so fine. Lovely hands. Beautiful boy. His mother I think is very lucky. As are you. I think perhaps you are more his aunt than his mother, no?"

She smiled at Hania, who smiled back.

"His hands suggest he will be a special boy, even if he…well, I think so. I can tell."

"Do you have any children?," Hania asked, then caught herself. "I'm sorry, I should not have…"

"No. No, it is all right," said the German Woman with a slight laugh. "I will have a baby late next spring. I hope it will be a boy. That would please my husband."

"I am sure he will be a beautiful baby."

"Yes. Yes, I am sure. Like this one." She handed Jakub back to Hania.

"You are not from here."

"From Germany. My husband, he is an attaché at the Embassy. Do you know what that means?"

Hania shook her head no.

"It means he is always busy. Too busy."

"He must be important."

"He has many responsibilities. And these days... He is always busy. You must look after the baby, my Fraulein. Like a good aunt, no? These days you must look after him."

Hania stared at the woman, whose gaze seemed far away, distracted. The woman said nothing for a long moment, then shook her head thoughtfully.

"I should go. My husband does not like me coming here but I find it quite beautiful. So: it is getting cold I think; it is time."

The German Woman stood to leave.

"A beautiful child. As I said to you, he has your eyes. I think he is lucky to have you, young Fraulein."

She started away.

"Your baby..." said Hania. The German Woman turned. "Your baby will be so also."

The German Woman stared at her, smiled slightly, nodded, then walked away, disappearing down the path.

*

Autumn turned to winter, with its snow and freezing winds. Nevertheless every day Hania rose early at the same time as her father went to work so that she could make the hour journey to her school, then on to her Aunt and Uncle's where she continued to look after Jakub, just beginning to take his first steps. She rarely went to Krasinski Park. If she took the baby out, it would be to visit the shops on Nalewki Street for her aunt or mother. If the day was somewhat warmer she might push the baby carriage as far as the Vistula and sit watching the river race by in the late winter's day sunshine.

Aunt Lea invited Hania, Shaul and her parents to a performance at the Femina Theatre where soprano Maria Ajzensztadt sang songs of Schubert, with Aunt Lea accompanying. Hania found the evening magical, despite having heard Aunt Lea practicing for weeks before the concert.

In the final days of winter, as spring was just beginning to awake, Hania's mother Zivia appeared in a small role at the Nowości Theater, with the VYKT, in the operetta play *Shulamis*, as she had hoped, playing one of the citizens of Jerusalem at the Grand Temple. The performances were a great success in the community, although did cause some outrage in the newspapers and with certain politicians because of its setting and claims that it was too political, too Jewish, for the propriety of many of Warsaw's citizens. Regardless, seeing her mother flushed with excitement and anticipation at each night's performance over the week was a joy for all the family. Hania kept a photograph of her mother in the play beside her bed in a place of pride.

Hania continued her studies at Miss Pozner's with the diligence and hard work that her parents expected of her, although her friendship with Alicja never waned. While the days were short the two girls had less time to spend together, particularly when the cold winds were blowing through Warsaw; Hania had to rush home after looking after Jakub at Aunt Lea's. But as the days began slowly to lengthen and the weather eased, the two friends took up where they had left off, wandering in Powązki or the Jewish Cemetery, staring in the shop windows up on Nalewki and dreaming of all that they might buy when they were rich and beautiful, for the moment instead satisfying themselves by purchasing bagels from a street seller on Chlodna Street, scoffing them down as fast as they could.

One day when the girls were out walking Alicja noticed two young men in their school uniforms from the Gymnasium some streets near to the girl's own school watching them, then following. The boys nudged one another, whispering, full of bravura, smoking cigarettes, trying to act rather indifferent although not invisible; they were hardly invisible.

"We will see if they are cowards or not," muttered Alicja, as the girls pretended not to notice.

The two young men followed the girls and made the odd surreptitious glance in their direction, but after a while must have grown bored and disappeared.

A few days later, however, they reappeared and again followed the two girls, heading to Powązki Cemetery to stroll amongst the statues and graves as they had the year before.

"I think they are following us again," said Hania.

"Good. We can see how brave they really are."

The girls continue walking into the great old cemetery. The two young men hesitated, then followed. A game of find me if you can developed, with the two girls disappearing and reappearing behind mammoth crypts and the teenage boys losing them, finding them, losing them, until the girls managed to come up behind the two others and half-scare them amongst the late afternoon shadows, all four of them eventually breaking into laughter and racing along the quiet necropolis paths.

This happened in afternoons once or twice more. Finally on one such afternoon the four collapsed in laughter at the foot of one of the crypts. They sat for a few minutes not saying much, when suddenly Alicja jumped up.

"I will come back," she said to Hania while looking at the older boy, Romek. Romek hesitated, then he too jumped up and the two of them disappeared amongst the crypts.

The slightly younger boy, Arie, suddenly went very quiet, unsure how to speak to Hania, whether to sit or stand, move or freeze. Arie was a thin, small young man, someone still uncomfortable in his own skin, and particularly uncomfortable around those of the opposite sex. Hania understood his shyness, but her own prevented her from trying to overcome it.

Arie finally found the courage to speak.

"They say there may be trouble soon. Maybe even a war."

"Do you think so?"

"The Nazis want Poland. They hate the Jews."

"Are you afraid?"

"Me? No. No, I'll fight for Poland. We will see them off."

"I hope that will not happen. My father and mother are worried."

"Mine too."

"Maybe things will be all right. You have to hope."

"Maybe. I don't know."

"I guess I am a little afraid."

"...I guess perhaps I am too, just a little."

Arie looked at her, then away.

"It is all right to be...It is all right," Hania said. Then she was silent, watching him, wondering where Alicja had gone to, wondering should she believe her own words.

Arie did not look up at her, not knowing quite what she meant. The truth was he did not know either. They sat in silence for a few moments when Alicja and Romek reappeared. Romek seemed flushed and ill at ease. Alicja looked slightly cross.

"Come, Arie, we should go," the older boy said to his friend.

Arie turned and started after Romek, who had already started to walk away. The younger boy turned back for a moment, looking at Hania and Alicja.

"See you again," he said, then quickly turned and followed his friend.

The girls watched them go. Hania looked at Alicja, the older girl's expression proud and haughty.

"Cowards," she said; "I thought so."

Hania followed her out of the cemetery, then Alicja turned around to walk back to her Uncle's apartment, while Hania continued on her walk back to Zoliborz. In the days that followed the two boys were nowhere to be seen.

*

A few weeks later Hania was again with Jakub in Krasinski Park when she saw the German Woman sitting in almost the same spot where she had last seen her. Hania smiled and walked over.

"Hello," said Hania. "We have met here before."

The German Woman turned to look at her, needing a moment to remember. Her expression was of someone slightly lost, a woman struggling. Only then did Hania realize that the pretty German Woman had been quietly crying.

"The Jewish girl who looks after her beautiful cousin. Almost like an aunt or a mother."

Thinking she should not have come over, Hania started to withdraw.

"I am sorry, I just wanted to say hello and…"

"No. It does not matter. Come. Do sit. Please."

Hania hesitated, then sat down.

"May I?," the woman asked, then picked up Jakub before Hania could respond.

"He has got very big. Still beautiful. Still…Yes. Beautiful boy."

She rubbed her hand on Jakub's cheek tenderly. Stared at him, then away, frozen with her own thoughts. She put him back in the baby carriage. Smiled weakly at Hania, then turned her face away again, her thoughts carrying here elsewhere.

Hania noticed that the woman was not pregnant. She was not sure if she should say something. The German Woman seemed to sense what Hania was thinking.

"No. I'm not. I lost it," she said. "This winter I…I lost it…"

Although she could not see the woman's face turned away, Hania sensed the woman's tears. She took out a small embroidered handkerchief she kept in her coat and handed it to the German Woman, who glanced back at Hania now, then looked down at Jakub. She shook her head, just slightly, with a quiet, pained sigh.

"Thank you… My husband, he has tried, he…I am not sure he knows how I…I…I am not sure he grasps what I…"

"I am sorry."

"…My husband loves me, but he does not understand things. He spends more time with his assistant Herbert than he spends with…Men and their foolish ideas, they sometimes do not see what matters even when such yearns to be seen…It was not meant to be, you see. It is unfair, no? All these mothers here, these Jewish children…All of it."

"But perhaps you will be pregnant again. Soon. You might."

The German Woman looked at her, smiled just slightly. Then the smile disappeared and she looked away.

"We will leave Warsaw soon I think. Some things in life you cannot prevent. You have no control."

Hania stared at her, said nothing, knew not what to say.

66

"You should leave too, Fraulein."

The German Woman glanced at her, then up at the sky.

"Dark clouds. I think it will rain. You should go."

The German Woman stood, looked at Hania.

"I think you should. I am sorry."

As she walked away, Hania called out to her:

"When you have a child, he will be as beautiful as his mother. He will."

The German Woman turned, looked at her for a long moment, nodded, then turned and walked away.

A month later Hania and Alicja out pushing Jakub as usual again stopped at Krasinski Park, sitting together on a bench, laughing and chatting quietly, with many other mothers and their children seated around them. Alicja had a small Sida camera that her Uncle had given her for her birthday and she took some photographs of the mothers sitting on benches cooing at their children. A young man passed and she asked him to take a photograph of Hania and her. As he looked through the viewfinder, Hania rested her head on her friend's shoulder. Alicja grinned broadly. The camera clicked.

"There," said Alicja. "Friends forever frozen in time."

"Friends forever," agreed Hania. She leaned over to check on Jakub, looking up at her, smiling. She ran her fingers over his little cheeks lovingly, lifted him out of the carriage, resting him in her lap.

"He could pass for your child," laughed Alicja.

Hania smiled at the thought. She looked up then and was surprised to recognize the German Woman, smartly dressed, walking towards her. Uncertain, Hania stood up with Jakub in her arms just as the woman reached them. She stared at Hania, smiled weakly, nodded to Alicja.

"Such a beautiful boy. How sad."

Hania stared at the woman, confused, becoming aware of pronounced silence around them, with many of the nearby mothers either staring or with their eyes cast down. Behind the Woman standing now before her she noticed at the park entrance gate a car waiting; emerging from it, then marching towards them, came a man in a black uniform. The German Woman turned and saw him as well. At first

67

Hania did not recognize him. Only at first.

"My husband. They all must wear uniforms now. Everyone has their orders. Their duty."

She looked back at Hania, at Jakub held tightly. The German Woman tried to smile, but Hania saw only sadness. Only emptiness.

"He does not want me to come here, my husband. He says it is not for us. But I want to see the boy one more time. I insist we look to see if you might be here again. And so you are."

The German by now stood beside his wife, staring at Hania, at Alicja, still seated, who stared back with a hardened face, refusing to stand. He turned to his wife.

"We should go."

"Such a beautiful child, is he not?," the German Woman said to her husband.

The German said nothing. His wife pulled an embroidered handkerchief from her bag, handing it to Hania.

"I also need to return this to you."

Hania reached out and took the handkerchief from the woman without taking her eyes from her. The German Woman hesitated for just a moment, holding still the small, ironed piece of linen.

"He has your eyes," she said to Hania.

"Sturmbannführer?"

A rather large, heavy man also in an army uniform had appeared. The German turned to him, nodded. The man stared for a long moment at Hania, then turned back towards the car. The German turned to his wife.

"You have done as you wished I believe, my dear. Come."

The German Woman stared at her young, handsome husband. Although his expression seemed thoughtful, his face seemed somehow hardened, cold. She nodded, turned back one last time to Jakub, gently touched the baby's face, nodded at Hania, then turned and walked back towards the waiting car.

Hania sensed she would never see this woman again.

The German watched his wife retreat, then gazed back at Hania and Jakub, and at Alicja, whose expression remained defiant. The German then turned and started away, hesitated, turned back once again, extended his arm above his head, his legs stiffening, his back straight, his voice without warmth.

"Heil," was all he said. He nodded, turned one final time and walked to the waiting car, which pulled away after he climbed into the back.

No one in the park watching said a word. Not a murmur.

Hania was afraid.

*

Spring months turned to summer, the days growing longer, hotter. With her classes in break, Zivia asked Hania to spend more time at home sewing with her and looking after Shaul in her free hours. Hania continued to visit the apartment on Twarda Street and to help with Jakub, but over the summer Lea had fewer students to contend with so Hania was needed only for two days a week. As always she looked forward to these days, leaving early for her usual meander in Powązki Cemetery, heading back late so she could spend time with Alicja.

The two were now even more inseparable, often chatting or singing, sometimes simply walking along streets looking at people or in shop windows. Alicja's father had cancelled his planned return during the summer and her uncle paid her little mind. In Hania there was someone Alicja could talk to about her hopes and plans and schemes. Hania always listened without contradicting or making fun or doubting. Both girls allowed themselves to dream. Both imagined the possible, reinforcing one another with 'why not' and 'I will go too.'

After the encounter weeks earlier in Krasinski Park, Hania chose not to return there. But she and Alicja discovered the joys of the Saxon Gardens in summer, where Warsaw's well-off would stroll in the late afternoon sunshine, taking in the beautiful manicured lawns and flowers. As the weather grew hotter than they had remembered from years gone by the two girls would take off their shoes and socks to sit with their bare feet in the cooling fountain waters, talking about everything and nothing as young women their age were wont to do. Or they might stroll to the Vistula and sit in the green grassed-in areas buttressed up against the constant hubbub of Warsaw, sitting quietly, watching the waters flow, pretending the worries and cares that had started to permeate every corner of the city simply did not exist.

One afternoon Hania's mother, after much begging, agreed to let her daughter leave the sewing so to spend the day with her friend. Alicja had a glint in her eye as Hania met her outside of her Uncle's apartment. She knew a way to sneak into the Kino Napoleon, the new cinema house in Trzech Krzyży Square in the basement of a large building. The girls waited until the lights had gone down so they would not be seen, then sneaked in and somehow found seats in the crowded great balcony, with its opulent purple upholstered armchairs each decorated with the letter N. They could not imagine a more wondrous royal palace anywhere, not even in America, they said later.

They sat opened mouthed with amazement when the film appeared on the giant screen, Hania never having been to a film before. Everyone in Warsaw seemed to be talking of Michal Waszyński's *Vagabonds*. For several years Hania had laughed with delight when listening with her family to the two stars, Szczepko and Toňko, in their hilarious Sunday night weekly radio broadcasts of *Lviv's Merry Wave*. Both girls found seeing the two stars on the screen simply magical. When the film was over they quickly escaped the theatre before their presence was noted, singing the film's jubilant *'Only in Lviv'* together as they skipped back home.

But despite the seemingly careless days of summer when Hania would roam the streets with her closest friend, or entertain Jakub while listening to her Aunt Lea playing the beautiful Chopin melodies in the parlor below that somehow brought gentle coolness into the house, wrestling with the hot breeze whispering through so many open windows, events happening in Poland and at its borders were never far from anyone's thoughts or fears.

Hania's mother and father, indeed almost all of the adults she knew, talked of little besides the gathering storm coming out from Germany. It seemed daily more soldiers in uniform appeared on the streets. In May there had been a mass demonstration of workers in the city; Hania watched thousands marching through, cursing the German Nazi government with slogans and shouts.

Many thought war had become inevitable. The British had promised to help Poland in the event of such, but no one could be certain that they would do so, given what they had done to Czechoslovakia in 1938. Rumors and distrust were everywhere. General Stachiewicz had ordered fortifications to be built on the border with Germany, which demanded that the free city of Gdansk, or Danzig as Germany insisted, be handed back to the German state. Riots there had become almost commonplace, with the Polish minority often beaten or killed.

The girls tried not to let this world deflect from their own plans and dreams. Hania and Alicja wanted freedom, insisted on it, pretended that the world beyond was not theirs, that they would break free, be free. No one would touch them. No one would hurt them.

As they had on so many previous occasions, they ran in Powązki and played catch me if you can amongst the crypts and statuary, simply being themselves, laughing, denying the ugliness of the world around them that they tried so hard not to acknowledge. They ran and laughed and hid and fell down together, almost like lovers, until they could no longer talk, felt they could no longer breathe.

"Do you think it will be all right?," Hania finally asked her friend.

"Of course it will," answered Alicja.

Hania looked at her, then up at the sky. Alicja, lying beside her, took her hand.

"Of course it will," she said again, more emphatically. Hania again looked at her friend.

"I love you, Alicja…" She could not finish the sentence.

"I know," Alicja said. Smiled. "I know."

They got up, a hint of laughter between them, and started back to the avenue. As they emerged from a crowd of crumbling graves onto the road they saw a group of five boys sitting on fallen gravestones nearby, smoking cigarettes. The boys looked at them, then at one another.

"Well what have we here?," one of them said; they all stood up, their manner threatening.

"Would you look at them," another said. "Dead faces. The dead have risen from their graves."

And still another: "Hold on, I think they are Jews. Are you Jews? I think they are Jews."

The two girls quickly turned, ignoring them, walking away. But the boys, once started, were hardly ready to end their taunts.

"This is not the Jewish cemetery, Jews. This is for Poles. You are not Poles.

You do not belong here."

"Germany only threatens Poland because of the Jews! What do you think, Jan? Jewess whores in our cemetery? I don't think we should allow that."

The boys approached threateningly. Hania and Alicja walked more quickly, but the boys continued. They started swearing in unison:

"Whore, whore, Jewish whore. Whore!," they shouted.

Suddenly Alicja whirled around.

"Yes? Yes?," she screamed. Then louder: "You think so? You think you are all so brave? You think so!"

She roared at them like an otherworldly spirit: mad and frightening. At first they smiled. Then she screamed, even scaring Hania. Her screaming refused to stop. Refused to capitulate.

"She's crazy. Crazy Jew whore," one of them said. He threw a rock. And they all picked up rocks. As they did, Alicja raised herself to her full height and stood her ground. A rock hit her in the head and a cut opened over one eye, but she did not move. The boys went silent.

"I'll show you crazy," said Alicja, almost growling, fierce. She reached into the bag she had with her, and to Hania's astonishment, pulled out a knife.

"Crazy? Come on then! I'll cut the little teats between your legs straight off and make you squeal like pigs! You want to threaten girls? I'll make you into one."

Alicja began to run towards them, her arm outstretched, her hair wild, screaming with fury. The boys laughter waned; they clearly did not know what they had unleashed, as if this girl might be one of the dead come to take revenge, so fierce and controlled her anger. They turned and ran, disappearing around some gravestones. Alicja had no intention of allowing them to get away easily. They ran; she ran. They ran faster, but not as well. The last of them, the smallest, tripped and fell as the others disappeared. He started to stand when Alicja caught up with him, kicking him onto his back. In a heartbeat moment, she was on top of him, just as Hania caught up with her.

Alicja had her knife at the boy's throat. He genuinely looked terrified.

"Alicja! No! Don't Alicja! Don't!" Hania shouted.

Alicja raised the knife, not taking her eyes from the boy.

"Don't," Hania said again, quietly this time.

Her friend hesitated, then slowly lowered her hand and tossed the knife away. Still she held the terrified boy pinned to the ground. She stared at him.

And she slapped him. Hard. Once.

Hania saw tears in the boy's ashamed face.

Alicja slowly climbed off him.

"Go," she said firmly, with strength that could frighten. "Never let me see you again."

The boy stood, looked at her, turned and ran.

Alicja, with blood still flowing down the side of her face looked at Hania, picked up her knife and marched back towards the road. She stopped, looked at her friend.

"It will be all right," Alicja said. "I will always defend you. Always. Remember that, Hania. You understand?"

Hania nodded, still shaking. She walked over to her friend, carefully wiped the blood away. The two girls stood one in front of the other, staring, silent, for the longest moment. Both somehow understood, each the other. It was enough.

Hania did not see her friend for the remainder of the summer. What had happened frightened her. But the thought of losing Alicja's friendship frightened her more.

She had wanted to try to see her again, but it was not to be. Late in August Hania returned home from being out much of the day with Shaul to find her father at home, ashen faced. The Germans and the Soviets had signed an agreement not to fight one another, he explained. Instead they would split the spoils of their treachery. Those spoils were Poland. War, he told her, was inevitable. Those most in danger were the Jews, for there seemed little interest from the Polish government, or any government, to do whatever possible to protect them.

Uniforms were now everywhere. Hania's mother and father told her that she and Shaul were no longer to go out during the day. Hania was frightened her father would go away with the soldiers who were mobilized several days later, but her father said he would not be called up because of his age and because his work at the PZT state radio works was too important for the Polish government.

Hania had to stop going to her Aunt and Uncle's, could not see Alicja. Her parents rarely smiled now. Although they tried to protect their children, their worry was obvious. The streets grew quiet. The soldiers departed for the Western frontier. Hania did not know what to think, what to feel. She knew only that she was afraid.

Everyone was afraid.

"Surely our army will defend us," she said to her father. "Our government will resist the Germans. Surely they will."

Her father said nothing for a long moment. Finally he tried to smile.

"Yes, my Hania. It will be all right. You will have your school and your friend and Warsaw will be safe. It will be all right."

She heard his words. And she heard the doubt in his voice.

That night her father went to the synagogue to pray. Her mother lit candles at home. She said they should all trust in God, that their family, their friends, that all Poland would be safe, that their prayers would be heard.

The next morning, the first day of September, Germany invaded Poland. The War so many feared had begun.

*

After the first few days of September rumors were rife that the German Army had broken through the Polish line and that the Polish Army, or what remained of it, was in retreat. Word came over the radio that both Britain and France had declared war on Germany in response, but for those in Warsaw this offered no hope of reprieve or salvation, as defeated soldiers returned to Warsaw streets, wounded and broken.

Men overturned tram cars for barricades. Civilians took whatever they could find as arms, preparing for a long siege, intent on defending their city. Hania's father stayed away long hours, overseeing the manufacture of radios to get to the troops still able to fight and to those civilians desperate to find ways to contact others in countries that now seemed so far away and unable to come to their aid. Marek would return exhausted in the evenings only to attend meetings or to host them at the apartment with others from their community, arguing into the small hours how they might best defend their families and neighborhoods, how best they

74

should protect their fellow Jews who had particular reason to fear the German onslaught. Resistance plans were drawn up, discussions of evacuation, but by then it was too late to think of such. Barely more than a week after the German tanks and aircraft crossed the border, Warsaw was mostly surrounded. Checkpoints were everywhere. People were frightened. They had cause to be.

As matters went from bad to worse, her mother insisted that Hania and Shaul remain henceforth only in the apartment. When necessary Zivia went out to try to find food, although everything was in short supply. Hania convinced her on a few occasions to be allowed to help. She was shocked to see streams of refugees pouring into the city, hiding in doorways or in empty buildings, desperate for shelter. A few times her mother stood in front of their building, keeping to the doorway and shadows for protection, handing out tea and bread to those who passed. Most had nothing with them but the clothes they wore.

Soon, however, the Sterns had to stand in the long lines at the bakery themselves, like everyone else, fearful that when they might get to the top of the line, the bakery would be empty.

September 16th was Rosh Hashanah, the Jewish New Year. Her mother argued strongly that they should recognize the holiday despite the travesty around them. Late in the afternoon, Hania helped her prepare a meal so that they might try to find a least a little joy in the holiday, that they all might pray together, that they would be protected from the darkness at the edge of their city. While her father was at the synagogue, Hania and her mother put out some herring, bread and butter, some tomatoes and carrots that Zivia had kept for the day. They heard planes flying overhead as their father came in, telling them they must hurry to the cellar: the Germans were strafing the streets with machine gun fire from their fighter planes. As they hurriedly gathered their meager foodstuffs to take with them, they heard banging at the door. Her mother looked at her father, who told them all to wait in the side room. He opened the door a crack only to find Aunt Lea, Uncle Michael and Jakub. They had left their own apartment locked up, deciding they should come try to celebrate with the Sterns. Half way on their journey to the edge of the city the shooting started and bombs began to fall. Many places in the Jewish quarter were on fire.

The Elsters remained with the Stern family in their small apartment for the days that followed. The adults all felt it best for the time being to remain in Zoliborz, although conditions continued to grow worse. Food became scarce, often limited to tins of sardines or pickles, the only things they might have to eat. Word spread that the Soviets had now invaded eastern Poland, tearing the country in two. By September 20th the water in the apartment ceased working and the radio that Marek had set up in the apartment went silent.

Still the streets appeared somehow safer for the moment. Lea and Michael discussed returning to their apartment on Twarda Street, but Hania's mother begged them to remain, at least until after Yom Kippur, the Jewish Day of Atonement. They could not be certain what would happen, or what they'd find.

The night of Kol Nidre, the holiest night of the year for the Jewish community, Hania's father and her Uncle Michael attended the synagogue together. By the time they returned, German bombs had started to fall nearby. The Germans had decided to save their worst onslaught until this holy Jewish day.

Warsaw shook beneath the bombs. The two families spent the night in the cellar, its walls shaking with the explosions, the dust refusing to settle on the floor. The next day, September 23rd, the Germans continued with the most intensive bombardment anyone had known, or could have imagined. The targets seemed primarily the Jewish district south of Zoliborz, targets with no military significance. Hania could only imagine what might have happened to her Aunt and Uncle had they returned to their own apartment days earlier.

In the middle of the day the bombing stopped; Marek and Uncle Michael ventured upstairs to the street. After a few minutes they rushed back to tell their families to come witness nothing short of a miracle. Outside the sun was out, but in the midst of what seemed to be a fine, quiet day, heavy snow mixed with large hailstones had begun to fall. Neither Hania's parents, nor Aunt and Uncle, nor the neighbors who had appeared from the cellars and doorways, could ever remember having seen anything like it. Some said it was an intervention from God, an act of earthly contrition to recognize the Day of Atonement. Perhaps it meant they would be saved from the horror brought upon them by the German bombs.

That did not happen.

Later in the afternoon, the bombs began again, with even more fury, more destruction…and more death.

Fire raged during the night. Thousands lost their lives. Hania, the Sterns and the Elsters resumed their prayers, surrounded by fear, sheltering in the Sterns' apartment building cellar with the other residents, covering their eyes and ears against the explosions that rocked the streets and buildings around them.

And in the few final days as the siege continued, as the German bombing continued, hope evaporated.

On September 28th word spread that Poland had capitulated. All left the safety of the cellar to witness those Polish soldiers who had remained in Warsaw, their heads lowered in exhaustion and defeat, leave the city to join their comrades who had survived as prisoners of war.

For Hania and her family, for all their community, there was only fear.

Over the next day or so the streets were largely empty and an uneasy calm returned. Michael and Lea decided it would be best for them to return to their own apartment building to see what remained, to await what might happen. Marek agreed to walk with them to their home in the Jewish district. Hania, her mother and Shaul were to remain in the apartment in Zoliborz, but Hania begged to go with the Elsters and her father. She was desperate to find Alicja, to hug her friend, to cry with her. Marek finally relented. All began the journey from the suburb into the main Warsaw center, uncertain what they would find.

At times Hania led the way, knowing some of the back streets and paths through Powązki Cemetery where they might be safest along some of the small back roads leading into the district. In many of the shadows of the cemetery she imagined she saw Alicja, remembering how the two of them would run amongst the crypts and the narrow paths, laughing together, dreaming, alive. Now she sensed only death, saw only death and a great deal of destruction. Buildings had been bombed. Windows shattered. The city she thought she knew was the same city no longer. The wounded. The dead. Blood. Crying. Stunned silence. This is what she saw. What she breathed. And what she knew was that she was witnessing the death of Warsaw as she had lived it.

Arriving finally at Twarda Street, all were relieved and grateful to find the

Elsters' building standing, with only superficial damage, the apartment itself empty and safe but for the dust from the month's destruction. Lea walked into her parlor where her piano remained upright in silence. She opened the cover above the keyboard, stared at the black and white keys. Hit one, another, then looked away. Hania, holding Jakub in her arms, could see that her Aunt was crying.

"Come," Lea said, collecting herself after a silent minute; "we could use some tea."

She went into the kitchen and found tea hidden in the back of a cupboard. The water in the house remained shut off, but there was enough in a large container that they had kept aside to make a strong pot for them all, heating it over a fire that Uncle Michael lit in the oven. They sat in silence, drinking, each to his own thoughts.

After a while Hania turned to her father.

"Papa," she said, "I need to see Alicja. I need to know she is safe."

Her Father looked at her, and nodded.

"Yes. We will go to her house then back to your mother."

Promising to return if it was safe in the next few days, Hania and her Father thus left the Elsters amidst their own thoughts and silences. Walking along Twarda Street, they passed Miss Posner's School at Number 27. The building, like her Aunt and Uncle's, had suffered little but the most superficial damage. It looked empty, however. The glass on the upper windows had broken and curtains blew in the breeze. Hania wondered if she would ever return there, would ever immerse herself in books and lessons again. All seemed bleak and unknowing.

Desperate to see her friend, Hania marched towards Nowolipki Street, her father's eyes darting left and right, keeping a wary eye out for any potential dangers they might encounter. Once or twice he pulled Hania into a doorway. Several of the people they saw had slightly crazed, terrified faces. Her father knew that frightened people could do frightening things and that any uniforms approaching were unlikely to be those from the defeated Polish army.

Although he tried to hold her back, Hania started to run, desperate to make certain her friend was safe, desperate to find...something. Some hope. Something... Her father hurried behind, trying to stay with her.

"Hania!," he called. "Hania, wait!"

"It is just the next block! Just there."

She ran. She turned the corner into Nowolipki. Rushed down the street. Her father Marek raced after.

She came to a sharp stop. He caught up, looked at her. Looked at his most beautiful daughter. Young woman, no longer child. Too soon had childhood disappeared, as had all innocence. Too soon.

This he saw. Looked at her and saw.

This girl he had watched grow, had had dreams for, so much hope for. He looked at her, at her beautiful green eyes, staring straight ahead, and crying now, and knowing. He looked at her and wrapped his arms around her, kneeled down and held her tight, and only wanted to wipe her tears but knew he could not wipe her tears, could never wipe her tears.

Hania did not look at her father but rather only stared at the scene before her. She felt her tears track along her face, unstoppable, unstopping.

And she felt only the pain of these weeks, and the weeks that would undoubtedly follow, and all that she would have to suffer. The pain and anger and hurt and fear and terror and longing and loss that she would no doubt come to know. No doubt feel.

She did not know that anything could have ever felt quite as she felt now. Standing there, tears welling in her eyes, falling. Standing there, looking beyond.

Looking at the collapsed floors and ruins and rubble of the apartment house where her friend Alicja had once lived, now reduced to concrete and dust and broken wood and metal. Reduced to nothing by a bomb dropped from the sky, dropped by those who hated her, hated her friend, hated... Just hated. Hate.

She saw this all before her now.

And felt her father's arms wrapped around her.

And felt great emptiness.

And saw that nothing remained.

Instead she saw only life extinguished. Heard the wind blowing without a voice, her throat empty and dry and all the words gone. And she saw only nothing. Nothing left to see.

Dr. Kazimierz Palinsky, D.N., PhD
   (Consultant Psychoanalyst, Babinsky Institute/ Kobierzyn)
Personal Case History: The case of Hannah K.

14 August 1947

Although the first analysis evaluations in the case of Hannah K. in these initial months of her confinement at the Institute suggested a likely propensity to schizophrenic affinity, I was never of this conclusion from the moment of my first meeting with the patient. I strongly suspected that much of Hannah K.'s behavior was like a self-imposed exile, rather than a more complex breakdown or mental disorder. Whilst her silence and refusal to engage certainly disabled her ability to function daily in any sort of normal capacity, Hannah K. never, during any of our consultation periods once I had taken up her therapy, struck me as disorganized in any way, nor suggested even the mildest of hallucinatory behavior, nor indeed ever suggested confused or delusional emotional instability. Rather I sensed that much of her behavior was likely the result of severe trauma experienced while living 'feral' on the remote family farm, but equally just as likely due to traumatic experience much earlier in her life, particularly suggested by a premature or unexpected loss of virginity resulting in possible sexual uncertainty or even fear, as noted subsequent to her first physical examination here at the Institute. Such patterns of behavior might well concur with discourse in Freud's 'Studies in Hysteria', as we know.

My notes and reflections indeed indicated that some of Hannah K.'s mental state was reactive and very possibly defensive, likely stemming from what Dr. Freud discusses as the basic conflict underscored by the ever present imbalance between one's psychological ego and id—and more importantly, returning to Dr. Freud's most seminal works, best described in Hannah K.'s case analysis as between those concepts of Eros and Thanatos: the instinct to love, i.e. to live life, and a very strong desire for Thanatos, the metaphorical death instinct in her personality which rationally wanted to condition her to conform, to take over— humanity's perpetual conflict. It is worth noting here the influences both at the

Institute and further afield of the work of Ivan Pavlov and his studies of neuro-conditioning, currently much in vogue both in the Soviet Union and indeed in our own country, of particular concern to me given some of the suggested therapeutic approaches by certain colleagues with regards to this patient.

I however continue to be of the opinion that in the case of Hannah K., her ego has led her to a self-destructive parameter in which speech itself, language, most specifically communication with others, ceases to hold any moral value in its constant struggle with love and thus the possibility of a healthy life in which Eros and Thanatos are in equilibrium.

Effectively, one cannot help but wonder if the psychoanalytic notion of this patient's super-ego has become weakened due to an unspecified traumatic encounter or encounters. Her ability to make what is effectively a moral case to engage positively and constructively with society through the desires innate to the id has for all essential purpose been sublimated by the desire to disengage: and by disengaging, by withdrawing, to thus end her life as she knows it, certainly removing her ability to embrace life and love. Her silence is effectively her complete embrace of the Thanatos side of her personality: Death within, seeking to embrace Death without.

I considered that progress was being made with Hannah K., albeit only very slowly. I felt that we had begun even in silence to find a centre ground in which, through mutual acceptance, we might together and in partnership generate the hope necessary to develop the relationship I sought, empathetic and positive, with mutual respect, so that slowly but surely I might begin that process of gathering information through memory and dream recall in order to begin to understand the issues weighing on her emotional well-being.

I could not hope to commence what Adler referred to as Phase Two of psychotherapeutic treatment, which is to say through questioning and dialogue utilizing the preferred Socratic methodology to evaluate with the patient the consequences of her life before, the actions that defined and resulted from possible primary trauma, and therefore to look at alternative understandings of that trauma, enabling her life to move in a different direction; and thus also to engage with the qualities I remain convinced are within her, but dormant: namely the qualities of the id, the acceptance and awakening of her libido, of human desire and of her female temperament.

Although I had felt I had reached a breakthrough with her return of the notebook and its single blackened page some two months previous, I spent the following weeks witnessing no further progress whatsoever. I continued to offer her the notebook and encourage that she record thoughts in images or in words, but to no avail. We seemed to have moved no further forward; indeed it could have been argued that the patient was moving backwards.

I began to look for other tricks that might push the patient into a reactive stage. I would sometimes wear a tie, as normal, but sometimes she would find me with no tie and collar undone. I would polish my image before her arrival, or at times purposely create a figure of disarray. No matter what the trick, she would at most look at me for a few instants, then resume her seated pose on the sofa, back straight, eyes towards the window and escape in thought from the consulting room. On one occasion she opened the door to find me reposed on the sofa upon entry. I encouraged her to sit in my chair just beyond my line of sight. I proceeded to tell her about a dream I had had that previous night, a dream in which I was on a journey somewhere unknown and was agitated because I was unclear where I was going. I had seen a door in my dream but was terrified of opening it as I did not know what lay behind, whether darkness or light. Thus I awoke in fear, with sweat on my brow. I asked her what she thought such meant, thinking that perhaps if we traded places she might find a means to respond.

When I asked her what her opinion might be, did she have such, and turned to her, she was looking not at me but at the desk, where her notebook sat at its edge. She looked back at me, then stood, walked over to the notebook, picked it up. She stood there for a brief moment, then put it down again and left the room. She had turned it to the page that she had drawn, her only 'comment' to date, leaving the ink blackened page exposed.

Again I felt in this manner she was talking to me. And in my expressing my own unconscious fear she might yet relate her own.

I tried yet another tack for our next arranged session. When Hannah K. knocked at the closed door, I told her she should enter. She opened the door and stopped mid-step: she saw me across the room, in a headstand against the wall. For the first time, I believe, she truly did not know how to proceed.

I insisted she come into the room, told her to sit in the chair.

"Sometimes I see the world upside down," I told her. "Or at least I think I do. I wondered if it might look right side up if I was upside down instead of it. What do you think?"

She did not answer. But neither did she take her eyes from me.

I then explained that I had once read a book about so-called Indian swamis who stood on their heads to find emotional and intellectual enlightenment. I wondered if in doing so I might become enlightened about our process.

"For example," I said, "my name is Kazimierz Palinsky. Let me repeat that. Kazimierz Palinsky. Your name is Hannah K. Yes?"

She did not answer.

I repeated what I said as my face grew redder and redder. I said my name several times and asked her her own name several times, to no avail.

"I am looking for enlightenment," I said. "I am looking for a way to reach you and for you to reach me. So to start at the beginning: my name is Kazimierz Palinsky. It is who I am. Now, who are you? How do you think you might respond to such a simple but fundamental question?"

Only silence.

At this point I unintentionally lost balance and fell, knocking over a book and small lamp on a table. I stood, righted everything, looked at her and shrugged.

"Perhaps it is not such an interesting idea after all," I said. "I am not certain my fellow doctors here would approve anyway."

I chose then to dismiss the patient, as I indeed had a noticeable headache and explained as much. She stood and started out of the room.

But she hesitated at the door. She turned, looked at me as I was straightening my tie. Her head shook, just slightly. I stood there looking at her and heard for the first time her soft voice, heard the words that I knew had been captured within, finally released.

"My name is Hannah K***," she said. "Hannah K***. That is who I am. And you..."

She hesitated. My still red face must have said a great deal.

"...You are a fool."

She turned and left the room.

The breakthrough.

Joseph Babinski Specialist Hospital/ Institute of
   Neuropsychiatric Disorder, Kobierzyn (Krakow)
Patient Identification: 46-10/276
Patient Name: Kielar, Hannah
Patient Birthdate/Locale   04Apr1924/Nowy Wiśnicz
Consulting Psychologist: Dr. (hab) K.Palinsky, D.N.,PhD.

Interim Monthly Patient Report
16 September 1947

Subsequent to last month's interim report to the supervising medical committee, I am pleased to report that the patient, H.Kielar, has made noticeable progress in both her mental state and in her psychotherapeutic consultations with me.

The techniques used were traditional in nature, without recourse at this point to any attempt at deep analysis. The initial exchange consisted at first of little more than a mutual acknowledgement of identity and a recognition of the nature of the patient's confinement, as well as suggesting the possible parameters of the patient / therapist relationship.

However, subsequent to that initial exchange, H.Kielar has started to open up and engage, slightly, but with some continued progress at each further session. Her verbal responses are generally monosyllabic at times, but she does acknowledge her surroundings and will respond to very simple questions such as 'how are you feeling today' or 'do you like the sunshine' or 'what did you eat for breakfast' or 'is your accommodation satisfactory?'

The intention of these exchanges, minimal though they may be, is very slowly to establish a bond of trust between psychotherapist and patient. It is not at this point advisable, in my opinion, to begin the process of probing more deeply. However what is clear even from such minimal question and response is that the patient, far from demonstrating deep rooted psychosis, in fact proffers behavior that suggests

84

a strong intellect and an emotional strength of will that allows her to maintain silence over a considerable length of time for the very specific purpose of the avoidance of societal engagement. This in my opinion is not the response of schizophrenic disorder, even mildly so, as had been at one time surmised, but rather is the result of a depressive, neurotic disorder and utilized at the very least as a primary defense mechanism.

I remain of the opinion that H.Kielar is the victim of some significant trauma, that only with psychotherapeutic treatment will such trauma be addressed and ultimately overcome. I continue further of the opinion that, as per pervious suggestions from various colleagues, psychosomatics potentially imposed in an attempt to pacify the patient's personality and thus control her mental state would not result in a favorable therapeutic response, that the required attribute on behalf of this therapist is more than ever one of patience. My conclusion is that H.Kielar has now commenced her journey along a desirable pathway towards societal reintegration and recovery, but that such will only be available to her through a very slow process of analysis and eventual discussion with an ultimate goal of self-realization and thus self-acceptance, recognizing there will be undoubted pitfalls and no doubt minimal regressions in the process. Whilst I have yet to gain the patient's unmitigated trust, it is my opinion that with gentle probing and dialogue, approached with warmth and a push into active participation on the part of H.Kielar, indeed with gentle humor as well, through a process of Socratic intervention the patient will indeed take the first steps towards rehabilitation and stable mental health.

K.Palinsky
September 1947

Warsaw, 1940-41

She hated having to put on the armband every morning. The armband with the yellow Star of David sewn on by her mother's hand. But it was required. So much was now required. Hania stared out of the window in the room she shared with her younger brother Shaul, opposite her parents' room. She would soon have to go out. She did not know if it was yet safe to go out, but in the spring sunshine with all the refugees now in Warsaw there would be many others about and it would be safer to move in a crowd.

So much required. So much changed.

They had hoped when the bombing and the shooting ended they would be safe in their apartment in Zoliborz. It soon became obvious they were not. The Germans had started rounding up Poles to work in their factories and workhouses. Jews were treated particularly badly. Many had been shot on sight for no reason whatsoever. Theirs was truly a harsh winter, harsh not simply because of the terrible cold that seemed to go on forever.

Even when they remained in their own apartment, they were not safe. Because they were Jews, forced on penalty of death to wear the armbands, they were often targeted. On several occasions German soldiers or Polish thugs appeared at the doors of each apartment in their building and demanded entry. They systematically went through every room, taking what they wanted, threatening anyone who spoke. They tore family photographs into pieces, removed furniture and paintings from their frames for their own, stole all of Zivia's jewelry and any money they could find; even Shaul's toys were taken or smashed.

At times there was little choice but to go out to buy food, always in short supply. They would stand with their neighbors for hours in lines at the food shops for the few vegetables still available. They would collect the two small pieces of meat per person they were allowed each week, unlike in the strictly Aryan districts that still had decent supplies at a third of the cost. Prices increased almost daily for Jews. White bread cost four times the black bread that had soon appeared, tasting of sawdust and potato peelings. For those who could afford things some shops had supply. But for most the cost proved insurmountable for all but basic foodstuffs, and these were limited. Many now sold their finest belongings on the streets before they could be stolen, having to accept a few zlotys from the Nazis or Polish Police for things worth ten times that amount.

At the beginning of the new year, Hania's father Marek was ordered to return to his job at the PZT radio works. Many men had been pulled off the streets and sent to forced labor camps in the countryside, but his job was considered essential for the Nazi war effort.

Marek was issued a pass that allowed him to travel through Warsaw to the factory on Grochowska Street. Jews were no longer allowed on most trams outside their own district; on those trams on which they were allowed to travel German and Polish police would often board and throw them off, or beat them for sitting in a seat, or looking in a particular way, or simply for existing. Nowhere was safe. But for Hania's father the travel to work was no different, as he preferred the walk. He had to be careful on his journey, a walk that he had always done, although it took longer: only one bridge across the Vistula remained after the bombings.

The previous factory managers had all been fired and the Germans had taken over the works. Marek was told he would no longer be considered a foreman. He was to work under sharp eyes for eleven hours a day, manufacturing components for the German military, but at least he had a job that paid minimal amounts.

He returned home one night soon after starting again, covered in cuts and bruises, an eye black and half shut. Hania burst into tears, although her father assured her it was nothing. The new managers had wanted to make certain Marek knew his place, so he was roundly beaten. But he considered himself one of the lucky ones. Other workers had had their fingers and hands broken, or worse, which meant they could no longer work. And if they could not work they could not eat.

There was another reason that Hania's father felt himself fortunate to have the job at the factory. After that initial beating, because he understood the components and assembly better than most and his skill was obvious to his supervisors, they left him largely alone as long as he did his job and did it well. He therefore always worked as hard as he could; it got him little leniency, but it also meant managerial attention tended to ignore him as often as not. Many of the co-workers at the factory were not aware that he was a Jew; those who knew, even those fellow

Jews, largely kept their distance and their thoughts to themselves, at least for the time being. This made it easier for Marek to make various tubes and components disappear. He found during the very short break in the middle of the day allowed to workers that he could hide one or two fragile triode tubes, or batteries, or pentodes at a small break in the fence, where there was a hole beneath some snow and rocks, as long as he was careful not to be seen. Later, protected by the dark winter's night, he would pick up the valuable components on the walk home. Radios were a Godsend to so many desperate for news from the rest of the world, and desperate for hope.

Once a week Marek did not have to report to the factory, as the Polish supervisors decided to keep to the working week that allowed them to be with their own families or friends. On one such day off the Sterns walked from their Zoliborz suburb to Twarda Street, the first time Hania had been there since she had witnessed the ruins of her friend Alicja's apartment building. As they carefully crossed the boundaries of the Jewish district Hania saw that barbed wire had been put up to separate the northwest part of the district, a border adorned with signs saying 'Danger Plague Zone! No Entry For Soldiers!' Her father explained that while typhus was now a very real danger there had also been rumors in the German controlled Polish newspaper that the Nazis wanted to create a ghetto in Warsaw as they had in Lodz and Krakow and other places already. This was the first step in its creation, an excuse of an epidemic for those in the world who could still watch what was happening in Warsaw. The world had not yet forgotten them. The Nazis wanted it to seem as if life under their dominion continued as normal. It was anything but normal.

Her parents decided it safest to try to walk amongst crowds of people, although they would no longer have been able to take the paths through Powązki Cemetery where Hania and Alicja had played, even had they so wished. A barbed wire fence had been erected to stop Jews from entering; indeed they were forbidden to go into any parks, green spaces or areas reserved for Aryans. They could have walked through the overgrown Jewish Cemetery, but Marek knew with the constant flow of ever increasing corpses being hastily buried in common graves it was no place to stroll.

With great relief they reached Twarda Street. Aunt Lea burst into tears when Hania's mother embraced her. Jakub's sweet smile had made the fearful walk through the district all the more bearable.

The Jewish Council, the Judenrat, and its president, Adam Czerniakow, had been ordered by the Germans to act as the mouthpiece to the Jews of Warsaw and to issue decrees at the behest of their Nazi overlords. Because of the stream of refugees seeking refuge and assumed safety in the city, the Judenrat had set up department after department to address each aspect of affairs in the Jewish community. The Nazis had ordered that all Jewish property be registered, had frozen all Jewish bank accounts and started closing all Jewish businesses. Synagogues had been shut or destroyed. More and more edicts were being handed down and more and more barbed wire appeared to separate the Jewish population from their former Aryan neighbors. The Judenrat had to find room for the thousands of Jews arriving from other countries let alone the countryside now appearing on the streets of the Jewish district; many were forcing their ways into apartments. Epidemics had indeed become a possibility.

Uncle Michael, although forced to cease his architectural work, managed to 'play the music box', as they jokingly said in the area, with certain members of the Council whose palms might be greased, as well as having successfully bribed various Polish police and even some of the Germans. He had therefore been given a job overseeing the clearing of some of the bombed buildings to help make room for the influx of those from the country. He and Lea still occupied the two floors of their apartment themselves, but they knew it was only a matter of time before they would likely have to give up rooms to strangers.

With what was happening, with so much danger on the streets, Michael and Lea proposed that the Sterns move into the Twarda Street apartment and take over the large second floor room. The Judenrat actively sought to keep certain concert venues and restaurants open for Jews with the acceptance of the German occupiers, so Lea had little time to look after Jakub and needed Hania's help. Michael and Marek both still had jobs, as did Zivia who could work in one of the seamstress workshops in the area. Hania's Aunt and Uncle argued that they would all be safest if they stayed together.

There were other reasons that Michael and Lea wanted the Sterns to move to Twarda Street. It had become apparent that the Jewish community had to find a way to retain contact with the outside world. Given Marek's work and his readiness to smuggle out radio components from the factory, Hania's father would be invaluable in the future secret struggle that was beginning to find quiet murmurs of resistance. Indeed, those voices were already beginning to organize: both Lea and Michael had joined the nascent Jewish underground.

The adults spoke in hushed words while Hania was upstairs with Shaul and Jakub. Hania heard enough to know that her Aunt and Uncle, like her parents, felt there would come a time to resist, that they had made contact with the Polish underground already responsible for small acts of sabotage and even assassination. Hania knew her father would also be of use to the underground because of his work. He was trustworthy; this and silence were a highly valued gift. While her parents wanted to keep her ignorant, and therefore as safe as possible, she nevertheless overheard some of what they said. She would say nothing, she swore. But she knew. And knew that knowledge could be dangerous.

There was another reason too why Hania hoped her parents would agree to her Aunt and Uncle's proposal. The Nazis had decreed that not only must all synagogues close, but there would be no more schooling for Jews. Books could no longer be bought. Education was forbidden. Teachers caught teaching were often executed in front of their students. Miss Posner's school at Number 27 never reopened and now housed refugees from the countryside, but already secret classes were being held in apartments, cellars and attics in various parts of the district. Hania had received word from a teacher of her own class. She knew it would be far easier and far safer to continue with her secret education if the family lived at Twarda Street. As the Germans had declared that any Jew of fourteen or over was required to work, Hania was young enough to have an excuse to help with Jakub, to study with classmates, yet still could help her mother in the workshop as needed. So when her parents agreed to her Aunt and Uncle's suggestion, Hania felt relief and indeed a sort of happiness for the first time in so very long.

*

They had lived in Twarda Street for several months, as the winter cold softened to spring. The weather changed for the better. Their lives did not.

Too many times Hania saw Jews insulted and assaulted on the streets. German and Polish police would cut the beards off religious Jews or beat them for not getting off the pavement quickly enough. Many Poles showed kindness, often protecting Jews in their homes when they could, but equally there were those who informed on others at any opportunity, stealing from former neighbors, hating in ways once unknown. Refugees arrived with nothing but what they had carried on their backs, living on the streets, more and more often dying on the streets, their corpses left on sidewalks for hours or even days until the funeral home workers would collect them at night, piling them onto carts and burying them in open pits in the former sports field next to the Jewish cemetery. Murders had become commonplace both from Nazi tormentors and Polish gangs carrying sticks and knives, beating their victims until they could cry out no longer. Many newly arrived, the poorest, orphans, begged in doorways or amongst the ruins of collapsed buildings. Starvation was in evidence on every street. Somehow pedestrians learned to ignore the beggars or the dead, to hide their feelings, to embrace indifference. Dignity, even humanity, was sacrificed on the altar of survival, but still madness overcame many.

While many Jews suffered, many in the community grew wealthy and powerful off the suffering. Two of the most successful men now making their fortunes from smuggling were undertakers Pinkiert and Wittenberg. Graves in the Jewish cemetery had become like gold dust, with the gold coming to the pockets of Germans and many Poles, some of the Judenrat and the two undertakers who paid bribes for control.

In April the German press announced that the Lodz ghetto had been sealed off, and that Krakow was 'free of Jews.' The German authorities ordered the Judenrat to commence building a three meter high wall around the boundaries of the Jewish area so they could close off the Jews from the rest of Warsaw: Jews were subhuman and required isolating. The formal creation of the Ghetto had begun.

Hania's father and Uncle Michael secretly set up a radio in the attic of the apartment house, creating a hidden room behind a brick wall, brick that Uncle Michael had carefully taken in darkness from one of the collapsed buildings where he worked during the day. Certain trusted neighbors would gather each night to listen to the BBC in particular, Uncle Michael translating from English for those listening. All found the news grim, heartbreaking. By May the German army had overrun Belgium and Luxembourg. Rotterdam was bombed. Holland invaded. The march to France continued unabated. What remained of the British forces escaped from Dunkirk. Two weeks later, as the temperatures soared in Warsaw, Paris fell.

All this was hard news for the Jewish population. The Nazis had taken control of Europe, which meant the Nazis could, and did, begin to act with impunity. Hate, suffering and death were now ever present and in the open for all to see. And experience.

For Hania, going out remained always perilous. But in a strange way the streets of the constantly guarded Ghetto, with its twenty-two gates being slowly reduced in number, felt somewhat safer, at least from the gangs of Polish thugs who had roamed the area. She often carefully went to one apartment building or another where her teachers would secretly give their lessons to her and other students, some of whom became close friends: Edzia Blum and Noemi Geller in particular. Sometimes they would meet in the doorway of one or other's building, then walk together carefully to the appointed apartment where the lessons might be held, each keeping a lookout up and down the street should any German soldiers or particularly vicious Polish policemen be about.

More and more gangs of orphan children roamed the streets, begging for food, often smuggling through the barbed wire that separated off the Aryan districts from the Jewish streets. The three girls were making their way down Lezno when they saw three Polish policemen and two German soldiers chasing a group of ragged orphan boys down the street. One of the smaller boys ran into Hania, almost knocking her down, then jumped behind a mattress standing upright in a doorway to hide, unseen. A Polish policeman ran towards them and grabbed Hania by the coat.

"Where is he?," he demanded.

Hania shook her head, terrified.

"The little thieving smuggler: where did he go?"

"I saw no one," Hania replied, her voice quivering.

The Polish policeman raised his hand to strike her, when another policeman called out to him.

"Chimczak!"

The policeman Chimczak turned to see the third policeman and a German soldier dragging a boy in rags away. Chimczak hesitated, then pushed Hania away, turned and marched off. After the police had all disappeared, the girls, white with fear, called out to the skinny boy hiding behind the mattress, who emerged, smiling. He walked over to Hania and pulled from his torn, filthy shirt a red apple, holding it out for her.

"Thank you," he said. "Simcha Gitler. You ever need anything, I am your man." He tipped the ragged cap on his head, then hurried away.

The girls looked at one another. Edzia laughed, partly from fear, partly from the encounter.

"Your man! I think Hania has an admirer. Be careful of that cap on him, Hania. No doubt full of lice."

Noemi on the other hand was not smiling.

"Do you know who that was?"

"That boy? Simcha Gitler?" Hania asked her.

"No. Not the boy. The one they called Chimczak. The Polish policeman. Most people call him 'The Magician.' You do not know?"

Hania shook her head. Edzia's laugh quickly disappeared as she looked over her shoulder.

"That was…?" Edzia's voice trailed off, realizing.

"The Magician. People knew him once as a magician entertainer of children, sometimes in the squares of Warsaw or at their parties," Noemi explained. "Now that he is a policeman he reveals his true nature beneath his smile."

"I heard a story about him," said Edzia.

"Not a story. Not magic either," said Noemi. "A few weeks ago it happened, before the Nazis ordered the Judenrat to make the wall, although there was already a fence. You know the Café Hirschfeld?"

"Where the rich Jews go," Hania nodded.

"Yes, and the Gestapo, and the smugglers, and the collaborators like the

'Thirteen', Jewish scum who bleed the community dry," Noemi added. "So the Magician now in his police uniform, he stands at the corner near the café, on Sienna Street, and some children recognize him from before the days of the Ghetto. A father and a little girl approach. The Magician, he smiles, bows at the pair, reaches into his coat and takes out a handkerchief. He waves it in the air, puts it over his hand, whisks it away and there is a flower that he gives to the girl. 'Would you like to see another trick?' he asks her and a few people stop to watch. 'A Jewish trick, for your father this time.' Of course the little girl, she nods. Again he takes the handkerchief and throws it over his hand. Makes a motion with his other hand, magic dust, recites magic words then throws off the handkerchief. This time he has a pistol in his hand. He smiles and shoots the father twice in his brain. Poof! Poof! Everyone stands in shock and the Magician, he bows and says 'Death is a Jewish Trick', then walks away. He simply…walks away."

Hania said nothing, staring at her friend. Edzia looked at the ground as if afraid to meet Hania's gaze.

"My cousin," Noemi continued, "he works at Pinkiert's, collecting corpses on the streets at night. He hates it but it is the only job he can find. He picked up the father in his cart. No, not a make-believe story. Nazi magic. Make sure you hide if you see the Magician."

"That boy, Simcha…" Hania muttered.

"He's alive," said Noemi.

"For now. But if he is caught smuggling," said Edzia, not finishing her sentence. She did not have to finish it. They knew.

Late that evening Hania's father and Uncle Michael had disappeared to a meeting in another part of the district. Hania could guess what it might be about. Up in their rooms Shaul was asleep and her mother's door was closed. Hania had fallen asleep herself, but sleep did not come easy. She awoke in darkness and lay in the bed, Shaul's rhythmic breathing unbroken and somehow peaceful.

As she lay on the bed, Hania heard soft music. Quietly she got up from her bed and stole down the stairs to her Aunt and Uncle's rooms below. In their reception room beside the bedroom, with only the moon bringing light inside, Hania's Aunt Lea sat at her beloved piano, Jakub asleep in his carriage beside her. She played gently, pain and sadness seeming to emanate from every note.

Hania sat down at the bottom of the stairs, embraced by the night's shadows, listening. Each phrase, each note touched her deeply. Overwhelming. She felt the tears begin to form, then fall, quietly, one after the other. She could not stop them. Tears for the father shot in front of his young daughter, and for Noemi's cousin who had had to push the body away in a cart. Tears for the boy the German soldiers and the Polish policemen had taken away. Tears for the skinny boy in rags, Simcha Gitler. Tears for all the dead and for Alicja, the friend who was gone. Tears for the living. Tears for those who suffered, and would suffer still, would suffer further. Tears for herself. Tears for the heart that had to harden. Tears for what had been lost. The music. The shadows. The tears.

*

With so many people still flooding the Ghetto, the Judenrat made a regulation in July that each room must be shared with four people. Uncle Michael 'played the music box' once again to a Jewish Council housing affairs official so that he, Aunt Lea and Jakub might have the downstairs bedroom to themselves, with the piano in the small reception room. He successfully argued that Lea performed a service with her concert performances that she gave for nothing at the Judenrat's request so needed to keep the piano. Nevertheless they agreed that a young woman who worked as a nurse at the Ghetto hospital could sleep on a mattress on the floor beside it.

Hania and Shaul moved into the larger upstairs bedroom with her parents. A car mechanic named Josef Schipper, a big, crass man, took the other bedroom. Schipper made Hania feel uncomfortable at best, the way in which his eyes followed her, so she kept her distance. She knew some people thought he might be an informer because he had a pass to work on Nazi officials' automobiles. Hania's father did not believe this rumor; he said Schipper was simply good at his job and thus the Nazis kept him working on the Aryan side. Nevertheless he and Uncle Michael were even more careful when disappearing into the attic to listen to radio broadcasts, particularly with more people now living in the building.

Hania's mother had been ordered to work in a Ghetto factory sewing uniforms for German soldiers. The hours were long, the work hard, cruel even. She did not want Hania to have to do the same, so Hania spent as much time as possible with Jakub. Hania would take the child out for long walks in the middle of the day, trying to keep away from any German soldiers or Polish policemen she might see in the street. Or as long as Schipper was not up in his room she might sit quietly and tell Jakub stories of wondrous bike rides she had taken with her mother and Aunt Lea to the enchanted Kampinos Forest, with its fresh air and green, green grass and trees, a most magical place where the kindest of magicians lived. Now she could only dream of the memories of those bike rides. And a memory of trees.

She would sometimes sit too at the piano with Jakub, encouraging him to push on the keys, making sounds that seemed to fill the little boy with joy, as if the notes spoke a language that entranced him, that somehow brought peace into his confusing, hungry world. Or sometimes she would take him to the community food kitchen that had opened some streets away, where Aunt Lea occasionally worked making the thin potato or cabbage soups that had become a Ghetto staple for the starving and almost starving. Aunt Lea would slip her niece a few extra bits of potato or an old carrot to put into her son's carriage seat. Hania would help stir the large pots or cut the few vegetables that might go into them, while keeping a close eye on Jakub who sat on the floor playing with utensils, watching his mother and cousin with his adoring, wide green eyes.

By September Hania and many of her fellow students again started class, encouraged by the Judenrat despite the Nazi edicts. She would carefully attend the secret lessons in the mornings, with her aunt taking Jakub. Then in the afternoons she would take the child out to walk, or perhaps to buy 'stinking fish' as everyone called them, the tiny little fish covered with flies, decaying, that had also become a Ghetto staple.

Hania's father also encouraged Hania when she was out to help the newly formed Toporol Society in its push to plant vegetables on tiny plots where buildings once stood. Her father said this might bring the family vegetables in days to come. Although occasionally some of her father's colleagues would give him food for his family, or some of their former Aryan friends or neighbors outside the Ghetto would find ways to send food to them, her father warned such generosity would become harder for everyone. They had to find ways to keep from starvation, as was already the case for so many in the Ghetto. So he managed to find seeds for Hania to plant in a small plot of dirt on the site of a collapsed building. This also gave Jakub the chance to feel the earth and crawl in a bit of dirt and weeds, as if normality might be just within reach.

Hania's morning class was held in a large second floor apartment in a building on Sienna Street, risky because it was near high barbed wire that separated the ghetto from the Aryan side. Hania, Edzia and Noemi, with other classmates, had to sidle between doorways and back courtyards to avoid being spotted by any guards. Luckily her Uncle Michael was now working just across the way on the Ghetto wall, having been ordered to oversee some of the building works by the Judenrat, in turn ordered to be raised and strengthened by the occupation Nazi government. Although Michael had to be careful, as guards kept an eye on the builders, they were not so observant that he couldn't direct where certain stones might be placed without mortar, keeping these positions marked out in his memory as potential openings for smugglers or communications with those he knew in the Polish underground.

The afternoons, however, were often Hania's: to study, walk with Jakub, plant vegetables, sometimes to meet with friends and talk about all that they might one day do once they were grown and free. They refused to believe that the life they now lived would go on forever. They refused to stop dreaming. It was all they had.

An early autumn light snow started to fall one day at the end September. Returning home that afternoon, Hania passed a group of boys sitting on the curb of the cobblestone street, rags on their feet to protect them from the snow and cold weather. One jumped up as Hania passed, hurrying after her. She turned to see a skinny young boy in rags grinning at her.

"Did you like the apple? Well? Did you?"

Simcha Gitler. She remembered him.

"The boy behind the mattress," she smiled. "I had almost forgotten what a real apple tasted like. Where did you get it?"

Simcha shrugged.

"I can still taste it. Thank you."

She then continued walking; he remained at her side.

"I can get another. I can get many things."

"How can you? You do not look like one who would get a pass out of the Ghetto."

"There are ways. Through the wire or the wall where stones are loose. Underneath sometimes. Ways."

"Simcha, isn't it? Don't, Simcha. If you are caught you will be beaten or worse. Don't do it."

"But I can, if you help."

Hania glanced at him.

"It is not safe."

"You do not have to go. Just keep an eye out, tell me when I can make a dash for it."

"You mustn't. It is too dangerous now."

"I have to. I cannot let them beat us. Don't you see? It is all I can do."

Hania shook her head, both with fear for herself, and for him.

"No. I am sorry."

Hania walked quickly away, dismissing the boy. She turned the corner only to see two German police, their backs to her, leaning against a parked car at the curb. She froze on the spot. One threw down the cigarette he was smoking. She felt a hand grab her and pull her into a doorway behind. Simcha put his finger to his lips. They heard a commotion and carefully peeked around the wide stone entrance. From a building a couple doors down two men in plain clothes pulled an old religious Jew from a building. They tried to force him into the back of the car.

"No! I will not go! No!" said the old man, struggling with all his strength.

One of the men then pulled him backwards away from the car.

"No? You do not want to ride? Good. So you do not ride. Jews should not ride anyway, so why not!"

He nodded to one of the uniformed police, who reached into the back seat and pulled out a rope. Three held the old Jew while the fourth tied the rope around the old man's legs at his feet, then tied the other end to the rear of the car.

"Now, you do not ride. You fly."

The four Germans jumped into the car while the old Jew tried in vain to pull at the knot tying his legs together. The car started and jerked forward. The rope grew taut. The old Jew fell on his face into the thin layer of snow. The car skidded, then raced away, pulling the old man after, his clothes, his beard, his face tearing to a bloody pulp. Faster the car drove, zigzagging faster down the road, finally disappearing.

Hania and Simcha emerged from the doorway. Hania stared at the trail of blood tracking through the light layer of snow over the cobblestones, then looked at the boy, her face angry, her eyes set.

"Yes. All right. I will help."

The boy Simcha led Hania to one of the fifteen ghetto gates that now remained, the wall running down the middle of the wide street separating the Ghetto from the Aryan side. Polish Police stood at the crossing barrier. Their German police overseers sat by a small fire in front of a guard hut. Hania and Simcha hid across from them, in the shadows of a building wall, unseen, waiting until the evening settled in, but still two hours before eight o'clock curfew. One of the guards turned and looked in their direction, then away. Hania felt her stomach tie into a knot when she saw his face, recognizing the Magician. Simcha glanced at her.

"My Polish friend who almost caught me. The Magician. You know of him? Yes, you do."

Simcha kept his eye on the crossing, waiting a few more minutes. Finally: "Down the street, there, maybe one hundred fifty meters, the bottom stones in the wall are broken, hiding a small opening. I can get under, crawling on the ground. Every night a Nazi car passes through the gate. The driver, he gets out, talks to the Magician, gives him a cigarette. When the driver returns to the car the Magician always cuts in front so he can open the door for the driver. That is when you take two steps out, here. Two steps only, then back into the shadow. Then I know it is safe and I have enough time to run to the wall, to crawl through. You understand?"

Hania nodded. "I will wait here until you return."

"No. You do not wait. You leave. That is all you do. Nothing more."

"Then how do I know you are safe?"

Simcha looked at her. Smiled.

"Two steps, but you do not wait," he said again. "Nothing more."

99

Before she could say anything further, he disappeared. Hania remained hiding in the shadow of the building, shaking with cold, shaking with fear for herself, for the boy. Fifteen, twenty minutes. Then, just as he had said, a Mercedes came to the crossing. One of the Polish guards lifted the barrier. The Mercedes drove through, stopped. The driver, a big, round man, got out. The Polish Policeman she knew now as The Magician walked over. The big round German shared a joke with him, pulled out some cigarettes. They spoke for a minute or two, smoking, then both walked back towards the car. The Magician jumped in front of the driver, opening the car door for him. Hania quickly took two steps out from the shadow of the building. She hesitated, then as agreed, took two steps back.

The car started up, pulled away. The Magician looked around, right, left, then walked back to the crossing barrier shelter. The Mercedes passed just in front of Hania, still standing in the shadows. She did not know if the boy Simcha had crossed under the wall or not, but something else distracted her, and frightened her. As the Mercedes slowly passed, the driver turned his face and looked directly at her. She felt certain he had seen her. And for a moment, she did not know why, but she felt certain she had seen him before.

The car did not stop. After it disappeared she hurried from her hiding place and ran back to Twarda Street, arriving well before the curfew hour.

She heard nothing further of Simcha the street boy. But four days later, emerging from the food kitchen into its courtyard, she carried Jakub over to his push carriage. When she pulled away the cover, she found a red apple hidden beneath the thin blanket on the carriage child seat.

*

The students in Hania's class of girls met in a large apartment on Sienna Street, across from the wire that cut the street in half. One or two kept lookout, in the event that any German or Polish police might be seen in the area. Their teacher, a large formidable woman, Mrs. Garfinkel, had left Krakow after her husband had been killed and made it to Warsaw with relatives. A strict teacher, she nevertheless could be warm as well, knowing that her students, just like herself, faced the daily struggles of the Ghetto, indeed struggled just to survive. She particularly emphasized science and mathematics. She told them these subjects would one day bring them good jobs away from the hell that the Ghetto had become.

In the middle of a lesson one morning a girl who had been keeping watch down the stairs ran in to say that a car of police had pulled up in front of the building. The girls quickly hid their few books and papers and pulled out meters of the heavy grey material that they kept in just such circumstances, with several scissors, thread and needles. They sat sewing just as three Polish policemen entered.

Hania felt immediately ill. She and most of the others recognized one of the policemen: the Magician.

"What is this?," he demanded.

"These girls learn to repair uniforms for the German army. The Judenrat has requested we do this," Mrs. Garfinkel answered, her voice strong and commanding.

"Sewing uniforms. We are to believe this? If you sew, you have money. Maybe jewelry. You keep jewelry and money here. Where is it?," said another of the policemen.

"We have no money. Nothing of value. We sew, nothing more."

"Liar! You hide money and jewels for others!"

"No. We sew."

The Magician pulled out a gun, pointed it at Mrs. Garfinkel. The other two policemen pulled out their guns as well.

"You have it on you," he said.

"No. No, I do not!"

"Remove your clothes!"

"I most certainly will not."

The Magician cocked his head to one side, scowled. He walked over to the teacher, stared into her eyes. Grinned. And he slammed his gun into the side of her head. She fell, and he kicked her, again and again. She lay bleeding and broken, moaning in pain. He pulled out a knife and bent over her. One of the girls began to cry. He put the knife inside her dress and pulled, cutting through the cloth.

"Now, all of you remove your clothes. Do it!"

Several of the girls started to cry. Hania felt tears welling up, but would not let them see. She refused to let them know.

Mrs. Garfinkel remained on the floor, bleeding, unable to stand. All the girls, shaking, began to remove their clothes.

"Hurry up! Everything! You too! Now! And stand against the wall."

The girls slowly removed every piece of clothing they wore, trying to cover themselves with their arms, their hands. Many now cried. They turned to the wall to avoid the horrible leers of the three men. One of the Poles grabbed an older girl and turned her around to face him. He put his gun between her legs, pressing against her genitals.

"Now, tell us, where do you hide your jewels and money? Maybe here? Eh? Eh?"

"Enough! That is enough!"

The policemen turned around; some of the girls also turned their heads, hearing the new voice. Standing at the doorway entrance was a big man in a black Nazi uniform, and beside him an Officer.

Hania turned her head to look at them. She looked hard, thinking back, and she remembered.

The big man had been the driver of the car at the crossing. She remembered his face. And remembered where she had seen him before that. He was the driver then, and so was now, for the Officer standing behind him in a Nazi officer's black uniform. The Officer she remembered from Krasinski Park in what felt like a world ago, an age ago. Before the world changed. The German Woman's husband. Hania remembered her. She remembered him. She remembered his salute. She was afraid.

The German looked around the room. He stared directly at Hania, then turned his eyes away and glanced at Mrs. Garfinkel lying on the ground.

He looked at the Magician, at the two other Poles.

"Pigs," he said coldly, without emotion. Then to all: "Education is not allowed. Take her to Pawiak Prison to be dealt with. But you do not touch her. My order. Understood?"

The Magician nodded sullenly.

The German looked at his driver. "See that these girls are not hurt. You remain until they dress, then they go."

He turned and left the apartment.

"Get dressed!," ordered the Driver. The girls picked up their clothes, still trying to cover themselves. Two of the Polish policemen grabbed Mrs. Garfinkel, bleeding, broken. As they pulled her towards the door, one of them said something under his breath, then continued from the room.

"What does that mean, Misio?," the German driver angrily asked the Magician, following the other two police and the teacher out.

"…It means a child's stuffed bear. He says you are dragged about by your Officer like a big stuffed bear."

The Magician shrugged, glanced back at the girls with a cruel smirk, shook his head, turned and walked out. The Driver looked back at the students.

"Dress and leave here. There is no more school."

The girls, many still weeping, quickly stepped into their clothes and buttoned their dresses.

"He is a big fat Misio," Edzia said quietly after glancing behind her and seeing that the German Driver had walked out of the room. "Stuffed Misio. What do you think they will do to Mrs. Garfinkel? They cannot prove she is a teacher."

"She will be all right," said Noemi, almost desperately. "She has got to be all right."

Few of the girls believed it. Many still in tears, they left the room in several small groups, afraid.

Hania, as one of the oldest, was one of the last to leave with her two friends. They came out onto the street, into the sunshine. Sucked in the clean air. Tried to hide their distress. They noticed, down the road, stopped at the curb, a car parked. A familiar Mercedes.

"We must go," said Hania. "Quickly." The two other girls looked at her, at the Mercedes parked down the road, and the three quickly hurried away around a corner then cut through a courtyard and crossed through the ruins of a collapsed building, making certain they could not be followed.

That night Hania told her father what had happened. He asked her if the Polish policemen had touched her, or any of the girls. She explained how a German officer had appeared and ordered them to leave, taking Mrs. Garfinkel to the prison with them.

"Tomorrow night after work Uncle Michael and I will go to the Judenrat offices. We will try to get your teacher released. We will complain against these police but it will do little good; not all Poles are like them, but many are... You must be careful, my precious myszka. Even inside these walls the Ghetto is not safe."

In the morning Hania went to the community kitchen to help her Aunt. That afternoon Lea was playing piano at the café, so Hania said she would go look for her friends, taking Jakub with her. But her friends were not to be found. Instead Hania went to the small parcel of dirt in the ruins of a building, that space she called a garden and had planted seeds. She often went there to see if they had grown, or died. She sat on the ground surrounded by weeds and a few sprouting green tops, with Jakub beside her. The boy sat quietly, occasionally muttering the few words he could now say. Hania looked at him; he stared back at her with his eyes wide and adoring, his expression very serious for a child so young.

"'ania."

"Yes, my Jakub. My lovely Jakub."

"'ania live."

She stared at him for a long moment, then nodded. "Yes," she said; "'ania live."

She stood, held out her hands to the little boy and helped him to stand, then picked him up in her arms. She turned, and gasped.

Standing directly now in front of her, a tall man in a black uniform. The German. He grabbed her shoulder. Stared at her. His eyes then fell to the child, who was looking at him. Jakub smiled, unafraid, unaware.

"'ania live," said Jakub.

Hania's heart missed a beat. She wanted to cry out, but had no voice. Her face must have showed terror, because The German removed his hand. He stared at her, at the child, for a long moment. Then he finally spoke.

"My adjutant, he is my bloodhound. He finds anyone, even a girl who wishes to disappear. He thought he saw you before. Then yesterday. He has a good memory of faces. As do I. I remember you. I remember this child. He has grown. What is his name?"

Hania tried to find words, but still no words came.

"His name," the German repeated, calmly, not raising his voice.

"Ja...Jakub."

"Jakub. Jakub...My wife, she talks about this child still. You met her. You were kind. In Krasinski Park. Do you remember this?"

Hania nodded.

"Good. My wife she talks about your Jakub. His green eyes. About you."

The German glanced around him, at the pathetic garden, the crumbled ruins of the building. Looked around at the Ghetto surrounding them.

"Come," he said.

Hania hesitated.

"Come. You are safe. No Polish police now."

The German turned and started to the street. Hania followed, holding Jakub tightly. Parked at the curb beyond was his car. The one Hania now called Misio got out from the driver's seat and opened the rear car door. The German looked at Hania, gestured to the car.

"Get in."

Hania gulped, afraid.

"Do not be afraid. No harm will come, I promise. Get in."

Hania knew she had no choice, and would get help from no one even if someone saw them. Terrified, holding Jakub, she climbed into the back seat. The German closed the door, then got into the front seat with the driver.

"Your home, where is it?" asked the German. When she did not reply he turned in his seat, staring at her, his face set but not angry. He nodded slightly at her, in part with encouragement, in part making certain Hania understood she had no choice but to answer.

"Twarda Street. Number seven."

"The boy too or are you now his mother?"

"His mother is my aunt. We all live there."

The German stared at her for a long moment, then turned to the Driver, who nodded but said nothing. The car set off at speed.

Several minutes later they came to a stop in front of Hania's building. Those passing gave the car a wide berth as The German emerged and opened the back car door for Hania and Jakub. She got out, holding the boy tightly to her.

"Show me."

Hania looked at him, then turned to go inside. The German followed. No one appeared in the corridor. Hania unlocked the door to the apartment downstairs. Turned to look at The German. He nodded slightly, indicating that she should continue in, and he followed, leaving the door to the apartment open.

Hania walked into the reception room where the Nurse's mattress lay on the ground at one side and the polished piano sat close to the window, silent, on the other. The German stared around the room, at the piano. He nodded towards the closed door of Hania's Aunt and Uncle's bedroom. Hania opened the door. The German walked over, looked within, staring quietly at the few belongings, the bed where they slept with Jakub. He walked over to the piano.

"Whose is this?"

"My aunt, she plays, concerts and cafes and...she plays."

The German looked again at Hania, nodded towards the mattress.

"Who sleeps there?"

"A nurse who works at the hospital. She lives in this room."

"With the piano. A Jewish nurse?"

Hania nodded. "We are ordered."

The German stood looking at her for a moment, then turned and walked over to the piano, removed the cover protecting the keys. He hit a single note. A second. Listened. The sound disappeared into silence. And fear. Without looking at Hania:

"The woman who was your teacher, you and the others..."

"What happened to her?"

The German did not answer the question. Instead:

"Did she ever tell you the story of Jakub, the Jew? Do you know it?"

Hania said nothing.

"Jakub found a way to Heaven. A ladder. You are a Jew: do you know your Jewish bible? Maybe she taught you this?"

He now turned to Hania, who still did not answer.

"The only way to heaven is the ladder. Jakub knows this. A way out. To heaven... I will tell my wife I found you. And the child with green eyes. Here: take."

He stood still by the piano, held out his hand. In it were two small sugar sweets.

"For you, the boy."

His stare pierced her to her very core. She did not move. He watched her for another moment, then put the two sweets on the piano keys, looked at her one more time, then marched out of the room. A moment later Hania heard the car start up and pull away. She looked over at the piano, but her feet felt nailed to the floor. She held Jakub ever tighter in her embrace.

She did not tell her parents or Aunt and Uncle about what had happened. That evening her father and Uncle Michael made enquiries at the Judenrat offices. They returned late, careful to avoid patrols as it was past curfew. Hania had been waiting for their return. Their expressions were drawn, tired. Her father's face revealed much. When he said that Mrs. Garfinkel had been executed that morning, Hania left the room and went up to her bedroom where Shaul was asleep. She got onto the mattress with her younger brother, pulled his sleeping warmth to her and closed her eyes. Sleep did not come for hours.

Three days later some soldiers came to the apartment and took the piano away.

*

In late September the Nazis declared the entire Ghetto to be a quarantine area. Typhus had indeed become rampant. Nightly the funeral workers carted bodies away to open pit graves. Then at least the Nazis and the Polish police kept a slightly greater distance from the Jewish population. It did not mean the violence eased, but life fell into a pattern where people understood how they might stay alive. At least for the moment.

Hania's mother spoke to Miss Pozner, who recommended an illegal school for Shaul and found another teacher for Hania and many of her classmates, with their class held in a community building on Grzybowska Street. The tuition was expensive but Hania received a scholarship, leaving only Shaul's fees at his school. Her parents saved what they could; even then they could not always afford to pay for her brother's education, when the cost of what little food they could get seemed to double every day.

The Ghetto had been separated into two parts, known as the Large Ghetto and the Little Ghetto, separated by Chlodna Street. At the corner of Chlodna with Zelazna Street a passage between the two parts had been erected, high walls on either side between which Jews could pass. Chlodna Street itself was for Aryans only. A carefully guarded exit was in the middle at Zelazna. Glancing through the opening as she pushed Jakub in his carriage from one part of the Ghetto to the other, Hania could only think how different these two worlds of the Ghetto from the rest of Warsaw had become, separated only by a wall. She would then walk up to the food market on Leszno Street, where she might see meat or chicken, even fresh carp for sale, but costing twenty or even thirty zlotys per pound. Few could afford such luxury; her family could not. For a time she knew hunger, until it became so commonplace that she ceased to be aware of the emptiness always there.

Sometimes Hania would go to a free concert where her aunt performed, or a play with her friends. Her mother, despite the longer hours of work and inevitable exhaustion, acted for several weeks in a comedy at the small Yiddish art theatre, Azazel, on Nowolipie Street. Hania delighted in seeing her mother smiling with the joy of it, with the laughter of the audience. Laughter might be all they had left.

She and her two school friends also went to see a group of young people from Lodz, the LZA, perform songs, dance and do comedy routines at Weisman's former dance studio on Panska Street. The three emerged singing and trying to tap dance themselves.

Hania did not see The German again. But while she did not see him, she once found some sweets in Jakub's push carriage, and another time on the mat outside the apartment door as she was about to go in. He was around, somewhere. Watching. She felt frightened but refused to hide away, always glancing over her shoulder, right and left, just in case. Sometimes too Noemi or Edzia would say that they had seen 'Misio' driving past; when this happened Hania would turn and walk in a different direction, keeping a close eye out in case the car should be nearby.

At the beginning of October the Germans announced the start of what they called a resettlement 'Aktion'. They ordered all ethnic Poles to leave the Jewish Ghetto; all Warsaw's Jews were henceforth to be rehoused only in the Jewish district. Thousands were forced to move into the Ghetto. In Hania's building, where some fifty people had been living, there were now over two hundred residents.

On November 16th, the police carried out a major series of raids and arrests, forcing the resettlement of yet thousands more Jews who had been hiding throughout Warsaw into the Ghetto boundaries. That, or they were shot. The same day they banned all radio stations, newspapers, cut telephones and any communication with the outside world. They shut thousands of shops and food stores owned by Jews, or handed them over to ethnic Poles. From then the Ghetto was sealed. Almost no Jews would be further allowed through the crossings. Those who did manage to cross, although not through official crossing points, were mostly smugglers, often crawling through tunnels that had appeared in the ruins of collapsed buildings where the cellars might be joined, or they would crawl through the sewers. Some were successful. Many were not. If caught, they were shot. Many children died this way.

Marek Stern was informed that he would no longer be allowed to work at the PZT factory. The Ghetto wall closed him in as well. He was a Jew. Jews could not be trusted. Her father told her it was for the best: outside of the Ghetto it had become too dangerous, pass or not.

His biggest concern when he returned that night from his last day was that he had had to leave some radio components buried outside the factory gate, components that the Jewish underground desperately needed. Now they would have to remain outside where they were hidden.

Hania listened as her father and Uncle Michael discussed what options they had. They could try to get word to their Polish underground contacts, get them to try to retrieve the batteries Marek had hidden, but it would be fraught with danger. They decided the risks were too great; the components would simply have to remain buried at the factory, hopefully to remain undiscovered. A great loss.

"Simcha Gitler could get them."

Her father and Uncle Michael looked at her.

"Simcha Gitler. But I do not know where he is. I do not know if…" Her voice tailed off.

"Who is this?," her father asked.

Hania told her father and uncle about the street boy, Simcha Gitler, who she had first seen around Lezno; how on their second meeting she had helped him smuggle into the Aryan district by keeping watch at the barrier on Sienna Street. She thought her father would be angry but he only furrowed his brow, then said quietly:

"This was not wise, Hania."

"I had to help him."

"Perhaps."

"I have not seen him since. I do not know where he is."

"Or even if he lives," added her uncle. "Sewer rats, children smugglers, the German and Polish police catch them every day. Many have been killed. Too many. Children."

"Children?" questioned her father, looking at her Uncle. "They are no longer children, not in the Ghetto. The Germans have extinguished childhood. They have cut its throat."

Hania looked at her Father and Uncle. "He did not die. Not this boy."

"And how do you know this?"

"I know. I simply…know."

Her father again looked at her Uncle Michael. Neither said anything further, or ever raised it. Hania did not remark again about the boy or the components. She knew her father did not want it discussed, did not want her to know more than necessary: it would not be safe. But at the meal of soup and bread a week later her father took out a handkerchief from his tunic, unwrapped it, and passed around a small quarter of an apple each to Hania's mother, to Shaul and to Hania, keeping a quarter for himself.

"Where did you get this?," asked her mother, incredulous.

"From Hania," he said, looking at his daughter with a wry smile. "Something she grew."

Nothing further was mentioned, but Hania felt a slight glow within.

*

Marek Stern took on jobs as a glazier and repaired bicycles for those who could afford them. Uncle Michael lost his job overseeing the remaining works on the wall; the Nazis no longer trusted Jews, having realized that some of the bricks used had been placed without mortar. Using his pull, Michael was appointed as a janitor in a nearby apartment building, a job that not only gave him a small income, it also gave him access to various adjoining cellars and attics, a network of passages that would likely be useful in the future. With his skills he could devise ways of movement and potential escape without knowledge of the Polish or German police.

Hania's mother now worked with Aunt Lea at the community kitchen, where Hania would still help when she could. German and Polish Police became more and more cruel. Beatings were commonplace. So too murders. Smugglers, adult and child alike, increasingly risked their lives crawling through sewers to bring back food or any goods they could get their hands on from the Aryan side where life went on as if nothing had happened. Desperate, starving, homeless and without family, many children now lived on the streets. And died there.

In January the snows fell particularly heavily. Hundreds, perhaps thousands froze in doorways or on the sidewalk. People bundled up in what little clothes they had, pretended not to see, or saw but could no longer feel pity.

None of the apartments had heat. Any loose wood found was set alight for a few moments of warmth. Marek and Michael, with some of the others in the house, would often go to the secret room in the attic to turn on the hidden radio. Sometimes her father allowed Hania to listen as well.

One night there was commotion and the big mechanic, Schipper, burst in. The men around the radio went silent.

"What?," said Schipper. "You think I don't know? You think I am a fool? You are the fools. Have you not seen the Nazi's newest toy? They have a truck that goes up and down streets and can detect radio signals. They find radios. Is that what you want to die for? Not me, I can tell you. That truck I have seen four blocks away this very night. So now what?"

Michael looked to Hania's father for comment.

"It is possible," said Marek. "They could easily do this. It is not difficult."

"We should hide the radio then."

"No. It is no longer safe. No, we have to dismantle it. Take the components from here."

The others in the room looked at one another, then nodded. They knew the cost, and the cost was great. Hania's father gave instructions and that very night they scattered the parts in secrets places throughout the Ghetto.

Two days later German soldiers burst into the building and searched high and low for any contraband. All of the residents were forced to stand in the hallway under guard while the Germans searched. After two hours, the Germans left, having found nothing. As they went out, Hania saw her father give a small nod to Schipper, who had most likely saved all their lives.

They should have been safe then. The radio was gone. But they were not safe. Some of them, but not all.

Not Marek Stern.

Uncle Michael had gone to the Judenrat offices on business, when he heard that the Germans decided to arrest any Jews who might have worked at the state radio works factory and therefore possibly the sources of contraband radios. They would all be questioned at Pawiak Prison.

Michael ran all the way back through the snow to Twarda Street, pushing people aside right and left. He was too late. He arrived just as three men were putting Marek Stern into a car. Marek caught his brother-in-law's eye when he appeared, warning him away. Too much risk. Too dangerous. Both men knew what this meant.

Hania was with her Mother and her Aunt at the community kitchen. Jakub was sitting in a corner, playing with spoons, Hania kneeling beside him, making different sounds by tapping the metal on different surfaces. Jakub's face lit up with joy as he listened. She would always remember that moment, kneeling there, when her Uncle Michael burst in, desperate to tell them what had happened, to warn them. He said he was going up to Pawiak Prison to try to help Hania's father, to plead, but Hania's mother stopped him.

"Not you. A man will not be safe. Talk to your contacts at the Judenrat. Beg them. I will go."

"We will both go, Zivia" Aunt Lea said, taking off her apron. Her mother hesitated, then nodded.

"Take Jakub, get Shaul from his school," she said to Hania. "Take them to the apartment and stay there. Keep your door locked."

Hania nodded, saying nothing, nearly paralyzed with fear. She did not know what to do, except what her mother ordered her to do.

They waited for hours at the apartment. Uncle Michael returned early in the evening with no news. As the hours grew longer, his fear, let alone the others', became all too evident. Hania took Shaul upstairs to her family's bedroom and got into the bed with him to try to get warm. She could not stop her shaking. Shaul finally fell asleep against her. She refused to let her own eyes close.

She lay beside him, silently shivering. She could not stop. The minutes became an hour, another, another. Still the shaking would not stop.

Around midnight Hania heard muffled noises from the floor below. After a few minutes, her mother quietly entered the room and closed the door behind her. Hania could see her mother's shadow through the darkness. Her mother just stood there, not moving, saying nothing. Finally Hania saw her mother remove her leather shoes, walk to the bed and get in beside her. Shaul woke and her mother pulled his thin body to her other side, put her arm around Hania and pressed her daughter's head to her breast.

Hania felt her mother's tears fall from her face to Hania's own.

"They have…taken your father. They will not take us. We will not die; we will not. We will resist them. Your father would want us to be strong. Do you understand? He has gone somewhere warm, and gentle, and safe and he will wait for us there. One day we will see him in a better place. A much happier place. We must be strong for him now. That is what he would ask of each of us. You must do this for him and for me. Do you understand what I am telling you, my angels, my children? Do you understand?"

Hania felt her own tears, hot against her cheek, as hot as the warmth she felt in her mother's presence, her brother's presence. She knew it was all right to cry. She cried.

"Yes, mama," was all she could say.

She cried.

*

They paid Pinkiert's to retrieve his body, then take it in a cart with others from the radio works also shot that day. They followed the cart with the bodies piled up as the undertakers forced an old horse to pull it to the Okopowa Street entrance of the Jewish Cemetery. As none of the families of the dead had enough money for a private grave, the bodies were laid out side by side in a common grave and covered with a white linen cloth. Zivia Stern insisted they all remain strong and held herself from crying tears of anguish. Hania could not do so, leaning against her mother who held her tightly, just as Hania held her brother's hand tightly in her own. Her Uncle Michael and Aunt Lea followed behind them to the cemetery, as did others she knew, and some she did not. Her friends Noemi and Edzia, some other school friends, even her new teacher came. A Rabbi led the cart filled with bodies, then said Kaddish over the dead when they had been lowered into the pit and laid out in a line. Hania, her younger brother and her mother stood by the open pit for a few moments in silence, painful thoughts singing silently in their ears, then turned and walked away.

Once they were gone the white linen shroud lying over the bodies was removed, to be washed and used again. And again. And again.

It was replaced by a thin layer of lime thrown over the corpses, the long pit in which lay the bodies of men, women, children not filled with earth but awaiting the next arrival of the dead.

*

Joseph Babinski Specialist Hospital/ Institute of
   Neuropsychiatric Disorder, Kobierzyn (Krakow)
Patient Identification: *46-10/276*
Patient Name: *Kielar, Hannah*
Patient Birthdate/Locale   *04Apr1924/Nowy Wiśnicz*
Consulting Psychologist: *Dr.(hab) K.Palinsky, D.N.,PhD.*

Interim Monthly Patient Report
12 April 1948

I would like to commence this report into the progress of H.Kielar by paying tribute to Dr. Nowak,, whose untimely death has been a sincere blow both to the Institute and to myself personally. I know he took a very particular interest in H.Kielar's well-being. Whilst I had certain disagreements with Dr. Nowak, particularly with regard to his enthusiasm for bi-lateral frontal leucotomy, I remain grateful for his introduction to the work of our respected Polish psychiatrist Dr. Lucjan Korzeniowski, who as all will be aware provided in-depth pathological and psychiatric analyses of Poland's nine primary neurosurgical cases at the Department of Neurosurgery in Warsaw. I refer in particular to Dr. Korzeniowski's perceptive descriptions of great and medium improvement in five of the patients who had undergone the surgery beneath the guiding hand and knife of neurosurgeon Dr. Jerzy Choróbski. Dr. Nowak was kind enough to bring this work to my personal attention. It was therefore appropriate indeed that Dr. Korzeniowski should have offered such plaudits in his funeral oration for our own Dr. Nowak, whose loss is a loss to us all and whose own work in neurosurgical treatment stands in good stead with the likes of his colleagues Drs. Korzeniowski and Choróbski.

I believe it worth commenting, taking into account above, on the relation between Dr. Nowak's suggested treatment for H.Kielar and my own alternative and at times contradictive path of analysis, following on from groundwork set out by Dr. Adler in Vienna. In an interesting conversation I had with Dr. Nowak, he argued for the advantages of bi-lateral frontal leucotomy treatment as the means to return the patient to rapid syntony. My concern with such treatment, in which some patients I acknowledge may have shown improvement as discussed and analyzed in the subsequent recent articles by Dr. Korzeniowski, remains that it has been applied primarily to patients with medium or severe symptoms of confirmed schizophrenia. I was never of the opinion that such diagnosis was appropriate in the case of H.Kielar, but rather that her illness stemmed from symptomatic neuroses that have become sadly commonplace in the populations throughout Europe as a result of the atrocities of the recent years of conflict, of which here in Poland we are more familiar than most.

I continue to be of the opinion that the argument for necessary psychosurgical personality change as means for the improvement of a patient's well being in fact works only to the severe detriment of patients of median or severe neuroses. As with most patients of such disorder, H.Kielar is, in my opinion, a young woman of subtle sensitivity and, in my recent conversations and work with her, a person of great moral conscientiousness who has suffered greatly because of her experiences of the social 'disorder' of the last decade, as well as the potential abuse of her Kielar father, the loss of her Kielar mother, and subsequent isolation without social structure or support. In my determination she is an example of the dangers of possible unwarranted trepanation, which in the most accepted arguments can lead to unexpected and undesired psychological change, even to the extinguishing of dynamic personality. I believe that such results in tragic loss.

While this was the nature of many of my discussions and indeed arguments with Dr. Nowak, I have to say he was always a fine mentor and valued colleague and he will be terribly missed.

In keeping with the paradigms set out by Dr. Adler, after months of coaxing H.Kielar forward, with ever illuminating discussions between us, I can confidently say we have reached that stage of Dr. Adler's methodology in which therapy consists of Stage Three analysis in order to seek an understanding by the patient of psychological insights into her own feelings and goals. In order to gain such insights it continues to be necessary to unravel these prior to their reassembly through positive psychological engagement.

The committee will of course be aware of Pierre Janet's exploration of the splitting of consciousness between the normal self and secondary self. Dr. Freud naturally took Janet's theories in a different direction, seeing such splitting of consciousness not as an innate weakness but as the result of psychological conflict. In the last decade or so, however, it is noteworthy that Dr. Freud returned to his initial interpretations of such in the Outline of Psycho-Analysis, exploring this strategy of the psyche as the splitting of consciousness within the confines of the neurotic rather than simply symptomatic of the schizophrenic.

I believe this is the case with H.Kielar and one area that I now explore with her. The external traumas of her experience of loneliness and likely abuse by one or both of the Kielar parents resulted in an inner conflict, a splitting that she found difficult to tolerate; only now through therapeutic dialogue does she begin to come to terms with a new lifestyle of common sense and social engagement.

My hope is that, through analysis, through exploration and self-exploration, H.Kielar will come to the conscious conclusion that her own interests remain rooted in social engagement by means of cooperation and contribution. Once she begins to define her own personal goals in relation to her improved psychological health, once she defines her own pathway to such goals, I believe she will move away from the life style in which she was trapped by her own neurotic state to the pathway on which both of us, analyst and patient, have now embarked. From this analyst's point of view, the journey the patient finds herself on is one of self-understanding of what she does feel as opposed to what she should feel, working towards a goal of what she can be capable of feeling, and experiencing, and accepting that she will feel in the years to come.

K.Palinsky

April 1948

Private and Confidential
Dr. Kazimierz Palinsky, D.N.,PhD
  (Consultant Psychoanalyst, Babinsky Institute/ Kobierzyn)
  Personal Case History: The case of Hannah K.

9 June 1948

The patient Hannah K. continues to exhibit improvement in her mental health and greater control over her neurotic tendencies, although I note occasional lapses into mild to middling controllable melancholia, unsurprising considering her initial mental state more than a year previous. We continue to carry on

117

sessions of four to five hours per week. As agreed, we now first meet weekly in my consultation room for a two hour period of personal and mental history discussions. Sometimes we share a cup of tea and talk; sometimes with her agreement I attempt traditional analysis where she will lie quietly on the lounge and talk of her hopes and fears, her dreams and memories. I sit behind taking notes, then reread to her what she might have said, asking her questions to elicit her own opinions on such thoughts and their potential meaning. I find her mental agility to be surprisingly acute for her sex and have to admit to enjoying the challenge of her intellect.

Once a week we also stroll outside on the grounds of the Institute whilst the weather is warm and comforting, engaging in discussion which I acknowledge seems to be to her liking more than traditional analysis in the consultation room. We might talk about her past or her memories from growing up on the family farm near Nowy Wiśnicz, although she continues to be hesitant in her response. When she does proffer information, the details sometimes change from one session to the next, which makes me wonder how truthful she is being. She does not strike me as purposely deceitful, although at times she describes her mother and father in ways that are not always consistent: warm and loving, then becoming harsh and cold. There clearly is motivation behind many of her responses.

More often than not we speak of the weather, or her opinions of the other doctors (she was, unsurprisingly, always uncomfortable around Dr. Nowak, although saddened to learn of his demise), or the flowers, the birds, the food (her appetite remains simple, although I am pleased to say she has put on a slight bit of weight and no longer suffers from malnutrition as was certainly the case at our initial encounters last year.)

As to what happened during the War period in Nowy Wiśnicz, she keeps many of her recollections or experiences to herself. Certainly she is guarded in her comments, particularly about her relationship with her father. She has on more than one occasion claimed she cannot remember him which would seem to be a defense mechanism.

I noted on many occasions that she forgot to bring the notebook I gave to her in order to record thoughts, memories, dreams to our consultations. I asked her

118

about this and she promised to bring it to the next consultation but then discovered the following week in the consultation room, or on our morning amble, when I asked her to produce the said notebook she had lost it. I gave her another, but once again the item was lost. In fact this happened on several occasions over numerous months. I finally asked her why she seemed so often to lose the notebooks, or claim that she wrote down a memory or dream but then lost the paper that she tore out to record such, or had intended to record her thoughts but lost the pen with which to write such down.

I asked her what this act of forgetting, or losing things, might mean? "Perhaps I am simply forgetful," was her first reply. Yet when I asked her on several occasions to describe herself, a quality of forgetfulness was never mentioned. I pointed this out and wondered if there might be some other explanation or meaning. It could be that she prefers not to confront memory, to confront her past, but that is often not the case. She talks easily about the property in Nowy Wiśnicz, about her mother who she often calls Helena instead of mother, about her father, although she often says she remembers little, suggesting the possibility of an abusive parent. I did ask her to describe her father in a single word, in an unguarded moment. The word she said was 'lost.'

I put it to her that by losing something, whether notebooks or pens, paper or language, something or someone, it suggests the need in turn to find such item or person: that without losing there might be no need to find. One might necessitate the other. Could it be that she perceives herself as lost, but in the very process of being 'lost' she needs to be found? It suggests a need for valued existence: as long as one loses, one needs to find; and as long as one needs to find, existence itself matters. A validation of her own being.

Memory, I suggested to her, may be lost, and by being so may need confronting, remembering, in order to move on. Did she not think that was the case? She hesitated in her response, then replied that she did not a agree. Memory was not needed for life to continue.

Once Hannah K. began to open up and engage, while sitting behind her in my consultation room as she lay quietly on the lounge, as our exchanges began to take on greater depth, I asked her how she would define life in a word. Her answer:

119

death. I asked her if she thought one needed the other; her response was that one is always stronger. I put it to her that life and the desire to love should be stronger. She turned looked at me for a moment and did not smile. Then looked away.

"Love?," she asked, then answered her question; "Love is death. An acknowledgement of need that cannot ever be fulfilled. Taken."

"Then you do not believe in love?," I asked candidly. "Or in the possibility of love?

At first she hesitated. "Love may be a gift to give," she said, "or a gift to take, or a whimper, or a hope, or survival, or a passage. Love was taken, just for a moment. Love flew from the window. Love suffered."

"Are you speaking of love, or sex?," I ventured.

She did not look at me this time, but remained motionless on the lounge for a very long moment before replying. Finally, she clearly decided to reply.

"I listen rather than speak. That is all I can do, Doctor. All I care to do."

All of this suggests a neurotic mind in conflict with itself and again compels the suggestion of some sort of abuse: psychological and, given my knowledge of her torn virginity, physical.

A morning some two weeks subsequent, whilst out walking and admiring the manicured grounds and flowers around the Institute, I asked Hannah K. to describe the world she remembered, the world of the farm where she grew up: to describe the house, the land, the trees, the barn, the animals. She described things as material presences, but without texture, or color. I asked her why she thought this was. It was not a world of color, she told me. There was only black or white, and shadow in between.

Lying on the consultation room couch recently, Hannah K. told me of the dream she had had the night before. She said it was snowing and she could see through a window her father and her mother and indeed herself, another Hannah who she gazed at from afar, working outside in the snow. She knew she was hungry and they were desperately trying to gather food so that she could eat. But the snow all around meant they could not find food to bring for her. They came into the house and said it was her fault that they could not find food, it was her fault that the snow was falling. Had she not been hungry it would not have snowed and they would have had enough to eat. She said in her dream they made her go outside; there all she could see was snow over everything, nothing further alive. The house disappeared, her mother and father, her mirror self, the animals, all she saw was snow. She walked and walked and finally she came to a place where all around her was white, in the middle of which there was a tall black well. She said she climbed the wall of the well, then sat at the edge. Because she was so thirsty despite snow everywhere, she reached in, pulling up the bucket so she could drink. And when the bucket reached her hands, she saw there was not water in the well, but blood. She looked into the well and saw there the body of her father and her mother, the priest Father Daněk who came to the farm and took her away, and children she thought she knew, herself, all in the well, their faces floating then disappearing. She said she saw my face as well.

I asked her if she knew where the well was, and she said there was just such a well, albeit not with a high surrounding wall on the farm in Nowy Wiśnicz. She described it to me. I asked her why she thought she had to climb the wall to the top of the well in her dream; this seemed unusual. She thought for a moment, then said perhaps it was because it contained that which she did not choose to see, but ultimately she needed to make herself see. Climbing the wall was not an act of contrition but rather a forced act of enlightenment, whatever the cost might be. Ultimately an act of freedom, thus free will.

I partly see this dream as a representation of Hannah K's sexuality and its loss in perhaps a moment of violence. I also would suggest that the pulling the bucket towards her, a bucket full of blood rather than water, is a symbol of menstruation and the trauma that might result from such. But I see my own presence in the dream an illustration of transference. I asked her what she thought the dream might mean. She suggested she thought it meant she should have been in the well instead of the others. She felt responsible. I asked her if in fact it suggested that in the act of drinking, in the same way she lost things so that they need be found, so that she would be found, she was finding in this dream those that she perceived as being lost now being found and reaching out to her to do so. I wondered if such might in fact be about her own need to be found rather than lost, her need to embrace memory so to move forward, while simultaneously suggesting her own journey from childhood into womanhood and the trauma often resulting from such. But I remained intrigued by the presence of others in the dreams perhaps suggesting something more fundamental, something arguably more traumatic. Could it not be the case that, seeing the faces of those she knew within the well beginning to disappear, she feared that she may lose them, as she lost notebooks? My own place in the dream indeed suggested to me this very interpretation.

Walking in the gardens several days later, I again brought up the dream that she had so vividly told me in the consultation room. I put to her once again that perhaps to face all that she had seen, and had to see, that what might indeed bring her to self-enlightenment was to remember, to embrace memory. In this way faces are not lost, do not disappear.

"There are no memories," she replied. "There is only snow, the well, the black and the white. That is all."

Then she added rather cryptically these words:

"There is no more of then. Only now. Only Hannah K***. Remember. That's what she said, what she told me. I must remember that, that alone. Only Hannah K***. That is all there is."

She was holding a flower she'd picked in the garden, a small rose. She dropped it back into a flower bed and looked down at her hand. There was a streak of blood on it from where a thorn had pricked the skin. She stared at her palm, held it out to for me to see.

"That is all there is," she said again, then turned and walked away, bringing the morning's walk and session to an end.

For the next three sessions Hannah K. spoke not a word but regressed into silence.

Warsaw, 1941-42

The bombs began to fall from the sky. On the afternoon of June 22nd the Ghetto walls shook and many buildings collapsed or burst into flames. This time the bombs came not from German but from Russian planes, dropping their loads on the railway station just south of the Ghetto, and beyond. Germany had invaded Russia, putting an end to the fallacy of non-aggression. The War came closer.

For almost a week the bombs fell; again it was often the Ghetto that suffered much of the damage. And the death. Warsaw was in a state of siege. The curfew was extended. Hania and her family spent most nights sheltered in the cellar of their apartment building, crowded together with the many residents caught between the fear of an explosion from above and the hope that the Red Army would instill pain and death on their own Nazi tormentors. She felt the heat. She breathed the dust. She remembered mostly fear.

The banned underground press communiqués appeared more often on the streets, giving lie to the official German paper in which the authorities suggested that the 'Red Barbarians' caused no damage to German military installations, but only to Polish residences and hospitals. The Red Army planes in fact succeeded in destroying Okecie Airfield, stretches of train track, some munitions factories in the area; in the process many innocents died. For a short time most in the Ghetto felt hope, something not felt for many previous months. But before long, the Red Army began to find itself in retreat. Life then continued much as it had been in the Ghetto before Germany attacked Russia, yet growing harder and more dangerous by the day.

The streets were awash with people as the Germans deported more and more Jews from the towns and villages, forcing them to live behind the Ghetto walls. Some 450,000 people now lived in this small enclosed area, often dying of starvation, sleeping in any available space they could find in apartments or on the streets. Thousands of starving humanity, considered sub-human by their tormentors.

Only nine crossings through the ghetto wall remained open. Of those that did, only those Jews who crossed were the smugglers who crawled through the secret tunnels and sewers and the hundreds of misfortunates rounded-up as 'workers' for forced labor camps, marching out with resigned terror in their faces, knowing this would be a death sentence.

The lucky ones were those who worked and lived on the grounds of the new guarded Schultz textile workshop just outside the Ghetto wall, at the far end of Nowolipie Street. Some viewed these men and women as slaves, but they had passes protecting them from the frequent round-ups and murders by the ever violent police. Thus many envied those forced to work at the Schultz workshop; work for them apparently meant life.

Typhus became rampant. Every evening Hania's mother had Hania and Shaul strip off all their clothes so that she could inspect for lice, fearing that any of the lice she found would bring the disease. But if typhus was the fear, hunger was the reality. Without Marek Stern's small income, Hania's mother needed to find work that paid so the family would not starve. Thanks to Uncle Michael, Zivia found a job at the Judenrat organized sewing factory at 21 Ogrodowa Street, working now twelve hours a day for four zlotys a week and a single meal of thin soup and black bread that she would often bring home for her two children, tasting mostly of sawdust or even wood shavings. Four zlotys bought almost two pounds of potatoes. Almost. And nothing more.

Hania helped her Aunt Lea at the community kitchen while also looking after Jakub for much of the time, sometimes bringing a vegetable or two back for the family—usually a blackened carrot or turnip. Luckily some of the vegetables she had planted managed to grow almost enough for the family to eat. The authorities rationed food and each person was allowed 180 calories a day, one-third the amount received by those living outside the ghetto walls, so any small vegetable that Hania might add to this felt like a feast for them all.

The two families, the Elsters and the Sterns, also moved into the single room that previously had been Hania's Aunt and Uncle's. Where two hundred or so had been living in the building, now four hundred lived. Uncle Michael did his best for them all, helped by his janitor's income, but often his pull could not ease their situation; he had little left to use as bribes.

While many of the hidden radios disappeared, many still remained despite the best efforts of the Nazis. In this way word quickly spread in September that Kiev had fallen as the German Army continued its advance. Zivia now had to work still harder, sewing winter uniforms for the Wehrmacht military machine. Her life depended on it, as did the lives of her children. Every stitch she made, she told Hania, felt like a prick into her heart, and the blood would not stop. Every prick she gave herself reminded her of Marek and the pain she suffered with his loss.

September 23rd, the eve of the Rosh Hashanah holiday, offered no celebration for the two families sharing the meager New Year's evening meal of thin soup, even with the two carrots Hania brought home from her small patch and the added small pieces of meat they had saved to buy. Without her father there to say a prayer, his place at the table seemed ghostly and without joy.

The following morning Uncle Michael came home from the synagogue with even worse news. The Nazis had ordered the Judenrat Council's President Czerniakow to deliver five thousand Jews to be taken to labor camps outside Warsaw; it was rumored that the Germans intended to close off some of the Little Ghetto, perhaps even to liquidate it. They were all at risk and had to be very careful on the streets. The Judenrat had organized a Jewish Police force that could be as brutal as their Polish counterparts, particularly the so-called Blue Police that operated in some precincts.

Hania had not seen The German or his 'Misio' in the months following her father's death. But if she hoped that perhaps he had left Warsaw for Russia or some such place, she knew in her heart that this was unlikely, knowledge confirmed on one occasion when a small bag of sweets, covered by small stones, appeared on her small vegetable parcel half hidden in the ruins of the destroyed building. She knew who had placed the sweets there. At first she stared at them, then felt the bile rise within her. She vomited, then gave the sweets to a group of homeless street children covered in rags she saw nearby. She ran home with Jakub in her arms.

Her class began again in the autumn with a new teacher. Thanks to President Czerniakow having somehow successfully convinced the German authorities to allow some schools to open legally in the Ghetto, Shaul had a Komplety School to attend organized by the Judenrat. Hania would walk him there every morning, then continue on to her own class several streets away, depleted somewhat as a few of the girls had died of typhus or been ordered to a workshop. Or been killed. Her friend Edzia Blum was amongst those who had not survived the disease.

In the afternoons Hania would go to the community kitchen with Jakub. While the weather was warm, if it seemed safe, she would take him by the hand and walk in the crowded Ghetto streets to the kitchen, or perhaps to her small plot with its few remaining root vegetables, always careful to pull back into shadows if she saw police or any soldiers. Or a German car passing. She never stayed there long alone, or with Jakub. In October the Germans put out an edict that any Jew caught outside the Ghetto would be executed; at the same time any non-Jews still remaining in the Ghetto were to leave immediately. They closed further streets near the Chlodna Street crossing between the Large Ghetto and the Little Ghetto, as well as forcing many tenants on Zelazna and Sienna Streets to vacate their buildings. The family knew it was only a matter of time before they too would be forced to move. Michael went to his housing friend at the Judenrat Council offices, who said he would be unable to help. But after a night meeting with his contact from the underground movement who he referred to as the "Commander", a small apartment on the third floor of a building on Dzielna Street in the Large Ghetto was found. There were two small rooms with an interior short corridor between, at the back of the building overlooking a large courtyard of many other surrounding buildings. One of the rooms had once been a bathroom, although all that remained in it was a sink that brought up no water; everything else had been pulled out. The rooms' previous occupants had died of typhoid. The previous janitor, an Aryan, had only just left. Uncle Michael was appointed such, no doubt assisted by his underground connections because of his involvement in the Resistance.

The two families moved their few belongings from the Elsters' once proudly owned apartment in the beginning of November, as the winter weather began to bite. Hania, her mother and Shaul put a bed in the small room that would become their home. Zivia and Lea scrubbed and scrubbed the rooms, desperate to remove any trace of the previous occupants or the disease that took them. Aunt Lea and Uncle Michael took the slightly larger front room with Jakub, as occasionally they would hold clandestine meetings or Uncle Michael might be working with others in the attic accessed from the stairway two floors above their own; thus all felt it best they should have that slightly larger room instead of the smaller room down the corridor to the back.

One of the men Hania often saw in the outer stairwell or heading to the attic with her uncle, who only went by the name Yitzhak, was one of those who often came in the evenings, speaking quietly with other adults; Hania suspected he was the one her uncle called the Commander, but said nothing.

Aunt Lea taught music two days a week in the cellar of the Femina Theater on Lezno Street, where she had access to a piano, and spent the other days helping at a different public kitchen not far from the new apartment. The lines of people waiting for a single bowl of soup seemed to grow longer daily, and Lea had even less time to look after Jakub. Because so many of the workers might be away with illness, or possibly held by the police, Hania again would help her aunt whenever she could, both by keeping an eye on her young charge, ever more attached to her almost as much as he was to his own mother, and by serving the hundreds lined up outside, waiting to eat something. Indeed, anything.

On one afternoon in late November a long line of people stood outside the community kitchen, with its few tables, waiting for their daily ration of thin soup. Three girls ushered people slowly inside where they could sit and eat, while Hania and another took bowls from Lea and other women cooking in the few large pots they had, stirring the thin liquid over two open fires. Two women would put a single ladle of liquid into a bowl, which they would hand to Hania and the other young girl to carry as quickly as they could to a counter, handing out a small bowl of liquid with a small piece of black bread to each hungry person they could feed. No one had money. No one had anything. But at least the meal was hot.

After each hungry man, woman or child finished his or her bowl it was brought back to the counter to be filled again. With so many now waiting, all the kitchen cooks and workers had to work as fast and as hard as they could. Jakub sat below the counter, at Hania's feet, playing quietly with a small pot and a tiny doll that had once been Shaul's.

Hania moved quickly, passing out bowls, pulling them back when empty. She went out of her way to be courteous, trying to smile, rare enough these days in the

Ghetto and hard enough for her.

"Extra special, today," she would say. "You may even find some carrot instead of leather."

She was only half joking. More than one shoe had been boiled for flavor and nutrition. Hania walked the few steps into the kitchen area and grabbed three more bowls, then carried them out.

"Our specialty," she said. "Ghetto goulash. Here you are. Enjoy. Eat slowly; it will last longer. Here. You will not find any better in all the Gh…"

She did not finish her sentence. The bowl she was holding fell to the floor. The other girl behind the counter looked at her, shocked at the waste, but Hania was silent, her mouth open, her eyes wide.

"Hania?" the other girl whispered. Hania said nothing. Instead she stared at the face whose hands had reached for the bowl now fallen, at the face of the young woman from her past. A ghost. The dead. Hania stared in shock at the drawn, slightly older face of her friend, Alicja Leder.

"…Alicja?," Hania gasped in a half whisper. She shook her head. And started to cry. "Alicja?"

The girl stared at her. If surprised, she did not show it. She stared at Hania, then dropped her eyes, turned and, limping, disappeared around the counter and out of the room.

"No! Ali…" But the girl was gone.

Hania grabbed Jakub, hurried back to the kitchen, put him down near Lea.

"I have to go! I have… I will be back."

Hania rushed from the public kitchen, hesitated, and hurried to the right, pushing past the multitude of people. She came to a crossroads, looked up and down, again chose to go where the crowd was thickest. She pushed, ran, pushed, hesitated. And knew. A little ahead she saw her, hurrying along but slowed by the supporting crutch because one leg did not move naturally, one leg that was clearly made of wood from the knee down. Hania saw the girl from behind: now taller, now more woman than girl, but a figure she nonetheless knew.

Hania took a breath, another, then hurried forward until she stood just behind the hobbling figure.

"Alicja, please," she said quietly.

The figure in front of her stopped. Hesitated. And slowly turned.

Alicja.

Hania threw her arms around her friend, who stood statue-like, not moving, until she too finally put her arms around her younger friend. A dead girl risen, and alive. Hania could not hold back her tears. And could not let her go.

*

"We hid in the cellar as they dropped their bombs. We thought we would be safe. But we were not. I think it was the third night: a bomb fell directly onto the building. My uncle died immediately beneath falling concrete. I had been sheltering beneath stairs. Somehow they stopped the stone from crushing me, kept me from death, but my leg was trapped. I must have passed out. I do not remember. When my eyes opened some men were carrying me out. They took me to a Jewish hospital. My leg was crushed. They had to cut. They did not have many drugs. I remember screaming with the pain. I remember...little."

"But you lived. You lived."

"Did I?"

Although Alicja had been hesitant, Hania had convinced her friend to go with her to the collapsed building courtyard where she kept her small vegetable plot. She knew they could talk quietly there, somewhat away from the crowds on the street.

"Yes," said Hania. "Yes.... Your father?"

Alicja shrugged. "I don't know. Dead I suppose. I will never know."

Hania looked away, then quietly: "I have lost so many. My father. People I have known. Friends. I thought I lost you. I thought I lost..."

"I miss our adventures through Powązki Cemetery. Krasınski Park. I think I even miss Miss Pozner's school and some of the girls there."

"I continue to go to a class some mornings," said Hania. "In the Little Ghetto. Some of the same girls. Noemi, Vera Kleiner, a few others. You could join us."

"No. Not for me. All that is past."

Hania said nothing for a moment. Then: "But, how do you get by?"

"I get by. I have...I have a job. Enough to eat. Sometimes at the kitchens if I need, but I have enough."

"Where are you living?"

Alicja looked at her friend, then away towards the few vegetables still growing in the dirt of the small plot, avoiding the question.

"Those are yours?"

"All that remain. A couple carrots. A few turnips. Maybe more next year."

"Next year…"

Alicja was quiet again. She rubbed her leg below the knee, obviously somewhat uncomfortable.

"After they… I spent a long time in the hospital. A carpenter there, he made this for me. Not the same, but I get around. I had no one so the Judenrat sent me to Korczak's orphanage. You know it?"

"On Chłodna Street. Everyone knows Dr. Korczak."

"He recently moved the orphanage to Sienna Street. The Germans move everyone. Even Janusz Korczak. We called him Dr. Janusz. He said Dr. Korczak was too formal. Gentle. Kind. Not like so many others. He tries so hard with all the children. Tries to bring…hope. I spent a year there. Maybe a bit longer. But when they had to move to another street…I could not stay longer. I needed to breathe, some space. The other children…"

Alicja shook her head.

"And where did you go?"

"…Not now. Another time. I get by. It is enough, Hania. It is enough for any of us…Tell me, your little Jakub?"

"Growing. I keep him with me most days. He was at the kitchen, under the counter, pulling on my dress. He likes to play with pots, make sounds. His music he says."

"Like his mother. Her playing such beautiful music on the piano…It made me feel anything was possible. I hope she still plays."

"The Germans took her piano away. She stared at the empty space for hours, but she never said a word. She gives lessons now sometimes at the Femina Theatre. Sometimes concerts. Perhaps you would like to go. We could go together."

Alicja simply looked at her friend and smiled, slightly, then looked away.

They stared into the distance, at the people walking, beyond. Where there should have been noise, there was only silence.

"This is not what we dreamed, Hania. Playing statues in Powązki Cemetery. Not what we dreamed."

"We still can. We still have to believe. Faith."

"…Faith."

They sat in silence then, looking at the tops of the few turnips growing near their feet. Looking at the past in their memories. Searching for a future. Wondering.

*

The weather turned ever colder, with the worst of winter approaching. The Nazis ordered all Jews to surrender any fur coats, collars, muffs, even any odd bits of torn fur to them by the beginning of the New Year, although few but the best-off could only dream of such clothing. Collection centers had been set up. Some people were forced even to relinquish their long underwear, often having to undress and stand naked in the snow while Nazi or Polish police took their warmest clothes. Rumor had it that the Nazis wanted to use the furs to sew into the boots of their soldiers heading east into Russia.

Hania continued to see Alicja, who often appeared bearing small gifts of food or woolen underclothes, despite the Nazi edicts. Sometimes her friend would suddenly appear at the community kitchen when Hania was working but would refuse a bowl of soup. She said she had enough of her own. Aunt Lea was shocked and quite pleased to see Alicja again, even said a quiet prayer for her. Alicja might wait quietly outside the community kitchen until Hania could leave, then stroll with her and Jakub, sometimes chatting, sometimes just walking in silence. With corpses often piling up on the sidewalks, talking was not always as easy as silence.

Alicja visited Hania's apartment room once or twice, bringing some lumps of coal for the small iron stove as the cold crept in through the thin window overlooking the courtyard below. She seemed to have her own resources and although tired and thin she did not seem to be in need. Hania tried to ascertain where Alicja lived, but her friend remained vague for reasons Hania never really understood. Hania followed her once and was surprised to see Alicja make her way back to the ruins of her one time building on Nowolipki. Alicja disappeared amongst the rubble and collapsed floors of the one-time apartment building. Hania would have followed, but with Jakub holding her hand it proved impossible.

Late one afternoon in December, the night already setting in, walking home with Jakub holding her hand and her brother Shaul at her side, Hania was surprised and rather disturbed to see Josef Schipper, the mechanic, emerge from her building, cross the courtyard and disappear to the street. She held back for a moment, then went inside, meeting Uncle Michael coming down the stairs.

"I saw Mr. Schipper just now," Hania said. "He was here."

"Yes. They ordered everyone to leave the building on Twarda Street. He has a workshop not far from here now. He has been helping me with something. Come; I want to show you."

Michael scooped up Jakub in his arms. Hania and Shaul went with him up the flights of stairs to their apartment. The two older children followed their uncle into the rooms and stood silently staring at the single room in the apartment. Their own room, and the short internal corridor that led to it, had disappeared. All that remained was the sink that had previously been in their room, now on a wall where the corridor had been, sparkling clean and plumbed.

Hania and Shaul looked at one another, worry in their faces. What would this mean? Would they have to find somewhere else to live with their mother?

"But…we have nowhere to sleep now," Shaul said.

"I do not understand," Hania added.

"Wash your hands in the sink," suggested her uncle. "Go on."

Hania walked over the sink, turned the faucet. Nothing.

"Still no water."

"No. No water. But watch."

Her uncle stood beside her and reached under the sink for a moment, then gently pushed the side of it. The entire sink and the wall behind tiles swung to the side, revealing a hole. Uncle Michael had made the corridor and their room into a secret room. The children walked through as they normally did. Their room with its bed and their few belongings were still there; in fact there was more space, and a bit more light from the window, as the sink in what had been the former bathroom was now in the other room.

"A hidden room," Hania said with a grin.

"Yes. And I hope well hidden. Now you must both listen to me: if ever we have an emergency, if the police come, the soldiers, you two and Jakub, your mother, perhaps all of us can hide in here. But you must be quiet as mice if that happens. Do you understand?"

Hania and Shaul nodded. They understood well.

"It will only be closed off if we have to. Let us hope we do not ever have to, yes?"

Hania turned and hugged her uncle. She had come to love him very much; she knew he did this for them, for Jakub. She knew that he did it for her Father's memory as well. And she knew he was afraid, but staring in the face of fear he refused to allow it to defeat them.

In early December the clandestine radios announced that America had entered the War. For the thousands and thousands of Jews in the Ghetto, this inspired some hope. But they had hoped before, only to learn that the German Wehrmacht had marched steadily into Russia, even now on the doorstep of Moscow. The War may have slowed but the only army in control of Warsaw and indeed of all Poland was the German Army.

The red brick walls surrounding the Ghetto were made even higher. The Jewish Cemetery also was now walled off; even that had become forbidden to the denizens of the Ghetto. The brutality continued, if possible worse than before.

Hanukah and the holidays came with little joy. On Christmas Eve Hania swore she could smell the odor of real cooking fat and cooked delights coming from the Aryan side of the wall. For the Jewish population it simply meant surrender of their warmest clothes at the collection centers, or if lucky enough some were able to sell their precious warm furs to Poles who somehow yet managed to sneak into the Ghetto and buy Jewish family treasures for next to nothing. For those who sold however, such at least meant food and perhaps staying alive that much longer.

In the large courtyard across from the Sterns' window a bakery was hard at work over the Christmas period. Uncle Michael, having kept the courtyard clean and the rats away in his role as janitor of their building received two white loaves of bread as a gift. Hania asked Alicja to join them for their New Year's feast of bread and the stinky fish that had become so prevalent. Surprisingly she did, although would only stay until early in the evening. The Sterns and Elsters welcomed her warmly. Almost incredibly she brought four pounds of potatoes with her, which must have cost her more than thirty zlotys. The Nazis had gifted the Ghetto a large consignment of potatoes a few weeks previous, which amazed everyone, until they discovered the reason why: the potatoes had been sent to the eastern front soldiers but had frozen and blackened. Nevertheless on that New Year's eve Aunt Lea smashed these potatoes and made the most delicious pancakes they had ever tasted, so they all agreed.

January turned bitter cold but still Hania and Shaul trundled to the Little Ghetto every school day morning, even as the snows fell. The Nazis had decided the Jews should no longer be allowed to walk across the single crossing at ground level between the two ghettos, so built a three story high wooden foot bridge over Chlodna Street, guarded at both ends where daily thousands crossed. The people of the Ghetto referred to it as the Bridge of Sighs. One of the German guards, called Frankenstein by the Jews, became infamous for the violence he showed to anyone who hesitated on the walkway, or even looked at him the wrong way. Often people were beaten until their bones broke or they collapsed in pools of blood. Hania and Shaul made certain to hurry as quickly as they could from one side to the other if Frankenstein was on the bridge.

Once she saw Frankenstein on the street with the Magician, standing over the motionless bodies of two emaciated figures. The Magician did a little pirouette on one of the corpses and laughed. Frankenstein kicked the other, and when the corpse moved, apparently still barely alive, the German guard took out a pistol and shot the unfortunate in the head, stepped on and over the corpse, then walked as if nothing lay there but the sidewalk itself. In his eyes that was all there was.

By February the cold had turned bitter. Hania continued rising early to go to the Little Ghetto and to her class, but Shaul's class stopped for a week because there was no stove to heat the room for the young students. Hania would return to the apartment to check on him, then go to help her Aunt Lea in the community kitchen. Occasionally she would join her friend Noemi and a few of the other girls for a reading and study group. She tried to convince Alicja to join them but her friend always had excuses that her work prevented her from such. Hania assumed Alicja had a small job in one of the Ghetto workshops but remained secretive about many aspects of her life.

Returning from her class early one afternoon, as the snows fell, Hania walked up the flights of stairs to hear voices in the apartment. She walked in to find her mother, unexpectedly there, with Aunt Lea and Uncle Michael, talking quietly.

Hania looked from one to the other.

"What? Mama?"

"Your brother is ill," said her mother, her eyes tired and exhausted. "Typhus. It does not seem too bad right now. I must stay with him, however, Hania."

"But I will stay with him."

"No. No, not you. It is better that I do. He needs to be isolated but we have nowhere else to take him. Aunt Lea and Uncle Michael agree you must sleep in this room with them. But we cannot be without the money I make. You will have to stop your studies for now and take my seat at the factory. You are capable with the machine. We cannot risk that I will lose my place there. Do you understand?"

Hania nodded. "Can I see him?"

"No, Hania. Not now. I hope soon. Not now."

Hania found the work at the factory difficult and came home exhausted at night. The supervisor was understanding, seeing to it that Hania always had a little extra soup in the meal she had during the short break. Luckily Hania learned quickly and worked hard. Each evening when she returned she would ask about Shaul. Her mother would say he seemed slightly improved but slept much. Uncle Michael tried to get some medicine from the few hospitals still open. He talked to the 'Commander' to see if any 'friends' on the outside could help. But no medicines could be found. The Nazis had tightened their grip on the Ghetto. Those medicines that the smugglers managed to bring in went to the richest only, or for the so-called 'Thirteen'--those of the Jewish criminal elite, perhaps for some in the Jewish police as well or kept by the Judenrat council members as their own.

Her mother allowed Hania into the room after four days to sit beside her brother one night while he slept for a short time. Hania stared at his small frame, red spots on his face and chest, the blanket pushed away from his sweating body despite the cold. He opened his eyes at one point to look at her.

"I love you, Shaul. I love you, little brother. Get well for me. For Mama."

He kept his eyes open for only a minute or two, saying nothing, then closed the again and slept.

The next night, walking back through the Ghetto, Hania kicked the heavy melting snow at her feet in anger as she walked.

"Why?," she asked aloud. "Why does this have to be so? Why?"

Various people passing stared at her, then turned away. Mad people were common enough now on the streets.

Hania could not stop the tears from falling. A small torn cloth she wore as a scarf blew off in the cold wind. She turned and knelt to pick it up. Standing, she saw behind a car stopped some distance back at the curb. She could make out little through the darkness, when inside the car a match struck to light a cigarette. She saw Misio's face in the shadow thrown by the small flame.

She stopped breathing for a moment, then turned and ran.

She arrived at her building, checked to see if she had been followed, then ran up the several flights of stairs and burst into the room. Aunt Lea sat there, alone, holding Jakub to her. Hania stopped in her tracks. She saw the false sink and wall had been opened, revealing the short hidden corridor entrance to her own room. She saw tears in her Aunt's face. She saw pain, and felt it.

"Shaul?...Shaul?" she shouted now.

"Your brother died this afternoon, Hania. I am so sorry."

"No. No!..."

"Your Mother and Uncle Michael wrapped his little body and took him to be buried."

"No they can't."

"I am sorry."

"But they can't. No, they…No…"

"They had to bury him quickly. Without the Jewish Cemetery now, and this disease…they had to bury him in a grave with many others at the sports field. You have to be strong now Hania, for your Mother, for Jakub, for all of us."

"No. No, she…No!" Hania screamed. But no scream could bring back her Father, and no scream now could bring back Shaul. No scream could shut out the cold. No scream could shut out the pain.

*

Lea scrubbed the secret room clean with Hania's mother. They said nothing between them, their sadness so overwhelming. At first Zivia wished those first days to remain alone in the room they had all once shared. Hania therefore slept with Jakub pulled tightly to her, holding the small child to her own breast, listening to his soft, quiet breathing. Sometimes at night she would hear cries or screams from other apartments overlooking the courtyard or beyond. Sometimes she would hear her Mother, pacing back and forth, back and forth, back and forth.

A week or so after Shaul's death, Hania rose in the middle of the night and walked through the hole behind the sink, down the short interior corridor to the back room. Her Mother stood by the window overlooking the courtyard in the darkness, her arms at her side, her form swaying slightly like a thin towel drying in the wind. Hania walked over and took her Mother by the hand, then lay down with her on the mattress, covering them both with blankets to keep them warm against the cold Ghetto air. Her Mother's body felt ice cold, near death itself, but slowly took on the warmth of the blankets and her daughter's youthful form. From that night on Hania slept at her mother's side.

Zivia said little after that and a silent vacancy remained in her eyes and her face. She would sit for hours, becoming days, staring out the window, lost in her thoughts and memories. Sometimes she would talk to herself or have a non-existent conversation with her husband. "Marek," she would exclaim, "why do you need to work so hard? We need you here. Hania and Shaul, we need you here." Or she might turn to Hania late at night and say to her: "I hear Shaul crying again. Tell him Mama is here. Will you tell him for me?"

Hania, lying next to her mother, would nod and try not to let her tears be seen. Her mother would smile then. "He's such a good boy. A bit of mischief, maybe, but a good boy." Then she would turn to the wall and sleep. In the morning she again would sit at the window, sitting in silence. More and more she withdrew into silence.

Hania returned to the sewing factory in her mother's stead. Uncle Michael did the best he could, but between his work, his meetings, his own worries, he could not afford to support them all. Hania had to cease her studies, but she understood her responsibilities. She had become a young woman now and the privilege of study was hers no longer.

After several weeks of twelve hour shifts at the factory, the fears of encountering police or seeing the likes of Frankenstein or the Magician or The German on the streets, of hurrying past shadows and hollow faces of the Ghetto residents, then the restless nights of fear and loss, Hania too had grown thinner and felt exhausted. Her single joy was seeing Jakub in the evening. He would take hesitant steps when he saw her coming up the stairs, then would run into her arms and hug her when she walked into the room.

Hania crouched over the sewing machine in the factory one morning towards the end of March when she looked up and realized her Mother stood beside her table, watching. Her Mother touched the heavy grey material beneath the needle, ran her fingers along the line of stitch as if inspecting it. She nodded approval at her daughter.

"You have done good work, Hania. I am proud of you. But now I shall take over for you."

"Mama," Hania said, "you do not have to. It does not matter."

"No. I need to work now, my daughter. I need to forget."

Hania stared at her Mother as the supervisor came over. Her Mother explained that she had been recovering from illness but it would be best for the family if she took the machine over. The supervisor considered, looking at Zivia's thin frame and drawn face, the emptiness in her eyes, then finally agreed with both mother and daughter that Zivia would work three days in the week, and that Hania would take the machine the other three days.

The air had grown warm with each passing day; Hania gasped for breath like a drowning woman as she emerged into the sunshine. She had not seen Alicja since Shaul's death and was desperate to talk to her friend. Although Alicja had always been vague as to where she slept, Hania remembered following her to the collapsed ruins of the building on Nowolipki and hoped she might find someone around there who knew her, or knew where she worked or lived.

Walking amongst the crowds on the sidewalks, many simply wandering aimlessly hoping for handouts of food, careful to avoid any passing Jewish policeman's glance, or worse should she see a Polish or German policeman, Hania crossed part of the Ghetto to the building where her friend had once lived with her uncle, a building of which little remained but fallen concrete, twisted metal and wooden beams. She climbed over some fallen stone and found a passage through the ruined building to what must have been a courtyard in the back. Hania discovered here, amidst the ruins of what had once been rooms in apartments now exposed to the elements and half fallen to the ground as rubble and dust, evidence of people living and a number of people milling about. She approached an emaciated woman trying to nurse a baby, sitting alone amidst the rubble, staring at nothing. Hania had thought her a young woman, but when she drew closer she realized the woman's hair was grey and her face drawn.

"Do you have any milk? I do not have any milk for him," she said.

"No. I'm sorry, I…" Hania was not sure if the baby was alive or not.

"He may die. My baby may die. Maybe he should die. I don't know. Maybe he should die."

"I'm sorry."

"He's beautiful, my boy. Look: is he not beautiful?"

The woman held out the bundle for Hania to see, and only then did she realize that there was no baby in the folded rags. All that this woman coddled was a child's half broken doll.

"I'm sorry. He is…beautiful," Hania said quietly.

"Yes. Why are you here?"

"I have a friend, Alicja. I am looking for her."

"Alicja."

"Do you know her?"

The woman did not respond.

"She uses a stick. One of her legs is made of wood so she needs a stick."

The woman looked away, then back at Hania.

"On the other side. In the back. Maybe there. Maybe not. You do not have milk? You cannot give milk? My milk is all gone. My baby needs milk."

The woman turned away, rocking the bundle that perhaps once held a child, but now held only loss.

Hania walked through some collapsed rooms opened to the elements at the back side of what was once the apartment building. The rooms reminded her of catacombs and the crypts of the graves where she and Alicja once played hide and seek and tried to frighten one another. The building around her had become a crypt. A living cemetery.

She saw no one. She came to a broken stairway that led down into what once must have been a cellar. Twisted metal and a wooden beam acted like a handrail and she carefully made her way to the floor below, again partially open to the elements. She found down here recesses like collapsed rooms. In one a blanket was drawn across the opening. She pulled it aside to reveal a mattress, some candles and a small stove. A torn dress hanged off the remains of a broken beam. She reached up to run her fingers along the material. She could not be sure who it belonged to, if perhaps someone lived here.

A rustling behind her. Hania turned, gasped and cried out, just slightly. Alicja, leaning on her stick, stood before her, staring at her.

"Alicja! Alicja…"

"You should not be here, Hania."

"I wanted to find you. I wanted… I wanted you."

"You should not have come here."

Alicja stared at her friend. Her expression then softened after a moment.

"Come. We will sit in the sun. The warmth will do us both good."

Alicja led her friend back up the stairs and out to the open air. They sat on stones in the sunshine, their legs hanging below them, swinging slightly back and forth in the slight breeze like two carefree girls. The girls they once were. The girls they should still have been.

"You are not living here?"

Alicja said nothing at first.

"I come here when I need to be alone. No one bothers me. Where I stay there are so many others, I feel like I cannot breathe sometimes. The Germans, they make it harder to breathe. Every day."

Hania nodded. She understood what her friend meant. She then told her about Shaul, about the disease. She told her about her mother and having to work at the factory to bring in the few extra zlotys each week. She talked about her father, about missing him so much that it hurt to wake each day and to fall asleep each night. She told her how she heard her mother talking to him and how she wished she could talk to him as well. How she was afraid she would forget what he looked like, then forget what her little brother looked like. She told her about the old woman nursing the doll on the other side of the collapsed building, how the woman said she had no milk, how she was afraid she would never have milk herself and if she did would never know what it meant to nurse a child. She told her friend that she did not want a child anyway, not here, not in this place where she would die before she grew old, or fell in love, or knew pain or loss or anguish like her mother did. She would never know what love really meant. Not really. She told her she once dreamed that, although Shaul was younger, younger than them both, he might grow to be big and strong and handsome and wealthy and intelligent, so that he would marry Alicja despite her being older. So that they would be sisters. Because she longed for a sister and longed for Alicja to be with her. Sisters not friends. Because Alicja meant so much. So very much.

Hania told Alicja she was afraid.

She was afraid.

Alicja listened, not speaking, not interrupting, just listening. Finally she put her arm around her friend.

"I know," she said. "I understand. And we are sisters."

"I cannot lose you too," Hania told her.

"You will not lose me. Not ever. Nor I you. I told you once I would protect you. Do you remember? I meant it always."

Alicja took her hand. And they sat in the sunshine. And they heard a gunshot, far away in the distance. And they sat.

*

Rumors began circulating in the Ghetto that the Germans might be planning to

141

unleash an extermination brigade on the Jews, the same brigade that had unleashed the pogrom in Lublin and that now would come to the Warsaw Ghetto to unleash a massacre. They were particularly worried that German guards at the wall would be replaced by Ukrainians and Lithuanians so the Germans could be shipped off to the Russian front. The Ukrainians were known to be especially violent towards the Jews.

There were also rumors spreading about a work camp outside of Warsaw called Treblinki. From the few Poles who had escaped from there or been released, the Jews heard rumors that a sister camp was being built by German Jewish slaves, that many were dying in the process. One could almost taste the fear on the streets.

On the 17th of April, while Hania worked at her sewing machine, a man from the Judenrat Council ran into the factory and said that everyone must return to their homes as soon as possible. All quickly left. Panic filled the streets. Stores closed. Confusion was everywhere.

Hania ran to the apartment. Her Mother, Aunt Lea and Jakub were already inside. Her Uncle came soon after. He said they must all stay in the secret room and keep as quiet as possible. Hours passed as the sky darkened into night. And as the night fell, they heard shots and shouting, sometimes nearby, sometimes from afar. They heard footsteps from the stairs outside the apartment as many rushed up to the attic and into the various passages between the houses that had been created there in secret. Later they heard heavy footsteps on the stairs, shouts and doors banging. The family were terrified.

In the early hours of the morning, peeking out the window, Uncle Michael saw German soldiers in the courtyard, kicking in the doors of the bakery across the way, pulling out a number of the workers and taking them away. Then, silence. The family remained in the room for the rest of the day, and that night as well.

In the morning people began to emerge from hiding places, but few would go out onto the streets, excepting those who had nowhere else to go. Uncle Michael learned from his contacts that several dozen bakers and printers who had been printing the underground Ghetto communiqués had been rounded up and shot. A few days later the German soldiers were banging on doors throughout the Ghetto with lists of names they wanted for questioning. By the end of the month sixty more had been executed: a few more bakers had been shot, as well as many who had secretly worked for the underground, their identities revealed by informers. No one could be certain who to trust.

But in early May the Ghetto quieted again. Things started to return to normal, if starvation and beatings could be called normal. Hania's mother returned to working at the sewing factory, with Hania taking her machine seat two days a week and helping out at the community kitchen or looking after Jakub on other days.

An official from the Judenrat came to see Aunt Lea, to ask if she would perform in a concert in an assembly room that had once been a synagogue. They had arranged for the piano from the Femina Theatre to be brought there in two weeks. More than ever the people needed to feel like normal human beings; thus a musical evening had been planned. Lea hesitated, then agreed. She took several days away from the kitchen to practice.

Alicja came one afternoon to the kitchen, waiting for Hania to finish her work. Alicja then led Hania, pushing Jakub in his infant's chair, to Chlodna Street bridge across from the small ghetto. She wanted to show her friend something she found bewildering, if not amusing. Although nervous at crossing the wooden Bridge of Sighs over Chlodna Street for a change the German guards did not beat any of the hundreds who passed. Frankenstein was nowhere to be seen.

Alicja led Hania and her charge up onto the bridge then slowly crossed. The Germans and Jewish police stationed at short intervals did not let anyone stop, hurrying people on, but Hania slowed slightly with Alicja purposely hobbling with apparent difficulty. Alicja nodded over the barrier on the bridge, towards the street. Hania looked over and was amazed to see that a very large light had been set up behind a large movie camera. The Nazis were making a movie about the Ghetto.

Hania walked to the other side of the bridge beside Alicja, then followed her to an abandoned destroyed house on Wronia Street. Making sure they were unobserved, they snuck through a passage into a small courtyard and stayed in the shadows. From here they could see into the back of a restaurant on Chlodna. Inside cameras had been set up. People sat at tables, eating and drinking. They could see large plates of food set out. Hania felt her stomach rumble.

In the centre of the room she could see a German officer organizing the camera around a table with faces she recognized as Judenrat officials, including President Czerniakow. Even from a distance she could tell that he looked ill at ease.

"Czerniakow too acts a part. This is what they show to the world of how Jews live in the Warsaw Ghetto. Liars."

"But surely no one will believe them?," Hania asked.

Alicja looked at her.

"People believe what they want to believe. And they will not believe what is beyond their ability to see in their hearts or their heads. As the Ghetto is."

They returned to the large Ghetto mostly in silence. As it grew late, the streets became more dangerous. Hania was anxious to return. She asked Alicja to join her, but Alicja said she had work. Hania told her about the concert in a week's time where her Aunt Lea would perform. Would Alicja come as well? Alicja looked at her friend, then away.

"I will try, but…I will see."

Alicja smiled for a brief instant at her friend, then turned and went her own way. Hania knew Alicja would likely not come to hear her Aunt perform. She suspected such would be too painful for the other girl. Hania felt much the same way, but knew her Aunt needed her support; her mother had already said she would not feel able to attend but that she would look after Jakub.

The days before the concert the streets of the Ghetto seemed somehow calmer. People felt less afraid of being on the streets. Uncle Michael had intended to meet Hania at the Assembly Room, but the Jewish Police had warned janitors and house leaders that they must never leave buildings unattended in case their presence was requested; by whom or what they never said.

Thus Hania went alone to the concert and took a seat on the aisle, hoping that Alicja might yet join her, unsurprised when she did not. Several young men stood guard outside the building to keep watch, should any Nazi soldiers or police appear. The large room quickly filled with people desperate for music, desperate to be transported in their imaginations to a better place. Desperate to feel normal. Desperate to feel alive.

The first to perform was Miriam Eisenstadt, who everyone called the Nightingale of the Ghetto. She sang two pieces to rapturous applause. She was followed by Artur Gold on the violin, who played a tango and a song 'Jásminy' from one of his recordings. Two men then pushed a piano forward onto the stage platform. Aunt Lea came out and sat down.

The room hushed and she began.

It had been a long time since Hania had heard her Aunt play, and perhaps longer since she had heard any of Chopin's Nocturnes. Aunt Lea had chosen two that she would perform. The first, Opus Nine Number One, took the audience's breath away with its beauty. When she began the second, Nocturne in C Sharp Minor, Hania noticed several people around her in tears. The music, Lea's performance, brought out the sadness so many felt and the beauty for which most desperately searched and painfully believed had gone. She played with all her heart. The audience responded with the silence of the deeply moved. She played as if her life depended on it. For most there it did in so many ways. Half way through the piece it slowed just a bit.

She raised her hand to touch the next note. It was then that there was a single, loud applause coming from the back. Slow, rhythmic, almost antagonistic. People turned. Hania turned. Many gasped. Hania felt her heart pound, then miss a beat.

Standing at the back was a German officer, and several German soldiers. She recognized him immediately.

The German. The German she knew and feared.

He slowly walked forward, clapping slowly, threateningly, as he did. A couple other soldiers pushed into the room at the entrance, holding two of the young 'lookouts' by the scruff of the neck, guns at their heads, bruises on their faces.

The German continued walking until he was two thirds of the way down the aisle. He stared at Aunt Lea, not taking his eyes away from her.

"Beautiful, Fraulein. Truly, beautiful. Do not let me stop you. Please. You should continue. You should. Your Chopin: a pity he was not German. I think in his heart perhaps he was. My apologies for interrupting. A young friend of ours has sadly missed an appointment."

The German stood his ground and looked to his right. Half way down the row of the audience, a young man sat slouching somewhat in the seat. The German stared at him without moving. Soldiers came to the far end of the row, their guns out. Two others came down the centre aisle, standing behind the officer. Still The German stood motionless, staring. Cold. The young man knew he was penned in. His face set, terrified, he stood up and slowly walked to the centre aisle. The two soldiers grabbed him roughly by the arms and pulled him away. The others at the back pulled the young lookouts from the room.

The German remained standing in the room, alone but for the audience.

"Please, Fraulein, you must continue. So…tragic, this music. Please… Please!" His was clearly not a request.

Aunt Lea turned back to the keys. Hania could see she was shaking. She began to play again. She missed a note, stopped.

"Pity," said The German. His face set, he turned and started down the aisle. But when he came to Hania, he stopped. He turned his head.

And he looked at her. Stared at her.

And her eyes met his. And she knew that he knew.

He stayed that way for a long moment, then turned his head again and left the room.

The audience sat frozen.

Aunt Lea sat frozen.

Slowly people stood and began to leave the room. Hania stood as well, almost gasping for breath. She walked out, desperate for air, almost faint.

Outside people dispersed quickly. The soldiers, The German, were gone. But on the steps just outside of the building, the body of the oldest of the 'lookouts' lay in a pool of blood.

Hania did not tell her mother what had happened. She did not need to. She went straight into the secret back room and lay on the bed. She had not waited for her Aunt to return. She later heard her come in and talk quietly with her mother, then Uncle Michael when he came up. Hania did not come out to the front room. She lay on the bed facing the wall. When her Mother did come in, she lay beside Hania and held her.

She only closed her eyes an hour before dawn at best.

She awoke a few hours later and came out. Aunt Lea, dressed to leave, sat with Jakub on her knee, staring out the window.

"I am sorry," whispered Hania. Her aunt put her finger to her lips.

She sat there for a long time. Hania did not move. Finally her aunt stood, put Jakub down. She came over to Hania and placed her hands on either side of her niece's face. She leaned over and gently kissed her on the cheek, looking into her deep green eyes.

"Yes," was all she said.

Lea put on a wrap and walked over to the door. Turned back to Hania.

"I need to be out. I will return later. Will you look after Jakub? He loves you deeply, Hania. As do I."

Hania could only nod.

Her Aunt started out, but hesitated.

"Last night the Nazis executed sixty young men from the underground…I hope the one they came for—I hope the music touched his heart. I hope he heard the notes in his head as he died."

Then she was gone.

Hania spent an hour telling Jakub stories: about the Kampinos Forest, and bicycles, and strawberries that he had never seen, and a kind farmer who gave her cheese, a word the boy also did not know, and about her Babka's special cake. She told him about playing hide and seek and tag with her special friend. She told him about the magic of Jakub's mother and father, wizards at music and buildings and art and all things good. She told him about her own father. About walking over the River Vistula in the morning mist. She told him about the love in her heart for her parents, and his, for her brother who had to leave them, and for the little boy himself.

She told him one day he would know these things. One day he would know the rainbow. One day he would find color in his heart and gift this to the hearts of others.

She told him this for an hour, and another.

She told him how she loved him.

She told him how she always would.

For an hour. And a second hour. And a third.

Jakub slept for a short time in her lap. She held his head in her arms. She held his heart in her own.

When he awoke she thought she would take him for a short walk. She needed air. She needed to see the sky.

She picked him up and carried him slowly to the ground floor. She allowed him then to take her hand. Together they walked out the front door and turned down the street.

And as they did, Hania saw at the bottom of the road a German Mercedes coming towards her, followed by a small canvas covered troop vehicle.

Hania knew.

She picked up Jakub in her arms. She turned and ran.

She ran as fast as her legs would move. Back into the house. Up one flight of stairs, another. She ran, breathing hard, holding him tight. She ran.

On the third floor she unlocked the door to the front room in the apartment and hurried inside. She carried Jakub into the back room, the secret room. She sat him on the bed, looked him in the eye. Fear spoke her words.

"Jakub, listen to me. I will be right outside. You must wait for me. You must not say anything. No sound. You must wait. Yes? No noise. Shhh! Not a sound? Yes? Yes Jakub?"

The boy confused, nodded seriously, his legs swinging on the mattress.

"No words. Wait."

Hania turned and ran back to the outer room. She pushed the sink and tiled wall covering back in place, hearing the latch click. She stared at it to make certain she could not tell anything might be amiss.

She turned and ran back to shut the door to the apartment, to lock it from within. She pushed the door shut.

But it did not shut. Did not close. A hand stopped her. And pushed it open.

Hania's heart stopped for a moment. She took a step back. And another.

The one she called Misio, a gun in his hand, blanket in the other, pushed the door open and marched in. Behind him walked The German.

Hania backed away, terrified.

The German stared at her. His face unmoving. His eyes cold. He looked around the room, then at the terrified girl.

"Where is he? The child? Where is he?"

Hania shook her head, saying nothing.

"Did you really think I would not know where you were? Where your family were? Did I not tell you we can find anyone whenever we want? Where is the boy?"

Still Hania said nothing.

Not raising his voice, but speaking very slowly: "Where is he, girl?"

"He is not here," Hania finally found a voice to reply, quietly, afraid. "He does not live here."

"You lie, girl. You should not lie. Not to me. Where is he?"

"No. I do not lie. I do not know. I do not…"

Footsteps running up the stairs outside, and Aunt Lea at that moment ran into the room.

Misio turned the gun towards her. She stopped in her tracks. The German glanced at her.

"So, I should have thought this. Chopin never sounded so…empty. Where is your son? Or did you abandon it to this girl? I think not. I think this child is yours."

"Not here. He is dead. Not here."

"Dead? Really?"

The German walked straight up to her. He took out his own gun from the belt at his side.

"Your son, Madam. I want to know where he is."

"I have no son. He died! He is gone!"

The German raised his gun to her forehead. He turned to Hania. Without raising his voice:

"Tell me where the boy is, or I will shoot her. Now. Tell me."

"No!" Aunt Lea screamed.

"You are a liar. You should not lie to a German Officer," said the German, in a low, calm voice. He swung his raised hand holding the gun and slammed it against the side of Lea's head. Hania screamed in fear. Lea, bleeding from her ear, fell sideways. Her head slammed off the iron stove that gave them heat in the winter as she fell on the floor. Her eyes closed, she did not move. Her breath, shallow.

The German stood over her unconscious body and pointed his gun at her head. He looked at Hania.

"First I will shoot the boy's mother. Then I will shoot you. I do not want to do this, girl. Where is her little boy?"

Hania hesitated.

"I," she tried to swallow but her throat was dry. She tried to breath, but could not breath. She felt urine trickle down her leg. She could not. She could not.

"I do not know."

The German looked at her, shook his head, started to turn, when in the deathly silence of the room came a child's cry. A weeping. Unmistakable.

"'ania.'

Unmistakable.

The German looked at Hania, looked around the room. He walked over to the sink. Stared at it. Tried to move it. Couldn't.

"Open it," he said to Hania. When she did not move: "Open it!" he shouted, raising his voice for the first time, simultaneously pointing his gun first at her, then again at her aunt on the floor.

Hania, her body shaking, trying to find breath, walked over to the sink and released the latch hidden beneath it. She pushed the sink aside, revealing the entry panel and hole in the wall.

"Stay here," The German said to the driver, grabbing Hania and pushing her in front of him towards the hole and the corridor beyond.

Hania struggled to take her steps along the short passageway and walked into the hidden room. Jakub ran into her arms. The German followed. He stared at the boy. He did not move. Finally he raised his hand and forced the boy, now crying, to look at him. He stared at the boy's eyes. His green eyes.

"Come in here!," the German shouted, and after a moment the man Hania called Misio walked into the room.

Without taking his eyes from Hania:

"Vermin. Take it."

Hania stepped back. The large man grabbed the boy and tried to pull him away. Jakub screamed. Hania screamed. The German grabbed Hania by the shoulders and wrenched her away, throwing her against the wall. The one she called Misio had the boy in his arms, struggling. The one she called Misio threw the blanket over the crying boy. Held him tight.

The one she called Misio left the room holding Jakub in his grasp.

Hania tried to stand. Tried to run after. The German grabbed her arm and again threw her down.

"You should not lie to a German officer. You are nothing but a Jewess. Nothing."

Hania stared at him. He took off his coat and threw it on the bed. Pulled his braces down from his shoulders. Terrified, she stared.

"Jewess. Girl? Or maybe not. Shall we find out?"

He grabbed Hania and pulled her up, towards him. He grabbed her arms. She fought against him. Struggled. Freed an arm and with all her remaining strength, she struck his face as hard as she could.

The German reeled back, just slightly. Hania stood, frozen. He turned, stared at her, and roared with anger. He grabbed her by her reddish blond hair and pulled it until she thought he would pull it out from the roots. Her head fell back against his pull.

"A Jewess. You are nothing. You want to see what you do? You want to see what the result of your Jewish lies is?"

He pulled her towards the window by her hair, with one arm around her neck. He took his gun from the holster in the belt and used it to shatter the window glass. Hania heard it break and heard the large pieces fall as he hit each one, fall three floors below and shatter on the ground in the courtyard. The German forced Hania's head over the edge of the broken frame.

She saw the courtyard below.

She saw her death.

She hoped he would throw her now.

She hoped it would not be painful.

She looked below.

And she saw in the courtyard one figure only; no one else in any of the buildings would dare be seen. One figure of a man in a uniform with a face she recognized.

She saw in the courtyard, looking up, the Polish Policeman she knew as the Magician.

And she saw in his arms, bundled in a blanket, the shape of a small boy, his feet sticking out.

The Magician walked into the otherwise empty courtyard. He threw the bundle onto the ground. He stood over it, then looked up.

The Magician saw her, saw her head pushed over the edge of the window, saw The German's hand holding her so that she could not move her face, could not move her eyes.

She could not move.

"Look!," he shouted at Hania. "Even that pig of a Polish bastard down there stands higher than the vermin we call Jew. You see? You see!"

She could not move. He made certain she could not move. He made certain she would see.

"Remember!," he shouted again. "You did this. This is what you did by lying. Always know that you did this! You did this."

He held Hania's head, although she tried to move it right, left. Tried to move. He held her head by her hair, her red blond hair.

Then he raised his other hand still holding the gun, raised it to the Magician, standing below. The Magician raised his right hand in a Nazi salute. The Magician turned back to the motionless bundle on the ground, with the feet of a boy sticking out from beneath a blanket. The Magician took out a gun from his belt.

The Magician pointed the gun at the bundle over which he stood, lowered it to the edge of the blanket where a child's head must have been.

And the Magician shot.

And shot again.

And shot a third time.

The bundle lay still. The bundle lay…still.

And that was all.

The German pulled Hania into the room and threw her own motionless with shock body to the floor.

"I will have him throw that child's body into the sewer where the Jews belong. You did this. He dies because of you. Always remember. You did this."

The German turned and disappeared from the room.

Hania tried to push herself up. She tried to reason. She tried to make sense. She tried.

And then she prayed she would die.

And Hania fainted into unconsciousness.

*

Later, she opened her eyes, then closed them again. She did not move.

*

And still much later, when she could not know, her eyes opened again. She realized she was lying on the bed, her head resting in a lap. She felt fingers gently massaging the back of her head, running carefully through her red blond hair. She felt compassion. She felt she did not deserve compassion. She felt she deserved only disgust, and hate.

Hania turned her head, just slightly, turned her eyes, just slightly.

Hania looked into the pained, deeply saddened face not of her mother, as at first she had assumed held her, but saw holding her in her lap, her arms holding her to her breast, her friend Alicja.

Alicja said not a word.

Hania's eyes fell back towards the wall, towards the floor. She did not move further. Her eyes closed. She slipped back into a black world without dreams.

*

She returned into a dark world of silence.

Joseph Babinski Specialist Hospital/ Institute of
  Neuropsychiatric Disorder, Kobierzyn (Krakow)
Patient Identification: 46-10/276
Patient Name: Kielar, Hannah
Patient Birthdate/Locale 04Apr1924/ Nowy Wiśnicz
Consulting Psychologist: Dr. (hab) K.Palinsky, D.N.,PhD.

Final Monthly Patient Report
12 September 1948

---

*After a lengthy discussion with Dr. Łados, we have agreed that this will be my
final official report as to the case of H.Kielar. I will continue recording and filing
case notes for as long as I remain her therapist and will happily discuss these with
the Committee.*

*The patient had for some time expressed a desire to reenter society. Although
we do not feel it quite the right moment for her to depart the Institute, we have
arranged for an initial temporary position for H.Kielar to assist at the Kobierzyn
Primary School for Troubled Children on Kwiecista Street under the tutelage and
guidance of counselor Dr. Marian Piekarski. The Committee will recall Dr.
Piekarski's exemplary work here at the Institute with our youngest patients and
her success in creating the Institute's adolescent wing prior to her opening the
Primary School here in Kobierzyn. Dr. Piekarski has agreed to employ H.Kielar
as an assistant at the school three mornings a week and will help oversee and
guide her reentry into the community. It is hoped that the patient will in due course
move from her quarters here on the Institute's property into accommodation in
town, all being well.*

*I will continue my work with H.Kielar, although therapy sessions will now be
reduced from five-seven hours per week to three.*

*I believe all will agree that the progress H.Kielar has made here at the
Institute, albeit at times slow, has been satisfactory. She has reached the stage in
her therapy in which her present behavior, substantially calmed but nevertheless
intellectually engaging with myself and, slowly, others, is now largely shaping her
future: that is to state the obvious. That future will be dictated by the goals she has
set for herself with the guidance of the Institute. Those include one day perhaps
teaching children, which she has told me in discussion was always an aspiration.*

H.Kielar's therapy will and should continue. In Adlerian terms, she is now working through that fourth phase of therapy, a phase of character rebuilding that seeks change, not radical personality change (through psychosurgical technique, for example) but through a stage of Emotional Breakthrough. As yet, I cannot say such Breakthrough has been achieved. As her therapist I tread most carefully on her past life in Nowy Wiśnicz. Attempting to explore the circumstances of her mother's death, H.Kielar has a tendency to shut down, as well as when trying to explore her feelings towards her father and his unexplained disappearance. Such events must be confronted before H.Kielar can move forward, can 'Do Differently' in order to find her stated goals.

The fact that H.Kielar was an only child has, I would suggest, reinforced her feelings of inferiority. And thus her silence. It also might go some distance to explaining her desire to teach, to become literally the 'head of the class'. H.Kielar exhibits classic characteristics of the only child: she waits for direction, needs support, views the world as a hostile place. But these characteristics have slowly tempered, leading me to suggest that she is ready to take her first tentative steps back into society, a suggestion supported by Dr. Łados.

I would at this point make one final observation. The patient arrived at the Institute unwilling to engage with language or emotion. I suggest she had taken on this catastrophic mental state when faced with the traumas of the previous years—her mother Helena's death as related in her notes from such information as supplied by Fr.Daněk and as earlier supplied by Fr.Zieliński prior to his own death, her father's unexplained disappearance, her possible physical abuse by one or both and in whatever circumstances her relinquishing of her virginal state— resulting in the very avoidance of responsibility for her own intimate acts of destruction: depression, neurosis, silence, evidence of fear and paranoia.

Now, after almost two years of slow recovery here at the Institute and with work yet to do in order to understand and accept the past, H.Kielar has begun to emerge from those events, from memory itself, in order to begin to put the past behind her and to look forward to a socially engaged and new future.

K.Palinsky

September 1948

PERSONAL FILE NOTE ONLY (re: Hannah K.)

16 September 1948

As mentioned both in the report to the Institute's Committee and in my filed case notes regarding Hannah K., I have been updating Dr. Łados as usual regarding this case and the little I have gleaned of the Hannah K's 'feral' days in Nowy Wiśnicz prior to her committal here at the Institute. Indeed Dr. Łados has kindly taken on the role of my own therapist and mentor in this and my other cases. As my therapist I have found him sympathetic to my concerns and conflicts.

I indicated to Dr. Łados that as Hannah K. has opened up more and more to me, she continues to hold much back. But I am also concerned that the issue of transference, whilst perhaps commonplace enough, demonstrates resistance between us; however rather than a parentification of our relationship, this may be an unsurprising attraction on behalf patient to therapist. Dr. Łados agrees with me that such may be a common occurrence, but that nevertheless extreme care must be taken at this stage of the therapy: it could as easily become a threat to such as it could become a useful tool.

We discussed the situation at length, and I volunteered to withdraw from the therapeutic consultations with the Patient if Dr. Łados felt that such transference might be too risky, but he did not counsel for such.

What I did not say to Dr. Łados is that it is not the Patient's transference that concerns me at this point in the therapy, it is the possibility for my own counter transference. I silently worry this is the real risk I must sooner or later address, and that I cannot at this point address through therapy either with the patient, or in discussion with him.

Warsaw May 1942-January 1943

Hania did not know how long Alicja remained with her. Hours became days. Alicja barely left her side. Alicja fed her soup as if her friend were a small child. She sat with her. Slept at her side. Sometimes she sang softly. Spoke softly. Memories. Hopes. Silence.

"Your mother is in the front room," Alicja told her. "Your aunt will be all right but she has suffered. Your mother thinks it best that she stay beside her for now. Your uncle too but he must do his job or no one eats."

Hania said nothing.

After a week or so, Alicja whispered to her early one morning:

"I must go today, Hania. I am sorry. You must be strong."

Hania was asleep when her friend left. She barely knew she had gone. She slept most of the time. She wept silently much of the time. Tears offered no solace.

When she finally emerged from the back room, the secret room, after many days she found her mother sitting beside her aunt, holding her hand. The eyes of both stared at nothing and everything. Her mother nodded at Hania, but said nothing. Her aunt looked at her, not with anger, not with emotion, but simply as one whose life had been thrown into a void and whose spirit had abandoned her. Hania walked over and knelt before them. Her mother put her hand on Hania's head, stroking her hair. Aunt Lea looked down on her with a vacant glance, confused, disorientated. Then away.

The following morning Hania returned to the sewing factory on Ogrodowa Street. Word had spread amongst those at the machines as to what had occurred. No one said anything. Everyone had their own tragedies to live, to relive. The Supervisor allowed Hania to return to her seat. June had become incredibly hot, made worse in the treeless Ghetto. The sewing factory stifled in the heat. Hania never noticed. She sat for the now required twelve hour work day, day after day. She wanted mindless work. Work without thought. Still sometimes her mind wandered. Broken glass. The sound of gunshots. Sometimes. And she worked the machine, often ignoring the afternoon meal despite her obvious weakness, the machine running tat tat tat, the grey fabric, sewing, sewing, machine needle grey material machine material, hearing still the glass break, feeling still her throat pushed against wood and broken glass, feeling empty. Breaking glass.

She would be empty too.

Despite the danger of walking through the Ghetto at night, Hania paid little attention to what streets she walked, what direction. She would return to the apartment by curfew, sit in a far corner or in the secret room alone, eating little, a bit of soup, some bits of potato or beet or turnip, some sawdust laden black bread. Although she told herself she had to care, she did not care.

Sometimes she returned to her small, carefully planted piece of earth to see if the carrots had lengthened, the turnips grown fatter. She told herself it mattered for the sake of all of them. She told herself they had to survive. She told herself they all had to believe. But despite such quiet words muttered to herself, she did not believe.

Sometimes in the back room, its window now without its glass, open to the day's heat, the air and death that had taken the most innocent of children, her mother would come to sit with her, sleep beside her. Sometimes too Zivia would pace. Or stand in the painful stillness of the room.

Aunt Lea no longer spoke. Her wound had damaged. Her mind had damaged. Her eyes said everything there was to say.

One night Hania woke to the moonlight and shadows, still hot. In the distance occasional shouts or gunshots or cries of anguish, a hot summer's night like as now all the summer nights. She walked down the short corridor and through the opening into the main apartment room. Her mother and her aunt lay on the bed, holding one another, asleep. Her uncle had gone.

Hania opened the apartment door and walked out to the stairwell landing. A window was open and she looked out at the moon. She wondered how long it would shine on the Ghetto. She wondered how it could be silent and not weep.

Below, the courtyard was empty but for a single figure, on his knees, scrubbing the ground. She knew it was her Uncle Michael, scrubbing at the blood of his only son, blood that had long since disappeared. Several times over the coming few nights Hania awoke and looked down at the courtyard. Each night her Uncle kneeled there, scrubbing. He could never seem to scrub enough. He could never clean the anguish away.

She cursed God. God had abandoned them, whatever the rabbis might say. God did not look upon the Jews.

Hania filled her days with emptiness at the factory. The machine and sewing; she saw little else. Knew nothing else. One evening she came out of the factory, stared at people walking endlessly, purposelessly by. So many people. Madness around her. Madness within her.

She wanted to scream. She could not scream. She hadn't the energy. She barely had life inside her.

Hania suddenly knew she needed to see Alicja again. She had not seen her friend in almost a month. Alicja was life. Hania needed life. Hania needed to pretend they could together return to their games in Powązki Cemetery and Krasinski Park. She needed to feed on it. She needed hope. She needed to feed.

She pushed through the throngs hurrying towards Nowolipki Street. Alicja had told her not to go there, but Hania did not know where else she might be. All Hania could think of was her friend's arms around her, telling her that all would be well, that life would go on, that she had to hope.

At the fallen remains of the building Hania once again found the passage through the collapsed ruins to the courtyard in the back. And once again she walked through the derelict, destroyed rooms of what had once been people's homes, rooms now like crypts for the dead. She saw no one else. At the broken stairway she carefully tread each step down to the cellar space, light fading from view.

Hurry then to the rear of the recessed collapsed rooms. To Alicja. Find Alicja, the only thing she could think. Find Alicja.

She came to the last recessed cellar alcove. The blanket had not been drawn across. She looked. She stared. She had found her friend. And found what she had not expected to find. Had not wanted to find. Could not have imagined she would find.

She saw the mattress on the ground. She saw Alicja, her Alicja, lying there with a man on top of her. She saw the man's trousers pulled down to his feet. His grey trousers. She saw Alicja's legs splayed apart, with the man lying between them. She saw the man pushing against her friend, brutally, pushing, harder, pushing between her legs with his body and his strength. Pushing with all the hate in a man, his form falling up and down, again up and down, her good leg and her other leg half flesh half wood splayed wide and his form pushing up and down. Hania saw one of his hands holding onto Alicja's throat. She saw her friend's closed eyes. She saw resting on a half broken table near the bed Alicja's walking stick and the man's grey uniform coat. She saw the uniform of a German Ghetto guard. She saw him entering her friend with his hard filthy hating manhood, over, and over, and over. Slamming against her. Grunting with hate and disgust and filth. Over, and over, and over. And his hand pushing at her throat.

And then her eyes opened.

And her empty stare turned, just so, until that stare met Hania's shocked face, Hania's eyes wide, her expression one of fear and shame and pain and loss. She felt the tears well, begin to fall. Her head shook back and forth. She heard the glass from the window fall and crash into the courtyard.

Hania heard the shots from the Magician's gun. One, two, three.

Hania saw the body of the beloved child not hers but almost hers, her Jakub lying beneath a blanket on the courtyard stone, blood spreading out now over the stone. She heard her own body as it collapsed against the wall. And heard The German saying: "You did this. He died because of you. You did this. Remember."

Hania remembered.

And she could not stop the tears now falling.

Alicja looked at her friend, looked into her friend's watching eyes staring directly into Hania's crying gaze, then turned her head away and closed her eyes.

With the German Ghetto guard pushing his hate and filth and death and power inside of her, his filthy body inside of her, pushing, forcing, over, and over, and over.

Hania turned away, walked back through the ruins of the collapsed building where the friend she knew had lived and the friend she knew had died, could only have died. She walked back through the catacombs of death, cold and without memory and empty of all that she would henceforth remember.

Hania returned to the apartment where her mother sat with her aunt and death surrounded them all. She returned to the apartment where Uncle Michael could be seen below, in the shadows, scrubbing the stone it the courtyard, over and over again, but could not make the loss or pain or memory of his beloved Jakub, the family's beloved Jakub, could not make the loss of all the beloved sons and daughters, fathers and mothers, aunts and uncles, and yes friends disappear, no matter how hard the stone was scrubbed.

And Hania lay down on the bed. And closed her eyes. And said nothing. And did not sleep.

*

July came. Rumors everywhere. Rumors that everyone in the Ghetto faced deportation. Rumors that the population had only forty days left to live. Terrible rumors about the work factory Treblinki, that people sent there died horrible deaths. Rumors that Ukrainian and Lithuanian Auxiliary Police had prepared to take over at the Warsaw Ghetto walls. Rumors of the guard Frankenstein on a rampage, killing any beggar he found on the streets. Some chose to have faith in God. Some chose to believe in rumors.

Still Hania went daily to her job sewing grey German Wehrmacht uniforms. Still Hania walked home at night, stopping only on occasion to pull up a few vegetables, now growing, but seemingly alone in growing in the Ghetto.

Returning one evening, Hania met Uncle Michael on the stairs.

"Come with me," he told her.

Hania followed him past the stairway door to their rooms and up the last two flights of stairs. At the top, a small hidden hatch to the attic had been pulled open and a ladder within pulled to the landing. Hania followed her uncle up the rungs and pulled herself into the attic space. Several men turned to look at them, then away. Michael led his niece to the far end of the large space, where he spoke quietly to her.

"I do not know what will happen. I do not know who will live or die. Your father wanted you, your mother, your brother to live. Your brother did not. My Jakub did not. But you must live, your mother. You must do everything you can, do you understand?"

161

Hania nodded, saying nothing.

He lifted some boards. Below was a narrow crawl passage amongst the floor supports.

"This leads to the adjoining attic. From there to the next. Five houses in all. In the third house is a cellar. If you go down, under the stairs at the ground, another trapdoor. In that cellar in the back we have created a bunker. There is food. If things get bad you go there. Your mother, any who can. You must move quickly. Quietly. If you see police, German soldiers, you hide. You give no one away. But you must save who you can. You must try to save yourself. That is what your father would want. Hania?"

She nodded.

"Good."

They returned to the apartment.

That night Hania lay beside her mother, staring out through the moonlight.

"Hania?"

Hania turned her head to her mother.

"Your friend Alicja: she has been good to you. A sister. When you see her tell her she should come stay here with us. She will need us. You will need her. Ask her."

Hania stared at her mother, then turned away.

"Alicja is dead," she said. And closed her eyes.

The next morning Hania went to the factory as usual. At noon everyone was told to return to their homes. Hania did so to find her mother pacing, her aunt silently facing the wall. Fear was all around. Towards the evening Uncle Michael returned home with a hammer and some boards. He went into the hidden room and nailed the boards over the window, then emerged back into the front room.

"The Judenrat just published a notice that all those not necessary to the effort will be deported to the East. Everyone. They say there will be food and jobs in factories. I do not believe them. Many do not believe them."

"What does it mean?," Hania asked.

"I do not know. We will find out. Tomorrow you will stay here with Aunt Lea and your Mother. You should stay in the other room. We all will."

That morning, July 23rd, at dawn Uncle Michael left early. Hania sat in the back room with her mother and aunt. They pulled the false panel in front of the short corridor, leaving them shut in. In the single room light streamed in through breaks in the wooden planks. They could hear whistles and shots from afar.

After a while, Uncle Michael returned and joined them in the secret room. He brought in some bread, soup, then shut all within.

"The Germans, many Ukrainians and Lithuanians too have sealed all the Ghetto gates. They are rounding up anyone on the streets. I have been told that President Czerniakow committed suicide last night. Apparently he could not bring himself to be responsible for the German Resettlement Aktion. They wanted a list from him. He wrote a note and said he could not be responsible for the deaths of five thousand Jews. We will stay in here as long as we can. We have food. We will not go outside. They have quotas. They are closing off street by street and searching for Jews. The Germans say every person should pack their things, one suitcase each, carry food with them for their journey."

"Where are they taking them?," asked Hania.

"Umschlagplatz, on Stawki Street. Hundreds there wait for trains to resettlement. They wait. Some are shot. We will stay here and be silent until we know what streets they close."

For the next few days they remained in the secret room. Hania slept on the floor, as did her uncle. Her mother shared the bed with Lea. Lea said nothing and seemed to disappear into nothing, her skeletal frame growing daily more angular, her hair turning thin and grey. Sometimes Hania woke and looked over at her aunt. She could see her tears even in the darkness. She could feel everyone's fear.

Uncle Michael broke off a small bit of board from the planks over the window. They peeked through and saw hundreds of people who would be resettled brought to the courtyard by Jewish Police, made to stand in several rows. Hours later they marched out in columns.

After several days their food supply had grown low.

"We could move into the attic passageways but there are many already there. The Judenrat no longer has food to supply anyone. The Germans want to starve us out."

"I should pull my vegetables."

"Too dangerous," said her uncle.

"You said we will need food."

"No, Hania. No."

Uncle Michael left at dawn to meet with some of his contacts. They had started to plan the first groups of armed resistance amongst those hidden in attics and cellars. They needed to plan for a future, should there be a future.

In the afternoon the streets below grew quiet. Hania decided she must retrieve the food she had grown in the ruins of the fallen building, despite her Uncle's warning. They needed everything they could collect.

"I will come back, Mama. I will come back."

Keeping to shadows and doorways, Hania left the apartment building to try to get to her small plot of dirt where she grew her few vegetables. If she saw a street blocked off, she backtracked and found a different way to go, often cutting through buildings that seemed recently abandoned, sometimes hiding beneath stairways if she heard voices or shouting. Sometimes she saw long columns of people, hundreds of people being marched away in the direction of the Umschlagplatz, guarded by Nazi SS soldiers. She hid as they passed, praying that they would not come looking in the shadows where she crouched.

Hours later, although it should have been only many minutes, Hania made it to the ruins of the building where she had her small bit of earth, her few vegetables that she knew would have to go some way to keeping them all alive. Waiting until dusk, she crawled into the open and started to dig. Several times she thought she heard shouts and she lay in the dirt, pretending to be a corpse, waiting until the shouts receded. She dug up everything she could, putting her small crop into the rags she had brought with her.

Once she was certain she had left nothing in the ground Hania hurried through the building ruins towards the road. When she got there she realized no one was around. She carefully looked down the street and saw that the Jewish police has set up a barricade on the road to prevent escape. German and Ukrainian soldiers were marching into buildings, pulling people out if they did not voluntarily emerge. She saw several buildings on fire. She saw furniture and clothes thrown into the street, abandoned. She saw soldiers strolling further down the road past a burning building and saw a man jump from above with flames around him, jumping to his death. The soldiers glanced at the smoking body, then kept walking.

Hania did not know what to do. She looked up another street but saw it too had been closed off and Jews were being forced from their homes. She returned to the ruins of the building where her small plot was and crawled beneath a collapsed wall. Here she lay motionless as darkness fell. She remained here through the night, hearing shots and screams throughout the ghetto.

At first light Hania crawled out from her hiding place. She carefully made her way back to the street. There was no one. Buildings had been cleared. The police and soldiers had moved on. Once again Hania started on her journey back to her own apartment building, avoiding any street where she saw a uniform, or indeed any movement whatsoever. But just as Hania turned onto Dzielna Street she heard the rumbling of motors and saw several vehicles driving in her direction.

Hania ran the rest of the way to her building. She rushed up the stairs to the apartment and pushed the door open. Uncle Michael and Aunt Lea stood in the front room.

Michael turned towards his niece as she ran in.

"Hania… We thought we had lost you."

"I went for food. I am sorry. I was trapped during the night until they left. The Germans, I think they are closing off the street. We should go into the attic."

Hania looked from her aunt to her uncle.

"Hania…," her uncle softly said.

"Mother?"

"She is in the room. You need to go in there. There are too many in the attic right now. It is safest here."

Hania, breathless.

"Come then. Before they arrive."

"Hania…"

Only at the moment did Hania see the two packed suitcases behind her Aunt and Uncle. She did not understand. She could not understand. She stared at them, then at her Uncle.

"What are you doing? We need to go inside. Mama?," she shouted.

"Hania, no."

"What, we…but we…."

"Hania, go within. I will shut the panel after you, make certain the seal is good. You must be with your Mother."

"I do not understand, you…"

"We are leaving. We have to. We think it will be safe. We will get word to you if it is. We cannot stay here any longer."

"No."

"We cannot stay, Hania. With Jakub now…with… We have decided."

"You can't!"

"I am sorry."

"No!"

They heard shouts from below.

"Come," gently said her Uncle. Hania was crying now. "Come…"

He took her arm and led her to the corridor behind the opening.

"This is what we must do. For us…" said her uncle. He struggled to maintain his composure. "Stay alive. Stay…"

He shook his head. He too had started to cry. And as she stood there, he began to push the false paneling closed.

Aunt Lea stopped him. She looked at him, he at her. She took a step into the corridor, stood directly in front of Hania. She reached with her hands and pulled Hania's face to her own, then kissed her forehead. In a whispered, barely audible voice, hoarse and shaking, Lea spoke for the first time since Jakub's death, staring into Hania's green eyes, green even in the shadows of the dark corridor.

"It… is time. It is not…your fault."

Perhaps it would be the last thing she would say.

Aunt Lea kissed Hania again, then shuffled several steps backwards. Uncle Michael closed the false panel door. The corridor was dark.

Hania, crying, turned and walked into the secret room. Her Mother sat in a chair, rocking herself slightly forward, backwards. Hania walked over and hugged her Mother. Her Mother did not resist, and did not respond. Hania then went and looked through the small gap in the wooden boards. Below, in the courtyard, she saw Aunt Lea and Uncle Michael emerge from the building and join the hundreds of others lined up. After an hour of waiting the German guards ordered the men, women and children to march out.

Hania saw the empty courtyard, the place where her Aunt and Uncle had stood. She saw that it was on the spot where their small son Jakub had been murdered. She knew her Uncle had been right: she could not see it, but she knew that there was still blood on the stone there, and it would never disappear.

*

Thousands were taken. Old and young. Infirm and healthy. Men, women, children. Some volunteered. Some were forced. Many were killed.

Hania and her mother remained in the secret room, keeping silent, waiting for nothing but the possibility of life itself. At times even that did not seem worth waiting for. Hoping for.

Hania knew she would have to go out to scavenge. After several days of keeping watch and seeing that the courtyard remained empty, she decided to open the secret door one evening, knowing she could move easiest in darkness. She closed the panel entrance behind the sink once more, leaving her mother within, promising to return.

Some of the apartment doors on the landings heading down to the street were open. Hania carefully entered rooms, hoping to find food. She found a rotting carrot or two, a small beet, some crumbs, nothing more. She decided to risk crossing the courtyard to see if she could get into the rooms of the old bakery. Keeping to the shadows and the edge of the buildings, hidden by darkness, she slowly made her way towards the bakery's former entrance. The last twenty meters she had to run in the open. She ran expecting a cry to ring out at any moment, a shout or whistle. But she heard nothing.

The door to the old bakery was locked shut. A cellar window was broken and Hania climbed in. Just below the broken window, a small table had been pushed up so she did not fall. She had brought a candle and matches with her. The room had clearly been ransacked. A few mice pecked at some fallen specs of grain. She walked over to the stairs leading up to the bakery and gasped when she saw eyes staring at her. Lifting her candle she saw the emaciated forms of two adults and two very small children, hiding, staring at her in terror.

"I am sorry, I...I am sorry. I thought there might be food. I am sorry."

They said nothing to her. Hania backed away, then climbed up onto the small table to pull herself out of the broken window. She felt a pull on her skirt and turned. The emaciated woman had followed and held out her hand to Hania, offering her a small bit of black bread. Hania hesitantly took it. The woman nodded, turned and disappeared back into the darkness.

Hania pulled herself back into the courtyard and again kept to the shadows. She started around to her own building's rear entrance when from nowhere a pair of hands grabbed her and pushed her against the wall. A Jewish Policeman stared at her, his eyes hard, his face set. He shined a torch directly into her eyes.

"Who are you?," he demanded.

"I...I..."

"Past curfew. You live in one of these?"

Hania nodded.

"Papers!"

Hania, trembling, pulled out her identity papers. The Policeman held the papers up, staring at them.

"These say you work at Ogrodowa Street Factory."

"Yes."

"What do you do there?"

"Sew. Uniforms. For the Germans."

The Policeman stared at her for a long time, then pushed the papers back into her hand.

"These may keep you alive. Perhaps not. Go home and obey the curfew."

He pushed her away. Hania ran back to her building entrance. She did not look behind.

For another week Hania and her mother remained in hiding in the secret room. Occasionally she saw police or soldiers searching the buildings around the courtyard. One morning she looked out and saw several soldiers kick at the door of the former bakery until the lock gave way. They entered. Many minutes later they emerged pushing several people in front of them. Amongst those were the family she had seen in the cellar. Hania knew she could not help them. No one could.

The heat in the room could be stifling. She looked forward to the night, to the relative quiet and emptiness of darkness. That evening she sat on the floor as her mother lay on the bed, sat and thought and tried to remember her father's face, her brother's face. They had almost faded from memory.

She heard noises from the apartment room beyond the panel. Footsteps. She waited. Listened. Heard them again. She stood and tiptoed down the small corridor. Listened. Silence, then again footsteps. And someone pulling at the latch on the other side hidden beneath the sink.

Hania backed into the bedroom and sat down on the bed. Her mother sat up. Hania took her hand. She heard the false panel being pulled away. She held her mother's hand tighter. Terrified now. She waited for them to come for her, for her mother. She would not cry. She would not scream out. She sat, her mother sat, both silent. The panel moving across the floor, the door to the secret room opening.

A moment, and a figure appeared in their room, staring down at them.

Not police or soldiers. The man she knew as Yitzhak. He stared at her, at her mother. Then nodded, just slightly.

"You cannot stay here. It is no longer safe for you. Bring your things. Any food you have left. Come."

Hannah looked at her mother, uncertain.

"Come," he said again.

They followed him out of the room and up the stairs. At the top landing he pulled up a loose floorboard, purpose-broken to size; he put a small clip on the end. He reached up and hooked into a small broken bit of ceiling board, pulling open the near-hidden hatch. He then carefully pulled down the ladder from above. They followed him into the attic.

With his torch illuminated now he led them through the attic to the crawl space. Looking back to make certain they followed him, all three crawled along the makeshift passage beneath the floorboards into the next building's attic. Hania saw several faces here, frightened faces, a couple from her building, a few she did not recognize.

Yitzhak pointed to a back corner where some blankets had been placed. He handed Hania a bit of black bread.

"You will be safer here. They have searched this building and there is no entrance into this attic from below. You can share what food there is."

Hania helped her mother settle in the dark alcove. She walked over to the other side, where Yitzhak kneeled, talking to two young men.

"Thank you," Hania said.

He looked at her, nodded. She started to turn away.

"I could have got him out. Your uncle." Hania turned back. "I told him I could have got him out, maybe your aunt. He said no. He chose resettlement. Perhaps they will be safe."

"Do you think so? Do you trust German promises?"

He looked at her, lowered his eyes.

"No."

She stared at him for another moment, then returned to her mother.

Hania and Zivia remained in the attic space for several weeks. Any food that could be brought in or found was shared. Sometimes Yitzhak would appear with men she did not know, waiting until one of the other adjoining attic spaces was safe to go back to the street. Some had passes allowing them the relative safety of the 'workshops'; others were 'illegals' who if seen would either immediately be sent to the Umschlagplatz for deportation or shot. Thousands died on the streets this way. Soon even the passes saying you worked at one of the workshops, or at Toebens or Schultz, or any of the other factories, offered no guarantee of survival within the Ghetto walls.

Hania knew that Yitzhak helped organize the newly formed Jewish Fighting Organization, the ZOB. More and more assassinations were carried out not only against Nazis, Ukrainians, Lithuanians, but against those Jews who profited from the exploitation of others in the Ghetto or who informed. Illegal newspaper sheets also appeared with reports of the battlefronts and reports about the deportations, about the so-called work camp Treblinki. Yet despite these reports, many continued to line up with their suitcases and march to the waiting cattle transport trains at the Umschlagplatz railway siding. Death was everywhere.

September 21st was the Jewish Day of Atonement, Yom Kippur. Everyone in the attic remained within its walls that day. One of the older men said a quiet prayer for all. Most everyone then prayed in silence. Hania sat quietly with her mother. Normally on this holy day they would fast. But now they hardly had to think of doing so; there was almost no food for anyone to eat had they wanted to.

That night word spread that the Nazis had just blockaded the streets where they had recently ordered all the Jewish police to now reside. The following morning two thousand people from those streets marched to resettlement. Only a few Jewish Police were allowed to remain. Most of those chosen for resettlement knew the fate that awaited. Few people would miss them; they had been as harsh as many of the others, attempting to please their German masters.

That next night explosions could be heard throughout the city, with bombs dropping from an air raid by the Soviets. Bombs fell on much of the Ghetto, particularly around the area of the prison. The Germans claimed little damage had been done, but Yitzhak said there had been damage to airfields and the train station. It did not stop the deportations.

At the beginning of October, following another Soviet air raid when the Ghetto was quiet, Hania left the confines of the attic in the morning while her mother slept. She intended to forage amongst some of the furniture and personal items that had been thrown out onto the street, hoping to find anything of value she might sell for food, before the Germans or Ukrainians or Polish Police ransacked the goods first, as they usually succeeded in doing.

She found little of interest and started back to the adjoining building when she saw groups of Ukrainian Auxiliary Police starting to blockade a nearby street again. She quickly ran into an adjoining building where she knew she could enter into the attic passageway network. She saw only a few people but warned all to hide: another Nazi roundup was beginning. By the time she reached the secret attic the streets all around were blocked off.

She warned those in the attic what was happening below, then went to sit quietly with her mother.

Zivia was not there.

Hania looked around the room.

Zivia was not there. Not there…

Yitzhak climbed in from a side passageway.

"My mother: she is not here. Where is she?"

He looked at her, his brow furrowing.

"She went to the room behind the panel in your apartment. She said you had told her to wait for you there."

Hania stared at him, taken aback.

"No I…"

She did not finish her sentence. She turned and rushed over to the crawl space back to her building. Yitzhak grabbed her arm.

"You cannot go out. The Germans have closed off the street."

She pulled her arm away, stared at him for just a moment, then turned. He knew she would not listen.

"Hania… if they search the houses, stay in the hidden room with her. Do not come back here. Do you understand?"

She nodded just slightly. One of the men in the attic stepped forward to stop her, but Yitzhak shook his head. The man looked at Hania then helped her into the crawl space under the floor and crawled in after her.

Hania inched her way to the attic of her own building, the man following. Once there he lowered the ladder for her. She climbed down. He pulled up the ladder and closed the hatch behind. Hania stared at the ceiling. The only reveal was the small catch, barely visible.

Her heart beat heavily against her chest as she hurried down the stairs to her apartment rooms. She heard heavy footsteps on the stairs below. She knew they were searching. She ran into the apartment, closing the door behind her. She pulled back the panel fronted by the sink and hurried inside, then closed it behind her, hearing the latch catch.

"Mama? Mama…"

Her Mother was not there. The room was empty.

172

She did not know what to do. She did not know what to feel. She heard voices in the outer room, searching. Searching. What to do? What to do?...

She sat on the bed, feeling ill, terrified. The voices grew quiet. The sound of heavy boots descending. What to do?

Hania pulled aside the small peep space from one of the wooden planks over the window and looked out. Several hundred Jews stood in rows in the courtyard, guarded by soldiers. A Ukrainian Auxiliary with a list checked through names. Men. Women. Children.

Hania looked at faces. A few she recognized. Most she did not. She let her eyes scan one row, then the next, then the next.

And then she saw her. Her shoulders slumped, her face expressionless, a shawl around her shoulders, her Mother stood at the end of one of the rows. Stood without expression. Or hope.

"Mama?," Hania gasped, wanting to scream. Whispering. "Mama?"

The Auxiliary marched up and down the rows of broken people, marking off names, calling out names. He stopped beside Zivia Stern. From the blocked window far above Hania could hear him yell at her mother.

"Name?"

Her mother mumbled a response.

"Your daughter. You have a daughter?"

Hania saw her mother stare straight ahead.

"Where is your daughter?"

Still her mother said nothing.

The Ukrainian Auxiliary pulled out his pistol.

"I said, where is your daughter?"

Her mother said nothing, but stared straight ahead. The Auxiliary started to raise his gun.

"Mama?" A voice near the building entry. "Mama?"

The Auxiliary turned as a girl slowly pushed over to Zivia, and stood beside her. A girl with one damaged leg, with its carved wooden calf and foot, who needed a stick to walk.

Hania felt a scream in her throat lock there. She could not breathe. She could not swallow.

Alicja took her place beside Hania's mother. Zivia looked at her, then nodded, just slightly at the Auxiliary. He hesitated, then shouted for the columns of people to march out to the street.

Hania stared in shock as the guards hurried the people away.

She fell onto the floor, fell onto her knees.

Her body shook with terror.

"No," she said, over and over. "No, no, no, no…"

Hania wanted to die. Hania was ready to die. She took a breath, struggled to breathe, struggled to move.

Then she moved. A step. Another. She hurried.

Hania unlatched the false panel and pushed it aside. She ran into the front room, then out of the apartment. She stumbled. She hurried. She tripped on the stairs and fell. She caught her breath, stood again and hurried. One step, two steps, another, another.

The ground floor; she quickly moved to the front entrance. Went through the door.

Rows and rows of people, hundreds, marching away, up the street. Hania hesitated, looking for her mother, for Alicja.

"Mama?," she cried out, but if anyone could hear above the shouts and orders of the police, no one responded. "Mama?"

Hania ran alongside the columns of people, looking in the rows for her mother. She could not see anyone she knew. Jews looked at her and away. Still she pushed forward, pushing some aside, desperate. Desperate.

A hand roughly grabbed her shoulder. An Auxiliary Policeman pulled her sharply towards him. Stared into her face with hate.

"Get in with the others. Walk!"

He pushed her to the end of a row of people. He walked beside her, forcing her to stay in the row he marched beside. Other deportees joined them from different streets. Soon there were a thousand people, then two thousand. The Auxiliary remained beside her, indifferent to her but preventing her from moving except in her row of those marching beside.

It took almost an hour to reach the Umschlagplatz. Several thousand people were penned in, others immediately shoved into cattle train transports as they appeared. Wives were separated from husbands. Families torn apart from one another. Some people screamed. Some cried out for their loved ones. Some tried to run away and were shot. Others collapsed and were beaten. Hania was pushed to a pen on the next door grounds of the former hospital that served as a holding area and told to sit. Her Auxiliary Policeman disappeared. She looked all around for her mother, for Alicja, but could not locate them. They sat for an hour, two, three. No food, no water. Finally they were allowed to stand, to mill about, just slightly.

Hania pushed through people, searching, searching for her mother. She saw a few faces she knew. Some faces from her factory. One of the men who she had seen in the attic. A family from another building. Josef Schipper the mechanic. She pushed through, desperately searching.

She pushed into the main yard, still searching.

And then she saw her Mother. And she saw Alicja, still at her side. They were in a crowd of a hundred or so people herded towards a cattle car.

"Mama!," Hania shouted and pushed through crowds of people. "Mama!"

Hania pushed towards the train wagon and heard a male voice scream at her to stop. She did not stop.

"Mama!"

Her mother was being pulled up into the transport, helped by Alicja.

"Mama!," she shouted, terrified.

As her Mother started to disappear into the train, she turned. She gazed around, as if she heard Hania. Hania saw her eyes drop, her gaze drop, as Zivia turned away again.

"Mama!"

Beside her Mother, Alicja. Alicja turned. Gazed around. And her eyes met Hania, standing in the yard. And she saw her. And their eyes locked.

Hania could not breathe.

175

Alicja stared at her, stared at her friend. She shook her head, just slightly. Shook her head no. And her face said: I understand. And her eyes said: it is so. And her body said: it is time.

And her lips formed a single word: live.

Then she, and Hania's mother, Zivia Stern, were pushed inside, as the guards closed the train transport door with a loud bang. And locked it.

Hania, cold, motionless.

Hania, without life.

A hand came down heavily on her shoulder and whirled her around. An Auxiliary.

"I said stop! I told you stop!"

Hania held her ground. Stared at him. Said nothing. Could say nothing. Empty. Stared.

He hated her eyes. Her green eyes. Her stare. He pulled out his gun. He aimed it at those eyes.

"Nein!" She heard it from her side.

"I said...No!"

The Auxiliary turned his glance, just as he was pushed away, hard, shoved at the arm holding the pistol.

Staring at him with hate and command, a German officer.

Hania knew immediately. The German.

The German.

He glared at the Auxiliary.

"This girl is mine. I said, she is mine!"

The Auxiliary hesitated, then gave a fierce, ironic grin, raised his arm in salute, stood aside.

The German grabbed Hania's forearm forcefully and pulled her beside him. She resisted. He pulled her harder. She almost fell over. He would not let go. Roughly he dragged her behind him. They passed a big German soldier watching. Hania for a moment recognized Misio's face. She did not acknowledge it. The German dragged her behind him. Struggling, but dragged after.

The German pulled her toward the edge of the siding, along a cattle car, another. Pulled her. Dragged her.

At the rear of the cars he pulled her around the back side. Away from the waiting Jews. Away from the guards. He pulled her. He dragged her. A body lying on the ground, a Jew wearing a prayer shawl, his head lying in a pool of blood. The German stepped in the blood on the ground, still pulling Hania after him.

She could no longer fight. She could no longer struggle.

He dragged her towards the edge of the yard, opening to some buildings. He stopped here, threw her down. She lay on the ground, staring up at him.

No longer afraid. No longer alive.

He pulled out his gun. Loosened his tunic. Stared at her. Stared at her with hate like she had never seen. The hate of his power. The hate of his victim.

"Stand up," he said quietly, his voice shaking, his gun pointing at her.

She struggled to stand. But she stood. And stared at him. She wanted to die staring into his face. She wanted him to know her own hate. Her own disgust. Her own—indifference. She wanted to die with his face in her heart; this, she thought in this final moment when she could still think, this is what I deserve. Because she had killed Jakub. She had killed her Aunt and Uncle. Now her Mother. Now Alicja. She had killed them all. Because she was not at her Mother's side. Because Alicja had pretended to be her, had tried to save her. But she could not be saved.

There could be no salvation. And no redemption but hate. Now.

The German stared at her. He raised his gun, his arm outstretched. He raised his gun and stared at her.

And he pulled the trigger. Twice. He pulled the trigger and shot.

And shot above her head. Twice. The shots ringing in her ears, twice.

Dying twice. And living twice more.

"I do not care if you live or die. You are nothing but a Jew. I am leaving this hell on earth. I am indifferent who lives here, who dies here. But it will not be you. Not here. Not now. You will never see me again. Now go. Run."

Hania did not move.

"Run!," he shouted at her.

Hania turned. A step. Another. And she ran.

And she waited for the sound of the gun and the pain of the bullet that would rip through her brain, her back, her life.

And she waited to die. But she did not die.

She did not turn to look at him. She would never see his face again. She was not meant to die, not here, and she did not die. Not yet. She heard nothing else, felt nothing else. Nothing but the wind whispering in her ears, against her face. She felt the wind. She felt the pain of life.

And she ran.

Dr. Kazimierz Palinsky, D.N.,PhD
  (Consultant Psychoanalyst, Babinsky Institute/ Kobierzyn)
Personal Case History: The case of Hannah K.

17 February 1949

These will be my final notes in the case of Hannah K. for reasons that I trust will become clear.

Hannah K. continued to make slight progress in her therapeutic sessions and from all accounts from Dr. Piekaski has successfully settled into her assistant's role at the Kwiecista Street Primary School. In November, Hannah requested that she be allowed to leave her residence here at the Institute and find accommodation in Kobierzyn. This request was discussed first with Dr. Łados and then with the Committee as a whole, all approving the request without dissent. As therapist I too agreed, on the condition that a weekly therapy session continue, supported by both the Committee and most importantly acceptable to Hannah K.

With the assistance and advice of Dr. Piekaski, a room in a house for young women on Zamiejska Street was contracted by the Institute with monthly rent deducted from her small salary, to commence after the New Year. Dr. Piekaski also suggested that Hannah K's time at the school increase to three full days and one half day of each week. Hannah K. had succeeded in developing a strong bond with many of the children. Dr. Piekaski felt therefore that her work was most satisfactory and in such circumstances an increase in hours would be beneficial both to the children and Hannah K.

Dr. Piekaski related one story to me that I believe worth recording in these notes:

"At first," Dr. Piekaski explained, "Hannah remained quite withdrawn from the children. Children sense things, and sensed in this new Assistant some sort of mental confusion, or hesitation. Some of the children were drawn to her, recognizing themselves in this quiet young woman; others kept a distance."

"It was in the third week I believe that I began to understand the potential benefit to the children as well as to your Patient. We had been having a difficulty with one of our children, W. The child had been diagnosed with infantile schizophrenia with exhibited signs of savant ability. You are probably aware of papers in regard to this psychopathy, particularly Hans Asperger's lectures on child psychology and autistic psychopathy. In passing it is also worth looking at the American Leo Kanner's work on what he terms 'autistic aloneness' and the 'instance on sameness'. But I digress."

"At times we would have to isolate W., or ask him to remove himself into another part of the classroom. W. would accede to such, but might exhibit further anxiety by sometimes saying a single word to himself over and over, refusing to meet anyone's gaze, and had recently taken to banging his head repeatedly on the wall in the corner of one of the classrooms, upsetting not only to the boy himself but to the other children and to the classroom teacher as well."

"On one such occasion W., standing in the corner, started exhibiting this behavior. At that moment, Hannah K. happened to walk into the room. Before the classroom teacher could ask her to seek me out for assistance, Hannah K. on her own accord walked over to the other side of the classroom, pulled a chair up beside W. and sat down. She gently took the boy's hand and drew him into her lap. For the remainder of the day they sat like that, saying nothing, the boy W. now calmed. The teacher was able to get on with her duties and left Hannah K. with W. in this way for several hours. But she did say at one point she looked over and saw Hannah K. wipe away some tears from the child's face—and then wipe away some from her own."

"It was then that I knew that Hannah K. would do well here at the school, and so it has proved. The children have since taken to her. W. continues to shows symptoms of infantile schizophrenic behavior, but responds better to Hannah K. than to any of the other staff."

I have one other incident to relate in this case history, important I believe to be retained in these notes and equally as revealing at this point in Hannah K's therapy.

I have suggested my concern about the issue of transference between the patient and myself as her therapist, a concern I shared with Dr. Łados.

With this in mind, and after private discussion with Dr. Łados, I felt it would no longer be wise to continue as therapist for Hannah K., this at least part of my *reasoning. As and if necessary the Institute or I can recommend other therapeutic counselors and analysis for her. I continue to believe that this would be helpful for her, perhaps even wise. In this context I need to record my final session of analysis with her. Hannah K. had agreed to repose on the couch in my office and attempt to undergo analysis. She has always been quite resistant to this type of analysis but seemed open to it in this session.*

I wanted to try to get her to confront her father's disappearance, her mother's death as reported by Fr. Daněk. I asked her first what she felt about her father.

She shrugged. Again she said she did not remember much about him growing up. I then asked her what she thought about his disappearance.

"He is dead."

"Are you certain of this?" I asked.

"Yes."

"How did he I die?"

"Painfully. Deservedly."

"Why do you say this."

"It should be so."

"And what did he do that should make it so?"

She was silent at this.

"What did he do to you? Would it not help to discuss this?"

"No. Why would it?"

"Do you not think it best to look at these events, confront them, acknowledge them and thus to move on."

"I have moved on. I do not wish to discuss this."

"What about your mother? It says in your notes she died during the Nazi retreat from Krakow, from Nowy Wiśnicz. You were aware of her death?"

"Yes."

"Did you witness her death."

Hannah K. did not respond to the question. I waited several minutes, but she said nothing.

"Hannah?," I asked finally.

"I have locked this away, Kazimierz. Locked it away forever."

This was the first time, indeed the only time in almost three years of working with Hannah K., that she addressed me by my Christian name, rather than, Dr. Palinsky. I said nothing for several minutes, taking in the implications of such, particularly in relation to my stated concern of psychological transference. Finally:

"Did you dream last night, Hannah? Can you recall any recent dreams you'd like to discuss perhaps?"

She sat quietly for a moment.

"Why is it you ask about dreams?," she asked.

"Dreams can provide clues to the stories in our head: our troubles, our memories, the conflicts we are trying to address."

"You are trying to tell me, Kazimierz, that my dreams may open doors to those closed rooms, may reveal who I am from the past, may indeed help understand what that past means?"

"Effectively, yes. That is correct."

"But I do not dream."

"We all dream."

"No. I have no dreams. I have no nightmares. When my eyes close at night I see only blackness until the morning. I have no past to reveal, Kazimierz. None. There is no past. No memory. All has been locked away, the key thrown away. I only see here, now, and possibly the future. I will never return to the past. I will never see that door unlocked. That is all."

"Sometimes, Hannah, those doors open regardless and we need to understand what lies within. Do you not think that is possible?"

"No. There is nothing more to see there. Nothing more to understand. I no longer dream."

These were her last words that morning.

Thinking through my notes from the session, I realized I could no longer help Hannah K. as her appointed therapist. For many reasons, I am no longer in a position to do so. I will discuss my reasoning in more detail with Dr. Łados, but in terms of my involvement I think it now best to cease herewith consultations and analysis in the case of Hannah K.

21 February 1949

I had decided, with holidays approaching at the end of the last year, that I would take a short break from the Babinsky Institute and visit friends in London, who had invited me to share the holiday with them. I had been in fact been invited to present a paper on Polish therapeutic advancements since the War in London, which served as the perfect excuse; having received Party travel permission after appropriate guarantees were provided to the Foreign Affairs Ministry, supported then by Michejda's office at the Ministry of Health for my attendance at the London conference, I set out in mid December. Whilst the journey was longer than I might have otherwise wished, I looked forward to revisiting the city of my War years, seeing friends, enjoying London as tourist over the festive season, as well as giving my conference paper. I was surprised to discover, therefore, that I could not get Hannah K. from my thoughts, that in fact London held no attraction to me. Indeed I looked forward to my return and to my sessions with Hannah K.

In recognizing this, I knew that my own mental state had become one of confusion, and that I must withdraw from further analysis of her.

I had also not yet told anyone of the approach made to me by Professor Tadeusz Tomaszewsk about possibly joining the soon to be created Department of Psychology at the University of Warsaw, due to open next year, as a lecturer in the methodology of Dr. Alfred Adler. Despite my admiration and interest in the development of my work here at the Institute, this approach was well received and I have decided to accept the invitation, assuming appropriate Ministry permissions.

After coming to this conclusion, I felt I needed to inform Dr. Łados, and more importantly to discuss my concerns and extrapolations from my consultations with Hannah K.

I related to him the experience of my last session with her, but moreover discussed with him my concerns not only about psychological transference, which I had previously mentioned to him and which manifested itself, for example, in how Hannah K. began to address me in that final session, but more to the fact my *own confusion about the issue of counter transference and the inevitable feeling of growing emotional entanglement with the Patient. In his writings, Dr. Adler, of course, unsurprisingly recommends utilizing both transference and counter transference strategically and positively for the benefit of therapeutic treatment, for cooperation and hopeful improvement towards good health. Whilst I understand the arguments for such, I remained troubled by the situation.*

Being frank, I continued uncertain as to whether in the analysis and exploration of trauma in this case, I in fact extrapolated my own emotional turbulence into the therapy, resulting in unavoidable confusion. At what point, I posed to Dr. Łados, does the life of the therapist entwine with that of patient so that truth itself becomes victim? I told him what Hannah K. said regarding the analysis of dreams. Whilst I remain convinced that 'opening that door' should be absolutely necessary, at the same time I recognize that such truth, in her case, may necessitate keeping the door closed, possibly forever, in pursuit of general happiness.

Dr. Łados listened patiently to all I had to say in his role partly as my supervisor, but also as my own therapist, as a mentor and as a friend. He sat very quietly for a long period, then said the following to me:

"Kazimierz, my young colleague. My friend. Firstly I should tell you that I greatly admire Professor Tomaszewski, and I believe you must consider his invitation with the utmost seriousness. Although the post is not a particularly advanced one, it nevertheless will place you in a very prestigious institution and allow you to consider your research and preferred psychoanalytical pathway within an academic environment rather than as clinician. We at this Institute would be very sorry to lose you, I say without equivocation, but you must do what is best for you and your career."

"As for your former patient and the issues you express: in our profession, we spend years coming up with theories about the mind, about the intellect and the illnesses that define us as human beings. Ideas of transference and counter transference have validity. Of course they do. And they give rise to intellectual debate, discussion. Yes, I would agree give rise to confusion. Our role is to engage intellectually with these issues that so define the human experience: the mind, the

fears we have, trying to find a good life, a contributive life. It can be so difficult. So confusing."

"Counter transference may be an issue and I think you are right to withdraw as therapist from this patient, or former patient as she now is. She may need help in the future. She most likely will. And no doubt you will do your utmost to assist and to identify that help."

"But whilst we psychologists and psychiatrists spend lifetimes trying to understand the patterns of human behavior, the essences of intellectual and emotional lives, the human mind, trying to find pathways to—acceptance--if not happiness—it is so easy to forget the lessons we experience not simply through our training as doctors and intellects, but the lessons of the human heart."

"Perhaps, my young friend, you are experiencing the confusion of counter transference. But perhaps what you feel and experience is in fact the reality of the human heart. What you need to ask yourself, simply: is this something that needs explanation, this confusion, something that can be addressed by the intellect and psychotherapeutic analysis, by Freudian terminology and Adlerian discourse? Or is it the case that in fact you have fallen in love, with all its risks, and pitfalls, and potential pain and potential joy that such may bring? And if it is potentially the latter, then I would suggest to you that you must weigh what is within your heart with the utmost sincerity, for your sake and Hannah Kielar's."

"Love is not always an easy science to comprehend for people in our profession. It can be confusing, and confused. And you will have to separate out your professional expression, your professional experience, from the duties and needs of the human heart. But I have to tell you one thing, my young friend: the road you may choose may be difficult, but do not be afraid of the callings of your heart. It is easy to be afraid. But this, after all, is what makes each of us human, in all its profound frailty and confusion. Before you are a doctor, you are a human being. Never lose sight of that."

As I was leaving his rooms, I thought for a moment, and smiled. Dr.Łados looked at me quizzically.

"I was just thinking: Hannah K. had been living alone, feral in Nowy Wiśnick, arguably lost, until she was found by the young priest, Fr. Daněk. Then she came

to us and was lost again. Now perhaps she is on her way to being found."

Dr. Łados stared at me, then said: *"Tell me, my friend, are you speaking of your patient, or are you speaking of yourself?"*

I returned to the solace and quiet of my office to consider Dr. Łados' wise words and advice. I thought about Hannah K. About Hannah. I thought about my true feelings. I realized it is not just her quiet beauty that attracts me. And not just her vulnerability, which is somewhat hidden by her strength yet remains in evidence. It is not that I can help her or cannot help her. She has secret rooms in her unconscious that I am not sure will ever be unlocked. I cannot know, cannot ever know, if these rooms will be unlocked, if I might enter with her, beside her. Or if such will remain hidden. Need to remain hidden.

Rather I am drawn to her because each of us has our own secret rooms that sometimes we can enter, sometimes we cannot. I am drawn to her because, like her, I too have catacombs deep within that might remain closed. Or perhaps might open one day. I am drawn to her because we travel down the corridors of these quiet, desperate places together, not necessarily to enter, but simply to walk together so we do not walk alone. Amidst the turbulence we might find calm. Or we will not. Can we help one another? I would like to think so, but cannot be certain. At least, however, we can travel down the corridor one beside the other. And be there. And that is a much as one can hope for. That is the future. That is what truly draws me to her. It is what I can give. And yes what I can take.

Dr. Łados has in the past kindly offered that I may borrow his Pobeda automobile any time I should wish. A GAZ-M20 no less! Next month, my old university friend Szpilman has invited me to attend a concert he will perform at the newly reopening Chopin house in Zelazowa Wola. I will invite Hannah to join me, perhaps for a surprise picnic, and then the concert. And after I will ask her to be my wife. God willing, she will say yes.

God willing.

Warsaw/Nowy Wiśnicz

December 1942-January 1945

Hania Stern could not remember her thoughts when she ran from the edge of the Umschlagplatz. She did not know why he did not shoot her then. Why he told her to run. She could not remember hanging to the shadows, in doorways, in ruins. She did not know if she saw others marching in columns to the trains, if she hid, if they saw her, if they did not.

She did not know what to do. She did not know what to think, where to go, how she should survive. Why she should survive.

She remembered her mother disappearing into the cattle car. She remembered Alicja looking at her, shaking her head, turning away, pushed inside. She remembered the train door shutting, hearing its clang of the latch dropping, locking everyone in. Locking her mother in. Locking Alicja in. She remembered everything and yet she remembered nothing.

Somehow, without quite knowing how or why, she returned to the building that had been her home, her mother's home, Shaul's home, her Aunt's and Uncle's and Jakub's home. For a while. A short while. And somehow, without quite knowing how, without quite remembering anything, she found herself back in the secret room in the apartment with the panel hidden by the sink closed, alone.

She sat on the floor and covered her ears with her hands. She lay flat and took a blanket from the bed to cover herself. She closed her eyes but could not sleep. She slept but could not dream. She was no longer afraid. She was simply empty.

She remained in the room all the next day. In the afternoon she heard footsteps coming up the building stairwell. Heavy footsteps. She heard someone march into the apartment. She heard footsteps hesitate, come towards the sink. Stop. She heard someone breathing. Waiting perhaps. Knowing. She did not feel fear. She felt: nothing. After some time she heard voices in German from the courtyard below. She heard several men march up the stairs, kicking at doors, throwing bits of furniture against walls, out windows. She heard loud footsteps and voices as men came into the outer room separated from her only by the hidden panel. She expected now she would die. But she heard a voice, commanding, shouting.

"No one here. Come! I said there is no one!"

Hesitation, then footsteps receding.

After that, she heard nothing. She remained in the room for days, trying to forget everything but unable to forget anything. She heard in her head her Father telling her she had to live. She remembered her Uncle saying the same thing to her. "Stay alive," he had said. The last thing she ever heard him say.

The so-called 'Great Aktion' ended at the beginning of October. The Small Ghetto had been emptied and closed off. The remainder of the Ghetto streets were largely empty. Only those factory workers or remaining officials with markings imprinted on their bodies and haunting their souls were seen on the streets. More than half of those who remained, mostly the young, hid. Of the more than 400,000 Jews living the Ghetto before the Resettlement, less than 60,000 remained in Warsaw. Ten Thousand had been murdered on the streets. Almost 350,000 people had been shoved into cattle cars and sent for resettlement to 'the East', in fact sent to a camp called Treblinki.

*

A week passed, a second week. She noticed a few people going in and out of the courtyard below, not guards or soldiers but Jews scavenging in the shadows. She chose then to leave the secret room. She pushed aside the false panel. The door to the apartment was open when she emerged but she saw no one. She made her way outside. The street was largely empty. She walked, keeping to doorways and shadows. She saw furniture thrown out onto the streets, ransacked. She saw a baby carriage turned over, discarded in an alleyway. She saw open suitcases, bits of torn ragged clothes strewn about. She saw the Ghetto had been largely emptied.

Hania walked for the rest of the day, seeking food. Twice she saw uniformed guards directing skeletal, slave-like Jews to search through the rubbish for anything of value. A motorized patrol passed and she hid. Where once the streets had been thronged with crowds of people there was largely silence and emptiness, black crows sitting atop discarded rubbish and human excrement beside men like the crows sifting through the same rubbish on orders from their uniformed masters.

She made her way to Nowolipki Street, still keeping to shadows, doorways. The wide street was completely empty. Standing across from the ruins of an apartment building she stared at the concrete rubble. She could not bring herself to cross and find the pathway to the rear courtyard with its collapsed floors of apartment rooms. She stood. Stared. Waited. Then turned away.

Later in the evening a number of workers emerged from their factories, empty people without spirit, without life within them, slowly stumbling towards what remained of their rooms. People breathing without breath. Existing without spirit. It was living as if dead, without the relief of death. Hania knew she was one of them.

She could not return to the room. Too many ghosts. She too now lived as a ghost, here but not here. Hania continued up the stairs. The disguised ceiling into the attic was in place, so she found the broken floorboard and used it to pull open the ceiling panel as her uncle had showed her. The ladder too had remained above. She climbed up inside, walked to the back and removed the cover over the crawl space to the next room. She crawled her way along, then stood up into the second large attic. Again, no one. She found matches, a few candles. On some half-hidden shelves she found the remains of a bit of food. It would do. She no longer wanted to see…anything. She would remain. And die. So be it.

She lay in the back alcove where she had slept with her mother. She should have left but she had no will to leave, no will to be. On the blanket mattress she could still smell her mother's presence. Her mother was no longer present though. Except that in the darkest hours Hania began to see her, and talk to her, and sing to her, and whisper to her, and place her head in her lap, and suckle at her breast because she was born once more, lived once more, infant once more, and she was wrapped in her arms, her mother's warm embrace. Swaddled. There. Not there.

She knew she was going mad. She knew that she could see herself from the outside looking in. She did not know how long she lay in the attic. She did not know if she ate or starved, was weak or strong. She knew nighttime by silence. She knew morning by sunlight peeking through some broken roof tiles. She did not know days or weeks. She was only there, and this was all. Perhaps she had been in the attic a week. Perhaps a month. One day she heard voices from the next passage and attic beyond, in the third building. Terrified she put up cloth rags across the alcove to hide herself, hoping that the shadow would embrace her, protect her. She sat huddled on blankets in the corner, making herself as small as she possibly could, terrified now they had come for her, would make her return to the world. She did not want to return. Not here, not now.

Voices. Then gone. They did not enter, friend or solider, Nazi or Jew. They left her. She fell asleep. She did not dream. She was afraid.

The next day she again heard voices. Then they stopped. Not certain what she should do, she carefully inched over to the crawlway back to her own building's attic. Should she return there? Go back down the ladder to the apartment and hide in the secret room? Or out onto the street? Should she leave the building? Go to the soldiers and beg them to take her to the Umschlagplatz? Put her in a pen with others? Push her into a cattle car? Take her away? Set her free? Set her free...

She stared at the opening to the crawl passage. She backed away. Fear. Empty fear.

She barely felt the hand that grabbed her arm, barely felt herself whirled around, pushed forcefully against the attic wall. A young man, more boy than man, stared at her, a stick in his hands, waiting to beat her, about to slam the stick into her head. Make it quick, she thought for the instant she could think. Just make it quick.

"Who are you? What are you doing here?" He demanded she answer. He demanded to know. She said nothing.

She heard others in the crawl space, pulling themselves now into the attic room. But he did not turn away from her.

"Why are you here? I said..."

"That's enough, Janek."

The man boy, boy man turned.

"I know her. That's enough," said a man behind him.

The man boy, boy man named Janek lowered the stick, hesitated, then moved to the side. Hania stared at the voice, stared into Yitzhak's tired eyes. He said nothing at first. Then:

"How long have you been up here, Hania?"

She shook her head. She did not know.

190

"Your mother?"

Again she shook her head, just slightly.

"I saw you also marched to the Umschlagplatz. How did you get away from there?"

"Maybe she informs. Maybe she works for the..."

"Shut up, Janek."

Hania looked from one to the other.

"I...I ran."

Yitzhak stared at her for a long moment, then nodded.

"There is a passageway over there and in the next building a bunker down below. Some people there. Some food. You should stay there. The Germans have increased their patrols."

"No. I will stay here."

"It may not be safe here, Hania. The Germans will return. We do not know when, but they will return."

"I will stay here."

He looked at her, nodded slowly.

"We will bring you food. We will close off the first attic room and remove the ladder. It will be safer that way. Do you understand?"

Hania remained in the large attic room. She did not know for how long. Daily someone brought her food. It was perhaps more easily come by now, more easily scavenged from the secret places left by those who had departed. Not much, but more. Some soup. Warmth. Some black bread tasting of sawdust and mould. Something. Anything. Days of anything.

Sometimes she heard voices from the next attic along. Sometimes she sat alone. Sometimes others came and sat in the same attic space. Rarely did anyone say anything. They did not exchange names. It was not safe to exchange names. It was not safe to care.

Twice several young men spent the night in the attic space. She awoke one night and watched them. One turned a pistol over and over in his hands. His glance caught hers. She then looked away.

One night she sat in her corner eating, slowly, trying to make it last longer. Two young men were in the attic space. One left to go to the other room. The other sat for a while, also eating, then got up and walked towards her. Sat down again opposite her. She did not look at him. She said nothing but knew he stared at her.

Finally she looked at him. Small, frightened eyes. Thin. A face without hope. Fear. At first he said nothing. Then:

"You do not remember me."

She looked at him. Tried to remember. Could not remember. Shook her head, slightly.

"Arie Zalszupin. In the Powązki Cemetery. My friend Romek and I, we... We hid amongst the statues and sepulchers from you. You had a friend. The two of you, like sisters."

"Alicja."

"Alicja. Is she...?"

Hania shook her head.

"Your friend Romek?," she asked.

"...No."

"...And your family?," she asked quietly.

He shook his head no.

"I remember," she said, "you thought there would be a war. You said that."

He nodded. Looked away.

Footsteps entering the attic room. Yitzhak appeared.

"Arie? All right?"

"Yes."

"Tomorrow?"

Arie nodded, hesitantly. Frightened.

Yitzhak looked at him, at Hania. Then nodded.

"It will all be well. Stay calm."

He hesitated, then left them. Arie started to stand.

"Wait," said Hania. "Wait."

He sat down again. She stared at him. Still thin, small.

"What is tomorrow?"

"...An operation. I said I would assist this time. I have not gone with them before but we need to… Yitzhak said it will be dangerous but I must do this."

He realized he had said too much. Hania knew he thought that.

"You were afraid then, that time in the cemetery when Romek and… You were afraid then. Are you afraid now?"

He stared at her. He looked away. "Yes."

She could tell that fear indeed possessed him, that he was alone. She could tell he was a child made adult but not adult not man. Older but frightened still. She could tell many things. He looked away, silent, looked away and could not look at her. Words offered no comfort. After a long while he stood, turned.

"I should let you be."

"No."

She stared at him, at his still child's face although he was no longer a child, as none of them were; at his hands, shaking just slightly. At his pain. At his loneliness. At his fear.

"Come."

He stared at her, saying nothing, then dropped his eyes. He hesitated, then walked over beside her. She held out her hand to him and he sat beside her.

She put her hand in his.

"Arie" she whispered, not to him, not to herself, but to the ghosts. After a moment she stood and put the torn cloth across her alcove, wrapping them in shadow. She sat back down beside him, then lay on her side and pulled him towards her.

He looked at her, uncertain, lost. She brushed his hair from his brow with her fingers. Stared at him, into his eyes, his fear. She saw herself.

"I am also afraid, Arie."

Then she pulled him towards her, and held him to her breast, and lay there, and later undressed him and undressed herself, and lay there with him, and then she helped him to enter her, inside of her, and he cried, and she tore, and she bled, just slightly, and she wiped his tears. And held him tightly, tighter than she knew it was possible to hold anyone. Held him with her body and all that was inside her. Held him with her life. And her dying. And all that she was, and was no longer, and had once dreamed of being, and would be no longer. Not child not woman.

Felt the pain. She held with her arms and her thighs and her own tears and her own loneliness. And for a moment, just a brief moment, she felt human.

Later he slept. And she looked at him. And she cried for him. And then she too slept. She had not slept in so long. But now she slept. And perhaps she dreamed. And perhaps she did not.

When she woke, seeing light creep through the broken tiles above the attic, no one else was in the attic.

And no one appeared for the rest of the day. Or the following day. Or the day after that.

Then on the fourth day she heard the hatch opening at the far side of the attic room and Yitzhak appeared with some food for her. He carried it over, placed it on the blanket while she watched him. He turned to leave.

"Yitzhak? Arie, is he…?"

Yitzhak looked at her. He dropped his eyes. Shook his head.

"The Germans saw us when we returned. We ran. Arie was…"

He did not finish his sentence. He shook his head again. Pain in his face. Turned and left the attic room.

*

After days, perhaps weeks, they stopped coming. She sat in the silence of the attic and waited, but she saw no one, heard no one. She remained alone. She knew she was mad.

She remained, perhaps occasionally gnawing on a bit of stale bread, perhaps simply sitting. Or lying down. Or waiting. Finally she decided that she could not remain in the attic any longer. She could not die there. Not there.

She crawled back to the first attic room through the crawl space, but the ladder had been removed. She returned to the second, opened the back hatch and climbed into the third room. Still no one. Here she took the stairs down into the building. At the bottom was the entry to the bunker her Uncle Michael had told her about. But she would not go down there. She needed the light. Whether or not anyone was in there, she could not go down.

She left the building. She kept to doorways, around the edges of buildings, courtyards. To Nowolipki Street. No one around. She found the way through the

194

rubble and the ruins to the back courtyard with the collapsed building floors and ruins and stone and rubble. She found the stairs leading to what had once been a cellar, but open to the light. No one. She found the back rooms and furthest back she found the alcove, with its dust covered, filthy mattress and a few blankets and a small stove and some candles and torn cloth and nothing else, but the ghost of the girl she had loved once and who she thought had betrayed her with her enemy but had not betrayed her and who had taken her place, taken her name and stood beside her mother and had become her and who was within her and who she hated and loved and hated all at once, all at once.

And who was gone.

Hania lay down on the mattress, covered herself with the blankets, closed her eyes. And felt herself far away, floating away, until they could not touch her. Could not kill her. Could not cry for her or remember her or know her or touch her or tear between her legs like she had seen the German do or cry lying between her legs like she had felt Arie do, could no longer hurt her, because she could not feel, and did not feel, and would never again feel.

And she slept.

And she remained here day after day, with weeks slowly passing, as the winter set in. As the cold began. She would nibble on the black bread until there was bread no longer. She would nibble on the few vegetables she had carried here until they too were gone.

One morning, sitting on the ground beside the bed, she saw just peeking out from beneath the mattress a photograph. She pulled it out to find a photograph of herself with Alicja sitting in Krasinski Park. A lifetime ago. A world ago.

Then she closed her eyes. And she lay back on the mattress. And the frost covered her. And beyond the alcove she saw snow on the floor of what had been the cellar. And she did not see stars. And she ceased to care for anything and everything but for the photograph that she held against her breast, tightly against her small breast. Ever so tightly held.

This was how she was to die, she thought. This was how the world would end.

She felt the heat on her brow. She felt the fire all over her body. She knew she was sick. She knew she was dying. She was ready.

And one night, that night or another, she heard voices. And then they went away.

And one night, that night or another, she opened her eyes and she saw her Mother and her Father.

They went away as well.

And another night it must have been, or many nights, and Alicja was beside her on a bench, sitting beside her with a baby's carriage just there and Jakub asleep within and grass and trees and calm and freedom. Freedom. "I will always defend you," she heard her friend say. But then she was gone.

She saw all those she knew, all those she had ever known, sitting with her and praying and wailing and holding her hand and she said:

"I am ready, I am ready, take me, please, take me. Now."

And they nodded and said they would take her and said she might now find peace and her body and fire turning to flame turning to ice back to flame, and they holding out their hands to her, and she saw then that she was walking in the Kampinos Forest and saw the strawberries all around her and her mother on her bicycle and the farmer standing there with cheese for them and a slice extra for her and the air blowing through her hair and she smiled and she lived and she breathed and she knew she was safe she knew her Mother was there and her Father and Jakub and Alicja all waiting for her, all gesturing: come, it is time, come now. You are free. You are free.

And she opened her eyes and stared at all those looking at her, but there was only one looking at her with gentleness and she knew him and she smiled.

"Simcha Gitler," she cried out with a whisper. "Simcha Gitler do not go through the wall stay here where they cannot find you. Sewer rat. Stay here." And she smiled and closed her eyes again. And saw nothing further.

*

She did not know where she was. A room, somewhere. Tiny. A bed. Darkness. Damp smell. A cellar. But the stone here felt real, the blankets real. She was not dead. That much she knew.

"I thought you would die," he said and when she focused she saw the face of the sewer rat Simcha Gitler. But he was not dream, and not nightmare. He was here, in this place, staring down at her.

"You have been unconscious for many days. You must eat. Don't talk. Just eat."

"Where is this place?," she whispered, struggling to speak.

"Where I stay. Some friends and I carried you here."

"Carried?"

"You weigh nothing. A feather."

"Am I dreaming or is it really you?"

"I wish I could say this was a dream. Here: soup. You need your strength. You have been very ill. I thought you would die."

She ate and slept. Mostly slept. Sometimes when she woke Simcha was there. Sometimes a young woman her own age, who said her name was Miriam. They fed her bits of black bread and soup they made on a small stove in the room. Only slowly did she feel her strength beginning to return, and then but slightly. Sometimes Miriam got her up to clean her, make her walk a few steps. Such exhausted her.

She woke one day, or night, as she never knew which, to see Simcha Gitler sitting across from her. She stared at him. He had grown since she had helped him at the crossing so long ago, an age ago. He had a confidence about him still, although yet a boy.

"How did you know where to find me?," she asked.

He looked at her. Shrugged.

"Some of our people said there was a girl living in the ruins. I thought it might be you."

"Your people?"

"Jewish Fighters. ZOB. The Germans will return. We do not know when but next time we will give them a big surprise. They will see."

"Miriam?"

"Yes. She fights. Many women like her."

"I can fight."

He smiled, just slightly.

"First, get strong."

"You said you thought it might be me. In the ruins, you said it might be me. Why did you say that?"

He hesitated, watching her, then looked away.

"Not now. Now you need to rest quietly, eat, find strength."

Another day she sat up with Miriam when he appeared and pulled out two orange carrots and some bits of dried meat.

"Where did you get that?," Hania said almost in amazement.

"I never reveal secrets. A Hanukah gift."

"Hanukah? It is Hanukah?"

Simcha looked at Miriam, then smiled, just slightly.

"Two weeks ago. But it sounds better than Christmas I think. You have slept for a long time."

Miriam made soup from the carrots, added the meat to it. They ate in silence. Hania thought it was the best meal she could remember eating for many months. Longer.

The new year came and went. Simcha said they should celebrate the fact they were still alive. Hania did not see much to celebrate. She remained haunted by bad dreams, when she did dream. They never left her alone. Her fevers continued to come and go. She felt a bit stronger. She knew she would not die now, not this way, but while her strength did return, it only did so slowly.

One day Simcha came in and sat with her.

"Both Miriam and I will be away for two days. Perhaps three. We will leave food. Can you feed yourself?"

She nodded. "Where are you going?"

He hesitated. "We will return. I promise."

"You are very kind to me."

"Your father… I knew him. When they took him, they could have taken me too. But he did not give me up to them. And your uncle, he too gave me work to do. I do not forget. We will return in two days, three. I promise. "

He kept his promise. Both he and the girl Miriam returned together. They brought more blankets. Some sugar, preserves. It had turned even colder. He told her then that he had talked to others in his group. They had all agreed that Hania needed to be taken out of the Ghetto.

"I was a sewer rat when you met me," Simcha said to her. "Now I am the king of the sewer rats. We think we can get you out that way. But you will have to trust me. And you must get strong now."

"I can stay. I can fight."

"No.

"But…"

"No. We have decided. No."

"Hania," said Miriam, "you will not be useful here. But we have others on the outside. With the Resistance. Many Poles are helping us, supplying us. Your place is no longer in the Ghetto."

Hania remained in the hiding place for several more days, getting stronger each day. On the morning they were to leave, neither Simcha nor Miriam appeared. Hania heard from outside their hiding place sounds she had not heard in many weeks: marching, shouts, loudspeakers. Then she heard shots. And explosions. And above her head, somewhere, a battle raged.

Miriam appeared late in the day. She explained that the Germans and Ukrainians had returned to the Ghetto, announcing a new Aktion: all remaining Jews must pack their things and go to the Umschlagplatz. They had not expected resistance. They had not expected a fight. Most people went into the secret bunkers and rooms they had built, and the ZOB fighters defended the streets, set up barricades. This time they would not be sheep.

A little later Simcha also returned. They would not leave that night. Too dangerous. They would see what would happen the following day.

But the next day the Germans and Ukrainians returned and again were met with resistance. They decided it was still too dangerous to depart. They sat in the hiding place. They waited.

On the third day, Simcha went out, then returned a while later.

"We will go tonight. The fighting has moved up by Umschlagplatz. It will be the best time."

Later, Simcha and Miriam helped Hania leave the hiding place, a cellar in an abandoned building. It was the first time she had been out of the room in more than two months. The cold night air hit her like a slap in the face. She realized she was still weak, more than she had thought.

They kept to the doorways, carefully made it around a barricade that the defenders had built, now half destroyed. Simcha went ahead to make certain the way was clear, then led Hania and Miriam to a street drain that he quickly opened with a bar he had brought with him.

They climbed down into the sewer beneath the street. Simcha lit a weak lamp and Hania saw a walkway disappearing just along the river of sewage, a meter or so above it. The smell was overpowering.

They followed him through the darkness, down various passages and turns. At certain junctions Simcha hesitated, but he seemed to know the way well. They saw rats everywhere. Several times Hania thought she might pass out but somehow she steeled herself. They slowly made their way onwards. The tunnels were a labyrinth. More than once they were blocked by a row of razor sharp barbed wire but Simcha knew where it had been cut so that they could crawl through on hands and knees, holding their breath amidst the sewage. Twice she vomited, but she refused to stop. Several times too they heard the rumbling of vehicles above, or sounds from beyond. Then Simcha would turn off the weak torch he had and they waited. Shivering with cold, with fear, they waited still longer then carried on. In one place he held up his hands in warning, then pointed to a device on the walkway, some sort of explosive. They jumped into the sewage here and walked for fifty meters before they could pull themselves out.

They must have been in the sewers for several hours, taking each step slowly, listening, stopping, crawling, walking. Finally Simcha stopped near a metal ladder and climbed up to a cover. He carefully pushed it open, a bit more, peeking through, then climbed out and signaled for Hania and Miriam to follow.

They gulped in the air. Hania did not know where they were but knew she was in a Warsaw that she had not seen for years. Dark, without streetlights, without people. Compared to the Ghetto, calm.

Simcha hurried them along. They ran down the street, keeping as quiet as they could, then into a building. They silently made their way up some stairs and knocked on a door: once, then twice, then once, barely heard. After a moment a woman opened the door for them and they went into the apartment. After the barren emptiness of all her hiding places, it felt like a home.

"Go," said the woman, "wash."

Hania and Miriam went into the bath first and hosed one another down. It had felt like years since Hania had used soap, had been clean. She looked at Miriam's body, at her own. She could see one another's bones protruding through their skin.

They emerged, put on other clothes; the woman had put out some food while Simcha washed.

"I am sorry. I do not have much."

To Hania it seemed a feast.

She slept in a bed with Miriam, the first time she had slept in a real bed with a sheet for months. She slept for hours. She felt almost human. When she awoke, Simcha and Miriam sat at a table, talking quietly. The woman had gone, but returned later with some food that she put into a satchel. Later the woman took Hania back to the bedroom, looked at her for a moment, then opened a cupboard and pulled out a heavy coat.

"You will need this."

"Your kindness; I cannot take this."

"No, you must take it. You must live. You must."

The woman started out of the room, then turned to Hania again. She unclasped a small thin necklace from the back of her neck and handed it to Hania. On the thin chain, a cross.

"Take this. Wear it. If the Nazis stop you, it may help protect you."

Hania looked at it, at the woman, nodded.

She slept. When she awoke she stepped into the front room. A man sat at the table with Simcha and Miriam, talking quietly. Simcha held a pistol in his hand, turning it over and over, inspecting it. When Hania walked in, they all looked at her. Miriam then stood and led Hania back to the bedroom.

"It is best if you wait here, yes?"

"I am sorry."

"No. It is all right."

Hania sat in the room. She heard them talking in the outer room. The man

201

raised his voice a bit, clearly not happy. Simcha then spoke. She could not make out what he said, but she twice heard him say 'Marek Stern.' The man said nothing further that she could hear.

Later Simcha came into the room.

"It is settled. He will take you from Warsaw. You can trust him. You must do what he says."

"You are not coming?"

"Miriam and I must return to the Ghetto."

"But…I can fight, Simcha."

"No, you cannot. I made a promise to your father once that I would repay his kindness. There is something else…"

Hania looked at him.

"You asked how I knew it could be you when our people said a girl was living in the ruins on Nowolipki. I knew the girl there before. She had been with Dr. Korczak, as had I, at the orphanage. Alicja. She told me about you. She loved you. She told me your name. I knew it was you."

"Alicja?"

"She told me too that you saw her with the German guard. What you had seen. What you knew. She told me you had turned away, it was in your face. She said she had betrayed you."

"Alicja…she took my life. She took…"

"Wait. Do you remember Chimczak?... The one they called the Magician?"

Hania nodded.

"He disappeared. Not our people. Before he did, he almost caught me. The sewer. Alicja saw. She protected me. She did not have to. She could have been killed then. She offered to help in the only way she could. There was a German guard with him. She made this man promises if he left me alone. To him I was a child smuggler. He did not care. Alicja made certain he saw nothing, did nothing. She paid for this in the only way she knew how ."

Hania lowered her eyes. She understood.

Miriam later embraced her, handed her a letter.

"Take this," she said. "It is for my sister. Eva. Those you will be meeting: she may be there. Only one of us could remain in the Ghetto. I belong there." Then she embraced Hania and she and Simcha left. Hania had to let them go. There was never a choice.

Later the woman in the apartment closed the coat around Hania and gave her a satchel of food. She said nothing, simply nodded, and Hania followed the man whose name she was not to know into the dark night. They walked for several hours, keeping to shadows. They kept off roads then as best they could, finally coming to large swaths of forested area. Here they stopped to rest. The man took out some bread, offered some to Hania.

"I worked with your father," he said. "At the Grochowska Street factory. They treated him, the other Jews..." The man shook his head. "Not all Poles are like that. I showed him the hiding place at the perimeter, under the stones, for his tubes. If I had not perhaps they would not have... He was a good man."

They made their way into the forest as the sky lightened. At the edge of a clearing they finally sat.

"Now, we wait."

Hania soon fell asleep. She awoke with the man shaking her shoulder. A blanket covered her. Others had joined them.

"I must now return. The Germans, they left the Ghetto alone again today. They never expected to have to fight. But they will return. You must not. Never return. Go with God."

He stood up, nodded to her, left.

There were eight or nine in the group she had joined. Three were women. Some were Jews, although she did not think all were. A man who was older than all the others approached.

"Come; we will go further into the forest. Safer."

They walked for thirty minutes or so, deeper into darkness, then stopped. They sat down amidst some rocks, seeking warmth where there was little. Hania got up, walked over to one of the women, roughly her age.

"Eva?"

The woman looked at her for a long moment, then pointed to another girl sitting alone.

"Eva?... Your sister..." Hania handed the girl the note. She looked at Hania, took the note, stood and walked away, reading as if her life depended on it. Hania could see her crying. She went and sat down near the others. After a few minutes the girl, Eva, walked back over to Hania.

"Thank you," Eva said. "I...thank you."

"Miriam saved my life."

The girl nodded slightly, went to sit nearby against a rock and closed her eyes.

The older man soon came over to Hania, kneeled.

"My name is Henryk. You do not need to know anything further. We cannot take unnecessary risks. Tonight I go south with those two." He nodded towards two young men, younger than Hania. "You must not ask them their names, but they are my sons. We will need to walk ten days, perhaps two weeks. It will be difficult. We mostly have to travel at night. There are patrols. Cold. We will cross the border into Slovakia. We have business there. You will come with us. I know you have been ill. You are not strong. But for us you must be strong. You understand?"

They departed in darkness. The man called Henryk embraced those who remained behind. They did not exchange words. They did not need to. Everyone knew they would meet up again, or would not. This was enough. The girl Eva put her arms around Hania, but said nothing. She did not need to speak. Hania understood.

They traveled through the night, keeping to shadows, resting in open country. When daybreak came they rested in ditches behind hedges, away from roads. They waited until nightfall and again began to walk. They traveled this way for several days, sleeping in woodland or covering themselves with brush. They barely spoke. Hania struggled, often. One of Henryk's sons helped her. She knew she held them back, knew too she had to find reserves within her to keep going.

On the fourth day it snowed. They found an abandoned barn and hid within for the day, then remained there the night. Henryk said they had to be careful of leaving tracks in the snow. If someone suspected they could expect a patrol to start looking. Several times they heard motorized vehicles in the distance. Because of the silence all around, they could not be certain how close or far.

After losing a day they continued. Hours walking, saying nothing. Hania decided Henryk must have made the journey before. He seemed to know which direction to take, when they would be safe over open land, or on a back lane. They ate little, did not light fires. After another day, Henryk disappeared for an hour or so, then reappeared with another man. They followed him to a small farmhouse where a woman gave them hot soup to eat with bread and an egg. Hania stared at it, almost afraid to eat. The woman encouraged her with a gesture. Hania ate.

They walked again through the night. Rested again during the day. Walked again. Hania did not know where they were. One night they heard dogs in the distance. Henryk held up his finger that they must be silent, must remain where they crouched in woods. The dogs seemed to draw closer. She could tell the men were worried. But then the barking seemed to fall away. Henryk decided they should stay the night and following day there. It was not safe.

They walked. And walked more. Hania felt herself growing weaker. At times she stumbled. Henryk watched her, but said nothing. She was determined not to stop. But sometimes she had to stop.

At the edge of a farm one night Henryk told them to wait. She could see him making his way to the farm. She saw him tap on a window. A light appeared. A door opened. Henryk embraced a man holding up a lantern, disappeared inside. He was gone several hours, returning at dawn.

"It is all right," he said.

They all went to the farmhouse. An old man was waiting. Inside his wife had prepared some soup for them. She showed Hania where she could wash. Hania painfully removed her shoes. The woman looked at Hania's feet, bloodied, covered with sores. She brought Hania some balm, then went and spoke quietly to her husband, who in turn spoke quietly to Henryk. He came over to Hania.

"They do not think you will be able to continue."

"I will walk."

"Are you certain?"

"I will walk."

Henryk thought, then nodded.

"Rest. We go again tonight."

Again they walked through the night, and the next. Hania was exhausted. She knew the fever had started again. She knew she was holding them back. And she knew that they knew.

Still they traveled, almost walking into a German patrol by mistake. It was only at the last moment that they heard voices in German. They lay in long grass no more than a hundred meters from the patrol. They remained hidden that way for hours until the patrol finally got back in their vehicles and disappeared down a road.

Dawn would soon break, and they hurried to some woodland, sitting there for the day. Hania slept.

They traveled that night. After several hours, they stopped. Henryk spoke quietly to one of his sons, who nodded several times, then left.

"We will wait here now," was all Henryk said.

The sky grew brighter, threatening snow. Hania could see Henryk was worried. Still no sign of his son. The other son too had concern written on his face. Finally as the winter sun began to appear at the edge of the horizon, the boy appeared.

"I spoke to her. She agreed."

"Did you see anyone on the journey?"

The boy shook his head. Henryk considered, then decided they would risk walking in daylight. They walked for three hours, perhaps more, keeping in fields, listening for any sound that might be a warning. They saw only crows and in the distance, from a small village, smoke from houses. They walked away from it.

The ground began to rise into hills, becoming wooded. They came to a country road, waited, listened, then crossed, going uphill now. They came to some small fields. Henryk directed them around the edges, then into woodland. Treading carefully, they saw below a small farmhouse in a sheltered area above some fields. They circumvented the farmhouse until they were above it, walking about another three or four hundred meters until they came to a partly crumbling large barn, its roof largely collapsed.

"We will stay here now."

Again, Hania slept.

When she woke, the others had their satchels over their shoulders. She sat up and started to put her few things in her bag, but Henryk came over, stopped her.

"You are staying here."

"No, I can walk. I will not hold you back."

"We have decided. A woman owns the farm below. She knows you are here. Her barn. She has helped us before. We are not far from the Slovak border but the German patrols have increased. It is not safe to take you. The woman will bring you food, another blanket. It would not be safe in the house with her but she says you should be safe here. You can trust her. We will return from Slovakia and will come for you. Yes?"

Hania wondered if she would ever see them again. She did not.

*

It grew dark quickly and while the trees in the surrounds kept the wind away, the cold settled in. The loft in the barn had collapsed on one end but an old ladder still leaned against that part of the platform that remained. Hania carefully climbed up. Mice scattered. Once certain the remaining platform would hold her weight, Hania gathered clumps of rotting hay into a bed for herself. She lay down, thought of nothing, slept again.

In the morning she saw no one but a plate of sausage and cheese had been left for her. She knew she must try to eat although she had no appetite. She took a couple of small bites but vomited it up. She could not hold down food. The fever had returned.

She lay down again and slept.

*

When she next opened her eyes another blanket had been put over her and the plate had been taken. Her dress had been removed. Her body felt on fire, sore, tired. She could not hold her eyes open and again slipped into unconsciousness.

*

The woman stood on the platform staring at her. She was not large, not young. But she was strong. Hania could see that. She had no expression in her face, neither concern nor indifference.

"You have been unconscious for four days. You need to eat."

The woman put a small container of hot liquid down near Hania and a small bowl with a paste.

"Drink this. It will help. Bitter but bitterness is good. I will make more tomorrow. This salve put on your feet. There is infection. You must not walk for a week. Do you understand?"

Hania nodded.

"I will bring you food as you get stronger. I am alone in the house. The Germans come from time to time. Take what they want. Taxes. Perhaps a neighbor from the nearby village but not often. The priest too. You must be very careful. If you hear voices be silent. When you get stronger you can hide in forest. Leave no trace of your presence. They do not come up here but you cannot be certain. For now you must let your body fight the fever so it does not consume you."

Hania sipped at the hot liquid. She gagged but managed to hold it down. She slept.

*

The woman brought the liquid twice a day. After a week Hania finally began to find strength. The woman then brought her things she could eat: broth mostly, rich with fat, and bread. She brought up fresh straw for bedding, some warm clothes, took what Hania had to wash or burn. She said very little but kept Hania alive.

Soon Hania was strong enough to climb down the ladder, walk. She kept out of sight as much as possible. She remained near the barn, always listening for the sound of a motor, or voices. She saw no one else, heard no one else.

The woman brought matches one day, pulled out a small rusting metal basin from behind the barn.

"There is dead wood just beyond," she pointed. "You can keep warm with a small fire in this, but only when it is dark. If anyone sees smoke they could report it. Keep the fire low. In the morning take the ashes away. Never leave a trace you are here. You must always think twice."

Hania nodded. The woman went away.

*

Hania began to venture further from the barn. One day she made her way closer to the farmhouse. She saw the woman working, alone, digging in the field. She saw her gather hay and carry it to the house. She watched as the woman washed

208

clothes, fed the few chickens roaming around. Pumped water from the well behind the farmhouse. She watched the woman work and knew she worked hard.

Later, when the woman brought food, Hania said to her: "I watched you work. You can use help. I can do that."

The woman looked at her, shook her head.

"No."

The woman started out of the barn, but hesitated, turned back.

"What are you called?"

"Hania."

The woman stared, her brow furrowed.

"Hania?"

"Yes."

"Your given name, Hania?"

"Yes."

The woman stared at Hania for a long moment, then turned away. Looked towards the woods beyond, the path below, again looked at Hania as if she thought to say something. But she said nothing, turned and walked back towards the farmhouse.

In the morning she appeared as usual with soup and bread. She left it at the edge of the loft platform before Hania woke. Hania did not see the woman at all during the day, or that night. The food appeared. The woman did not.

The next morning the woman was there as usual.

"Above, where the water runs, if you continue through the trees for fifty meters or so, the stream pools in some rocks. You can wash there when you wish. I fill a bath every second Sunday. Tonight. You can bathe yourself after me. Behind the house."

That evening Hania walked down to the farmhouse. The woman had put a metal tub near the well. When Hania appeared the woman added more heated water that she carried from the fire in the house. Hania removed her clothes and stepped in, the first bath she had had in many weeks. She wanted to stay there forever. The woman appeared and took her clothes away. She reappeared when the water had cooled with a different dress.

Hania climbed from the bath. The woman stared at her for a moment, thinking.

"You walked here from Warsaw? You are a Jew?"

Hannah hesitated, then nodded.

"But you wear a cross."

"A friend gave it to me. For protection."

The woman stared at Hania, standing naked before her. Then she lowered her eyes and handed Hania a clean dress, went back into her house and closed the door.

*

Hania ventured into forest. She found the small stream of water where she could wash in the mornings. The water was freezing cold although the days had started to grow warmer.

Walking back down to the barn, she saw an overgrown path that she decided to follow. After a short distance it led to a cleared patch, now overgrown, where a rough cross, two pieces of wood held together by a small piece of wire, had been planted on a grave. Hania stared at it for a long time.

Later, when the woman brought her food, Hania stopped her before she turned to leave.

"Above, there is a grave. A cross."

The woman looked at her but did not say anything.

"Whose is it?"

The woman hesitated, looked away, then back at Hania.

"My daughter."

"I am sorry. How did she die?"

The woman just looked at her. She did not respond. She turned and walked back to her house.

*

Two German soldiers appeared on a motorcycle and side car. Hania hid in the trees, watching them. The woman came out of the house to greet them. They remained talking for some time. The woman nodded. The two soldiers eventually disappeared back down the road. The woman stood watching them go, then looked up past the house towards the trees. Hania did not think the woman could see her.

The woman however stood and stared, then walked back inside.

*

"I feel I could help," Hania said. "I can sew. I can work."

The woman put food down on the makeshift table in the barn, walked up to Hania, reached over and grabbed her hand. She looked at the palm, turned it over, then stepped back.

"You have city hands."

She left Hania alone in the barn.

*

The woman had gone into town for some supplies and to sell some meat she had cured. She told Hania to remain hidden and be vigilant. But when she was gone Hania walked down to the farmhouse. She saw that the woman had been laying up rows of earth where she had started to plant potatoes. A shovel stood against a fence post nearby. Hania began to dig. She spent all morning in the garden, mounding the earth. And all afternoon.

That night the woman brought food as usual to the barn. Hania had no hunger. Although stronger she was very tired.

"You will need to eat if you are going to help."

The following days Hania began to help the woman as best she could. The woman led her to a field away from the house where the grass needed cutting. She showed Hania how to use the scythe. It took some time until Hania felt she understood the rhythm. The woman watched her, then left her alone to the work. Hania cut. The work was exhausting.

Hania cut the next day as well. She had blisters on her hands, sweat on her brow. She worked until her muscles ached, then worked some more. She cut until the sun began to disappear.

She put down the scythe. The work was done. She saw that the woman was watching her from the bottom of the field. Hania did not know how long she had been there. She walked over to her. The woman stared at the cut field behind, then at Hania. She took Hania's hands, turned them over in her own to look at the palms. Saw the blisters.

"Come," she said. Nothing else.

211

Hania followed her towards the barn, but the woman gestured she should continue to the farmhouse.

Inside the single large room was dusty and cold. The woman lit a fire. She went over to a cupboard and returned with a small pot of balm. She took some on her fingers, sat down beside Hania, rubbed it into her palms. She then put a pot over the fire, heating soup.

"Tonight you will eat in here."

The woman poured two bowls of soup, cut some bread, then pulled out some ham from her cold store and cut two pieces. Hania stared at the meat when the woman put it before her.

"You will need to eat," the woman said. "If you are seen they will find ways to test you. To trick you. You must learn to be what you are not. Who you are not. Like the cross you wear around your neck. They cannot see inside your heart unless you let them."

Hania looked at her, hesitated. Then ate.

When they had finished, Hania started to leave but the woman stopped her. She stared at Hania for a long time. She got up, put more wood on the fire. Sat down again across from Hania. Said nothing at first, then:

"My name is Helena Kielar. My daughter's name was…My daughter was Hannah. Hannah Kielar. I suppose the similarity is but a coincidence if you believe in coincidence."

Hania looked up at her. The woman held her gaze, sighed, continued.

"I do not know if I do or not. She would have been about your age."

"I am sorry."

"I lived here with my husband and Hannah. He drank. I did not love him. Even then. When the war came he disappeared. Then he came back. He said he wanted to stay. He said he would work. I should not have believed him. I was foolish. I had to go to the village one day, to the market to sell. When I returned my Hannah was… I could tell what he had done to her. She said when she understood what he would do she tried to run. He beat her and he took her. He had then left and I never saw him again. I heard the Nazis arrested him in Krakow. I heard they tortured him for the sport. He died in pain. I felt pity for him. Perhaps I should not have done. Perhaps the world is unjust to all."

Hania lowered her eyes. The woman sat quietly, then continued.

"My daughter Hannah never recovered from this. She slowly stopped talking. Then she realized she was with child. She carried his child. She hated him. She hated herself even more. I was cutting grass in the field where you cut yesterday, today. When I finished the work I went looking for her. She was in the barn. She had hanged herself with a rope. I cut her body down and carried it myself to the small clearing that you found. I buried her with my own two hands. My Hannah."

The woman sat very still, staring at Hania.

"I could never tell anyone. She had committed two sins. She lay with her father. She took her own life. Two mortal sins. The priest would never absolve her of this. So I buried her, alone, where no one could harm her further. Sometimes the priest, Zieliński, visits here. He asks me about her. I say she is in Krakow. I say she does not send me news but I believe she is well. I say I am afraid for her in these dark times. I say she sends me money. I say she is a dutiful daughter. I say these lies out of necessity. One should not lie to priests, but I lie."

She stopped talking then. They remained this way for a long time, without words, watching the fire burn down. Finally Hania stood to walk back up to the barn.

"You have suffered too," the woman, Helena Kielar, suddenly spoke.

"Yes."

"There are no ghosts in the barn."

Hania thought, then answered: "There are ghosts everywhere."

As she turned, the woman said to her: "I have no time for priests. Or ghosts. Or for God. Anyone's God."

*

Hania worked with Helena Kielar over coming few weeks, helping to repair a wall, planting, washing, cutting, curing. Helena said almost nothing but noted that Hania worked hard even as the pain of such took hold. In the nights Hania collapsed in the barn, sleeping until dawn. Her body grew stronger, her muscles began to toughen. The bones sticking out from her skin receded slightly. Once Helena said she should stop, rest.

"I need not to think," Hania told her, and kept working.

On a couple occasions Hania had to hide when she heard a motor approaching or voices of a visitor. Helena never said who had been. Hania never asked. She had learned to keep to herself, to disappear as and when she needed to.

As the weather turned warmer Helena appeared early one morning pushing the hand cart, called Hania and told her to follow. She led Hania to a small pen beyond the high field where she secretly kept four pigs. She guided one of the pigs into the cart, tied a rope around its neck and pushed the animal away towards the woods. At a small clearing she stopped and drove the animal out. She wrapped the rope around the animal's feet, tethering it so it could not move at the edge of a ditch. She handed the rope to Hania to hold the pig, pulled a bucket and a butcher knife from the cart.

As the pig struggled and squealed, Helena wrapped one arm around its neck, leaned hard to stop the animal fighting, pushed the knife into the animal's throat and pulled.

Hania stared at the gushing blood, turned away and vomited. Helena put the bucket at the pig's throat to catch the blood.

"You need to watch. You need to learn."

Helena spent the day skinning the pig, cutting the meat. She and Hania dug a hole to put in what little offal Helena would not use, then put the rest into the cart. Helena kept some to take to the house to hang, but showed Hania a secret store in the woods where she kept food from the eyes of the Germans who came looking to take whatever they could find.

One day they were working and Helena seemed particularly thoughtful. Earlier than normal she said they had finished. She told Hania to come down to the house that night.

When Hania got there Helena had built a fire in the hearth. She put food before Hania. They ate in silence. When they were finished Helena put the bowls away, then walked to the far side of the kitchen and pulled away a loose stone from the base of the wall. She reached within and pulled out a metal box.

Again she sat across from Hania. She pulled out papers—identity papers, a birth certificate, a baptism certificate. Her daughter's papers.

"You are like her, in more than name. You know where you can find her papers if you should need them."

Hania saw that her daughter was born a year before her own birth. Perhaps from the photograph there was a similarity. She could not say.

"I will cut your hair, very short. Hers was dark, but once I cut yours short…"

Hania said nothing. Helena Kielar placed a chair near the fire and took out large scissors.

"Come sit."

Hania did not protest. She knew she had no reason to protest. She heard the sound of metal against metal, felt the pull on her hair. When she had finished, Hania's hair was shorter than any boy's. She looked at the red blond hair scattered on the floor. She did not move. She watched as Helena Kielar picked her hair up and put it in the fire. She heard her hair sizzle. Watched it flame and disappear. Her life going up in smoke.

The woman, Helena Kielar, stared at her, nodded slightly. She took a small bottle beside her drying herbs.

"This is drawn from sage and walnut bark. It will help your hair to darken as it grows. Her eyes were blue. That cannot be helped but hopefully no one will notice this."

She put some on Hania's scalp, rubbed it in. She looked at her for a long moment, then nodded.

"Take off your shirt."

Hania looked at the older woman, but hesitated only a moment. She removed her shirt. She put her arms across her small breasts, but then removed them and sat in silence, without emotion. Helena Kielar stared at her for a long moment. She walked over to her cupboard and took out a rag, twisting it. She looked at Hania, then handed the rag to her.

"Hannah had a birth scar, there," she nodded, "below her left breast. It is recorded on her identity paper. You need to become her. You need to be her if you are stopped, if you are caught. Unless you must speak, never speak. Forget your past. All of it. You must look only to this farm, to now, to the future. You must never trust anyone with the past. Ever. Not the Germans or the priest or police or officials or anyone. You were born here and you should die here. You have no life but the life I gave you, the milk you took only from my breast, the food you took only from our land, the breath and hope and sorrow that came from my being."

Hania did not respond.

"Put that between your teeth. This will be painful. Bite down hard. As hard as you can."

Hania did as she was told. Helena Kielar walked over to the fire and pulled a short iron poker from it. She looked at Hania, then walked over.

"It may be best to close your eyes. Raise your arm. Now bite. Hard."

Hania raised her arm. She refused to close her eyes. She looked straight ahead. The pain of the red hot bar against her flesh was excruciating. She heard the flesh sizzle as she passed out.

*

She lay in Helena Kielar's bed for the night. The pain would not go away. Helena Kielar rubbed a balm of honey and herbs onto the wound to cool the pain, but the pain remained. Despite it, Hania rose the next morning to return to the barn. Before she started out, Helena rose.

"Wait."

She reached for a book hidden on a shelf.

"Take this. My Bible. You need to read and remember as you will have once read your own, should they ask you. It may save you if you are discovered. Whether you choose to accept is up to you. Jesus Christ too was a Jew."

Hania returned to the barn. She climbed up to the platform, lay on the straw, covered herself with blankets. She let the pain infuse her. She wanted to feel the pain. She wanted to remember pain.

She still held the Bible in her hand. She opened the front cover and saw Helena's name written, Hannah's name. Where there had been another name at the top, the page had been torn, the name removed.

Hania closed the bible and pushed it under straw at the far side of the platform. She would not open it again. She did not seek redemption. She did not seek any God.

*

May, and the weather turned much warmer. Hania helped on the farm. She hid when she needed to. She worked to forget.

She was a ghost now. The woman Helena Kielar helped keep her alive, but she did not grasp life. She tried not to remember. Sometimes she could not but remember.

One morning Helena Kielar borrowed a mule from a neighbor and took the cart into nearby Nowy Wiśnicz to sell her hay and some food stuffs. She was gone all the day. She warned Hania that she must stay hidden. The Germans had increased their patrols.

Night approached and still Helena did not reappear. Hania remained hidden in the forest until she felt safe, then returned to the barn. She sat there until late in the night.

She finally heard footsteps approaching and Helena appeared, her way lit by a single candle. She stood at the entrance of the barn, raised the candle higher, casting shadow, until she saw Hania seated in a corner.

"I needed to speak to the priest. There were reports. I wanted to see if they were true. It was said the Nazis went into the Warsaw Ghetto in mid April. They did not expect the Jews to fight, but they fought. Bravely. There were many deaths. It took the Nazis a month. They ended it by burning the Ghetto to the ground. No one remains. Nothing remains. They killed everyone."

Hania did not move. She could not move. She said nothing.

"I am sorry, child."

The woman stood in the entrance for a long moment. Then she blew out the candle, turned, departed.

Hania sat where she sat. She did not move. She did not breathe. She did not think. Frozen. She sat.

*

In the morning she still sat. She did not sleep. She simply was.

*

In the afternoon she found some paper brown with age in the barn, and a pencil in her satchel. She sat down again in the shadows and started to write the name of everyone she ever knew, every name she could remember, everyone.

In small letters she wrote Marek Stern and Zivia Stern. She wrote Shaul Stern and Lea Elster and Michael Elster and Jakub Elster. She wrote down the Babka she never knew, the relatives she never had but knew existed. She wrote down the neighbors she remembered and the childhood friends. She wrote down the names of the butchers and the bread makers and the leather tanner and the coffin maker. She wrote down her school friends Noemi and Edzia and all the other classmates she could remember and her teachers. She needed another sheet of paper and still she wrote. Josef Schipper who she never liked, Yitzhak, Arie Zalszupin and his friend Romek, Simcha Gitler, Miriam and her sister Eva. She wrote anyone and everyone. She wrote down the faces and the laughter and the tears and cries. She wrote down the life she saw and the joy and the tragedy. She wrote down the music she heard, the piano playing, the words her mother spoke. She wrote the people on the street and the people hiding and the people who lived and the others who died.

She wrote Alicja and saw her friend's face and felt her embrace.

She wrote the Ghetto. She wrote it all.

Finally she wrote her own name.

Hania Stern.

She wrote it again, Hania Stern. And she stared at it. For a long time she looked at it, at all the names she had written. She looked at their names and saw their faces and looked into their hearts and looked into her own heart.

And finally she took out a match.

And she set the pages alight.

And she watched the paper burn. And smoke. And the paper turn to ash and fly up from her hand and disappear. And all disappeared.

She stood in silence, and muttered in silence the Kaddish she had learned and spoken often, too often, the prayer to remember, the prayer to forget. The prayer of tears. The prayer of the dead.

And Hania Stern disappeared. In her stead with her short dark hair, with her scar below her left breast, with her cross that meant nothing and with her green eyes that she could not hide, Hannah Kielar sat stone still in the shadows and refused to mourn. And refused to cry. And would live as she had become. And exorcized Hania Stern from her memory and her thoughts. Forever.

*

She only worked. She said little. She remained living in the barn. She did not ask for more. The woman, Helena Kielar fed her, watched her, worked with her, but did not demand more. The world slipped into silence again and sorrow, but she retained such sorrow within.

If she heard voices or motor vehicles or any sound other than the axe chopping wood or the pump pulling in water or the fire crackle, she hid. Sometimes she hid for days, even if it was unnecessary. Helena Kielar never questioned this. And never asked for anything more from the girl she knew only as her daughter Hannah.

Occasionally they shared a meal. Often they did not.

The year passed as had the previous. They were left largely alone. They worked. There were days Helena Kielar went to the town. And there were days Hannah, only Hannah now, walked into the forest, alone. Disappeared for hours, alone. She spoke only if she needed to speak. She did not cry.

Towards the end of the year, as the weather turned cold again, Hannah as she now was, spent more and more time alone in the barn, wrapped in blankets to keep warm, remaining in silence, living in silence, empty. Helena Kielar continued bringing food to her, or telling her to come below, sit by the fire. Sometimes she would go to the farmhouse. Helena went to the town one day as she had many times before. She returned to say that things were going badly for the Nazis, that they were starting to retreat.

"The War will come to an end. Maybe not now, not this month, but it will end. The Russians they say they are advancing. But they are no better than the Nazis. They are all the same. We are safest here. We will live our life and let Hell swallow all else."

*

A few days after the start of the new year Hannah as she now was lay under the blanket sleeping when she heard voices from afar. She jumped up, threw her blankets under straw and hurried down the ladder. She hid anything that suggested she was there, then quickly ran from the barn into the trees. Luckily it had not snowed for days. She left no tracks.

She remained hidden in the trees for many hours, waiting. Still she heard voices and laughter.

She finally decided to move from her hiding place. She carefully made her way towards the farmhouse, but keeping to the tree line, moving only slowly, ever slowly, staying behind low branches, keeping invisible. She cut through forest at the side and came to a grove of trees about fifty meters above the rear of the farmhouse.

She lay down on her stomach. She stared.

Below she saw four German soldiers. Laughing. Drinking. Drunk.

She saw Helena Kielar, her hands behind her, sitting, slouched, tied to the wheel of the cart. Her hair hung to the side of her head. She bled from her mouth. She was conscious, clearly in pain.

She saw the soldiers go in and out of the farmhouse, throwing out furniture, clothes, everything they could find. They drank from bottles. They found food from the farmhouse store and ate. They tore things apart, yelling at Helena Kielar, demanding food, money, jewelry. Helena said nothing. They pointed their guns at her, acting as if they would shoot. They did not shoot.

Hannah as she was, daughter as she was, saw them light a fire of the furniture to warm themselves. They carried out cloth and threw it on, broken wood, anything they could find. Still they yelled at Helena Kielar. Helena Kielar said nothing in response.

They drank more. Laughed more. They kicked Helena. Slapped her. They emptied the house.

Hannah as she now was did not know what to do. Three of the soldiers again stumbled into the farmhouse. She started to stand. She wanted to scream. She wanted to fight. She knew they would kill her, kill them both. She raised herself off the ground.

And as she did she saw the woman, Helena Kielar, looking up towards the woods. Towards her.

She saw the woman Helena Kielar shake her head, slowly, just slightly, as if warning. As if she saw her. As if in her face she said no, do not move, do not try, no. Live. Live.

And Hania now saw her mother pulled into the cattle car in Umschlagplatz, turning towards her, confused, crying.

And Hania now saw her friend, and herself from outside herself, from above, watching, and saw Alicja helping her mother up, then standing at the edge of the cattle car and turning. And Alicja's glance meeting her own. And Alicja shaking her head no. No.

And saw her friend Alicja mouth the word 'live' even as she was pushed within and the transport door closed behind, locked behind.

And she saw the woman Helena Kielar shake her head, just slightly, and even from the distance knew that her eyes teared and she said behind those eyes no. Live. No.

One of the soldiers emerged from the house and walked over to Helena Kielar. He untied the rope and pulled her up. He pulled her to a small table and threw her over it. He took the rope and tied her hands, one to each table leg.

Laughing, he walked behind her and yanked at Helena Kielar's dress, tearing it off, so that she lay over the table naked. He opened his trousers, spread her legs. And he sodomized her.

His friend watched, laughed, drank.

And when the first soldier finished, his friend took his place and did the same.

And the two others emerged. And the third then did this. And the fourth.

And when he was done, he stood up and walked around, laughing. He kneeled in front of the bleeding, broken woman and said something. And she lifted her head, just slightly. And she looked at him. And she spat in his face.

The soldier stopped laughing. He stood up. He stared at her. Cocked his head one way, then shook it as if in pity.

And he pulled out a gun from his belt.

And he shot. And her body slumped. And he shot again. And walked away.

They had had enough. One of the soldiers untied the naked body of Helena Kielar and pushed her onto the ground. He urinated on her. Then he and another dragged her body by the feet into the farmhouse. They took burning wood from the fire they had built, lit some material and clothes and threw it into the farmhouse after her. They watched as smoke began to filter out, then flames. They watched, drank. Watched.

And finally, as darkness fell, they stumbled down the road and disappeared.

*

Hannah Kielar, daughter, for she was Hannah Kielar, watched in silence. She made herself watch. She made herself know.

She did not move from her place in the trees through the night.

*

In the morning she went down to the half destroyed farmhouse. She found the remains of Helena Kielar within.

She did not cry. She would not cry. She brought over the small hand cart and lifted the charred remains into it. She put a shovel into the cart, then walked from the farmhouse, pushing the cart in front of her, struggling to push it up hill. She walked past the barn, pushing it into the forest, struggling over tree roots and undergrowth, until she came to the small clearing. She spent the day digging a grave beside the grave with the cross on it, the grave of who she was and was not.

In the evening she lowered the remains of Helena Kielar into the grave beside her only daughter. She thought for a moment, walked back to the barn to fetch the bible that was not hers, did not belong to her, then returned to the open grave and dropped it beside the remains.

She stared at the open grave. She stared at death. She took off the cross around her neck and dropped it in as well. Then she filled in the grave and walked slowly away, alone.

*

She stopped working the farm. She chose not to leave. She knew where there was food and knew she had enough for some time to come.

Several months later, the weather again began to turn warm. One night in early May, she awoke in darkness past midnight to the sound a church bell ringing, then another, and another, until the valley erupted with the sound of bells.

She climbed down from the platform and stood at the entrance to the barn.

She knew the War must have ended. Or had not ended, because it never would, never really would.

She stood and stared up at the stars, bright in the night sky.

She decided then she would remain on the property as long as she could. She had died as Hania Stern and she would live as Hannah Kielar and she would not speak just as Helena Kielar had warned her, would not say, would not return. On that day all memory perished, disappeared into the smoke of her nightmares just as the names on browned paper had disappeared into air, into never was. Forgotten. The forgetting. Never was.

It would be her life, her future. It began then. At that moment. Time without names. Time without the past. Without knowledge. She would forget.

She knew nevertheless that in a secret chamber within her head and her heart memory would remain. But she would lock it in the chamber of her soul and not release it now, nor in the future. She would not speak its name. She would not speak.

Hannah Kielar turned and walked back into the darkness of the barn, the darkness of the night.

Climbed up the ladder steps to the platform.

She sat on hay that had become her bed.

She did not close her eyes. She did not sleep. She would not speak. She had nothing further to say. She would wait.

Second Movement

Furorem:
Pawel's Awakening

Warsaw

1968

Jan-Feb 1968

Ministry of Interior
Committee for Public Security
SB / Dep 1

PERSON OF INTEREST OPK File Warsaw Mok.75392

Senior Investigating Security Officer: WójcikM Dep1/WC
                                                    Mokotów/Wierzbno
Operative Personenkontrolle
P. Weisz
Current residence: Zawrat 14
- -

29.1.68

Henceforth official request to the OPK office of I.D. (Public Security M/W Dep 1) in the matter of Warsaw resident Pawel Weisz, hereafter Subject.

Subject is an inactive party member. There is no record on file of involvement in any student committee other than through academic affiliation. Further there is also no record on file of stated Soviet or Zionist sympathy or any kind of semi-subversive tendency towards reform liberalization, pro-Western political bias or indeed political internationalism. Political sympathies currently untested and unknown. Noted recent correspondence and relationship with Czechoslovak Prague Music Conservatoire, while not in itself unusual, but given the current levels there of reform and potential for sedition amongst certain elements of our Socialist sister country, opposed by our own Polish government and party apparatus, approval for OPK surveillance therefore requested from the Ministry and request granted.

*

My team and I have today commenced daily surveillance of Subject, who resides in a single bedroom apartment at Zawrat 14. Subject from birth record is thirty-one years old born in Silesia provincial district.

Subject is a former student who graduated the Higher State Music School, Warsaw with distinctive composing ability as well as higher levels in piano and organ composition (according to academic record) for which he received top prize in 1960, then remaining affiliated with HSMS as Associate and Teacher at advanced level. Current Higher State Music School address (as of 1966 upon completion of premises construction) Ulica Okólnik 2 in central Warsaw. Subject appointed to position at the school in the Department of Conducting, Composition and Theory of Music.

Subject left his apartment building at 08.36. He is approximately 1.7 to 1.8 Meters in height, with light brown short hair, of slight build, wearing brown framed eyeglasses. He wore a dark navy woolen coat, gloves and hat with a light brown scarf. He carried with him a dark brown leather briefcase apparently full of paperwork, noted by the expanse of the sides of the case. This was to be expected given that this is the examination period at the School as indeed at other Warsaw universities. Subject proceeded to buy a newspaper at a kiosk across the street from his building entrance then waited at the trolleybus stop until he boarded Trolleybus 54, which ferried him to the music school. He disembarked in front of the school building at 09.17. Before entering main entrance Subject was seen shaking hands with three people: Professor T.Paciorkiewicz, identified elsewhere as Dean of the Department to which subject is attached, Associate Professor A.Sienkiewicz who we understand from records had been Subject's supervising teacher and advisor in the early student years when Subject first entered into the Higher State School of Music (1956 per submitted administrative record), and a young woman, today identified as one of Subject's composition students, Marta Ptaszyńska. Only Sienkiewicz has been previously identified as a person of interest, with a separate OPK file terminated in 1965.

Subject disappeared inside and did not emerge from same until 17.49 that afternoon. Subject reappeared alone at the entrance and ran to catch Trolleybus 54 back to his residence at Zawrat 14. However after waiting for only a short time at the Trolleybus stop, having no verbal exchanges with anyone else, Subject seemed to change his mind and proceeded to walk back to the apartment residence, a journey of some 57 minutes. Subject seemed noticeably preoccupied; explanation for such unknown. One of my team followed Subject from a safe distance for this journey and reported that no exchanges were made with any other persons during this walk. Subject entered his building at 18.07. Subject did *not leave the apartment for the remainder of the evening, at least until termination of the surveillance at 23.32 on 29.1.68.*

As per signed approvals of requesting Officer ID (Mokotów/Wierzbno) my third team member DB succeeded in gaining entrance to the apartment at Zawrat 14 in the early afternoon of 29.1.68 and inserted an agency CLD with record facility into the single unit telephone in the Suspect apartment's entrance. No further CLDs were requested or deemed necessary. DB also had time to photograph certain papers spread out in the apartment, all of which seem to refer to musical composition work. It was noted that within the apartment is a semi-sophisticated tape recording reel to reel piece of equipment of standard make (Wollensak T1500) that conforms to the Subject's employment and acceptable held personal equipment criteria as prescribed in the advance personal expenditure agreed with the school and the relevant Education Ministry. It has been noted that Subject is a recognized Warsaw based composer of growing repute and that such electronic recording equipment would be in keeping with his position and from what can be gathered to his musical composition work although such could be used for other purposes as well should he so intend. Thus this equipment is duly noted in the event further examination or reference is advisable.

Installed CLD equipment tested and in good working order. No incoming or outgoing telephone calls logged or recorded during evening of 29.1.68.

-MW, Senior Investigating Officer (SISO)

*

Pawel sat in his office stirring his coffee, staring at the spoon going round and round in the cup, his mind floating as if on a cloud at once white with hope, and grey with storm. Storm raining confusion. How often such confusion, unspoken, he thought to himself?

"Mr. Weisz?... Mr. Weisz?..."

A young student sat opposite his desk, in expectation and nervously awaiting Pawel's response.

"Um? Oh, Szymon, sorry. You were saying?"

"The accents of that third phrase: in your opinion is the contrast strong enough or does the repetition need greater pronouncement?"

"No, I think it is good as it is. Sorry. Your examiners should agree."

"…Yes. Good then. I understand."

"Sorry… my head today is in a different space I think. We will pick it up again when I see you next Tuesday, yes?"

"Of course. Thank you."

The young man, Szymon, grabbed his sheet music and left the room. Pawel watched him go, then sat quietly with his coffee. He should have been thinking about the students' work, not his own. But it was his own work that demanded his thoughts at that moment. And the coffee.

Pawel took his papers and scores from the locked cabinet at the side of his desk, laid them out at the table, stared at the music sheets. His composition 'With Memory for Twelve Musicians' in Four Movements for each of the four seasons reached out to him, but did not touch. He had been working on what he called his new synergy piece whereby he combined traditional Polish folk music with his own interest in sonoristic post-tonal chromatics, all technical and of his generation. And yet… He saw the notes and composition before him, the sounds, the included voices. He saw them with his eyes, heard them in his head, but something was lacking. Something he could not then put his finger on. He wanted to throw the composition onto the fire, start afresh. But start where?

He pushed the score aside. Turned on the reel to reel Nagra III tape recording machine and put the heavy earphones over his ears. He heard the folk songs he had collected from villages in the east country, the two women singing. Heard neither the words nor the out of tune voices but rather the emotions, the joy. Planting in the spring sun. Heard them singing of being girls again, of youth and love making and hope. He knew he could bring this music to score and transform it into something new, fresh, breaking it down into its most basic assemblage then reforming it like a cubist painting into reimagined elements as if from the ether itself. But there was something he could not yet find, could not yet express. Technically, yes. The emotion, however: how did he transcribe the emotion? How did he resurrect the past in ways that not only engaged the intellect, but might engage the heart as well?

Pawel turned away from the desk, listening to the singing envelop him through the earphones, out of tune, yet music of life, rebirth expressed. Listening, he stared out of the window towards the street below, the people rushing back and forth. He did not see them struggling as they worked their ways across the cold of the Warsaw winter landscape. He saw instead the spring warmth, the workers planting the earth in the countryside, raising their voices. He was lost in these voices. Saw the notes as they rose before him, notes that he would translate and transcribe into something modern, emerging reborn from songs and experiences of long ago.

He whirled around, surprised, when he felt an unexpected tap on his shoulder. He had been so lost in the songs reverberating in his head that the world around him had disappeared and he hadn't heard Sienkiewicz come into the room or call his name.

"Arkady, sorry."

"In a different world, Pawel?"

"In a field with two peasant women."

"Sounds enjoyable. I hope they are young and beautiful. How is it going for you?"

"Slowly. The summer section, good. But spring… I don't know."

"I am certain Vivaldi too struggled with his seasons."

"Yes but he had more musicians to score for without such complications, as well as melody and rhythm. I am stuck with microtonality and a discordant cello line."

"You could always compose then for a Western rock and roll band. Most are also discordant I think."

"I had not thought of that."

His mentor smiled.

"You need someone to bounce ideas off, Pawel, argue with, I am down the corridor as always. And there is vodka. Always the most important part. If you can take a break there is someone I want you to listen to."

"Recording?"

"Not this time."

Pawel nodded, got up to follow his mentor and friend. They walked down the stairs into the corridor of the main building then to the back extension classrooms and rehearsal spaces. At a rehearsal room along the ground floor corridor Sienkiewicz looked through the window in the entrance doorway, then entered, followed by Pawel.

Seated in the second row, Pawel's Instrumental Department colleague, Anna Wójcik, turned, nodded, then turned back to the young man with the violin standing near her, tuning the instrument. Pawel and Sienkiewicz found two seats at the back.

"So, the Chaconne, when you are ready?"

The young man shrugged. He stared at her for a moment, looked away, considered, then rested the violin between his shoulder and his chin and began to play.

Pawel sat back to listen. Intently. Unexpectedly after the first phrases he sat forward in his seat, his back straight, his brow furrowing, his hearing and thought intensely engaged. Bach's Chaconne movement at the end of the Partita No.2 in D Minor, a work he knew well. A masterpiece of solo instrumentation, truly a rich and layered experience of music and for most creating intense musical emotion, transcribing grief and loss into one of the most challenging pieces ever written for the instrument. Pawel had played a transcription on organ for his graduation prize. It was a piece close to his heart. But hearing it from this young man, almost mastered and captured as it was, almost flawless—almost in a way that even those flaws provoked questions--proved eye opening.

After some five or six minutes, Anna told the young man to stop.

"It is very good. Yes. Impressive, young man." she said. "I want you to relax and let us discuss that repeating bass line."

Sienkiewicz turned quietly to Pawel, gestured that they should go out. Once the door closed behind him he smiled broadly at his younger colleague.

"So?"

"He is good, I will give him that. Not perfect. Some missed moments. Very raw in a way. Undisciplined. But dynamic."

"Yes, he is good. Very good. We both know it. I thought you would be impressed."

"An instrumental student?"

"No. He is not one of ours."

Pawel looked at him, slightly confused.

"I don't understand, Arkady."

"He is not a student here, that young man. Anna heard him playing at a student club and asked him to come in. His former teacher had written to her so she went to listen to him play. She saw something in him. I think you and I might agree."

"He is not a student?"

"No. Robert Mandeltort. He studies at the University of Warsaw. Politics, I believe. Politicians do nothing but create wastelands. Music on the other hand produces the richest of tapestries. Such a waste of talent I would argue. So would Anna. We want to convince him to come here. I want you to assist."

Pawel looked at his grinning mentor. He agreed the boy had something special. Musically, certainly. But something else… something…

"He is good," Pawel agreed, smiling.

"As I said. Yes. He is that. And besides the Bach, he has a taste for your kind of modern. Before I went to find you, he was playing Penderecki. I would say he out Penderecki's Penderecki."

"I am not certain Krzysztof would appreciate it."

"Oh he would probably agree and laugh heartily. Then throw one of his prizes at the boy. I thought you would like him, Pawel. And I want you to keep an eye on him. Coax him. Convince him that he would love us."

"I have my own work."

"That is what matters most, I agree. But I think this Robert would be good for you. For you and your work. And for him. I think so. Besides, he is not a student here, not yet anyway. So for now, socialize. I think that too would be good for you. A social life that is."

"Arkady, I do not need…"

Pawel was about to protest, when the door opened and Anna emerged.

"Ah, Anna, a word," says Sienkiewicz with a wry grin at Pawel, and started down the corridor with her. Turned back to Pawel for a final comment.

"I think you do, Pawel. I think he is exactly what you need."

Pawel sighed, shook his head, then reentered the practice room.

Inside, the young man, Robert, sat on a stool, drinking from a glass of water, deep in thought. He looked up when Pawel came in.

"May I?" asked Pawel, pointing to a seat. Robert stared at him, shrugged.

"You seem to have rather entranced some of our staff. I heard some of the Chaconne; you play very well. Impressive."

Robert shrugged again. "Nice enough music. I am not trying to impress. And it is not my sort of choice."

"What is your choice?"

The young man stared at him. Smirked, just slightly.

"You are Weisz."

"Pawel Weisz, yes."

"I thought so. I heard you once."

"Did you?"

"Warsaw Autumn Festival, 1966."

"You are interested in formal modernism then…along with Bach?"

"Interested? I suppose. But your piece did not much move me, Professor. With respect."

"…Well, it did not move a lot of people. With respect or not. I am not certain it even moved me. So, would you care to play something else for me?"

The young man Robert shrugged yet again, picked up his violin in the case on the ground beside him.

"Perhaps something that moves you," says Pawel.

Robert Mandeltort looked at him, hesitated, grinned just slightly, and began. Pawel, motionless, watched, listened, his face serious but without expression. The young man began to play a Rolling Stones song almost as if in jest. Pawel did not move in his seat, just stared at him play. After a few phrases, the young man stopped. Grin oozing with irony.

"No? Perhaps this is more you, Professor…"

He started up again, this time playing from the Beatles.

Pawel shook his head, just slightly, stood to leave.

"You said something that moved me," Robert said, lowering the violin. "Great artists."

"Mr… Mandeltort, yes? Mr. Mandeltort, while I can easily grasp what you think of me, I should let you know I have heard better renditions of 'Paint it Black' from far better musicians. As for the Beatles, you are correct: I have always had a soft spot. And 'Help' is something I most definitely could use at the moment in my work, unlike yours perhaps. I am certain you will do well playing at your University's club. The girls will love you. Good day…"

Pawel started towards the exit.

"I have no time for girls who love me," Pawel heard Robert say, but he did not bother to turn around. As he reached the rehearsal room door, however, he heard the violin start to play again. Pawel hesitated. Listened and hesitated. Then turned and stared. The first notes of the Sibelius 'Violin Concerto' surrounded the room, surrounded the teacher, then took flight, held not by gravity but released into spirit itself. Pawel watched as this young man, Robert, this intense young man with spirit and irony in his face and magic in his finger movements, closed his eyes and got lost somewhere in the music. Pawel sat down again, completely taken in by the beautiful piece, taken in too by the emotive, almost flawless performance. This young man has talent, he thought. Yes. This young man indeed has something…

*

He waited at the trolleybus stop that evening, only to change his mind. When he needed to think, he chose to walk back to his small apartment even when the weather was cold. He did not notice the weather. The walk gave him a chance to reflect, to hear music in his head and find secrets to unlock chord structures and constant shifting layers. But on the walk that January evening he heard only Bach and Sibelius. He considered this Robert Mandeltort: his arrogance, his talent, his rebelliousness. But rebelling against what? Against whom? Pawel tried to focus on his own work in progress. Tried to listen to the two singing country women in his head. But as much as he tried he heard only the Chaconne.

Arkady Sienkiewicz had suggested he was not looking for Pawel to take on the role of educator, mentor. Not at this point. Arkady had said he wanted someone to help the young man to make a decision. To capture him in a way. To reel him in like a beautiful salmon that tries so hard to work its way upstream. Fighting upstream. Risking all. Good for the young man. But good for Pawel too, he had said. Why did Arkady think Pawel needed someone on his own journey, as he had put it? What might be gained in this, this relationship with the talented but raw Robert Mandeltort? Pawel looked for answers in the Warsaw streets he knew so well, he had come to think of as his own but that he knew were not really his own. They were no one's streets, built from the ashes of war. What had Arkady really meant?

He reached his apartment building. Took the stairs up to his rooms. Walked in and made himself a cup of tea. Sat and thought some more. He had asked Robert Mandeltort for a phone number. On behalf of the Music School. They wanted to consider him as an applicant. Did he want to apply?

"I do not know," the young man had said. Pawel heard him even still. His voice even still. "I have not decided."

"Confused?"

"These are confusing times."

"If you give me your phone number we might discuss it."

Robert Mandeltort had looked at him, at Pawel, had cocked his head and smiled. And wrote down his number as well as his address.

"I will give it some thought myself," Pawel had said. "I need to consider too if you are right for us as well as we right for you."

"Of course."

Pawel had nodded. "Oh, Mr. Mandeltort, in passing...I prefer the Rolling Stones to the Beatles."

Pawel turned to leave the room after their short discussion.

"Weisz: a German name?," Mandeltort had called to him as Pawel was half way out. Pawel turned back.

"Prussian. Silesian. Not German. Why?"

The young man looked at him, nodding slowly.

"No reason. Mandeltort is a Jewish name. At least it was for my grandfather. Still is I suppose. Not that it matters."

"No," Pawel had said. "Not that it matters."

Mandeltort had nodded without taking his eyes from Pawel. Pawel then turned and left the rehearsal room.

Now, in the quiet of his apartment, he wondered should he ring this young man, this Robert Mandeltort. But why? What would he say? You are undisciplined. You have talent, raw, unstructured; let us mold you? The teachers you mentioned, from your childhood, your youth: they were good but they could not bring you to the next step, the next level. So let us explore your talent. Let us use your talent. I can use your talent? I can teach you composition to see you fly, in tandem with myself, like two Warsaw swifts in their acrobatics above the streets of Warsaw? I can compose for that talent perhaps? Your violin sings. Let me listen to the song.

The Bach. He heard the Bach. He went over to his collection of LPs, found the Partita transcribed for organ performed by Karl Richter, stared at the cover and put it on his player. He sat down to listen to the music. To lose himself in the music.

He would not telephone this Robert Mandeltort. Tomorrow, perhaps. Not tonight. Not tonight.

Tomorrow.

*

He rang him from his office that following morning. Would he care to meet for a drink? But that evening was not good for Robert Mandeltort. That evening he was to attend the National Theatre.

"To see the play?"

Robert Mandeltort had laughed. "Perhaps," was what he said.

This was all he said. They arranged to meet the following week instead.

Ministry of Interior
Committee for Public Security
SB / Dep 1

PERSON OF INTEREST OPK File Warsaw Mok.75392

Senior Investigating Security Officer: WójcikM Dep1/WC
Mokotów/Wierzbno
Operative Personenkontrolle:
P. Weisz
Current residence: Zawrat 14
- -
7.2.1968

Investigating team first became aware of increased Subject contact with U.Warsaw student agitator, part of so-called Komandosi group, in repeated phone contact with University of Warsaw politics student RM. RM is the only son of Zionist official EM, returned from Soviet Union in 1952 (Second Polish Army in the USSR, laterally transferred to Kazakhstan in 1944) in the Ministry of Light Energy; a file on EM as person of interest already exists in the Ministry of Interior. RM noted attending the Higher State Music School on invitation from teacher Anna Wójcik, not currently under surveillance, after correspondence with RM's former violin teacher now in retirement in Krakow. RM appeared at the school with a document case and violin apparently only for purposes of possible entry recital to the school. The following day our team noted several attempts by Subject to contact RM via home telephone, recorded with analysis through the CLD placed as earlier requested in Subject's Zawrat 14 apartment telephonic equipment. Once contact was established Subject invited RM for 'discussions' at his office that day. RM informed subject of his intention to visit the National Theatre; thus Subject arranged to meet for discussions the following week.

Subject did not make any overt or covert attempt to attend the National Theatre himself, nor had any involvement in the events leading to the student demonstrations on night of 30 January following the final performance of 'Dziady' as per General Government Order that culminated in numerous arrests. Protesting students shouted and held hand painted signage against government policy that closed down the 'Dziady' performance, determined as counter to Poland-Soviet relations given its negative image of Russian historical occupation, *clearly no longer relevant to the present state of mutual respect between our two great Socialist countries. Although RM was not one of those student agitators duly arrested at this protest, it is noted he was photographed participating in student violence on that evening when those attending made illegal threatening speeches at the Mickiewicz Monument during latter stages of their illegal protest. In recorded conversations Subject did not approve of RM's attendance. Subject particularly spoke against the unacceptable violence that occurred at the monument to playwright Mickiewicz, author of the National Theatre's play 'Dziady' (written some 100 hundred years ago it should be pointed out) that the Government had ordered shut down.*

Because of this contact with RM, however, and RM's previously noted affiliations, we have requested from senior Security officer ID that surveillance be increased not only on the group of student agitators reference 'Kommandosi' group that includes RM, but that special OPK purpose surveillance be placed on both RM as well as increased surveillance on his father, the Zionist EM, at the Light Industry Ministry.

Subject has further met with RM both at the Music School and on two further occasions: at the so-called Zodiak Café at the Association of Polish Architects and at the Prasowy Bar Mleczny, said Milk Bar near Lazienki Park in the south of Warsaw not far from the apartment residence of the EM (RM) family apartment. Neither Subject nor RM made any attempt to disguise the discussion or purpose of these encounters. Surveillance team was able to place an officer near enough to Subject at both meetings in order to take notes of conversations, which seemed to focus on certain musical compositions and works by particular composers.

We now expect liaison between our unit and other Security units to maintain observation not only of RM but the 'Kommandosi' group as well, in particular those individuals and groups highlighted by recent communications from Interior Minister and Head of Security General Moczar in his recent memoranda in support of and in relation to the 'Partisans' and other Polish heroic nationalists who have expressed such disquiet with the current agitation and broader concern at potential support within certain elements of government for such.

--MW, Senior Investigating Officer (SISO)

Pawel decided to walk back to his apartment. He then had the idea that perhaps Mandeltort might care to join him. They had met several times already to discuss the possibility of Mandeltort matriculating in the State Music School in the autumn, but Mandeltort remained hesitant. Although he was grateful to his former teacher who had retired to Krakow for making the contact with Anna Wójcik in the first instance, he was not convinced that the Music School was his future. While he admitted loving nothing more than his violin and the music that came from it, Mandeltort's confusion as to his future and to the needs of his family and friends still left him doubtful.

Pawel wanted Robert Mandeltort to join him at the school. And perhaps further. He wanted that violin and the music it might create to somehow belong to him. He could not explain it but the feeling had consumed him since he first heard Mandeltort play. Robert had said he would be at the university cafeteria that afternoon with friends, so Pawel decided to see if he could find the young candidate protégé there.

It did not prove difficult. The politics student cum musician, or musician cum politics student—Pawel could not be certain which at this point—was at a far table in the cafeteria, arguing with a group of friends when Pawel entered. Robert looked over and smiled with that particular irony that he often showed when Pawel approached.

"Maestro," he announced. "Comrades, meet the State Music School's Papal envoy, Pawel Weisz, who is trying to push me into becoming a Penderecki priest instead of the thorn in the side to Gomułka and Moczar and the rest of those apparatchik buffoons."

"Don't forget your father," said one of the young men.

"Zionist Polish puppet of the USSR, thus a better kind of buffoon," smiled Robert. "So, Professor, meet some of my friends: the lovely Daria Wojewoda here is the love of my life, our intellectual standard bearer and our resident beauty queen; Stefan Marcin is our film director par excellence who cares far too much about capitalism to ever be a good Pole and considers himself our own Polish Stanley Kubrick—or is it the good Dr. Strangelove, I cannot remember; Daniel

Maślanka over there is our scribe in word and verse, our top agitating sign provider and also our resident pervert…"

"I thought that was you, Mandeltort," laughed the one called Maślanka.

"Yes, yes, probably all of us," smiled Robert. "And the rest of these misfits… they are not worth introducing. So why are you here, Maestro? Come to join the Kommandosi or are you fishing for my musical talents for a wedding? I would say Bar Mitzvah Klezmer music but not with your German heritage."

The students all start to laugh. Pawel acknowledged their humor with a nod of his head and a shrug of his shoulders.

"I did not mean to interrupt you, Robert. My mistake."

"Not at all, Maestro. I am just leaving these hooligans. Give me a minute. Comrades, I do not think the Professor here is a government spy but you cannot be certain these days. He says he prefers the Stones to the Beatles but I find that suspect. Say goodbye, corrupted studenci."

The others, smiling broadly, nodded at Pawel, who gave a slight wave and waited just outside the building until Robert emerged.

"What did you have in mind, Professor? A coffee or something more sinister?"

"I am walking back to my apartment. Your direction I believe. I thought you might like to join me. I like Warsaw this time of day. Good chance to clear one's head. So I walk."

"…Sure. Why not."

Although the wind was cold, neither man felt the need to hurry through the streets. At first they did not say much to one another. Rather they took in the winter sights and smells of Warsaw as workers rushed around them from offices or places of work to return to their homes. Eventually, as they walked, Pawel tried to explain to Robert why he preferred to walk instead of taking the trolleybus, what he found in the streets, in the passing of cars and buses, in the people rushing on their way. It was a time of day that Pawel had always liked, particularly in winter when the cold and snow on the ground deadened sound in such as way as to isolate the unexpected sights and the sounds consequently produced, like the separation of the different phrases of music for each instrument, inspired not with harmonies but with expressions of atonality and cacophony that created a sort of statement of place, energy, the modern.

It was his music.

Robert listened, smiling occasionally, nodding. And clearly not impressed.

"I understand what you are telling me, Professor. I see it. Hear it, even. I just do not accept it."

"And why is that?," Pawel asked him.

"All this, this Warsaw…it is but artifice. A city built from ruins of the War to look like the city before the War. Its facades, its vision. But it is not the vision of the city. It is the vision of Canaletto, who painted Warsaw as it was in the 18th Century and from his Warsaw rose from the ashes in 1948 or thereabouts. But this is not life, not history. Artifice."

"It is the modern."

"It is interpretation. Art. Same stone, same street names, same design. But the lives are gone. Life itself gone. Art without life."

"I look around the streets here," said Pawel, "and I see plenty of life. Our brave new world. It is as real as Warsaw in 1920 or 1820. It is the Warsaw of today."

"You sound like a mouthpiece for First Secretary Gomułka. Or perhaps Minister Moczar, it is hard to tell these days while they compete against one another for the true heart of Poland."

"What do you mean?"

Mandeltort considered, weighed his words. His smile disappeared.

"You want to create through music an image of Poland that is dynamic, modern. This work you said you are in the process of composing, 'For Twelve Musicians'?"

"'With Memory For Twelve Musicians'"

"Yes. But memory of what? Your memory? The city's? Your setting, a movement in the countryside amongst the peasantry perhaps. Your memories? I do not think so."

"It is about the music. The music speaks to the memory."

"And does it also speak to the emotion? The life? The human?... I am trying to understand: is it that the score you are creating should speak to memory, or memory to the score? I see in Polish politics much the same. Gomułka stood up to

Stalin. Then Stalin dies, there is a thaw in our relationship with the West, Gomułka promises a new face of socialism. But that face? Where is it? Then you have **Moczar and his so-called 'Partisans' now challenging** Gomułka, talking of 'true patriots' as those who remained here to fight the Germans, not those like my father who fought with the Russians and returned to rebuild Warsaw and Poland, but for what? For the façades around us that try to suggest to the rest of the world that the phoenix can rise from ashes? And yet the strife remains. Meat shortages, food price increases, now a sugar shortage. This is our Poland. And meanwhile they struggle one against the other, Gomułka against Moczar, while the workers, the students, the true face of a socialist alliance are nothing to them."

"And you thus presume that what I compose compounds this artificial face of socialism?"

"I simply wonder if this music will come from the heart, the soul, or is but artifice. A pretense at emotion but lacking it. A pretense of who you are. My question is simply: does this work truly reveal you? But we shall see, eh Professor?"

"I prefer Pawel, please."

"…Pawel."

"And tell me, your theatre protests that has caused such chaos…"

"Chaos can be good. In both music and life."

"Perhaps. But I fail to see what you hope to achieve with a protest for the closing of play written a hundred years ago simply because it is anti-Russian in nature."

"It is not that the play is anti-Russian. The Russians kept my family alive, saw my father promoted, enabled our return to Poland, remember? It is a protest against censorship and police brutality. Dejmek, the play's director, he has been dismissed from the theatre. Did you know that? We have to stand up against such actions. Is this wrong?"

"No. The principle, of course not. What is wrong is that it keeps you from music. Your music."

"Mine or yours?"

"You have the possibility, Robert, to be one of the greats one day. Your talent is natural. Raw perhaps. Undisciplined. But certainly natural."

"I had a good teacher in Yashvilli is all. And my mother as well."

"No. More than that and you know it. Your violin is not the gift. You are the gift."

"There are no gifts when we are muzzled. Article 83 in the Constitution guarantees freedom of expression, whether in music or speech or drama. Without that we are lost and the Moczars of the world win."

"Moczar and Gomułka only care about power, not the students. It is their struggle you fight."

"No. It is about the voice we have in the future. Not a revolution, a voice. You know, Pawel, there can be no second movement in your composition without the first. This is the first."

"At least there is music."

"Music as truth, or as artifice? An interesting question, I think. Not just a question of art. A question of politics. Perhaps I am wrong, Professor...Pawel. The question should not perhaps be does the music reveal who you are? Perhaps it is the more fundamental question: who are you?"

*

Pawel spent the weekend hidden away in his apartment, listening to tape recordings, looking over the composition work he had completed on the 'Twelve Musicians' piece. But the more he looked at the entire composition, the more he found he questioned himself. Questioning himself as Robert had questioned him. Perhaps Robert's challenge had been correct: had artifice taken over from truth? Pawel's work could be challenging. Dynamic. Sometimes beautiful. But was it truthful?

He cursed this Robert Mandeltort, this young man who had got under his skin. He cursed that he had to pretend that Robert's own confusion, torn in ways between music and politics, between the fundamentals of art and the inevitability of society's intervention, did not affect his own work. Of course it did. He blamed Robert when he should be blaming himself. He blamed the notes before his eyes. He blamed the country for demanding results over artistry at this point in its history. He blamed everything, everyone, for feeling so at sea.

He could not sleep that Monday night. Could not close his eyes. He lay in the darkness in his small room, staring into that darkness. Seeing notes and phrases and the voices that sang to him but he could not hear them, the patterns repeating as if trying to tell him something but he could not distinguish their meaning. He lay there lost in the cold night, desperate to push forward, the rhythm desperate to count time, defy time, forward, splitting sound, splitting notes and musical phrases and tone and harmony and performers, one becoming three becoming six becoming twelve. Twelve musicians in spring summer autumn winter. Take them together. Take them separately. Move them out of phase, one following the next, one challenging the next until you get—what? Chaos? Chaos can be good, he had said. Robert.

Again, Robert.

Pawel felt haunted. Why should he feel so? Why should this young man make him feel so? Why should the sound of the violin echo as it did in his head, before his eyes, the music? Always back to the music.

And then he knew. Then Pawel knew where it must take him and why. Then finally he heard what he had been wanting to hear, what he had needed to hear.

The following morning he returned to his office at the School of Music. He was to give two classes that week. He cancelled the first, claiming ill health, and convinced a colleague to take the second. Pawel locked himself away in his office and began to work, listening again to all the recorded song he had kept, but reviewing all of his earlier work as well, a short life-time of composition, making notations, putting down ideas' and diagrams, arrows leading to a centre. He assigned himself a practice room and spent hours working on compositions for the piano, then transcribing them for other instruments, for voice. He stopped going out except to move from practice room to office and office to practice room. Recording. Listening. Transcribing. Composing.

He could not return home that night, or the next. It was as if a fever had overtaken him. He lost track of time. He worked hour after hour. When he was not at the piano he sat in his office staring at sheets of music, or listening to the reel to reel recordings he had made. He worked in the library examining scores of masters: Bach of course, but also High Church Music, Western avant-garde,

Brahms, Stravinsky, then to find attachment in space, the Rolling Stones, then Jazz. He soaked up Jazz, spending hours listening to Miles Davis in the library. Then Chopin too. The beloved Chopin, late at night. Like Davis's jazz, speaking from the soul, late at night. Listen, he told himself. Understand, he muttered. Feel, he demanded.

Feel.

Robert. Damn Robert.

At night when the corridors were empty he unlocked the key to the practice room, his practice room, and sat at the piano, playing, listening, composing. Over and over and over still. The pianos in the school were of far better quality than the keyboard he had in his small apartment. He needed to hear the sound fully, rounded, the strings echoing their notes as if alive. They had become alive.

Late at night he would go to his office to eat something and sleep, when he slept, on the floor. But for hours he sat first at that piano, weighing each note to see if it held him down, or allowed him to fly. He sought only flight.

He worked this way for days. Composing. Recording. Throwing out. Rerecording. Sleeping. Starting over. Listening. Listening was key. In the key of G. Key.

Late one night he awoke in a haze to find Arkady standing over him, staring.

"Pawel, you are going mad."

"No. I am working."

"Same thing. The students are grumbling. Your fellow teachers want you sent to an asylum. And I, I want you to eat something. And to sleep in warmth."

Arkady left the office and returned a few minutes later with a bottle of vodka, some bread and jam and a blanket from his own office.

"I used to do the same thing but that was to escape my wife. It was always cold. So you need to stay warm and get drunk. Then eat. Tomorrow my wife will make you some bigos and I will bring it to you. And pierogi. Then you can use the vodka to wash it down. And for goodness sake do not let any students see you here. We have enough problems."

Another night passed, and another. A long week passing. Pawel finished the Movement 'Spring' as a companion to 'Summer', one counterpoint to the other.

He worked into 'Autumn' while shivering at night in his office and spending hour after hour at the piano. His wrist grew tired as he wrote phrase upon phrase, command upon command first for one instrument, then transcribing for the next, then for the voice, then the composition for another of the twelve musicians, and yet another. Music surrounded him. Inhabited him. Haunted him. He closed his eyes for 'Autumn' to see the leaves begin to fall and the women sing of the harvest and the children grow weary even as the days grew short. He saw the coal miners of Upper Silesia with their deep bass tones and full bar rests suddenly elevate into powerful A notes. He heard the shipyard workers in Gdansk with their strong arms and baritone beliefs. He heard the scythes in the wheat fields in the South, their labor in alto harmonies, rhythmically cutting in the old way before the mechanical machines arrived to change their lives. He heard the families picking hops in the East, the mothers lullabying their infants at their breasts in soft mezzo soprano while the older children loaded the hops onto trailers behind tractors that their fathers drove, singing in harmony as one. The notes. The songs. Broken apart into separate elements, separate phrases and note lines, then rearranged, transcribed for one instrument, counterpoint composition for another. The voices calling out in song and adulation of a sort. Music. Everywhere music.

Then it was time to explore 'Winter', to look at death, so necessary so that life could be reborn. And for the first time in a long time Pawel heard melody, quiet melody. He felt appoggiaturas in his gut and knew he now had to rest the notes even as he had to rest his soul and longing, here, to hesitate then find a new voice, the next note demanding attention, there, now find the C but fall to that B^b in the third bar, why not, and a half step only to A. To A, blessed A, in the higher octave, higher still. He heard life. He heard death. He heard his mother. He heard his birth.

Pawel knew where he was headed. And he knew why.

And he knew that this is what Robert had done to him, for him. He did not know why Robert, only Robert, but he knew it was so.

And it was the music.

The music took over his life. And spoke to him, finally. And spoke to him loudly, lovingly, taking him away.

*

"It is still very raw."

"I understand."

"It is not ready but it is the direction that matters."

"I understand, Pawel."

Arkady Sienkiewicz stood in Pawel's office, holding up one sheet of music, another. He furrowed his brow, listening to the notes in his head. Taking them in. Looking at repeating themes and meaning. Hearing the music. Arkady grunted. Went back to the page before, then to the next. Shook his head, just slightly, whether with approval or disapproval Pawel could not tell. When he got to the pages of the fourth movement, to the 'Winter' section, Arkady said nothing. Instead he stared intently at one page, another. Finally he dropped this page before his eye line to look over the top at his onetime protégé.

"Hm...Truthfully, I do not know if this is a step forward for you or a step back. You used to disdain of melody. But here... And yet you bring melody to minimalism, and minimalism to melody. Interesting."

"Bad?"

"No. Different. For you. But good I think. Not bad. Not revolutionary, but alive. That matters. Yes, I think it does."

Pawel said nothing. He looked down at the floor, considering what his friend was trying to say.

"Come."

Pawel looked up. "What?"

"Come with me. Come."

Arkady turned and walked out of the room. Pawel hesitated, then jumped up from his chair and followed. Arkady walked down the stairs and along the corridor without looking back at Pawel, following, then stopped at a practice room. He unlocked the door and Pawel followed him in.

Arkady sat at the piano and placed the music in front of him, the music of the final movement. He stared at it and began to play. Slowly. Staring at the sound surrounding him, floating on the air, the notes around him. Repeating where he was meant to repeat. Hesitating, then playing further. He stopped at a few points along the way.

"I would hold the A note here longer. A beat longer. I see your appoggiatura notation; good. But you need greater emphasis. And there, I think that needs greater clarity."

He went through the score for the 'Winter' movement, working it. Playing it. Sometimes stopping, repeating. Considering. When he had worked through the primary melodic lines, he stopped after the first expansive repetition.

"How do you see it? This movement? The most unsure. And also in its way the most melodic. Beautiful, even," Arkady wondered, staring at the sheet composition.

"This last part of the movement, from there… I want to transcribe it only for violin. The violin takes over. It reaches inside of us. I can use the whole range of the instrument. The other instruments, the voice, they all speak to one another. But here, this speaks to us. To us only. That G, there, an open note, and the A and D too. They give us earth, in contrast to the earth of voices. They become the voice. The people. Dying in winter, reborn for spring. The people dying but never dying because they cry out to live, to survive. Humanity."

"You have become a humanist?"

"I see the conflict. Artifice and emotional truth. Here they combine, from the death of winter in this movement to the very possibility of rebirth in spring. Twelve musicians at first discordant, searching, until harmony is reborn from the death of music itself."

"So violin."

"Violin."

"Hm… You know, Pawel, the Prague Conservatoire concert for August has been given the go-ahead on their end."

"Yes."

"You will be ready to take this work?"

"I think so."

"And the violin: does that have to do with Mandeltort?"

"I think he could bring something special to the work."

"He has not agreed to enroll in the Music School. Not yet anyway. Has he agreed to participate in your piece?"

"I have not discussed it with him. It is just a thought I had."

Sienkiewicz grunted again. Smiled. Shook his head. Considered.

"You are stretching yourself, Pawel. Seeking something. That is a good thing. If it is ready, I would recommend trying it out in Prague, assuming the Ministry approves the cultural exchange. And yes, I agree Mandeltort would make it special. Possibly more than you, my friend, although this movement certainly has something—traditional, and yet modern. It will raise eyebrows. I am not entirely convinced, but neither do I think it an incorrect step. I have to give you one warning, however: Mandeltort is that warning. Things are happening over at the University of Warsaw. Murmurs of discontent in the government. Students. Politics. We here in the Music School, we are Culture. The Government wants Culture. As long as we focus on our art they will likely leave us alone. Particularly the musicians, with our heritage. I am not convinced that will be so at the University. It is not the students they fear, our ministers, they fear one another. For some anyway, they despise where others come from, who they are, what they are. So many returned to Poland who had not remained in Poland to fight during the War. They fought from afar, not from within, and many despise them. Consider them false Poles. Particularly since the Arab-Israeli War last year. The Jews. Always the Jews for them. Are they anti-Semitic? Some are. For many however it is simply an excuse, but a convenient excuse. The rumblings are getting louder. You in your office, perhaps you have not noticed. I have. Others have."

"The students may find themselves in the cross fire," he went on. "I want Robert Mandeltort to enroll here at the School. In his violin I hear Culture. I hear music. The most beautiful music. But you must warn your Mandeltort to keep away from trouble. I know where his family come from. And I know there will be some who want to see him and those like him fail."

Pawel nodded. He not only heard the warning, he agreed with it.

"When you came to us all those years ago, talented but without focus, I thought then you would make something special of yourself, my friend. You have always tried to do so in your work. But you have lacked voice. Your own voice. I think perhaps now you are beginning to find it. Perhaps you owe it to that boy. Perhaps though you owe it to your own awakening self-awareness. Whatever pushes you

250

forward, I look forward to seeing where it takes you."

It was snowing and dark when Pawel later emerged from the Music School to return home. He chose not to walk back to his apartment. Too tired. He only had to wait for a few minutes before a Trolleybus came along. He easily found a seat near the rear. He sat quietly watching the buildings pass by. He could feel his eyes heavy with tiredness. They closed for a few moments and he felt his head heavy with fatigue drop once or twice, until the trolley stopped with a bit of a jolt to let on others.

Pawel opened his eyes and noticed a young woman sitting opposite, smiling at him. He acknowledged her with a nod, then looked out the window, when she spoke to him.

"Long day?"

"Yes. Long few days. I guess it has caught up with me."

She was quiet for a moment, then continued.

"You do not remember me."

He looked at her, tried to place her, but could not.

"I am sorry…"

"I was with Robert and the others, the cafeteria."

"Of course, um…"

"Daria. Daria Wojewoda."

"Miss Wojewoda, yes. My apologies. The tiredness has made my mind a bit flat."

She shook her head, smiled.

"He called you the Professor. Robert. You teach at the Music School?"

"Hardly a professor."

"Robert spoke to me about your work. He said you are a talented composer. Very new wave, he said."

"That I do not know… Your Robert is the one who is talented. He is a wonderful violinist."

"You want to see him enter the Music School?"

"He could go very far. When he wishes he plays with great beauty."

"I have told him that. But Robert… He listens to everyone, listens to no one. I do love him though."

"Oh, are you…?"

"What, together? Lovers?" The girl Daria laughed. "Hardly. Confidante maybe. Lover?" She laughed again. "I have known him since we were both small. Our fathers returned from the USSR to Poland at the same time. They both fought for the Russians during the War. His father went into the Ministry when he returned. Mine, a doctor. They both had dreams of rebuilding Warsaw. A just, new city. Robert and I, we are almost brother and sister."

"I see."

"He has spoken of you to me several times. He says you talk only of music. He says music is your life."

"I suppose it is. It could be his."

"Your parents as well?"

"…No. They died. The war."

"I am sorry. They would no doubt have been proud. Robert's parents encourage him. He does not always listen to them either. Right now, he wants many things. To rebel, to play his violin, to see Socialism as his father sees it, to reject Socialism as his father sees it. Robert calls for something human and with possibility. He wants to challenge the world. To believe… He thinks he is right."

"Perhaps he is, I cannot know."

"He is a child. My little brother, I call him. But a well meaning boy who, yes, plays beautiful music when he wishes."

"Along with Rolling Stones anthems."

She laughed.

"There is this."

Pawel started to stand. "My stop," he said.

"Mine too," she said, standing as well. Pawel followed her out of the trolleybus.

"Cold," she said, pulling her collar around her, as they started to walk.

"Warsaw in February."

"Um…Until the thaw. Of every kind. I go this way."

"And I that."

"Saturday, I am having a party at our apartment. My parents are away. You should come, Professor."

She tore a piece of paper from her notebook, wrote down an address and telephone number, handed it to him.

"Do come," she said. "Robert will be there. We can educate you, Professor. See how the studenci politicize. And party, not like Gomułka and his kind of Party. We will make you one of us."

"I do hope not, Daria. I prefer the turmoil of music to the chaos of politicians, of any sort."

"Come anyway, Professor Pawel Weisz. Robert would like that. He has told me. So would I."

She smiled again, nodded, turned and walked away.

*

He saw a few faces he knew; most he did not. All were young, or seemed young to him. All certainly seemed in high spirits.

The door was open when he got there. Several students were sitting out in the stairway. Daria saw him as he walked in and greeted him with a large smile.

"Here you can be Pawel. I will leave the professor at the door. I am happy you decided to join us. Robert will be pleased. He is in the other room."

Daria introduced him to many of the people sitting around, talking. She referred to him as a composer who teaches at the State Music School; she said happily he was neither a politician nor an activist for a change.

They worked their way into the larger sitting room. Pawel saw Robert in a corner, laughing and talking with several others.

"Professor! Daria said you would come tonight. We are blessed," Robert exclaimed with a wide grin.

"Apologies, Pawel, I did try. I will get you a drink."

Before Pawel could say anything she disappeared.

"Here, sit here. Move over, Mirek."

Space was made for Pawel on a sofa. Pawel sat, smiled. Daria reappeared with a large glass of vodka.

"To your health, Pawel."

Several raised their glasses. They had clearly been drinking for a while. Several, including perhaps Robert, were slightly drunk and showed it.

"We were talking about the meeting at the Polish Writers Union a couple days ago. Do you know about this?" Robert asked.

"No," answered Pawel.

"Wonderful. Four hundred writers in the room all condemned the government for banning 'Dziady' and dismissing Dejmek from the National Theatre. The writers are on the side of the students, and so they should be. Na Zdrowie!"

Several raised their glasses with Robert, savoring the moment—whether the moment of the vodka or the Polish Writers Union, Pawel was not entirely certain.

"It was magnificent," said a young woman nearby. "The writers blamed Minister Moczar and his Partisans supporters for trying to take away our guaranteed free speech."

"Moczar, the others, they are all anti-Semites. They blame everything on Jews," said the young man Mirek.

"Anyone who is not a Partisan these days is a 'Muscovite'. I guess that makes us Muscovites. I have never been to Moscow. In fact I do not think I have ever been out of Warsaw," said yet another student. All those around him were laughing.

"I love what Stefan Kisielewski said in his speech to the other writers about the government's censorship. He called them a dictatorship of dimwits. Now everyone in Warsaw is calling them that. Gomułka will be vomiting his barszcz." Pawel remembered this young man as Daniel Maślanka, also from the cafeteria, who was the group's 'writer'.

"And what do you think, Professor?," asked Robert.

"I think the government will not be happy. And will not back down."

"More than four thousand people signed the student's petition that our representative Irena Lasota delivered to the government. They will hear our voices and they will witness our protests," said the woman student.

"They will hear," said Pawel. "But hearing and listening are two different things."

"Then we will make them listen," said Robert. "And after, we will make music. And drink vodka! Perhaps Pawel Weisz here will compose our anthem."

"And you will play it, Robert," said Daria, who had reappeared, "instead of us having to listen to you drone on and on about Moczar this and Gomułka that."

"Alas, it comes from being a Muscovite and one of the terrible Jewish intellectuals they are so afraid of. Na Zdrowie!" Robert downed his vodka, as did others.

"Come on, Pawel, I will rescue you now. These hooligans talk too much politics. What we need is music, music and art," said Daria

"Daria is right. Give us music. Come on, Robert," Mirek shouted.

"Later. Later," he said.

Daria pulled Pawel up from the sofa. He followed her into the small kitchen. Other students nodded at him.

"Daria?," came a call to her from the other room.

"I will be right back," Daria sighed to Pawel. "Get some more to drink."

Pawel smiled. The girl disappeared. Pawel poured himself a very small glass of drink.

"I know your work," Pawel heard behind him and turned. He recognized the student Stefan Marcin, the young man who dreamt of becoming a film director, Robert had said. "I have heard it performed at the Music School. Very interesting compositions, Weisz."

"Thank you. I apologize that I cannot say that I have had the opportunity to see your work."

"In time, in time. Everything is new, Professor. Are you interested in music for cinema?"

"I cannot say I have given it much thought."

"You should. Soon cinema will be our greatest art form."

"I do not know if Bach and Beethoven would agree."

"Well, within reason then. The art form of our Century."

"Perhaps."

"Have you seen Antonioni's 'Blow Up'?"

"Alas, I have not."

"You should go to see it. Pure genius. A question of reality, of what one sees, hears, doesn't. The American jazz musician Herbie Hancock did the score.

Excellent."

"Interesting."

"I hope to shoot my first feature film next year when I complete my studies at the university. Your work would perhaps add something interesting to it, I think. Like Godard's work with Solal in 'Breathless'. Your work too has elements of jazz about it I believe."

"Elements, yes."

"Another great art form, jazz. We should talk some time. Here…"

Marcin took out a pen, found some paper, wrote down a phone number.

"You never know where art can take you, whether concert halls or cinema halls."

Pawel raised his glass to Marcin. As he did, he heard music beginning from the other room. The first notes Pawel thought were from a phonograph, but he quickly realized it was not a recording. The sound of a violin could only mean one thing.

Pawel wandered into the other room. Others had wandered in as well and sat wherever they could find room.

Robert had taken out his violin. He had played a few notes. Stopped.

"Come on, Robert. Play us a little tune. One of your favorites," said a voice sitting in a far corner.

"Go on, Robert," someone else said.

"Yes Robert my lovely, play for us," said Daria.

Robert laughed. Shrugged. He thought for a moment. He looked straight at Pawel, standing at the entrance to the small kitchen. Stared at him. Smiled. Drew his bow… and began.

After the first few notes, Pawel recognized what Robert was playing. Chopin's 'Nocturne in C Sharp Minor," Pawel knew, was one of the most beautiful of the Nocturnes. Robert played the slow, sad introductory first movement with a depth of feeling that Pawel could only think of as extraordinary. Immediately the apartment went completely quiet. When he played the second section of the piece, Robert played as if no one was in the room, as if he could see beyond, into the heart of Warsaw. Into his own heart. Yearning. Reaching. The notes from the violin touching the very souls of his young audience there. And by the time Robert came to the delicatissmo of the C♯ major note at the end, it seemed as if breathing had stopped in the room. Everyone stared at him, especially Pawel. Robert looked around the room, smiled ironically.

"Well," he said, "that was one way to shut you all up. But in honor of my friend Professor Weisz, some levity. For you, Maestro!"

Robert placed the bow against the strings, and began again. As soon as he drew his bow across the instrument, everyone recognized what he was playing. And everyone began to sing, drunkenly, the Beatles 'Yellow Submarine."

Everyone but Pawel. He stared at Robert, shook his head, walked back into the kitchen, left his now untouched glass of vodka and walked out of the apartment, the voices singing loudly behind him.

Pawel walked down the three flights of stairs. As he got to the bottom, he heard someone following. Ignoring this, he let himself out of the front door into the night. Snow was falling.

Just as the door started to close behind him it was thrown open and Robert emerged, panting.

"Come on, Professor. Don't leave us now. Look, don't go."

Robert grabbed his arm. Pawel turned angrily.

"What do you think you are doing, Robert? Do you do this for my sake? For your friends?"

"It was a joke."

"No. Music is not a joke. Chopin is not a joke. You, you are the joke."

"Oh Professor…"

"Do not call me that. I am no one's professor."

"Pawel, look, I am sorry."

"Your Chopin…No one I know can better that. No one. And you know that to be true. But then you…you decide to destroy it? To destroy beauty? Your beauty?"

"I thought you might see the humor."

"There is no humor. There is only the waste of your talent."

"Pawel…"

"No. No. I have spent weeks exploring my imagination for my new composition and I finally thought I discovered a fourth movement to this strange and wonderful piece. You know what it is? A violin solo. Something—rich, embracing. Challenging. You know why? For you to perform with us when we go to Prague. Music. Rich, dynamic music that is human and asks the questions we dream of asking in our heads and our hearts. And you could ask such a question because you bring something to music. But then you throw it away."

Pawel turned away. As he did, Robert grabbed his arm and pulled him back. Pawel turned towards him to vent his anger. Robert hesitated, then grabbed Pawel's shoulders.

And kissed him.

Pawel was shocked. He jerked away. Stared at Robert. Stared, speechless.

"Pawel…"

"You are drunk."

"Of course. We are all drunk." Robert reached for him again. As he did, Pawel pushed him away, hard, and took a step back.

"No!"

"Pawel, please."

"I am not like that."

"Are you not? Are you really not like that?" Robert seemed to fluctuate between anger and laughter. He reached for Pawel again.

"No."

"You are hiding Pawel. From me or yourself? Look at yourself. I know what I see. Who I see. Who do you see?"

Pawel stared at him. Shook his head back and forth. Turned and marched away.

"Pawel, wait. Pawel…" Robert started after, slipped and fell on the walk. Laughed. "Pawel…"

Pawel did not stop. He marched into the night. He did not turn around.

*

When he returned to his apartment, Pawel did not turn on the lights. He took off his boots. Lay down onto his bed fully clothed. Lay quietly. He felt broken. So he told himself. In truth he did not know what he felt.

Mar-Apr 1968

Ministry of Interior
Committee for Public Security
SB / Dep 1

PERSON OF INTEREST OPK File Warsaw Mok.75392

Senior Investigating Security Officer: WójcikM Dep1/WC
                                        Mokotów/Wierzbno
Operative Personenkontrolle:
P. Weisz
Current residence: Zawrat 14
- -

4.3.1968

CONFIDENTIAL/HIGH PRIORITY

See attached photograph Subject outside of apartment building Dr. WW, father of student agitator/further subject DW, evening of 2.3.1968,

-MW, Senior Investigating Officer (SISO)

*

Daily report yesterday filed has detailed the events of Saturday, 2.3.1968, with regards to the Subject's attendance at social gathering residential apartment Dr.WW, not in occupancy on this occasion but hosted by daughter/subject MW; said gathering primarily U. Warsaw students, many noted with affiliation to the 'Komandosi' group previously referred for surveillance.

This follows on from File submission note/photograph submitted by my unit attached to this report, photo of 2.3.1968.

Although my own team was unable to provide direct surveillance, through citizen informant providing appropriate information to one of our fellow investigating teams we have been able to receive detailed commentary on the gathering; his report attached herewith.

Subject departed the gathering well before any of those present. Team member DB had been delegated surveillance operative for the evening outside the building in which the gathering had taken place. Subject emerged from building followed immediately by previously noted Komandosi member RM. What transpired next please see file attached photograph. To date team has found no evidence of any personal involvements on the part of Subject. Although from record he is 29 years of age, perhaps surprisingly he has formed no sexual or romantic liaison to knowledge, at least not that has been observed or recorded.

RM has been noted from other surveillance to have engaged in certain homosexual acts in breach of the present law, evidence of which is held on file.

Upon emerging from the MW apartment building, RM followed the subject out and embraced him. Surveillance revealed likely intoxication on part of RM. It should be said that Subject seemed much taken aback by the actions of RM and indeed both argued against and rejected such advancement.

However at this time surveillance can neither confirm nor deny Subject's sexual proclivities. We therefore place the photograph on file for further evaluation.

Finally in the matter of subject RM: informant noted that RM is able to command great attention and respect from his fellow students by means of his musical talent. As informant notes in his report, RM's unprepared musical interlude at the social gathering resulted in surprisingly silent respect and even adulation. This could in time become a more significant threat than that demonstrated from some of his colleagues.

Given RM's political opinions and given the student protest now planned for 8.3.1968 as per notices placed throughout Warsaw, seeking support of common workers for such event, it is highly recommended that RM surveillance continue and that the attached photo be placed in his file for potential prosecution, should his anti-government views and his Zionist Muscovite background threaten the policies and stability of our Socialist nation.

-MW, Senior Investigating Officer (SISO)

*

Pawel was surprised to see police directing truckloads of Civilian Reserve Militia to side streets. He should not have been surprised. He knew that the University of Warsaw students had planned a protest in front of the library later in the day. They had put up posters and notices all over Warsaw about their protest. These ORMO militia in concert with police did not bode well.

He had avoided Robert. Decided that the young violinist had simply been drunk, had been goading him. He would say nothing further of what had transpired or how it had confused him. But now he was concerned.

Pawel decided to make his way to the University, hoping he might find Robert despite what had happened, might warn him to keep away from any protest.

Much of the University had closed down, however, including the cafeteria room where he had encountered Robert and others before. Pawel saw a group of students with placards, including the boy Mirek who had been at Daria's apartment. He hurried over to him, asked him if he had any idea where Robert might be.

"They are meeting at the old Hybrydy Club downstairs. Do you know it?," Mirek said in response. "Hey, Composer, are you going to join our protest?"

Pawel did not answer, but turned and hurried away. It took about twenty minutes to walk to Mokotowska Street, to the old tenement that had been the popular haunt for avant garde artists, musicians and filmmakers, then eventually student dissident voices for a decade. Over the previous year it had fallen into indifference and disrepair after the original organizers renounced Hybrydy involvement. When Pawel got there possibly two hundred students were milling about, preparing signs, laughing and starting to head to the University.

Pawel pushed his way into the crowded room downstairs. Standing on a table shouting slogans and instructions a student energized the crowd. Young people applauded, cheered. There were shouts of 'down with censorship' and 'we want Mickiewicz', although the playwright of *Dziady* had been dead for over a hundred years. The student on the table was shouting 'Down with Gomułka, Down with Moczar'.

On the far side of the room Pawel spotted Robert, laughing with some of his friends. Robert saw him as he approached.

"Professor! Are you going to come protest with us?"

Pawel pointed to the student on the desk.

"With him leading you? You think the government will listen to his slogans and shouts?"

"I do not know who he is, but if he leads of course we will follow. You know the government has removed Adam Michnik and Henryk Szlajfer from the University? Other students too. Daria has been told her bursary is terminated. Daniel Maślanka is also forbidden to return. They target the Komandosi. I will no doubt learn the same. We cannot allow this, Pawel."

"And you think you will change things with your protest?"

"The workers will join us. We are not seeking revolution, just a human face for our dreams of just socialism. That is what we seek. That is what we will get."

"They are bringing in Citizen Militia reserves to greet you. Do you really think they are going to join your protest, Robert?"

"Of course. Why not?"

"Don't be a naïve fool. They are not here to support you. You will find yourselves abandoned."

"No. You are wrong."

"Listen to me, Robert. You are a musician. You have a brilliant future ahead with your violin. These protests risk throwing all that away."

"And you think music will bring joy to the human face we are asking for, will bring freedom to speak out? They banned 'Dziady'? What next? Mozart? Bach? You?"

"I am asking you, Robert, do not do this."

Robert looked at him, smiled, shook his head and shrugged.

"I am sorry, Professor. Right now my beloved violin must be silent. Tomorrow maybe it will be free to sing as it needs to sing."

Pawel stared at him, at the others ignoring him. He knew his words were in vain. The student on the table was shouting again, then started to lead those in the room in the 'Marseillaise'.

Pawel turned and walked out.

He walked up to the Music School. The administration had abandoned classes for the day, anticipating potential disturbances. Pawel went up to his office. Sat quietly. Shook his head in dismay. After a while he took out the 'Twelve Musicians' composition. Tried to concentrate. He stared at the fourth movement, the 'Winter' movement, at the violin solo he had heard so movingly and loudly in his imagination. He thought about Robert, about the magic in his hands when he played. He thought about life through music and music through life. He thought about what it meant to be young, to have dreams, to want the world. He felt old. Thirty felt old. He felt on the wrong side of history, the wrong side of desire. He wondered if perhaps the young violinist could be right and he, Pawel, wrong. About so much. About art and music and life. And love. He wondered.

And he did not know what to do.

Pawel had to try once more. He would go to the university. Take Robert away. He had to try. He stood and hurried from the office. He met Arkady in the corridor.

"Pawel? Are you all right?"

"I thought I would see…I thought…"

"We kept our students away. We cannot afford problems today. Let those at the university have their protest. We can support them from afar but this is not our fight."

"Is it not?"

"We can fight with our music, Pawel. We can protest in song and harmony and pushing authority in our own way."

"Do I tell that to Robert Mandeltort?"

"He puts his career at risk. Is that what you want to do as well?"

"I do not know what I want, Arkady. Truly."

Arkady Sienkiewicz, his friend, looked at him long and hard.

"You need to be careful, Pawel. You have much ahead of you in your career. Here in Poland. Other places as well. It is a very great risk."

Pawel looked at his mentor. Nodded. He took in his message. But he knew he had to try to find Robert, stop him, watch out for him.

He walked quickly to the University of Warsaw buildings. A large group of a few hundred students in front of the library building had gathered, shouting slogans and singing. Pawel pushed through, trying to find Robert. He finally saw him near the steps, where amongst others shouting into loud hailers the same student who had stood on the table leading slogans at the Hybrydy seemed to push students to shout even louder, egging them on with protests and chants.

Pawel looked over towards a side street entrance to the courtyard. Police had appeared and marched towards the gathered crowd. Good humor became pushing and shoving. More shouts.

He had to get to Robert. He could not get through.

Some were pulled away by the police towards waiting vans. Cries and shouts. Pawel looked around. Pushed here and there in the melee. Everything had become fluid. Robert had disappeared. All around, much noise, shouting.

That is when several vans and trucks of helmeted ORMO militia raced into the library courtyard. The militia jumped down, their batons out. No one moved. Everything stood still, frozen in surprise, a moment of complete uncertainty. But Pawel knew. Hundreds of militia. He knew.

Where was Robert?

The student who had stood on the tables at the Hybrydy Club was the first to be taken. Four police grabbed him and pushed him towards a police van. At the same time militia in uniform rushed the students, swinging their batons, lashing out with their fists. Young people began to run in every direction. Many fell, blood pouring down their faces. Even on the ground the Militia continued their assault, kicking, slamming their batons down, screaming. The Militia and Police grabbed other young people and pulled them towards waiting security vans. Everywhere, chaos. From all direction, violence. Blood. Screams of pain. Broken faces. Broken bones. Madness.

Pawel was pushed down. He rolled onto his back and saw a face swearing at him, baton raised, cursing him. He waited for the blow, when the man standing above him was knocked aside and away by others rushing past. Chaos everywhere. Pawel closed his eyes, opened them, the assailant was gone. He got to his knees, caught his breath. Nearby he saw a young girl on the ground, blood pouring from a wound on her head, screaming in pain. Pawel stood, confused, but managed to run over to her and pull her up.

"Come on," he shouted. "Come!"

Students were running in every direction. Everywhere beatings without mercy. Pawel followed two students into an apartment building. Supporting the girl, seeing she was in great pain, realizing she might pass out, he held her tight, stumbling through the building entryway. Inside the building some of the students were crouching behind the door, terrified. An interior apartment door on the ground floor opened and a middle aged woman gestured that they should hurry in.

"Here. Come," said the woman and led them into a bathroom. She found alcohol to clean the girl's scalp. She and Pawel put on a bandage.

"She will be all right," said the woman. "Here, come, lie down in here. It is not deep this wound. No more bleeding. Lie down."

The woman led the tearful young woman into the bedroom, where she lay down. She looked up at Pawel.

"Thank you," she whispered, afraid.

"You will be all right. Rest."

Pawel went back into the apartment front room. The students who had run in with him sat on the floor, backs against the walls, looking defeated, terrified.

The woman whose apartment it was entered. "Terrible," was all she said. "Terrible."

Pawel remained with them twenty minutes or so before he left the apartment. Outside the building there was no one. Papers fluttered across the road. Placards lay on the ground stained with blood and footprints. From somewhere he heard crying. Further away someone screamed. Uncertain, Pawel turned away from the university, heading back to the Music School.

Crossing over Mikołaja Kopernika Street, Pawel saw many of the police vans parked, the security police milling around and laughing. He put his head down, walked quickly by without looking at them. Several police stared at him, but said nothing. As he passed, he turned his head and stopped in surprise. Leaning against the back of one of the vans, smoking and laughing with several police, he saw the student who had so provoked those at the Hybrydy, then stood on the steps of the library shouting slogans. Pawel only glanced at him, then kept walking. He understood... and he kept walking.

He returned to the Music School. Heard no one. Saw no one. Wanted to see no one. He went up to his office. Sat there, put his head in his hands.

"Pawel?"

Standing in the doorway, staring at him, his eye already partially closed with bruises in black and yellow, a cut on his cheek, stood Robert Mandeltort. His face was streaked with blood and dirt and tears.

"I did not know where else to go."

"My God," said Pawel as he jumped up. "I went to find you. I saw. What they did, they..."

"It does not matter."

"Does not matter?"

"You were right, Pawel. They came to fight. But they cannot fight us all. They cannot fight us forever."

"Don't be a fool."

"If that is foolish so it should be."

"Heads beaten? Young women terrified, blood streaming down their faces?... How can you be so naïve?"

"I am naïve? I am the one?"

"You think you will get what you want? That student, shouting to you in that Hybrydy this morning, shouting at you all to protest at the library: you said you did not know him. I saw him, yes? They took him away, but to be arrested? Then why did I see him standing with other police and militia later, smoking, laughing? Laughing at what, Robert?"

"Not so."

"Not so? They are using you. You and the others. You are pawns in the government's power game, no more. Your blood is not their blood. You are doing exactly what they want. And you are expendable."

"No, Pawel."

"Your blood for what? To say what you want? This is their game, not yours. Music is your voice."

"It does not matter who he was. It does not matter either what you think. Tomorrow thousands will march with us. You will see. And they will listen. And shout. That is what the government fears. What they will hear. They will acknowledge the law, the constitution, our right to speak. That is the music we need. You too, composer, professor, you too need to speak up. We can speak up together. Both of us."

Pawel shook his head. He did not know what to say to him. He did not want this young man hurt. This Robert he stared at, hurt. He looked at the cut on his face, at his eye.

"Wait here," Pawel said. "I will get a cloth."

Pawel hurried to a bathroom where he wet a cloth with some hot water, then returned to his office. Again saw no one else around. Closed the door behind him. He did not need questions.

Robert stood at Pawel's desk, looking down at the musical score laid out.

"This is what you composed? For violin? This movement is for your new work?"

Pawel hesitated. "Yes," he then said. "It is not finished. Here."

Pawel handed Robert the warm towel. Robert looked at it as if he did not understand and did not care, instead turned back to the music.

"This is..." He went silent. He seemed to play the music in his head.

"Robert..."

Robert held up his hand, silencing Pawel, while he read the notes. And heard the music in his head. And saw the music in his mind, his violin bow weaving the notes into a pattern of wonder before his eyes. In silence the music played. His violin played.

"It is beautiful, this. It is..." Robert shook his head slightly. Looked at Pawel.

"Your protest will get you nowhere, Robert. This, this is what you are. This." Pawel pointed to the score. Robert stared at him, saying nothing.

"Here," then said Pawel. He took the cloth from Robert, used it to stroke the wound on his face. Robert did not take his eyes from him. Barely could breathe.

And he took Pawel's hand even as the composer wiped away the blood and marks of tears and the pain.

And he kissed it. And looked at Pawel. And Pawel, uncertain, his head shaking back and forth, just slightly, his hand shaking, just slightly, said nothing, stepped back, just slightly, looked at this young Robert, this musician who explored the depths of emotion with such generosity and love. Then Pawel reached up and touched Robert's cheek, touched the cut, lightly. Tenderly. And Pawel leaned forward, just slightly and closed his eyes and brushed his lips against Robert's, and with his eyes closed he opened his mouth and touched Robert's mouth, his tongue to Robert's tongue, and brought him towards him, and held him.

And with his arms around his shoulders held him.

His hands on Robert's back. His fingers on his skin. His touch. His sweat. His warmth. Guided then. Led. His love. The pain. His sex. His heat. His body and soul. Pawel cried out. Need. Pain. Fear. He did not understand. He closed his eyes and did not understand and could not stop himself.

And all the while the music, there, playing, embracing. He heard the music. The music he heard Robert play now, then, forever. The music in his head. Winter. Death. Becoming spring. Life. Melody restored. Harmony allowed. Music.

He felt it. And heard it.

They both heard it. And knew. And were known. And loved. And felt each other.

Pawel pulled away. Robert's hands on him but he pulled away. He needed breath. No, he told himself. This is not you. This cannot be you. Pawel pulled still away, needed to… Away.

"No… I can't…No."

"Why do you fight against what you are? You cannot pretend any more. I know what I see, Pawel. I know."

He reached for him again. Touched him again. But Pawel pulled away.

"No. No! I cannot, this…I…I want to hear nothing else. I feel nothing else. I want…You do not know me, Robert. You do not."

Pawel stood up, quickly pulled up his trousers, walked to the door.

"You do not know yourself. Who you are."

"You must not go tomorrow. Not for me. Not for you." Pawel pointed to the music sheets. "This is who you are, not shouts and cries and protests and beaten heads."

But Robert shook his head.

"I know what I am, Professor. Just as you too know."

"Robert…"

"You know, Professor."

Robert said nothing more. He looked at Pawel. He looked away.

Pawel hesitated, then walked out of office. He felt sick. He felt lost. He walked quickly down the corridor. He went into the bathroom. He felt dead inside. He felt broken. He turned on the water in the sink. Threw water onto his face. Tried to breathe. Tried to be alive. Tried to die. Did not know. Did not understand. He looked up at the cracked mirror in front of him.

He thought he would be sick. He was not sick. He thought he would pass out. He did not pass out. He stared at his reflection and he did not know himself. He felt his eyes hot with disbelief and tears and fear. And he was afraid.

No, he did not know himself. What had he done?

Damn Robert. Damn him. Damn him. Damn.

When he returned to his office a few minutes later Robert had gone. Pawel looked at the score on the table where Robert had put it down. Pawel did not touch it. He took the key to the practice room that was still in his table drawer. He went downstairs to that room, closed the door behind him. Walked over to the piano and sat down.

He stared at the keys.

He gently touched a C♯. He let it resonate. He puts his hands on the keys. He did not play.

He sat there. In silence.

What had he done?

Who was he?

No music was heard.

*

Later, as the night drew in, Pawel left the school in silence. He walked over to the trolleybus stop. Stood to wait. The snow fell.

Three men approached him. One pulled out an identification card. Security police.

"Your identification," the man ordered.

Pawel said nothing. He was not surprised. He did not care. His face was blank.

He pulled out his identity card. The man looked at it, at Pawel.

"You have to be careful, Professor. Focus on music."

"I am not a professor."

"But of course you are. Professor."

Pawel wondered how he knew he was a teacher at the school. He wondered why he called him that.

Pawel stared at him as the man handed him the identity card.

"The students, running in and out of buildings, demanding this, demanding that. Freedom of expression, but freedom to express what, eh Professor? Spoiled Zionist children. Jews. They all need to go home. Go back where they came from. Where they belong. We all have to be very careful. All of us."

The man stared at him, intimidating. Then nodded. Turned, and the three men walked away. Pawel understood the warning. There would be no second.

The trolleybus arrived.

Pawel said nothing.

He sat on the trolley in silence. At his stop he descended in silence.

He returned to his apartment in silence. He went to his bathroom, where he stood holding himself up at the sink. Then vomited.

He wiped his mouth.

He went over to his bed and lay down. He did not sleep.

The following day students from the Warsaw Technical University also protested in support of their fellow students. They too were arrested. Many were beaten, jailed. Two days later, on the Monday, tens of thousands of middle-class Poles joined the students to march through Warsaw. Pawel did not join them.

Pawel tried to telephone Robert. A woman, presumably his mother, answered the phone. She said he had gone to Krakow, no more. She put down the phone.

In Poland the beatings did not stop. The government did not listen.

*

The protest that began with students spread quickly to cities and towns throughout Poland. Robert had been correct that many would protest. But only partially correct. From Krakow to Lodz to Wroclaw and Gdansk, students took to the streets. But while in some places young factory workers marched alongside

270

them, in others workers stayed away. Wherever the marchers took to the streets security forces met them with truncheons, batons, fists, sometimes worse.

It did not take long for conservative forces to use the media to turn the population against the protestors. Instigators were 'exposed' as coming from Stalinist and Jewish backgrounds. The anti-Zionist backlash created in particular by Interior Minister and Head of Security Moczar and his supporters took little time in catching fire. The purges followed soon, particularly against those labeled 'Intelligentsia': those in the government, academia, the arts, often with Jewish backgrounds, accused of being at best ambiguous towards Poland, at worst criminals. Most had come from the Soviet Union at the end of the War to rebuild Poland. Now they were deemed Poland's enemies by those who had fought from within. At all levels of government, the army, the universities, whether students or teachers, in former positions of power or weakness, men and women found themselves suddenly without work, expelled from jobs and schools with nothing unless they left Poland. While Secretary Gomułka tried somewhat to temper the anti-Semitism that had become rife, even though expediently labeled as anti-Zionism, those of Jewish ethnic backgrounds recognized that Poland wanted them to emigrate. Emigrate they did. They had survived the War years, the years of Holocaust, but Poland no longer saw them as fellow Poles however they had managed to survive. Three Million Polish Jews were murdered in the Nazi death camps. By the time Secretary Gomulka and Minister Moczar unleashed their anti-Zionist purge of 1968, perhaps only 30,000 Jews still remained in Poland, many who had returned from the Soviet Republics at the end of the War to try to make their homes in the Poland of their birth. In the following months, barely a fraction of them would remain, their safety and ability to work no longer assured.

At first, Pawel took Arkady's advice and kept his head down. Some colleagues, those of Jewish descent, decided in the current climate that they could no longer remain in Poland and began the process of emigrating. While no one in the Music School was expelled, the atmosphere in Warsaw for those in academia and the arts was toxic. In newspapers and on television the word went out: 'Zionists go to Zion' and 'We'll tear the head off the hydra.' Gomułka gave a speech in front of three thousand workers to announce that the Government would never negotiate

271

with protestors. He condemned those who were too 'cosmopolitan'. He claimed that what should only matter was loyalty to Poland, not ethnicity, only to come in for sharp criticism from Security head Minister Moczar. The anti-Semitism, couched as anti-Zionism, continued unabated. The music in the State School of Music may have played on, but the notes became decidedly hollow.

Pawel focused on his new work, refining, transcribing. For hours he worked on the final movement. He thought about other young musicians at the school who might bring the 'Winter' section alive, knowing there were many violinists amongst the students who showed talent, who he could coax into the heart of the last Movement, not just technically but emotionally. And yet he could not get Robert out of his mind. Could not because of what he knew Robert could do for the score with his violin. Could not because of what had happened. What he felt inside.

Robert did not contact him. Over the weeks he thought of telephoning several times, only to pull back. After the run-in with the security police at the trolleybus stop he had to think he was being monitored if not constantly watched. He could not quite comprehend why they would do so; he had to assume it was because of his involvement with Robert, with the student protestors, although he had not protested himself, regardless of where his sympathies lay. Did they know more than they let on? Pawel could not be certain. But what he did know was that it was safest that he kept a distance from Robert, and that Robert kept a distance from him.

For reasons of security.

For reasons of emotional security.

Pawel still did not understand what had happened to him that night in his office, why he had reacted as he had. He still refused to accept what it possibly meant. He knew that he was attracted to Robert, had been so since he first heard him play. He always thought it was the music. It should have been the music, only the music.

But there was something else, something that disturbed and upset him because he could not reconcile those emotions with the person he thought he was.

Pawel did his best to close his mind to it, to close his heart as well. As Easter approached, with all that had happened over the weeks since the offices of

Government began their policies of intimidation and repression, he knew he had to escape from all that surrounded him, from the voices shouting in his head. When the school broke up for its holiday break, Pawel took a train, then a bus, to the remote small fishing village of Dębki on the Baltic coast, far from anywhere, where he rented a room for a week in a fisherman's house.

Dębki was somewhere he could go for long walks on an empty beach, cold in the early April air, somewhere he could think, consider, work on his composition or future pieces. Somewhere he thought he could not be found. But even here he could not escape what was happening in the capital; even here politics were not entirely silent. Even here a musician might be suspect. Any artist was suspect.

And even here he could not ignore the turmoil inside.

After he returned, feeling constrained rather than rested, still ill at ease, still confused, Pawel found himself more and more desperate to speak to Robert, regardless of any potential consequences. In an odd way Pawel felt sheltered from this and felt Robert might be sheltered as well. So he told himself. Was it worth the risk making contact? Probably not. But Pawel could not remove desire and desire spoke to him all his waking hours. A desire to see the young violinist. To hear him play. To hear his voice, his passion. To feel his passion.

He tried again to telephone Robert several times, but oddly no one answered the phone. He became concerned, thought of contacting the young woman Daria, but worried he might have to explain more than he wanted. He waited. He tried to work. Tried to focus again on his students and the school but nothing else. But he could not shut out his thoughts. Could not forget what was within and what had happened.

An explanation, or shadow of one, came in a letter not to him, but to the school, through Arkady. Written not by Robert, the short note came from his father, explaining that he wrote on Robert's behalf, that given the current climate and unexpected circumstances Robert would not be joining the State School of Music in the autumn.

"A loss," said Arkady. "A sad loss. Perhaps for the best, but a talent like that…Perhaps he will take it elsewhere."

"No. No I do not know that he will. That is the worry."

"Such a terrible turn this country has taken," Arkady added then. "We musicians, we are relatively safe. Even as teachers of music. Not like writers, satirists, those who speak out."

"Not like the Jews."

"No. Not like the Jews. Tragedy returns to Warsaw, the tragedy of loss. We will lose the best. What about you, Pawel? Will we lose you?"

"Me? No. Why would I go anywhere?"

"Opportunity."

"My opportunity is here."

Pawel refused to let the door slam shut. Not yet. He had to see Robert; he needed to see him. He needed to understand. Deciding the risk had to be taken, Pawel took the 54 Trolleybus back towards his apartment, descending two stops prior to his own and walking to the address that Robert had given him some time before. He had made a copy of the final movement of 'With Memory For Twelve Musicians' as a gift. A calling card. A wish to persuade. And with his music briefcase in hand he looked like any other worker who might have left early from the office, or like the teacher that he was. No one stopped him, neither security nor regular police. If he was followed, he did not know it. He did not think so.

It was easy enough to find Robert's apartment building. He rang the entrance bell and was let in. He took the rickety elevator up to the fourth floor. He knocked, nervously, heard footsteps. Waited.

An older woman opened the door.

"Hello," said Pawel, with slight uncertainty in his voice. "My name is Pawel Weisz. I am a teacher at the State Music School. I was hoping I might find Robert here. I brought him some music and wondered if I might see him."

The woman stared at Pawel, silent at first, without expression.

"I know who you are. Robert is not…"

She was interrupted by a voice from a room behind her.

"Mother? Please. He should come in."

Robert's mother hesitated, then stepped aside, pointed to a back room. Pawel nodded his thanks, went slowly into the apartment, not large but comfortable, well lived in. Family photographs on the walls. Some non-descript art. He walked into the back room and came to a sharp stop.

Robert stood in the middle of the room, looking at him. Both of his hands were in plaster casts. He smiled at Pawel, weakly, with more than a hint of sadness in his face. The irony that so often came with his grin was gone, as was the spark in his eye.

"Jesus Christ," whispered Pawel.

"Not in this house I should think," said Robert, trying to joke, trying to smile. That did not come easily. "Please…" Robert gestured to a seat.

"What…?," Pawel started to ask, when Robert's mother interrupted him.

"I need to go to the shop," she said. "I will be back in twenty minutes." And to Pawel: "He tires easily."

Pawel nodded, reading clearly what she was trying to tell him. Before he could say anything further she turned and left the apartment.

"I must apologize for my mother. In normal times she would have happily greeted my friends. But these are not normal times."

"What happened to you?"

Robert shrugged. Looked away.

"After Warsaw I went to Krakow. A meeting of students to decide what to do. We formed a committee between universities to mobilize students throughout Poland. I went up to Poznan. They were waiting for me when I got off the train. Pulled me away. Their batons did nothing, but they crushed my hands. Both hands. They knew who I was. They knew everything. Workers Defense Militia: hah! They were security police. That is who they always were…My right hand… it will improve. My left…I have had surgery. The nerve endings were severed, it seems. It will heal. But I am afraid, Professor, I will not be able to perform your beautiful fourth movement in Prague. In fact I will not be able to play the violin again."

"Robert, I am so sorry, I…"

Robert shook his head.

"One day, perhaps I might be able to play a Rolling Stones medley for you. Or perhaps not. It is not your fault, Professor. You knew what they might do."

"No."

"You imagined. I did not imagine. None of us imagined. We thought the workers would join us. The workers did not. The others, they had been watching me. They knew how to hurt me."

Pawel felt as if he might break.

"Your beautiful violin…"

"Dead, Professor. Forever gone."

Pawel stood. He wanted to walk over to Robert. He wanted to embrace him. To feel him. To tell him what he felt inside, what he had probably always felt inside. To touch him. To cry for him.

But Robert stopped Pawel before he could take a step.

"Don't. Please…"

Pawel looked at him. Nodded. Sat again.

"Your life is not over, Robert."

"No. But my life here is. We will emigrate. We have no choice. Not really. They have removed my father from his position. They called him a Zionist infiltrator. They hate what we are, even though we are not. So we will go to Israel. What do we know about Israel? Perhaps I will work on some sort of collective kibbutz. As long as my hands do not have to grasp anything small, it should be fine. I hope there will be no music there. Socialism with a human face, finally. And no music."

"No…No, you can't, you…"

"They want us all to leave. My father fought in the War from afar, because he had dreams of rebuilding the Poland he loved. But they hate us nonetheless. They hate me because I thought it was right to speak out, to speak my mind. I thought it was right to believe our government and country could follow its path with dignity and humanity. Because I believed that speech, like music, should be free. Always free. So they hate me because music was part of my soul. And they destroyed that to keep me quiet."

Pawel did not know what to say. He looked away. He could feel the pain inside. And he knew at that moment that he had loved Robert, whatever he tried to tell himself, had loved this young musician who could bring tears to Pawel's eyes with the voice of his violin. Could bring light from darkness. He wanted to tell him and did not know how to tell him. He wanted to speak his love. He wanted to say he now understood.

"Robert, I…"

"No. Say nothing more. Not here, not anywhere. They listen. They will use anything they can against you. It does not matter. There is one thing more. One thing you need to know, Pawel. My father, he would have fought them. He is one to fight. They expelled him from his job in government. He would still have fought. But they came here. They came and threatened him. They had photographs. Photographs of me. They showed these to my father, to my mother. And now we will leave Poland forever. It is best."

"I do not understand," said Pawel.

"You were not…I have had relationships in my past. You did not know this. Why would you? That kind of relationship, it is still illegal here in Poland. They had photographs. They had been watching me for…for a long time. They threatened to arrest me. They threatened to arrest everyone I ever knew."

Robert almost broke here. Pawel froze in his seat. He thought he might be sick. His chest tightened, his breathing grew labored, shallow. He felt afraid.

"They photographed…"

"There was one of you, Pawel. Of us in front of Daria's building. They misunderstood its meaning. I explained but they said they did not trust me. Do you remember I came out to tell you to return? I was drunk. Do you remember how drunk I was? I almost fell over, I had had so much vodka. You caught me as I fell. Do you remember? Do you?"

Pawel knew that Robert was playing a role, a role for anyone who might be listening. Robert nodded at Pawel, coaching him, leading him.

"…Yes," Pawel answered quietly, broken.

"I was so drunk."

"Yes. You… you fell. I had to catch you. Hold you upright for a moment. I…I was angry and then departed because you had no control."

"Exactly. I did not know what I was doing. I was fortunate you were there, Pawel. I was fortunate that you did not get more angry. That you understood and held me upright or I would have fallen. I never said thank you. I never said…anything."

Pawel looked at Robert. He choked back a slight sob, feeling broken, afraid.

"Nor did I."

"It does not matter now. It is too late. We are leaving. The music is now dead. Forget the violin. I will."

Robert's mother returned as Pawel was leaving. Robert had showed him out. Pawel had asked him to write, to let him know where he was, but he knew Robert would be unlikely to do so. As Robert's mother came back into the apartment, Robert started to close the door with Pawel looking at him, desiring him, realizing he would possibly never see Robert again.

Pawel's shoulders had dropped. His head hanged slightly, his eyes focused solely on the ground. He started to turn when Robert called out to him one last time.

"Professor," he said; "Make beautiful honest music. Bring it to life. The music gave me hope. Always give such hope."

Those were the last words Robert said. Pawel took the rickety elevator back down to the ground floor. Left the building. He felt the slow tears, warm, on his face. He could not stop them. He knew he had paid a price that he would never recoup, the value of something he had not understood.

He walked and walked without knowing where he was going, or why. The spring afternoon became evening. The sky grew dark as night approached. Without quite knowing how, why, he found himself standing on the Slasko-Dabrowski Bridge, looking down at the waters of the Vistula flowing below. He remembered being told when he first arrived in Warsaw that another bridge had been here, the Kierbedzia Bridge, destroyed by the retreating German army in 1944. The Slasko-Dabrowski had been built on its pillars. It was as Robert had once said to him: artifice built from the ashes of what had been, without the past, without the humanity of the past.

Pawel opened his case of music that he had carried with him.

He removed the copy of the fourth movement of his latest work. He had wanted to give this copy to Robert, to get him to learn it, to play, to bring life from artifice. Now that life was gone.

He would find another violinist. There were other violinists, he told himself.

Some excellent students, as Arkady had said to him. But he knew that was a lie. He knew too he was lying to himself.

Pawel looked at the city beyond, the city that was not, that had removed life, that had now taken its toll on his life. He looked at that city that he had wanted to love as the lights even then were illuminating. Beauty but artifice. The path he was on. This path. This city not of life, but of a lie, of so much pain, so much death.

He threw the copy of the fourth movement, music that should have been his gift to Robert, Robert's gift to him, the music and all it represented into the Vistula far below. Watched the score disappear.

And walked on.

May-August 1968

Ministry of Interior
Committee for Public Security
SB / Dep 1

PERSON OF INTEREST OPK File Warsaw Mok.75392

Senior Investigating Security Officer: WójcikM Dep1/WC
Mokotów/Wierzbno

Operative Personenkontrolle:
P. Weisz
Current residence: Zawrat 14
- -
6.5.1968

    Subject left residence Zawrat 14 at 07.30. Did not stop at local trolleybus stop but continued to State Music School on foot, a common activity. Did not meet or talk to any other(s) en route to school and entered building at 08.38 without pausing to speak to anyone. As no installed CLD equipment in school office or surveillance (as preferred OPK request from office of Senior Official I.D., Public Security M/W Dep 1), it is not possible to comment as to any conversations Subject may have had while there, although to date no suggestion of undue correspondence or likely agitation on behalf of Subject.

    Subsequent to Subject's twenty-five minute meeting with former OPK interest RM at residence of family EM, recently dismissed from Ministry of Light Industry, Subject has not attempted to contact RM further, as noted from surveillance and through CLD surveillance of family residence EM (see OPK Person of Interest File Warsaw Mok 2437.) Events and recorded surveillance conversation at residence RM/EM are referred to in report of 30.4.1968 Subject file Warsaw MOK 75392.

    Subject departed State Music School 17.42 and spoke to no one upon exit. Subject again did not take the Trolleybus but without hesitation walked directly to resident apartment where entered 18.07. No recorded conversations through CLD recording took place on night of 6.5.68 and nothing further to report.

    -MW, Senior Investigating Officer (SISO)

Pawel threw himself back into his work. He taught his few remaining classes without much enthusiasm. He listened to his worried students who came to his office to discuss their own work. Sometimes he paid attention. Mostly he did not.

He refined and largely completed his 'With Memory for Twelve Musicians' composition. He found it gave him no more joy, but it had to be done. The Prague Conservatoire had announced the new composition by Pawel Weisz would be performed at two concerts and a workshop over a weekend at the beginning of August. Once he chose the eleven other musicians to perform with him, he would put in the necessary forms and application to the Cultural Ministry for approval. He knew he could not pull out now. He had a responsibility to himself. He had his career. He tried to care.

As the month progressed Pawel auditioned present and former students at the Music School to find those who could best understand and interpret his score.

He had always said the music was everything. Now it truly had to be everything. It should leave no room for anything else, for anyone else, but the work of his music students, his musicians, himself. So he told himself.

It also left him empty.

And it was all he had.

He tried to put Robert behind him. He tried to put him in a closed room in his mind. Lock that room. Lose the key.

But the memory would not be silent. 'With Memory For Twelve Musicians' became 'with memory of one musician,' one glorious musician who could have brought such—humanity—to that final movement of Pawel's piece. The loss was so very great.

But it was not simply the loss of a chosen violinist for the musical exploration and expression of 'Winter' in his work: winter, which equated with death and the possibility of life reborn, breaking free from dormant silence into spring. Pawel only heard the death of the movement. Not the hope it was meant to inspire.

He needed another violinist. He auditioned several at the school. Excellent musicians. None seemed right. None met his criteria. What were his criteria? He did not know himself.

He held off making a decision. He began rehearsals in a school rehearsal room, even then revising slightly, working with the musicians one on one, as a group, in parts. Listening to their comments, their thoughts. He transposed what was in his head and on the paper into other musical instruments, to the two voices that he had orchestrated for as well. All there, all working sometimes alone, sometimes together in point and counterpoint, without harmony. Discordant sounds working both against and for one another to create the images Pawel had always had in his head. The Poland he thought he knew.

Except of course that he did not know.

Except of course that he too now saw artifice rather than organic life, musical life. Experimentation, avant-garde exploration for meaning. What was meaning?

Through folk song and country traditional song revisited, broken apart, reinterpreted, reimagined over forty-seven minutes the various musicians explored eleven different chords, lingering on each chord to meditate on the songs Pawel had collected. Rearranging, tearing apart, reassembling. Assigning each to a different season. Within Pawel explored different rhythms and harmonies. He found from the past elements of jazz, echoes of the classics, a sense of the earth from sound. He explored the possibility of memory becoming the possibility of a future, hopeful and human. Seasons of the earth. Seasons of the human mind. Seasons that represented love and its loss. That was his intent.

And his intent began to take shape.

Yet it still lacked that final movement, death and rebirth. It still lacked the violinist who could tie all the movements together with both loss and hope, past and present, memory and foresight.

Such was indeed his intent. Yet it remained unfulfilled while Pawel sought the right person who could bring to the final quarter of the work all he needed. And knowing that he would never find such a one, not really.

Towards the end of the month, exhausted from the process, he climbed aboard the trolleybus to return to his flat. He knew that time grew short. He had to decide who would perform the violin movement at the end. He had to get all the paperwork to the Culture Ministry; approvals would take time in Poland. Arkady warned him that he had to make a decision. But he still did not know who, or how. He still thought of Robert, saw Robert in every phrase, every note, every rest. In his intent. His meaning.

And he knew within, secretly knew within it was his love that gave meaning.

He had not heard from Robert in a month. Pawel wondered if perhaps Robert and his family had in fact left Poland, as he had said they would do. He thought about trying to contact Robert, but knew he could not. Yet he could not get him out of his head. Ironic, he knew: memory for twelve musicians had become the memory of one who haunted him.

Pawel's mind wandered. Thoughts taking him away, confusing him. Moving on. He had to move on. Arguing various points with himself he practically missed his trolleybus stop. He had to ring the bell again, shout for the driver to stop so he could get out.

The driver finally set him free. He breathed in the spring air, closing his eyes for a moment, trying to set himself free as well. As he started away he noticed a figure moving in the other direction, nearly disappearing. He hesitated for a moment. Stared at her retreating back and was certain it was Daria Wojewoda. He remembered Robert saying she had been one of those who had been forced to leave the university. He remembered her invitation to her party after sitting across from him on the trolleybus all those many weeks ago. He remembered the night at her apartment. Robert playing Chopin on his violin. He remembered all of it. He remembered what he felt. What he felt still and could say to no one. Robert, unforgettable.

"Daria?" he called out. "Daria…"

If she heard, she did not turn. He took some steps toward the retreating figure.

"Daria?"

Still she did not turn. In fact she started to walk more quickly away. Hurriedly away. He could tell. She was running. Running from him.

He had to speak to her. He realized he had to hear word of Robert. Like siblings, she had said. Like brother and sister. He had to stop her, to ask about Robert, to know about Robert.

Daria, if it was her, disappeared around a corner. Pawel ran after. He reached the corner of the street, looked down the intersecting road. No one. She was not there. Had she been there? Was it her? He had to speak to her, had to. Robert.

Pawel started to run. He remembered her building. Not far. He had to see her, if it was her. If not, he would ring her bell. Ask to speak to her for just a moment. Tell me about Robert. How are his hands? Has he tried to play again? The music. Tell me about Robert. Tell me about his touch. Tell me does he remember. Tell me does he feel… something?

He turned another corner and saw down the road the building he remembered. The building Robert had emerged from that night, grasping Pawel's arms, his shoulders. He remembered, yes, he remembered and felt his kiss.

"Daria?"

She was at the doorway to the building. Fumbling with her keys. "Daria? Daria, wait! Please."

She started to pull open the door. Then stopped. Knew he was behind her. Knew he was there. She shook her head. She did not want to see him. Did not want to address him. Knew she had to. Knew she could not hide. She turned.

"Professor," she said, plainly, simply. Because it was her, she who also loved Robert, who had known him forever, children to adults, she who knew, who must have understood.

"I thought it might be you. I thought it was. I…"

"No. Yes."

"You are no longer at the University."

She sighed. "They took away my bursary. They asked me to leave. Many had to leave."

"I am sorry. So sorry."

"Poland. This is what it has become."

"I know. I know. It is terrible. I am so sorry."

"Why? Why are you sorry? Not for me. Do not be sorry for me. I believe in what I did. I felt. You are not them. You have nothing to apologize for, Professor. Whatever your feelings, they won. It is how things are."

"What will you do?"

She shrugged. Looked away, then back at him.

"We cannot stay here. Like others we will emigrate. My father was told to leave the hospital where he worked. It is not our country. Not now. Perhaps it never was.

I cannot say."

"It is what happened to Robert, to his family too," he said. "It should not have been this way."

She stared at him. Did not respond. He continued:

"I went to see him. I did not know. His hands. They… I did not know until I saw him."

She still stared at him. He could see she had started to cry.

"He will still play. One day. I feel it. His hands will heal. His heart will heal. The violin, the music. There will be music, wonderful, wonderful music. I know. I… Seeing him like that," Pawel said. "I felt so…helpless."

She was silent at first, then turned.

"I must go in. I must…"

Her hand shaking, she put the key in the door, pulled it open.

"Please," said Pawel. "Can we talk, just a moment longer. Robert…I need to explain. I need to…talk. Please."

She shook her head, over and over, started inside. She did not turn around then. Pawel watched as the door began to close. And watched as she caught it with her hand. Held it. Stood still for another moment. Then turned.

And he saw she was indeed crying.

And he watched as she opened the door again, and came back out.

*

Pawel did not return to the State Music School the following day. He cancelled all work and rehearsals with all of the musicians. He sent word that he needed to work on the composition more. All were surprised at first, but then accepted that such was typical of Pawel. He could be a perfectionist.

However he then did not return all the following week as well. He was due to be part of the examination adjudicators for some of the first year students but did not appear for that. Arkady became concerned. He telephoned Pawel several times, but the telephone was not answered. Arkady decided he would go to Pawel's apartment, so worried had he then become. He tried Pawel's telephone number one last time and on this occasion Pawel answered. He said only that he would return to the school after the weekend, that he had been working. He said he was not ill, just tired. Then he put down the phone.

The following Monday, Arkady passed Anna Bednarz, one of the promising student violinists, in the corridor. When he said hello to her she smiled and explained that she had joined Pawel Weisz's other musicians to work on the new composition with the composer, which she said she found exciting. She had so much respect for him she said. Had so enjoyed his teaching and mentorship. He was like Penderecki she said, seeking out something new for Poland. Something untried.

"Wonderful," said Arkady. "I am certain the experience will be excellent for all concerned. You will no doubt impress them hugely in Prague."

"I hope so," she answered. "I am very much looking forward to those concerts. I only hope our Composer is happy with his choice. I know it has not been easy."

"Your inclusion is richly deserved," Arkady told the young woman, who smiled, pleased, and walked away. Arkady turned back, went downstairs and found the rehearsal room where Pawel was indeed working.

"The maestro has returned."

Pawel looked up from his score. "I was never gone. Just busy."

"I understand. I gather Anna Bednarz will round out your musicians. She is very good, Pawel. She will no doubt do excellent work, particularly in that final movement of your composition. I know not Mandeltort, but she is an excellent violinist. And I hope sometime in the future you will be able to do something with that young man, when things finally calm down."

Pawel stared at the score, did not respond. Some of the musicians started to file into the room. Arkady nodded at them, then left the room, returned down the corridor.

"Arkady?"

Arkady turned. Pawel had emerged from the rehearsal room, was standing by the door.

"Um?"

"Robert Mandeltort is dead. He committed suicide two weeks ago."

That was all Pawel said. He walked back into the rehearsal room. He closed the door behind him.

Ministry of Interior
Committee for Public Security
SB / Dep 1

PERSON OF INTEREST OPK File Warsaw Mok.75392

Senior Investigating Security Officer: WójcikM Dep1/WC
                                Mokotów/Wierzbno
Operative Personenkontrolle:
P. Weisz
Current residence: Zawrat 14
- -
18.6.1968

Per OPK order 1775/13.6.68 office of I.D. (Public Security M/W Dep 1) surveillance re: Subject from File Warsaw MOK 75392 will be suspended with effect 21.6.1968, at which time installed CLD equipment will be disengaged although, as requested, not removed from site. This is to allow for possibility of future surveillance should such be deemed in public interest.

Subject has ceased any contact with former and current U.Warsaw student agitators and activists involved in the subversive anti-Poland activities and demonstrations that commenced March 1968. Subject did exchange comments with former U.Warsaw woman student DW (all accounts closed and University expulsion agreed as requested to U.Warsaw; see daily subject report 23.5.1968) but no further contact has been attempted with DW, who with family has applied to emigrate from Poland. It would appear that all other intentional or inadvertent contact with U.Warsaw students by Subject has ceased.

It is therefore the decision from the senior security officer I.D. that Subject for the foreseeable future should no longer be subject to OPK surveillance: the potential for disturbance caused by the Subject's activities is unlikely to become a threat to internal security, given particularly the recent emigrations and arrests of those primary agitators involved in the spring protests. As a ministerial decision regarding Subject's application to perform at the Prague Czechoslovakia Conservatoire remains open but likely, it is thought best that OPK surveillance cease until and unless Subject is deemed an internal security threat when at such later time that surveillance might become necessary for reintroduction.

For further information regarding Subject please refer to File Warsaw

MOK75392, or myself, Senior Investigating OfficerMW for any required comment. Subject's file will remain open for requisite twelve months for possible follow-up action or information.

Final reports for week to follow.

--MW, Senior Investigating Officer (SISO)

*

Pawel was not been particularly surprised. This was how things often were in Poland. However he had become nevertheless concerned when the exit visas and travel documentation needed for the cultural exchange allowing the twelve musicians to attend the Prague Conservatoire concerts in August still had not yet received official approval with less than a month before the planned exchange. Although he worried it may have had something to do with the events of the past months, he knew too that political events in Czechoslovakia caused certain anxieties to the more conservative Polish government that itself had marched away from reforms following the student protests. It was even possible that the approvals would not be granted despite the freedom of movement usually allowed to Polish nationals.

In the second week of July Pawel instead received an unexpected summons to the Ministry of Cultural and National Heritage, Department of Art and Cultural Education, the office of Minister K. Dąbrowski. Pawel duly appeared as requested, sitting in the anteroom of Dąbrowski's office for over an hour awaiting his appointment. He expected some intimidation; he knew this was part of it. So he sat quietly, kept his eyes closed as if indifferent, allowed his mind to wander.

Finally Pawel was ushered into the expansive room by a secretary. Dąbrowski sat at a large desk, reviewing papers, emanating importance, or at least self-importance. Across from him sat another man, a small unsmiling figure who did not look at Pawel.

"Weisz? Sit," said Dąbrowski, pointing to another chair at the desk. The other man present did not look at him. The Minister continued to read documents on his desk. Finally he looked at Pawel, folded his hands, sat back in his chair.

"The Department has been reviewing this request for you and your colleagues to attend the Prague Conservatoire next month."

"We submitted the documentation some time ago," said Pawel, determined to fight his corner and not be intimidated.

"Um, yes. The government has had many issues to deal with these many weeks, as you will understand. So: a cultural visit to demonstrate aptitude and creativity of one of our most interesting new composers. This is what I am told. What the State School of Music wishes to inform. I have to say I am not one who easily understands exactly where your work leads its listeners, Weisz. Still, clearly there is an audience for this sort of composing. I cannot say it is to my taste or liking. Chopin, yes, of course. But this modern music, this avant garde music, I find it inaccessible, hard to understand. Modern art."

The minister shook his head, never taking his eyes from Pawel. He wanted a response. He wanted to intimidate, in his way.

"They probably said the same of Bach or Wagner or Stravinsky in their time," Pawel answered.

"Be that as it may, you are probably correct. Our State Music School is highly respected and they are of course very supportive of your work."

He looked at his notes, and read:

"'Our new Penderecki,' they say. 'As did Lutosławski with his works and techniques in the 1950s, Weisz may well be the radical voice of this decade and the next that we have been seeking'…I am afraid I never cared much for either of these composers, although I cannot deny their accolades in certain minority quarters. Perhaps that is enough. Interestingly I read that your early work was in fact greatly influenced by Bach. How is it that you then followed this…different path?"

"Perhaps there are many paths to follow in music. In the arts. Many valued voices to be heard. Perhaps not all are so different as you imagine."

"Perhaps. But Bach?... But, then, who am I to say?"

Pawel did not respond.

"You have an interesting parentage, Weisz. We shall say Weisz, shall we not, as you wish. An interesting history, I see. You keep things to yourself. You are a valued cultural asset who cares more for music than politics. Would you say that is so?"

"I would say…I would say my life is music. It is enough."

"Indeed. It is why Gomułka insists we should smile particularly upon our musicians as Poland's cultural emissaries. Why we believe our support is in our interest as it is in yours. Musicians are more malleable than other artists, because music speaks quietly. Even yours."

The minister stared at Pawel. Provoking. Pushing. Pawel sat stone still, refusing to engage.

"So, as to your request. My office has been in contact with our comrades in Prague. They are very hopeful that you will attend, as you will know. Two concerts, I believe."

"And a workshop."

"To show them Polish craftsmanship. Polish genius perhaps. An original work I am given to understand."

"Yes."

Dąbrowski smiled, but there was no warmth in his smile.

"You will know, Weisz, that we in the Government have had to deal with, shall we say, small disturbances these last few months. Unpleasant matters. Nevertheless I assume you are aware of Secretary Gomułka's recent announcements on the matter?"

"No. I'm sorry."

"Ah, of course. Artists and politics do not mix well…Always best that way I think. So, the General Secretary has presented Minister Moczar with a promotion. Minister Moczar has thus departed his role as Minister for Internal Affairs after doing an exemplary job there. He is no longer in the cabinet. His policies might be thus refined. This is one of the reasons we have had to delay your request: to see how events might unfold. The General Secretary has expressed the hope, even the desire, that the issues that have troubled Poland these last many months have now come to a close. He has also moved to end once and for all the unfortunate voices of anti-Zionism that have done some damage to Poland's reputation abroad. Limited though those may have been, of course. I realize this does not affect you particularly, Weisz, given what you are, although it may be a welcome intervention by some at the State Music School. At least we hope so."

"I see," said Pawel.

"Do you? Hm. I wonder…The Government hopes for a return to normality, given the unfortunate events that have occurred over the last few months. And while our comrades in Czechoslovakia have their own issues that they must address we do feel it is wise to show our support for a sister Socialist state. Particularly at this time. Whatever I personally think of the Czechoslovak government's recent embrace of certain reforms, we feel it is best that they know that Poland remains an ally and friend. Therefore we are of course minded to approve this cultural exchange."

"That is good news."

"No doubt. You and your fellow musicians will receive the necessary approvals. Your passports will be issued immediately. As is normal in the case of such exchanges, the travel documents are for a standard year for the purpose of the exchange. We are also sending Comrade Dudek here to accompany you."

The man next to Pawel turned to him and nodded with a slight smile.

"Iwo Dudek," he said. "It would be a pleasure to join you, Professor. I have followed your career with interest."

"Have you?"

"Indeed I have. Professor."

Pawel knew well why this man would accompanying them to Prague. He knew he had no choice in the matter.

"Comrade Dudek I know has a far greater understanding of your work than do I. A connoisseur," added Dąbrowski. "I know he is looking forward to it."

"In fact, I requested it," said Dudek.

"And we feel it is the responsible action to take. Some of those with you: brilliant musicians, no doubt. But young. And young people can be so impressionable. They can follow the wrong path as we know. We want them to enjoy themselves. We then want them to return safely to continue their studies. But they need to respect Poland. Represent it in the best possible manner. It would be such a pity if their heads were turned at such a time of misgivings, shall we say, as there are in Prague. We would want no one to make a mistake. Even the appearance of a mistake. Would you not agree, Weisz?"

Pawel looked at the two men. He did not see a need to respond.

"Good then. All the necessary documentation will be processed in the next week. Dudek here will make arrangements with you as well. Good to have you on our side. We always felt you were one of us, so to speak. All that we know of you says this. A true Polish composer."

Pawel stood to leave. Dąbrowski and Dudek stared at him as he did. Pawel nodded his thanks, such as it was. As he started to turn:

"I believe, Weisz, you lost your original intended violinist. So I am given to understand. A friend, I also believe. I gather there was an accident. A terrible pity. Still, it is in our interest, your interest, that our musicians respect all that Poland has done for them. Reputations are so easily destroyed. I am certain things will have worked out for the best."

*

Arkady Sienkiewicz listened intently to each of the four movements in Pawel's new work. Pawel and his eleven other musicians played a rehearsal concert at the State Music School prior to their visit to Prague.

Arkady found the work very much reflective of the portfolio of compositional work that Pawel had produced the last several years. The methods Pawel had used to disassemble, then reassemble Polish folk music and historical song with motif, sometimes the spoken or song working in repetition, were nothing if not interesting. Arkady knew that Pawel continued to wrestle between tonality and minimalism. He heard a greater influence of jazz coming into the work, subtly, with great intelligence. He found the patterns that Pawel followed, finding meaning in certain notes, sounds, words in relation to the seasons, most engaging. Arkady did not find this new work Pawel's most dynamic composition. Hardly surprising given the events of the last months. But he greatly admired the struggle, the journey, the reach to a voice that was somehow new, somehow dynamic.

It was the fourth movement that most interested Arkady, however, this final movement that he found the saddest part of the work. He was not surprised that Pawel had abandoned the original movement he had listened to weeks before. Arkady had sat one night with Pawel, talking into the early hours. He knew all that had transpired with Robert Mandeltort—the protest, the beating in Poznan, the surgery. Pawel had told him that Mandeltort knew he would never play violin again, not in the way he had. And when Pawel talked about Mandeltort's death, Arkady knew this had a deep and probably lasting effect.

So it was no surprise when Arkady looked at the final score for the new work to see that the Fourth Movement had changed entirely. Pawel still used violin notes as a key component in the piece, and Anna Bednarz indeed performed admirably.

But whereas before the sound of the violin was central in expressing both the death of winter and then the possibility of rebirth in the final movement, now the instrument was incidental, working with the other instruments and two voices of all the musicians, instead of standing out from them.

The Fourth Movement no longer felt like a statement in its own right, a revelation of the loss of season and hope for the new. It worked well with the other three movements, of course, but in its way it was rather forgettable. It lacked the hope that Pawel had once composed for this final part of the work.

Arkady knew there had to be more to the story of Robert Mandeltort than Pawel had told him. He could but surmise what that was. He knew Pawel led a solitary, even lonely life here in Prague. He knew he had ghosts. He knew too that for that very reason he had pushed Pawel towards Mandeltort, because he could see in the young man's ability to play something remarkable, something incredibly moving. He knew Pawel would respond to such talent. He guessed Pawel had fallen in love with Robert Mandeltort. If so Arkady could understand why.

Now of course Mandeltort was dead. When Pawel told Arkady of the young musician's suicide, he said it must have been because of his inability to ever make miraculous music on his violin again. Perhaps. But Arkady guessed there was probably more to it than that. Listening to the full work and particularly the Final Movement in this rehearsal performance, Arkady understood the true meaning of what Pawel tried to explore and convey in the last part of his work. Arkady could almost feel with each note, each sound from every instrument, with chords repeated and the variations that transpired the weight of each stone that Mandeltort probably put into his pockets, into his case on his back, growing heavier, heavier all the time. The weight of things. And when the final percussion beat, held louder, stronger than all else in the final movement when it came, Arkady could almost feel the weight of those stones pulling Mandeltort further and further into the Vistula waters.

The final notes, like the final breaths, taken. Not beautiful as the road Pawel had at first started down, but now harsh and lonely. Arkady saw the loneliness likely ahead.

From a newspaper report Arkady read that Robert Mandeltort could not swim, so it was first thought that he might have fallen in. Or been drinking. But Arkady, like Pawel, knew this was not so. Mandeltort had made a choice. He would not have struggled, would not have fought. He would not have been able to. Arkady wondered if he heard music as the waters rose above him. He wondered if he heard Bach. Or Chopin. Or, indeed, Weisz.

A question no one would ever answer.

When the final Movement came to an end, Arkady then sat quietly and felt nothing but sadness. Sadness for the young musician. For his family. And mostly for his young friend Pawel, who would never have the answer. Who would always have that void.

Later, Pawel joined Arkady alone in his mentor's office over several glasses of Vodka.

"You leave on Thursday?"

"Yes. In the morning. We have a bus to take the twelve of us and our security friend."

"I know the Conservatoire people are pleased you can join their festival. I have no doubt this will lead to good things, Pawel. Na zdrowie."

Pawel clinked his small glass to his friend's.

"I have been in contact with Nadia Boulanger in Paris, Pawel. She hopes sometime to work with you. You could learn much. Perhaps that will be in your future."

"My future? My future in Warsaw." A statement, not a question.

"Of course. Poland is your future."

Arkady, smiling, raised his hand and pointed—pointed to the telephone, around the room. He was giving Pawel a message and Pawel understood it. More than ever he knew he had to be careful.

"Your documents allow you to travel, do they not? The Government likes its musicians to show their talent throughout the world. You could take a year to study with her, Pawel. Then return. It would be good for your reputation. Good for Poland. You should consider this. Carefully."

"And you, Arkady, would you not want to work abroad?"

"Oh, there was a time. But now…Poland will learn by its mistakes. Our life is comfortable here. My family is here. I am not as fortunate as you; you are still young my friend. If Prague goes well, the Cultural Minster will be happy, the Government, they will applaud you, support you if you wish to study abroad. You will no doubt give them reason to see you gain in reputation. Your ties are few."

Pawel listened, sipping his vodka now. Deep in thought.

"I almost forgot to mention: there is a young woman I know in Prague who will attend your concerts. I have written to her that she should make certain to do so. Adriena Pacovská. She wrote that she and her piano quartet will be performing in Vienna just after. A festival there. But she will remain in Prague a day longer to meet you. To offer her support. She can be very accommodating."

Pawel looked at his friend and nodded. He turned his gaze around the small office. Looked at the photograph of Arkady with his wife and two sons. Looked at the manuscripts, the scores, the papers and books scattered around. Looked at the life as it had become. And thought briefly about his own journey. About Robert. About loss. About memories and twelve musicians. So many memories. So many musicians. Pawel furrowed his brow and nodded. He looked back at his friend and mentor. Smiled, just slightly, a smile that spoke of loss and sadness. And understanding. They raised their glasses, clinked and downed the remaining vodka in silence.

*

The bus journey to Prague took most of the Thursday. Although Iwo Dudek claimed to have a strong interest in music and Pawel's work in particular, he barely engaged with any of the musicians on the journey, although did spend a little time flirting with Anna Bednarz until Pawel moved to sit with her in order to discuss the score. He knew she was grateful for the rescue. Dudek simply shrugged, moved back to the front of the bus. It was clear to all that Dudek was an SB officer, so it proved easier to ignore him rather than to engage.

The Conservatoire in Prague had arranged accommodation at an old pension hostel just a few minutes away from the music school, comfortable although hardly fancy. Pawel had hoped to have space to himself but Dudek insisted that he be included in the shared room with Pawel and the clarinetist, Bartosz. Pawel was not in much of a position to protest.

It also soon became apparent that Iwo Dudek had an ulterior motive for wanting to be included on the journey. Dudek confided in Pawel that he had an 'acquaintance' in Prague who he hoped to see, a woman friend from his youth. Pawel quickly deduced that Dudek probably had a wife in Warsaw who might not approve.

The evening of their arrival, despite his fatigue, Pawel joined the other musicians for drinks with their hosts and a number of students from the Conservatoire. Pawel would have preferred to withdraw. He did not like events such as this, but he knew he had to make his appearance. Surrounded by a number of interested students, Pawel explained how his latest work came to be, how he had recorded song and inexperienced voices throughout Poland, then broke them down into their primary elements only to find the essential notes, musical, emotional in sound as the basis for each movement of the composition. The students wanted to know as much as they could about this Polish avant garde artist in their midst for the first time, but they also wanted to know about events inside Poland and to talk about their own push for newly earned liberties. Pawel was careful to support the supposed reforms Gomułka had made for the Polish people, was careful to say as little as possible about what really had happened, was happening. He knew Dudek was listening, taking note. He preferred therefore to talk only of music: of Bach, jazz, American minimalism, atonal possibility, voice. The notes mattered. The composition. The story behind this remained silent by necessity.

While he was getting himself another glass of wine, a pretty young woman approached and introduced herself as Adriena Pacovská, a family friend of Arkady's. She came to rescue Pawel from the more enthusiastic students, for which Pawel was most grateful. They talked of his work, quietly, over a glass of wine, and about her own impending performance in Vienna with her quartet of pianists. They would perform a work by Dvořák but also a piece by Marek Kopelent, a proponent of new Czech music, whose music Pawel knew from the Warsaw Autumn Festival and admired. Pawel noted that Dudek soon became bored and wandered off, allowing him to spend more time speaking quietly with the young Czech woman without prying eyes and ears.

The two concerts on the Friday and Saturday nights went well for the Polish musicians. Both concerts were well attended and the reception after seemed very positive. They students tended to see in Pawel and his work a reflection of their own anti-authoritarian spirit and desires, a need to make statements in music about the possibility of a future without constraints that brought in elements of the past. Pawel was always careful not only to thank his hosts but to speak well of the Polish music trends and how these were supported by the regime in Poland. It gave him hope, he said, that even as music evolved, whether classical, or jazz, or even rock and roll, that the Socialist countries such as Poland and Czechoslovakia would always provide support and acceptance. He also went out of his way to support the Czech students in their desire to forge a new musical language and new possibility without expressing his regrets that events in Poland had only served to dampen such hope.

He noticed that Dudek was not in attendance at the second concert, that the SB officer did not join the musicians at dinner that night, which unsurprisingly bothered no one. And that Dudek only returned to the room in the hostel at midnight. Indeed the following morning at breakfast, Dudek extolled the virtues of the Czechoslovak capitol, remarking it only a pity that its government did not seem to know how best to control its citizens. Still, he told Pawel with a wry grin, perhaps that is not such a bad thing.

Pawel did not bother to comment.

During the Sunday afternoon Pawel led a workshop in composition and performance with a number of the Conservatoire students. The young pianist Adriena Pacovská had happily delayed her quartet's departure so that she might attend, at Pawel's suggestion.

That evening Pawel, in a thoughtful mood, sat at the small bar in the pension nursing a vodka when Dudek walked in and sat beside him, a look of amusement in his face. Pawel knew Dudek had been drinking as well, although was not drunk.

"So, Composer," Dudek said, "it would seem your stay here has been successful. Congratulations."

"They seemed happy."

"So they should be. A fine performance. I must admit, while I find your work interesting, hearing it once through on Friday was probably enough. But I found other ways to amuse myself last night."

"Good for you," said Pawel.

"Um…I noted you seemed to have found a particular admirer in that young Czech woman student. She seemed very taken with you."

"I do not know what you mean."

"Nothing, particularly. An attractive young woman is all. You spent some time talking with her. Like you, a pianist I believe."

"I am surprised you noticed, Iwo. You seem to be occupied with so much else."

Dudek smiled. Shrugged.

"Ah Professor, we all have our secrets. Me. You. In some ways we have a lot in common."

"I should not think so."

"No, it is so. It is why I have taken an interest in you for quite some time. The music, of course. But other things as well. Did you know, for example, that I grew up in the Warmia Voivodeship? I know that district is not quite the same as your Silesian Voivodeship, where your mother came from I believe. But not too dissimilar I would venture. No doubt you agree. No doubt. Of course, unlike you, my parents did not both die in the war. Professor."

Pawel stared at him, then away.

"Indeed I have often been fascinated by your music. Your evolution too. You were a lover of Bach, I believe. As was I. As I still am."

"The evolution from Bach to the work I do now is not as far as you might think, Dudek."

"Perhaps not. But then that is why you are the professor and my world is strictly that of audience. One who listens. Tries to understand."

"But does not. Understand," said Pawel, looking at the security officer, refusing in fact to look away from him.

"Perhaps not. Perhaps not. Still, we live in uncertain, difficult times. These last months: most unfortunate. We must look after our interests I say. Scandals can ruin a man as I have discovered. Even in government. Oh, yes… A minor scandal, such as one's background, or even a sexual scandal these days. My wife, for example: I should imagine she would only think the worse of me for wanting to say hello to an old colleague when I travel. She might have the wrong impression. She would be wrong, of course, but appearances…Who knows what might happen. Even if I were to say 'enough' of my beloved wife in Warsaw. Walk away. Disappear. Our Polish leaders rightly give us enough freedom to travel, to leave. With our permits these days we can go away for, what, a year without penalty. Without risk. But even then, a minor scandal can ruin a career, near, far. I would hate for that to happen to me, Professor. You would not know of such things, but someone in my position, with friends, family back home. Like you I am allowed liberties. But these can so easily be lost. To wind up with so little after working so hard. So I must be careful. It is always wise to be careful what one says, does, who one sees. Where one goes. Happily, we live in a good country. Even the Zionists are welcome there as long as they choose Poland, eh?"

Pawel stared at him, then away.

"You are wrong, Dudek. We have nothing in common. Nothing at all."

"Oh…I don't know, Professor. We are both composers, in our respected fields. Both creating music I think. In our own separate ways. Our own separate notes. Searching for answers. For direction."

Dudek signaled to the young Czech behind the bar to pour another glass of vodka for Pawel.

"I will not join you for another, Composer. I have an appointment, as you see."

Pawel followed Dudek's gaze to a heavily made up woman who stood in the doorway, nodding at Dudek. Dudek waved, then nodded to Pawel.

"That old colleague. Always a pleasure. I will be late back, Professor. Do not wait up. Enjoy your vodka."

Pawel watched him and the woman leave the hostel. He did not move from his seat.

*

In the morning there was a scramble to get on the bus for the long journey back to Warsaw. Dudek, with a splitting headache from a long if enjoyable evening, sat in the front seat as the various young musicians carefully loaded their musical instruments, along with their bags, then filed onto the bus. Dudek looked around.

He did not see Pawel.

"Where is the Composer?," he asked one of the students, who shrugged his shoulders. He turned to another. "Weisz?," he again asked.

"I have not seen him. He was in your room was he not?"

Dudek swore. He wanted to get on the road.

He walked back into the pension but did not see Pawel in the reception area. He went back up to the first floor bedroom. The blanket still covered the large form but when Dudek, annoyed, tapped on what he thought was a shoulder, he discovered that the blanket only covered ruffled sheets and towels and the pillow. Pawel was not there. Perhaps had not been there for hours. There was a note under the pillow however: 'Please tell Anna Bednarz that she played very well at the concerts. PW'

Dudek stared at the note. Shook his head. Tore it up and left the pieces on a table. Best such compliment would come from him, not Weisz. She was a good looking young woman. She no doubt would appreciate it if he said something personally. No doubt.

Dudek told the other musicians that Pawel would return by private vehicle as he had agreed to a further workshop. It was easier to lie. Secrets and lies; he had no problem with either. Sitting on the bus, he thought about Weisz. Dudek was hardly surprised. A little annoyed perhaps. Or perhaps not. Weisz was free to go as he chose. He would return, or he would not. His exit stamps allowed him movement for a year. If he returned he would find his position compromised in Poland. If he did not return in the allotted time, his citizenship would be revoked. In either case, Weisz was smart enough to know he would need to focus on music not politics. He was smart enough to know that a scandal, even outside of Poland, would only do his reputation damage. The Minister might be annoyed but the truth was that a Polish composer would only enhance Poland's position as a country that knew how to nurture its talent. Wherever Pawel Weisz might go, if he indeed found any success, he would always be a Polish composer. Wherever he might go.

Dudek sat back in his seat. Closed his eyes. As long as Weisz focused on his music, all would be well. And truthfully there was only the music. There was nothing else.

At about the same time as Dudek and the Polish student musicians crossed the border back into Poland, Pawel, Adriena Pacovská and her three other associate musicians crossed the Austrian border, having travelled through much of the night. There had been just enough room to squeeze in with them, given that he had almost no luggage other than his briefcase filled with music.

The Czechoslovakian border guard looked at everyone's papers and the Austrian formal invitation for the quartet to perform in Vienna. He looked at Pawel's documents. Adriena Pacovská explained that Pawel Weisz was a well known and respected composer who would perform with them in Vienna. One of the other guards asked to look through Pawel's case but saw only music, most of which had the composer's name on the various scores; therefore the story was most likely true. And even if not, this was really just a formality as the Pole had proper documentation and the guards had not received any communication to prevent such movement. After five minutes the four Czechs and the Polish composer were allowed to pass into Austria.

Pawel stared at the scenery, but took little interest. He felt nothing, when all was said and done. Certainly not trepidation or an undue sense of loss, as his friend Arkady could be certain to go quickly to Pawel's apartment and remove all the music, just as Pawel had written to him, in order to forward it at a later time. There was little else Pawel would need or want in the future.

He thought too about Robert. About what the violinist had done, and why. He knew he would keep Robert locked within him, his memory, for all his days. Memory with One Musician. Not twelve. One only. He wondered what would have happened if Robert had not died, had not suffered. He wondered if Robert had loved him. He hoped so. He could not know for certain, however. Would never know now for certain.

He closed his eyes, sat back. Wherever his journey might now take him, he would try to find some peace he told himself. He would look at music differently: not as an experiment, as a way to change the world, but as a way to enrich the world. To see it not as notes and cadences and alienation and atonal or polytonal or futuristic or artifice. Or artifice. No; he would henceforth seek out the human and

302

the voice, his voice, for a semblance of truth, as a semblance of love. Not that he would look to change style, or to cease exploring. He would still compose. But in the process he decided it was time to think with his heart as much as with his head. It was time to listen and to feel. To remember those who had gone before, and seek those who he was still to find. As he would.

So with his eyes closed, he stopped hearing the words and instead heard the music. He heard Bach playing in his head, in his heart. Then Chopin whispering to him. He heard the weeping of a violin and knew that is was the weeping of all he lost and the hope of all he would yet discover. He heard grief. He heard loss. He heard love. And finally, he heard hope.

It was enough for him.

*

Two weeks later, on the night of 20 August, 2,000 tanks supporting 250,000 Soviet and Warsaw Pact troops entered Czechoslovakia to put an end to the period of liberalization known as the Prague Spring. Amongst the Eastern Bloc invading forces that moved quickly into Prague were 28,000 soldiers from the Polish 2nd Army from the Silesian Military District.

It so happened that Pawel that night was on a sleeper train to France, so was unaware of the invasion until late the following day.

He did not comment on it upon his arrival.

Third Movement

Sacrificium:
Agnieszka's Supplication

Warsaw

2007

12 February 2007

Jewish Reference Archives Poland (Warsaw Office)
Dr. David Weinstein, Director

Dear Dr. Weinstein
I was kindly given your name by a mutual acquaintance, Professor Dorothy Sellin, of the Jewish Historical Institute. I wondered if I can come in to speak with you about an issue relating to my grandmother, Hannah Kielar, who died late last year. Dorothy suggested the JRA would possibly be an organization that could assist me with information.

I look forward to hearing from you.

Yours respectfully

Ms. Agnieszka (Aga) Janiec

*

Jewish Reference Archives (Warsaw Office)
Dr. D.Weinstein, Director

15 February 2007

Professor Dorothy Sellin
Jewish Historical Institute of Poland
Ohel/Polin Public Private Partnership

Dear Dorothy

Just to let you know I have received a note of introduction and request for possible information and assistance from Miss Agnieszka Janiec, who contacted us following a conversation with you. We will do our best to see if we can be of assistance to her.

I trust you and Walter are both well.

As always,
David

JRA Internal Memo

15 February 2007
From: David Weinstein
To: Beniamin Zuckerman

Ben:
See attached note from Ms. Janiec.
I would like you to deal with this, see if we can be of assistance. Miss Janiec is a rather well known actress. Professor Dorothy Sellin, who I know socially, advised her to contact us.

Keep me informed.
DW

*

19 February 2007

Dear Ms. Janiec
My name is Beniamin Zuckerman. I am a researcher with JRA (Warsaw). Dr. Weinstein has passed your note over to me. I would be very happy to meet with you to see if we can be of assistance in the matter of your grandmother. Should you wish to call the office, we can set an appointment.

Yours sincerely,
Beniamin Zuckerman

*

21 February

Dearest Mother, Father
A quick note to say thank you for forwarding the Za'atar, the dates and Halvah. All made it here safely and now I can enjoy a bit of Israel in my little apartment. The weather here in Warsaw has turned quite cold and I am missing the sunshine and beach of Tel Aviv. But all is good despite the cold.

Work continues to be interesting and sometimes saddening. A gift from Dr. Weinstein arrives tomorrow: an actress apparently, although unsurprisingly that means nothing to me. Alas, as always I remain your (relative) neanderthal son in matters of culture. I am not clear what she wants—something having to do with her grandmother. But we will see. Meanwhile my other file histories and research keep me occupied. A multitude of sadness and tragedy from the past, as you'll know. I will likely return to Israel for work sometime in the next month, perhaps a bit longer. I look forward to a short break there and to seeing you.

Please give both Avi and Mira my love. They owe me a letter.

Your loving son

Ben

*

Aga sat across the desk from him, sipping on the coffee he had brought from the kitchenette into which he had disappeared when she first arrived. He was younger than she would have imagined, far younger. Tall, quite handsome. Confident in his own skin. She made a habit of reading people. He had to be near to her own age, serious but easy going. He had a slight accent, although his Polish was fluent.

"My parents were Polish. They emigrated from the south of Poland in the 1960s. They did not know one another before. Met in Israel. I was born there but we speak Polish as well at home."

"You're far younger than I would have imagined. Although I do not know what I imagined."

He smiled again.

"I apologize if you are disappointed. Alas, Simon Wiesenthal died a couple years ago.

"No, I…Wiesenthal? You mean the…Oh, a joke. Yes. No."

He laughed. His laugh was gentle, not mocking. An easy personality.

"I will take it as a compliment."

"So why Warsaw? Hardly the weather?"

"I came here four years ago to finish research for my PhD. History."

"Polish history?"

"Medieval Polish history. Alchemy and its effects on the political class in the 14th and 15th Centuries. Very dull really."

She smiled. Shrugged.

"When I finished, academia was not for me. I approached the Jewish Historical Institute. I had hoped to be involved with the creation of the new Jewish Museum project they are building. But once the architects were appointed there was little need for a very good researcher. Or a bad one. I had heard that the JRA needed researchers to help set up new a new data base, investigate and research genealogies, reparations, that sort of thing. So, I applied and a year and a half later they have not fired me. At least not yet."

"And are you good? As a researcher here?"

He lifted his hands with a shrug.

"I believe you are an actress," he said. "Are you good?"

"Sometimes I wonder. I think I am still young enough to be lucky and lucky enough to be still young."

"Indeed. A good response. Perhaps we are not so different. So: how is it we can help you here?"

"I am looking for someone. My grandmother."

He looked at her, furrowing his brow just slightly. He could quickly look so serious in a charming way, she thought.

"I'm sorry, perhaps I misunderstood. I thought your Grandmother had passed away."

"Yes. She did. Last year. When she died my mother and aunt discovered a safe box at the bank where she had left a few things. Alas no secret fortune. But amongst the items was a large manila envelope addressed to me."

Aga reached down to her bag and pulled out a bound notebook stuffed with protective sheet protectors. She opened it and pulled out from the first a letter that she handed to Beniamin.

"Please," she said, gesturing that he should read.

Aga watched his face while he slowly took in each word, each thought. She saw his expression change from gentle interest to seriousness, a kind of quiet thoughtfulness settling in. When he had finished he put the pages down, looked away, stared out the window. Finally he turned back to her.

"You must miss her a great deal. She clearly loved you very much."

"...Yes."

"I take it you did not know what she tells you in this."

"No."

"You were raised...?

"Religion? Little, but what there was, Catholic."

He looked at her, nodded slightly. Finally:

"And what do you feel about what your Grandmother writes?"

"At first, confused. Perhaps curious. Perhaps hurt even."

"And then?"

"And then I went through the various papers. Names. Official documents.

Sometimes stories or diary entries, a fragment, recollections, thoughts. A cry perhaps. She wanted me to know. And there is much I do not know, much she does not tell. I think perhaps she needed to speak. Perhaps she did and I did not hear. Or listen. I need to listen now."

"What do your family think?"

"I have not told them. Not yet."

"Why is that?"

Aga hesitated. Thinking. Looking for the answer.

"My aunt has been undergoing chemotherapy. She is better but... No. That is not right. I could have told my mother, my aunt, but I am not yet ready to tell them. I need to find her first. Does that make sense?"

He smiled but did not reply to the question directly.

"And if this proves to be true, if you find out more, if you find her, as you say, then what?"

Aga looked at him for a moment, unclear where this was going.

"I do not understand your question."

"Are you hoping for...restitution? Property or art or money? Do you think if this is true the state owes you something?"

"No. No it is not like that."

"So what are you looking for?"

Aga stared at this young man, his expression so serious now, thoughtful. Just as he tried to read her, she tried to read him. Had she asked herself that question before she began making enquiries, seeking answers? She did not reply quickly. As she scrutinized his eyes, his hands folded now on the table: his face, his quiet.

"Answers," she finally said quietly. "The truth. Who she was. Maybe who I am. All that I knew was built on something that was...not."

"What do you know of the JRA?"

She shrugged. "Nothing, really. I approached a woman I had met before socially. She suggested contacting you."

"So," he smiled, "the JRA is a non-profit organization originally set up in the United Stated to try to bring a record of names, birth and death records, verifiable documentation to help illuminate in a small way Jewish life as it was in Poland

311

and elsewhere prior to the Holocaust, especially for survivors and their families. The Polish government is helpful now. It was not always so. Here in the Warsaw office I am part of a small division of the JRA. We help families try to trace what happened to their relatives, but also to discover lost personal property, real estate, effects, histories: mostly, as you put it, the truth. Most often Americans contact us, but not only. How much do you know about the Warsaw Ghetto, about the world your grandmother indicates she came from in this letter?"

"Not much," Aga said, shaking her head. "Sad, I know. My city, my history. Maybe my people now. Not much."

"An honest answer. Believe me, a majority of Poles, like many throughout the whole world, know only that the Holocaust was a terrible event, that six million Jews died, let alone homosexuals, Roma, political prisoners, countless others, to say nothing of the incredible loss of Russian lives. What gets lost in these statistics, beyond comprehension really, are the people. Their lives. Their histories. Their stories. History is no more than telling stories from time gone by, sometimes recent, sometimes long ago, embellished with a point of view. Stories matter. They tell us who we are. What we are. In Warsaw alone, more than 430,000 died in anonymity in Treblinka or on the streets, murdered, every day. Individuals, families, whole streets, a history torn asunder. Disappeared. As if such history never was. But…but it existed and seeks voice."

He hesitated, thought for a moment.

"I am sorry, my history hat often fits too large on my head. Trying to locate names, families, it is a long process, a difficult process. The Nazis kept amazing records and no records you might say. A dilemma. In some files, at Auschwitz for example, they recorded every detail: names, prisoner numbers, movements details, the numbers of lice found in a man's hair. Amazing. They kept records of records. But the real records kept as men, women, children marched into the gas chambers being told they would be deloused, then the names, the numbers, even the lice, these disappear into smoke like the people themselves. These records, the emotional records…these we do not have. You see first the Nazis sent in the men. The women and the children beyond, they often heard the screams. They knew. Still they too could not run, not escape. They too entered the false shower rooms.

312

And after they disappeared. Without their names. Without their identities. Without their very humanity. Buried in mass graves, covered in lime, later burned in furnaces. Ash. These stories are what matter, not simply the statistics; but these we do not always have…"

He shrugged. He was not giving a history lesson. He was the pain itself, removed by generations but refusing to forget.

"Even if your grandmother is telling the truth…

"If?

"Sometimes, people hope to gain the past, alleviate their own guilt or what they did, claim property. We can assist, but the courts deal with these issues now. Sometimes there is an issue."

"My grandmother was many things, but…not that. Not if you had known her, she…She was not an 'issue'."

"Forgive me; that is not what I meant. It is simply that the truth is never easily come by and not always black and white."

"Like life itself."

He smiled. Nodded.

"Like life itself. Here we sift through what information we can find. It is difficult. Your grandmother: after the War some lived. Most of those here in this country eventually emigrated to Israel, the United States, elsewhere. They could not stay. Under the Communists most came to feel they were not wanted. And they were not. But then not everyone left. Some found ways to make their peace here. Some changed their names. Some had forgotten. Or managed to forget. Or tried to convince themselves they forgot. I do not think you ever forget. Not really."

"No.

"Occasionally I have heard a story like your Grandmother writes here. Because of guilt, pain, for reasons we can only begin to fathom, a few, very few, never said, never told. Things we do not understand, will never understand."

Aga nodded.

"In here," she said, putting her hand on the folder, "my Grandmother left me many documents, mostly official things about Hannah Kielar, the woman I knew. Or thought I did. And then she wrote down at various moments some—events, stories, names. Fragments. A sort of diary. Reminisces. People gone, killed. Family. Explanations perhaps. I made these photocopies of all the originals, then tried to put them in some sort of order, tried to make a little sense of it all. I would like…an opinion. A sense of what might have happened. I can pay you…"

Beniamin smiled. "We are a non-profit. You can donate to the organization, or not. Leave it with me. I will go over these things. It may take some time. I will tell you what I think. Honestly."

"…She wanted me to know."

"Yes. And perhaps she wanted to know."

Aga stood, shook his hand. Held it for a long moment, looking into his face, finding the trust she needed at this point.

"Thank you, Mr. Zuckerman, I…I appreciate this."

"Beniamin. Or simply Ben. Please."

"Aga."

"Aga. You are working just now? As an actor I mean."

She laughed.

"Always acting, you wonder? An act. So, yes. In a play. Two plays actually. *Elektra* and *Iphigenia*. At the Factory. A temporary theatre."

"You must forgive me. I am not much of a theatre goer."

"It has been extended for another month. You should come if you can. There are a few seats still. I can get you tickets."

He smiled.

"You must be popular. Thank you. Let me see. I will come back to you on this when I can."

She nodded. Turned and left the room. She did not know if he would be able to help. She did not know what she hoped to find. She would wait to hear from him. She felt certain she would.

After that night's performance, once she had returned to her small apartment and showered, Aga sat at her small dining table, a cup of tea before her. She stirred it over and over again, her thoughts distant, questioning. Her Grandmother's various memories played out constantly in her head. Hannah had given so much, and given so little. Names mostly. Some stories, painful to read. The death of her father. The murder of her young cousin, who would have been Aga's own relative. Somehow an escape from Warsaw, then a life in Nowy Wiśnicz. How had she managed to leave? What had in fact happened to the woman named on her birth certificate as her mother, Helena Kielar? The reports from her doctor, later her husband, said Helena Kielar had died as the Nazis retreated. But how had she died? And why not Hannah as well? So many questions. No answers.

The tea stirred round, round, stirred around in her cup. She sat staring at it. Patterns without particular meaning.

Aga was exhausted. She knew she was. While pleased that the two plays had been extended by a month, she knew they were taking their toll on her. She had more than inhabited the two roles. They had become two aspects of her personality, in conflict with one another. Two characters who lived for one another died for one another hated one another were one another. Were one another. Characters in a play, characters inside of her. And like her Grandmother: Hannah and Hania. Hannah who she had known and adored. Hania of the secrets who she did not know. Could not know.

She hoped this Beniamin Zuckerman might find answers. Answers about her Grandmother's suffering. About her Grandmother's journey. The pain of it. The truth of it. She hoped if such truth could be found, it would ultimately lead to truth about herself.

*

He did not ring her until mid-March, apologizing for taking so long. Much on his plate. She agreed to meet him the following morning at the To Lubie café. When she arrived he had already found a small table on the quiet second floor, overlooking the street.

"Sometimes I think you need cheesecake and good coffee to start the day."

"And you get neither at the office."

He shrugged.

After the coffee had been brought to them Beniamin sat back in his stuffed chair, looking at her.

"So."

"So. So, I looked through the database, did an archive search, made a few

315

enquiries. The Grandmother you knew all of your life was Hannah Kielar."

"Was she?"

Aga stared at him. Then: "The birth certificates, identity papers, baptism certificate... most of these exist in the archives of the Krakow District, sub-district Bochnia. I believe they are authentic. I have written to the parish priest in Nowy Wiśnicz; I suspect if records were kept they will have the baptism recorded as well. Confirmation too, if she did. The Babinsky Institute in Kobierzyn is quite well known. Parts have been rebuilt. Many Jews were taken from there and murdered early in the Nazi occupation. Afterwards it reopened quickly for neurological and psychological disorders. I am waiting to see what records they might have of your Grandfather's time there as a psychotherapist. Your Grandmother's records I will not bother to request. These I know are confidential, even now almost fifty years later. But the few that your Grandmother left you again seem authentic."

"You have not told me about Hania Stern."

"Hania Stern. Yes. Well as you can understand with the Jewish population of Warsaw in the 1930s and 1940s, we work at a disadvantage. So many records were lost or destroyed; the Nazis did not keep a record of those who died. In those days, no database would have been big enough, you see. What we rely on often are accounts of those who survived, archives where we can find names, identities. The most famous are the Ringelblum Archives. Emmanuel Ringelblum kept diaries, as did a few others. These were buried in secret places in the Ghetto before it all burned to the ground and was demolished. The group that wrote down the records and hid them called themselves Oyneg Shabbos. The Sabbath Gathering, if you like. Ringelblum was a historian and at the centre of this group."

"So you can relate, given what you do," she said with a smile.

"No. Few can relate to what went on there. Few will ever know. Ringelblum and some others saw what was coming. They kept records, but they often disguised names, as you can understand. That these records have survived is in itself a bit of a miracle. But that is a digression. Another time, not now...I could find no record of a Hania Stern in the database and records we have. Not surprising. She was very young, according to your Grandmother. Nothing on Zivia

316

Stern or Marek Stern."

"What are you saying?"

"At this point? Nothing really. Pre-war housing records are hard to come by. The PZT radio works kept some records, but Jewish names were carefully removed or lost."

"Her mother: my Grandmother said her mother was an actress in Yiddish theatre. She performed in a Yiddish play at the...I need to look."

"I know. The play was called 'Shulamis', at the Nowości Theater. I am aware of this play. I am trying to see if somewhere in archives there might be a program, or something, anything. Most records give the name of the primary actors, but you never know. However, so far I have found very little I'm afraid. Now: I did find references to Michael Elster, who she says was her uncle. He had been a fairly well known architect before the war. And Lea Elster: she was interesting. A respected pianist and there are two or three mentions of her in some records. Birth certificates, or one for an infant Jakub..."

Beniamin Zuckerman shook his head.

"So basically there is little."

"No, basically there is nothing. Or almost nothing."

"You think perhaps Hania Stern did not exist?"

"That is not what I am saying," he answered without hesitation. "Not at all. I am saying I may find more, I may not. You need to understand what little I found in this short time does not paint a picture. And what I found is not hard to find. It is possible--and you must bear with me--it is possible that Hannah Kielar came up with a few names and for whatever reason created an identity for herself. She did need hospitalization after the War. She does not say why but some of the doctors did suggest schizophrenia."

"But not her doctor. Her doctor who became her husband."

"I do not think she was lying. And I do not think she made up the stories."

"But..."

"But I do not know, not at this point. She writes snippets, names that can be searched. She writes about the terrible murder of her Aunt and Uncle's child, but after that...she largely stops writing, recording that last period in the Ghetto,

317

except to say she escaped through sewers. Yes, a few names, but she does not say how she managed to get to Nowy Wiśnicz. Some of the names she lists without context may relate, or may not. But once she does get there, once she says she arrives at a farm near Nowy Wiśnicz, hard facts appear. Before…"

"Four Hundred Thirty Thousand."

Beniamin looked at her.

"Four Hundred Thirty Thousand Jews in the Ghetto you said. Almost all dead. Hard facts?" Aga shook her head.

"I know. I agree. But she gives enough to search, to see what comes out. There may be nothing."

"And there may be a life."

"And there may be a life. Yes. But I cannot do much more on behalf of JRA."

Aga was quiet for a moment. She nodded, smiled at him.

"I understand."

"No. You do not, not entirely. I would like to continue to search a bit. As I said I am a good researcher, just as from the reviews I read you must be a good actress. I have to go away for a couple weeks soon; work mostly. But I would like to continue, with your permission only however."

"What do you want for this?"

"Nothing. I am not Philip Marlow. I do not work on a retainer."

She looked at him for a long moment. His earnest face. His smile without a serious angle.

"Then why?" she finally asked.

"Because… Because if I were in your shoes I would seek answers, like you are doing. Because I would need to know. Because I would recognize that there may be no answers, no truth. But even a small truth, a small story, might bring life to the dead, and to the living bring…"

Beniamin Zuckerman hesitated. Looked away. Shrugged. Looked back.

"Peace perhaps," he said.

"Do the living need peace?"

"Perhaps more than the dead. Yes."

*

26 March 2007

Dearest Mother, Father

Just to tell you I look forward to seeing you next week. If there is anything you want from Warsaw, let me know. I would suggest pierogi from Zapiecek but no one beats Mother's pierogi. However you can be sure I will bring along a bottle or two of Wiśniówka to raise a glass for Passover. Anything else?

Remind me to tell you about the actress I have mentioned, Agnieszka Janiec. She appears in two plays running together here in Warsaw that I will go to see Saturday (yes, two in one day!), Elektra and Iphigenia. Apparently she plays the lead in each play but not the same character. The plays have had very good reviews, as has Agnieszka Janiec, so I am looking forward to seeing them—I just hope I do not fall asleep! You know me. I have done a bit of research into her family although it has not particularly led anywhere. Still an interesting story perhaps and an interesting woman. Work busy otherwise. Will need to spend some time at Yad Vashem but not until after the Pesach.

Your loving son

Ben

*

<u>*JRA Internal Memo*</u>
27 March 2007

From: Beniamin Zuckerman
To: David Weinstein

Hello David
I will be flying to Tel Aviv on Monday, 1 April (no joke!) for a two week holiday with my family, then will spend a week researching at Yad Vashem on behalf of three JRA clients, the Levins from Detroit, Mr. and Mrs. Black from Brooklyn and Rabbi Horowitz from Atlanta. I hope also to arrange those few interviews we discussed as well. I will keep a record and receipts of all expenses.

Also in passing I did put the name of Hania Stern in the index registry with a question mark, as we discussed. I have no idea if any more information will come to light but I'll indeed keep an open mind; you were right to have suggested this. Of course I will keep you informed.

I wish you and your family a Happy Pesach.

Ben

*

319

2 April 2007

Hi Aleksy!
Waiting at the airport to fly to Tel Aviv. Will drop this in the post before I leave.

Wanted to say thank you for pushing me to go to both Elektra and Iphigenia. A long day of theatre but well worth it. You were right about the theatre's location: a very interesting place.

I am so sorry you could not join me. Both plays were excellent. An understatement in my ignorant opinion. Certainly they gave me pause for thought. I must read the original source material. Aeschylus you suggest? The history interests me greatly, as you can imagine.

But more to the point: Agnieszka Janiec's performance. Both plays, such different characters: physical, sexual, painful. Okay, okay, yes she is quite attractive. But that is not the point, really. She seemed to encapsulate the conflict so inherent in both roles and I believe brought interpretations in her performances without a doubt influenced by some events in her personal life, of which I am aware through my own work. Another time perhaps to explain that to you. But I have to say her acting really touched me. At the end of the play she and the other actors were given a standing ovation, well deserved. Apparently she was too exhausted to come out a second time with the other actors to take the applause and I can well understand that. I had hoped to go back stage to offer congratulations, but I was told that she had fallen ill and could see no one. In fact then I read in the newspaper yesterday that she had collapsed after the second play and had been hurried to a hospital. Exhaustion, the article said. I am hardly surprised; a very physical performance and emotionally difficult I should think, let alone two plays over one day.

I hope and trust she will be well. I must get back in touch with her upon my return from Israel.

And we must find time for those beers you suggested. I apologize for having to cancel previous evenings myself. Have been so busy. I promise to catch up with you when I return at the end of the month.

So be well. Not too much alcohol intake in April (well, much but not too much: I know you!)

Until then

Ben

*

Stefan had driven her to the hospital immediately after the curtain came down. She could tell he was worried, sincerely so, but she urged him to return to the cast party. She sent all her love and asked him to let them know she was fine; just very tired. Her parents also came to the hospital that night and in the morning drove her home. They wanted her to stay at their house but she needed quiet. She needed space. For the next few days they, like Stefan, checked on her almost daily, but finally the phone stopped ringing and she slept. She felt like she could sleep for weeks. For two weeks, anyway, she largely did.

She began to feel stronger but decided she did not want to rush into anything new, not at the moment. Stefan had said he wanted to find something else to do with her, another play, but she knew he had been weighing taking on a television project in St. Petersburg and if he decided to do the project it would occupy him for the next year. Stefan said he thought she might be right for a part in the production but it held no interest whatsoever for her.

Aga realized she needed space. She wanted to think about the last months, about her Grandmother, her Mother, her Aunt, her life. She wanted to breathe. There would be time enough for a new project but not just yet.

So she read. She met her mother a couple of times for coffee and to shop. She thought about a holiday but decided against it. She enjoyed the spring weather in Warsaw and saw no reason to rush somewhere so she could lie on a beach or tread through museums. Her Grandmother's notes and her talk with Beniamin Zuckerman had made her realize she had much to learn. She wanted to learn. So she bought books. Thought. Rested. And let her mind wander, let her mind ask questions. She still had so many questions.

She was now not convinced she would hear from Beniamin again. She thought she would, but after so many weeks she could no longer be certain. So when she had a message on her phone to say he would like to meet she was perhaps more relieved than pleased. Ben—he insisted on that—suggested they meet at the JRA offices at the end of the month. She agreed. She realized that in fact she had wanted to see him again: curiosity in many respects.

"So," he said as he ushered her down the corridor, "thank you for coming."

"I am disappointed. I was looking forward to more cheesecake."

321

"Next time perhaps. This time the quiet of the office."

He closed the door behind him. He had a pot of coffee waiting, poured two cups as he sat down.

"I saw you, in both the plays. On the final night."

"Did you? I am pleased."

"Interesting plays too. Your performances—very moving. Really."

"A fan. That is kind."

"I do not understand these things very well. But somehow you seemed—well, more than just acting. The two characters not only came alive. They took you over. Does that make sense?"

She smiled. Hoped she had not blushed.

"You try to achieve that. If it comes across, then it works."

"Um... I had hoped to see you after but I learned you were ill. I read about it the next day. Nothing serious I trust?"

Aga shrugged.

"Tired. Nothing more. They ran some tests. All negative, happily. The play took over. It had been extended. Perhaps too much."

"Perhaps your Grandmother too?"

"My obsession?"

"Is it?"

"No. Yes. I don't know. What I do know, however, is that I have had little chance to grieve. Perhaps that played a part. I miss her. And then the—the stories as well. Raging tempest and I have needed to get out of the storm."

He nodded.

"I would have contacted you sooner, but I have been away. Israel. Holiday. Family. Work. In that order."

"Which was more difficult?"

"Family, to be sure," he laughed. "But the food was better. So...So. I wanted to talk to you."

"Did you find something?"

"Yes. Unexpectedly. It will not be easy."

He looked at her. He said nothing. She realized he waited for her response.

"I am stronger now, really. I have spent two weeks sleeping and a week shopping with my mother. As with you, family…"

"Yes," he smiled quietly. Thought for a moment. And began.

"As I said, part of my time away was holiday. Then I had a week, ten days or so of work. Not concerning your Grandmother. Or at least not intended."

"I see."

"Do you know Yad Vashem?"

She shook her head no.

"Yad Vashem. It means 'Memorial and a Name'. It is a place of pilgrimage in Jerusalem, a museum and a research centre about the Holocaust. They keep archives, documents, photographs, testimonies. There are seminars, collections, exhibitions. A wonderful place really. Painful. Thoughtful. Deeply moving… Anyway, I had research work to do at Yad Vashem. As a resource it is second to none. Some of our clients, if they do not have access, we go, research, seek names, documents, accounts. Information. It is hardly our only resource but probably our most valuable one."

"Did you find something about my Grandmother?"

"Yes and no. I was not there specifically about Hania Stern, so you should understand that. But I could not get away from her story, from yours. I brought your photocopies with me, in case I did have time to spend. There was not much I'm afraid. A couple names she recorded, as I said before, appeared again. Michael and Lea Elster, as I told you. She refers to a Nazi called 'Frankenstein" in some notes. His real name was Josef Blösche. And yes he was a monster. He was found in East Germany after the War and executed. I read many accounts of him in fact. The one they called the 'Magician' who she records as shooting her little cousin, I do not know."

"I do not care about them."

"No. Of course not. But names lead to others, so all names can be valuable, good or bad."

"Did you find anything about Alicja Leder? My Grandmother talks a lot about her friend. I think she loved her like a sister, the way she writes about her sometimes."

"No."

"I see."

"Not exactly."

He looked at Aga long and hard. She held his glance, read his thoughts.

"Go on, Ben, please."

"The name Josef Schipper. Do you remember it?"

Aga thought for a moment, tried to remember.

"She only mentions him a few times in passing: twice in a diary, some notes. So: here."

He opened his briefcase, searched through it, then pulled out a photograph. It was the photograph of an old man, a faraway look in his glance to camera. She could see he must have been a big man once, strong, but the lines along his eyes, his face looked only thoughtful, no longer powerful. Deep lines of considered grief. A weathered face of someone who had seen a great deal, suffered a great deal.

"This is Josef Schipper. He was a mechanic in the Ghetto. He moved into the Elster apartment building on Twarda Street."

"Oh yes, I do remember. She did not like him much she wrote. And she saw him again when they all moved to Dzielna."

"That's correct. After Hania says her father was killed. They moved to Dzielna Street. Schipper apparently moved nearby. I want you to hear something…"

Beniamin found a cassette tape in his briefcase and put it into a machine he had placed on the desk. He turned it on and Aga heard a man's voice, weak sounding, tired. She did not understand the words. They were in a language she did not know. Instead she listened to the voice, sometimes hesitant, sometimes demanding or insistent. Sometimes sorrowful. Somehow sorrowful.

"I do not…"

"No," said Beniamin. "I knew that. I simply thought you should hear his voice. Those things are important. He is speaking Hebrew. As I said, I had some research to do at Yad Vashem. In fact, Josef Schipper's name came up while searching for another client but I remembered his name written in your Grandmother's papers. One of the things they did, continue to do at Yad Vashem is to take testimony from survivors, from the families of survivors. Perhaps more than anything we have it remains the most valuable resource on the Holocaust. Firsthand accounts. Names. Memories. Those who bore witness. This tape in full is Josef Shipper's testimony."

Again Beniamin searched in his briefcase, then pulled out a folder.

"It takes time of course, but they make transcripts of the testimonies they have for later research. This is his. In Hebrew. But if you will allow me, I have marked some short sections that I would like to translate for you."

She stared at Beniamin's face, his expression. And as she had before, she saw the warmth there, not guarded, but full of empathy, determination and some sadness.

"Right, so…he explained how he was a mechanic with a business in a different part of Warsaw before the German invasion. A good mechanic, and despite the Germans being the enemy, they came to him with their cars and he needed the work. He justifies himself and that is understandable. Understanding is all important you see. And then he continues: 'I was living outside the Ghetto but the Germans forced everyone to move within its boundaries as they began to create first a fence, then a wall. For me, it was not so bad. The Germans needed their cars mended. They knew I was a good mechanic. The best. They were also stupid about cars. I was able to smuggle in mechanical parts, yes, but also bits of food, sometimes medicines, money hidden in the bowels of some of those cars. They never found out. If they had they would have killed me but I knew what I was doing, believe me.'"

Beniamin turned over some pages. "'Then the Judenrat found a room for me. I was a big man. No wife, no family, but a big man. And connected. So I was lucky. I had a room alone in a small apartment building on Twarda Street. I kept mostly to myself. Safer that way. And you had to be careful. I knew for example that some in the house had a radio hidden in the attic. The parts were smuggled in by one of the residents downstairs, Marek…um, Marek…What was his name? Stein I think. Marek Stein. He lived there in the apartment of his brother-in-law who I did not really know, with his family. A boy and a girl. The girl I remember was afraid of me. Maybe she did not realize how handsome I was.' He laughed there on the tape. I think he was joking."

Aga smiled slightly.

"He did not know the girl's name," said Beniamin, "but it could have been Hania Stern. He says Stein, but it was a long time ago."

"So she was there."

"…'Her father, the Germans discovered he had smuggled radio parts. They shot him at the prison. That must have been hard on them all, I…I don't know.'"

Beniamin looked back at Aga. She sat quietly. Looked down, away. Nodded slightly. He went on, turning over some of the pages.

"'After they forced us to leave the Little Ghetto, I found a space to work and a room on Smocza Street. The Ghetto was so crowded. Everyone was hungry, struggling, afraid. It transpired I lived around the corner from the architect from Twarda Street and his family. He was the one related to Stein. He asked me to help build some passages between attics in the buildings around his courtyard. Later I helped him and others build a bunker in one of those buildings. I do not know if anyone stayed in the attics or that bunker, but they could move from one to the other through passageways we hid. I also found supplies to build a secret room in his own apartment, behind a sink. He did a good job with that, being an architect.'"

Beniamin hesitated, turned over some more pages. He looked at Aga, sitting quietly.

"This is what I most wanted you to hear. But it is difficult."

If a question, she did not answer. She sat looking at him, then again nodded slightly.

"…'They had started what they called their 'Aktion'. Like everyone I tried to hide, but the Germans, the Ukrainians, they were everywhere. They broke into the building where I was living and I did not have time to get away or hide. They forced me onto the street with hundreds of others. Hundreds and hundreds of others. Eventually they made us get into columns and march to the Umschlagplatz. Some people had suitcases with them. They thought they would be relocated because the Nazis promised the Jews would be safe on a journey to the East. I had heard the lies the Nazis told and knew there would be no truth in them.'"

"'It took an hour, maybe two to get to the Umschlagplatz. More and more Jews joined the columns, guarded on either side. If anyone did not do as ordered they were shot there and then. So many died even on that short journey.'"

"'When we got there, we were made to wait many hours for the trains to be loaded. Cattle cars. They forced one hundred people into cars, threw lime on their feet that burned, shut them in. Cattle cars of death, I thought. Waiting for death. Carrying the Jews to death.'"

"'…I was in a crowd of people standing, not daring to say anything. Some people I recognized but no one spoke unless quietly. The guards shot anyone who did not behave as ordered. I saw people urinate, defecate where they stood. They could not move. I remember I was standing not too far from one of the train cars, waiting. I heard someone shout 'Mama! 'Mama!' I looked around and recognized that young girl whose house I shared in Twarda Street, the Stein girl. I had seen her at Dzielna as well, where her uncle lived. I think she lived there with him. I do not know what became of her young brother. She was in the crowd and yelling towards a car. I looked to see what she was yelling at and saw her mother being pulled into one of the cattle cars. I recognized her. A girl was helping her, a girl leaning on a crutch with only one good leg. It was all terrible. The daughter must have been separated from her mother. Then the Nazis threw in lime and slammed the door shut. Terrible. So terrible.'"

"'I looked to see where the young Stein girl was. She had been stopped by a guard. He pulled out his gun, pointed it at her. I thought he would shoot her, there and then. He would have I think but this German SS officer stopped him. I did not know the German officer or why he did this, but he pushed the Guard away. Then he grabbed the young girl. I saw him pull her away. Literally drag her. I watched them go towards the trains, but he did not put her inside. Instead he dragged her around to the back of the trains. I did not see her again but I knew what was coming. I wish I could have helped but no one could help.'"

Beniamin stopped, looked at Aga. She sat stone still, her face set. Beniamin hesitated a second, then read.

"…'After a few minutes, I heard a shot, then a second, from the direction where that German SS officer and the girl had disappeared. He reappeared a couple minutes later. His coat was undone. There was blood on his shirt. He was tightening the belt of his trousers. No one paid him any attention, although I looked over and saw the Guard, the same one who had almost shot the girl, stare at the German and shake his head with a big smile on his face. I hope it was fast for her. I hope she was not afraid. Such a terrible way to die. But everyone died so terribly.'"

Aga said nothing. She stared straight ahead as if seeing nothing, hearing nothing. Only her eyes reacted. Beniamin could see she was tearing, trying to keep control of herself.

"Are you all right?" he asked her.

Aga nodded, unable to speak.

"I... I did not know. I..."

"Thousands were taken to the Umschlagplatz from July to October, 1942. Thousands and thousands deported. Some three hundred thousand. Very few escaped from there."

"But she lived. Hania lived."

Beniamin did not respond.

"Ben?"

"I do not know."

"He must have let her go. She must have got away somehow. Escaped. She must have."

"Perhaps."

"You do not think Hania Stern is Hannah Kielar."

"She is. She isn't. So much of the stories meshes. Hannah Kielar knew the story well. How? Did someone else tell her the story? I can't think of another easy answer besides they are one and the same person. But to think she escaped? Almost every Jew there was killed if not on the cattle trains. But yes a few escaped or bribed their way out. Did he let her go? Perhaps. Perhaps not. Or perhaps she had help. I do not know."

Aga was silent for a long time. She stared at the photograph of Josef Schipper. He had known her grandmother as a young girl in the Ghetto. He must have known her.

"I could talk to him, I could…," Aga said, searching.

"Shipper died in 1991."

"…But he…he survived."

Beniamin looked at the young woman across from him. Vulnerable now. Reaching. Needing so much. He turned to the final pages of the testimony.

"'…so yes, I did not die. I thank God, and I curse Him every day. I did not die. The train journey was terrible. Some died in the car. Their bodies propped up against others; there was no place to put them down. You could barely move. You urinated, defecated where you stood. One young man broke a piece of the wood panel siding and somehow pulled himself through. But he did not make it. Horrible. Others gave up, if they had not already. Humanity reduced to…to nothing. The train journey to Treblinki took us two and a half days. No food. No water. We had to wait in the village of Malkinia for ten, twelve hours, standing crammed in the cattle car, in the heat. People fainted. Died. I do not know why we stayed there. Then the train finally reached Treblinki. Those who had not died were forced out. They separated men from women and children. Everyone was forced to strip naked. Some of the men, generally the strongest but only a very few, were told to go to one side. I was one of those. I thought they meant to shoot us there. Instead we were to become slaves for the Nazi machine and were driven to the far side of the camp. The lucky ones, if that was fortune, if Hell was fortune. But most of the men and the women and children, they were sent from what they called the reception to the bath house. They marched naked down the Schlauch, the pipe. This was a pathway lower than the ground level where they thought the outside world would not know. Would not see. Would never see…The Jews, they marched to the bath house…The house of death. The men first. You could hear their screams. The women, the children, all knew. Everyone knew. People I saw in Umschlagplatz, neighbors, some friends. All died horrible deaths. No one survived. I survived. I do not understand this still. I…The Nazis threw the bodies into huge pits and covered them with lime. Later, I do not know, perhaps four months, five months, they built the chimneys. I was part of a detail that had to open the pits again and take the corpses to be burned. The Nazis wanted no evidence. Only human ash. Nothing else. Nothing. I survived because I was strong. I… I do not know how I survived. Or why. I should not have survived. My heart, it did not survive. I live that nightmare every waking minute. No escape. I do not know why I did not die then…Perhaps I did.'"

Beniamin had come to the end of the transcript. He turned it over on his desk. He looked at Aga. She was weeping, crying in her silence.

"I'm sorry," he said.

She shook her head. Did not speak. Not at first. Finally she looked up at him.

"So am I," she said quietly. "Sorrow. Sorry. I did not…"

She could not finish her sentence. She could not find the words. No words. Silence…

*

Beniamin rang several times over the next few weeks. At first she did not take the call. She found it difficult to talk to him. Difficult really to talk to anyone. It was as if she found herself in mourning. Perhaps she was in mourning. For her Grandmother. But for the Grandmother she did not know as well as the one she had thought she had. For Hannah. For Hania. For the thousands upon thousands taken from the Ghetto. For the many. For the few. She mourned for them all and could not mourn for them all.

She spent more time with her mother and father. Her aunt. She could not tell them what she had learned, not yet. There would come a time. But not yet.

He rang her again at the end of the month.

"I am desperate for cheesecake. Help!"

"Beniamin, what do I have to do with your getting cheesecake?" she asked.

"Ben. And I have no one else as interesting to share it with. Besides, you have been avoiding me."

"I have not avoided you."

"Of course you have. Understandable. You do not like my Polish accent."

"Ridiculous. I do not know you."

"What is to know except I love cheesecake and will spend my future days very fat and it will be your fault. So let us meet so I can get fat with a smile on my face."

She hesitated.

"When?," she asked him.

"Tomorrow morning. So good, it is agreed."

The phone clicked off before she could protest.

He was seated upstairs when she arrived the following morning, with two pieces of cheesecake already on the table.

"You should eat. You look like you haven't been eating."

"Are you my mother now?"

"I bet she tells you this. She is a Jewish mother; she just doesn't know it yet."

"Maybe."

"Yes. Maybe. Or maybe not."

"Okay. You are right; she tells me this."

"You see?"

Aga smiled. He made her smile, almost despite herself. He was right about one thing: she needed to let go, break the chain. They waited for coffee, quietly remarking about the lovely weather and the delicious cheesecake and the bad dress sense of the American tourists who had just left the café and anything about nothing.

"It is good to see you smile."

"Smiling has been difficult recently."

"Yes. Still. The journey is not over. But nevertheless you sometimes need to smile. Life is like that."

She shrugged, nodded slightly in agreement.

"So, you wanted to meet. Have you learned anything new to pass on or was it simply your stomach talking?"

"Perhaps your eyes. A nice shade of blue green. Unusual."

"My Grandmother had green eyes too. You would have liked her."

"But would she have liked me?"

"I doubt it."

"Um, a pity…So, no I have nothing particularly new to tell you. But I thought it would be nice to see you. And…"

"And. And what?"

"I contacted a local historian in Nowy Wiśnicz with some questions. He responded. Seems nice. Helpful. I am driving down to see him Friday for a day or two."

"Research?"

"Yes."

"For me."

"No. For me. I get obsessed as well. Would you like to join me? Don't worry; it is not like that."

Hania hesitated only a moment. Smiled and shrugged.

"Yes. Why not."

"Good. Really?" He clearly had not thought she would say yes; not easily. "Good…"

Friday mid-morning he picked her up in his little rather rust-ridden Fiat.

"I call her Golda," he said. "A bit on the old side but she keeps running despite all and remains trustworthy when my Ferrari is not."

"Right."

They chatted only a little on the drive down. He asked her questions about her Grandmother, her family. He told her about his parents and siblings. They stared at the countryside. Each wondered what if anything they might find. About the strangeness of life that could change so with only a short letter. A secret revealed. Or was the secret but a lie?

Before two o'clock they arrived in Nowy Wiśnicz, a small attractive town in Lesser Poland Voivodeship fifty kilometers southeast of Krakow. A town of red roofed buildings best known for its gothic castle in the village environs of Stary Wiśnicz, two kilometers away.

They had little trouble finding the Museum of Wiśnicz Land, as it was known, given the size of the town. Inside they barely glanced at the museum's brass cannon, the photographs and various memorabilia, while they waited for Stanisław Walenda, who, the receptionist informed them, was running just a little late. When he arrived, Walenda showed them into a small side room where they could talk quietly.

"So," he said, "most people who come to Nowy Wiśnicz come for our castle, but I gather from your letter, Mr. Zuckerman, that is not the primary purpose of your visit."

"We hope another time."

"I hope so," smiled Walenda. "It is worth a visit. Our museum… well--stick to the castle. So: Helena Kielar. Unfortunately I do not have a lot to tell you. A little, not a lot. If you will wait here one moment…"

Walenda went to the door and spoke quietly to the Receptionist beyond. He disappeared out of the room for a short moment, then returned carrying a couple framed photographs and sat down.

"Every year in the old days the town held a harvest festival where the locals would meet to toast the harvest with drink and food, dance… Now there is but a farmer's market. Pity. Some traditions should have been retained. So: this is a photograph of the town square during the festival in 1930."

He looked at the notes on the back. Turned the photo over and pointed.

"Right, there. That is Helena Kielar apparently. Her husband, Kacper, and the small child there is her daughter, Hannah."

Aga stared at the out of focus photograph. The woman, Helena, was a plain, hard looking woman, unsmiling. But it was the little girl Hannah who Aga stared at. Did she look like her Grandmother? Aga did not think so, but she had no way of knowing, not really.

"About Kacper Kielar I found very little. He owned a small farm about twelve or thirteen kilometers from here according to the local land registry. When the Communists came to power much of the land around here was of course taken over, redistributed, nationalized. It seems from records that this property continued to be owned in the family name. The land registry file suggests the ownership after the War was still in the father's name but under law it would have likely passed to the wife, then the daughter if neither parent was alive. From the late 1950s I found district council letters that showed officials tried to locate the daughter without success. The farm was never put into one of the Communist collectives but the owners would have had to pay fines. However they could not find the owners. Perhaps the daughter's name had changed. Perhaps she no longer was alive, I do not know. The Communists failed with their collectives and the policy changed in 1956 under Gomułka. I suppose technically today the Kielar farm would still be in the family name. The provincial government wanted to make the area around it into state woodland and forestry preservation in the 1980s, but I think little came of that. Certainly there is no development up that way. Some walking trails, forest trails. Best sources for this are probably local farmers. I asked around a bit but came up with almost nothing."

He shrugged, then went on.

"Anyway, Kacper Kielar. Kielar apparently had problems according to local civil records. Was accused of stealing some pigs but not tried. A number of years later a neighboring farmer put in a claim against him for an unpaid debt. Also some drunk and disorderly charges for which he was fined. In truth nothing important. In the late 1930s he was a part of the local militia. This is him."

Walenda showed them the other framed photograph of a group of men wearing various mismatched uniforms, labeled as the Nowy Wiśnicz Defense Militia, 1937. He pointed to one of the men standing to the side, holding an old rifle.

"They were hardly much of a defense against the Nazis who marched through in 1939. From the archives, Kacper Kielar had in fact been thrown out of the militia for 'excessive drinking' prior to that. One can imagine. Other than this, I found nothing. He seems to have disappeared after the Nazis arrived. Perhaps he was killed, perhaps not. Certainly I can find no further record of him in the area."

"Even during the War there continued to be a Friday market here in the town. There are not many archives remaining from this time, but a few mentions of sales by H. Kielar for produce and meat sold and the taxes collected for the same, as well as taxes she paid for her land. The locals were good at keeping those kinds of records on behalf of the Nazis who governed around here. I found these tax records and market records for 1942 and 1943. Two receipts from 1944. I do not know if any of this is helpful."

He put the few papers in front of Aga and Beniamin.

"It is," said Beniamin. "Thank you for all the work you put in."

"The final thing I did find was an archive letter from Father Jan Daněk, who was the Parish Priest at the Parish of the Assumption Church here from 1945 until 1970. He died shortly after. I have made a photocopy for you. It is dated 23 November 1946 and was sent to the Superintendent of the Local Police."

Walenda took a photocopied letter from the file and set it before the two others. They read it together.

23 November 1946

Dear Superintendent
As we discussed, I delivered the girl discovered living alone and unkempt on the farm previously owned by Kacper and Helena Kielar, presumed to be their daughter Hannah, to the Institute yesterday. She seems in relatively good health, if frightened. She remained mute throughout the journey and I have to assume she does not have the power of speech. You will recall this is the young woman I found living wild on the property that Father Zieliński, my predecessor, had incorrectly assumed abandoned when he visited there last in 1945.
Although the young woman did not speak to me, she was able to communicate when I asked about the mother, Helena Kielar, who Father Zieliński had sought to visit, suggesting that this woman is no longer alive, God rest her soul. The identity of the young woman, who we both assume is the daughter Hannah, also was confirmed by Father Zieliński in 1945 and by her various identification papers that you authenticated at our meeting, suggested through gestures and a nod of her head that the mother had died at the hands of the retreating Nazis from the area in 1944. From what you told me there was indeed quite a lot of banditry as those soldiers retreated. In any event she seems to have lived alone since that time. God only knows what happened to her living there alone save with her mother during such a turbulent and painful time in our beloved Poland's history.
I hope perhaps you will find further information about her mother or indeed her father as there is little more I can do now.
Let us hope and pray to God that the hospital can help the young woman in ways that are not within our power. She is clearly damaged, and clearly alone.
In passing, I would like to thank you for sending your Constable, who with the further assistance of farmer M. Grzyb, kindly assisted in bringing the child into my care, so that I in turn could see her delivered to the doctors.
I remain your faithful servant,
God Speed,

Fr. Jan Daněk, Nowy Wiśnicz Parish Priest

"Tell me, is there a blood relationship to this family?," the historian asked them.

Aga hesitated. Looked at Ben.

"Perhaps. We are trying to establish that."

"I do not know the exact legal situation with the farm. There are lawyers here who might be able to assist should you need names."

"Thank you," Aga said. "At the moment that is not an issue. But if it becomes so…"

"Of course. If you want to go to the farm, I will write directions but whether

335

anything remains, I cannot say."

"One thing," asked Beniamin; "do you know much about any Jewish community here in Nowy Wiśnicz, what would have happened to them?"

"An interesting question. There was always a small community of Jews here, for a few hundred years at least. When the Nazis came quite a few more Jews arrived from Krakow and the surrounding towns. Most were ordered to transit to camps in 1942. They were never heard from again. As throughout Poland it was a tragedy. Some Jews did hide out in the area, in woods, forests, but few survived. As in most of Poland they were mostly viewed as outcasts. Now we have no such community."

"So some people might have helped the Jews at the time?"

"Some would have helped. People here were generous. Still are. But not all. Sadly."

"And Helena Kielar? Would she have been one to protect, hide people?"

"That I would not know. No one would now, or maybe the daughter if she was still alive. The property is at the end of one of the local forest reserves, much as it was then. It is possible someone hid there during the War. There was also a resistance underground unit that at one time operated around the area. One of the locals who unfortunately did not survive the War was involved. Henryk Pilichowski. He and his sons went into the resistance when the Nazis arrived. Rumor had it that he came and went from the area, smuggling arms from Slovenia into Poland. Local hero. He and his sons were killed in a clash with the SS at the border in 1943. There is a small memorial to him in the centre of town, near the courthouse."

Beniamin smiled. "Thank you; you have been a great help."

"I hope you find what you are looking for."

Following the directions that Walenda had given to them it took about thirty minutes to find the property, off the road from town and down various farm tracks leading up towards mountains into a forested area. Where there had once been farmland the forest now largely encroached. They came to a metal gate where the track came to an end, then got out and walked up into forest land.

After a hundred meters or so they found what must have once been a farmhouse.

The small house was largely a ruin. Two of the outer walls had collapsed. Brambles and ivy had taken over the flooring. Fallen bits of wood and stone littered the area. No furniture. No sense of life here. Nothing remained, barely even the outline of a home.

They walked behind what had been the house, looking up towards forest. A well and pump here, rusted. Ben pumped the lever handle once, twice. No water; just the high pitch from the scraping of rust. On the ground nearby, rotting, a wooden table with one leg missing. Nearby posts of what had been once some sort of animal pen. A rusted metal tub turned on its side, filthy, covered with a vine.

A life had been here. Or lives. No more. A story they would never know. Life and death of a house. Of a family. Of Hannah Kielar's family. And as Aga wanted to believe, Hania Stern's refuge. What had happened here? Secret stories now buried with the dead.

They walked amongst the collapsed ruins inside what had been the farmhouse. Below the outline of a window sill, broken glass. A small bottle, empty. Aga smelled it. Nothing. Ben ran his fingers along a collapsed beam. Stared at the black residue he picked up.

"There was a fire here, once, before it collapsed with time."

Aga sighed. She did not know what she had hoped to find, but whatever it might be, nothing now remained but the sound of the wind blowing softly through the trees and some birdsong. The building had been reclaimed, was being reclaimed still, by the land itself. So too the story of many years gone by.

They followed a path into the trees away from the ruined farmhouse that led up through the forest. They eventually found a small stream trickling gently down. They came to a small pool. Aga sat on a large rock, ran her fingers through the cold water. What had her Grandmother known in her life here? Had she been afraid all of the time? Had she found any peace?

Ben wandered away, disappeared into the trees. Aga sat for a moment longer, then followed the narrow path after him. She found him fifty meters further along, at a small clearing, kneeling, letting earth run through his hand, staring off into the distance. He nodded at a stone propped up a couple meters away.

"Marker."

"Of what?"

He shook his head, not knowing. Aga walked over to it. Saw some slight scratches in its surface, manmade or animal made perhaps. Behind it a decaying small length of wood with a bit of rusted wire cutting into its middle.

"Hallowed ground," she said for no particular reason.

"Yes. Maybe. Come…"

They again followed a narrow path through forest, heading back down now but in a slightly different direction. The path opened out into a fairly large clearing where the ruins of another building stood. It must have once been a barn. They could see the supports of a large door and in the building's interior foundations a collapsed rotting wooden staircase, some large beams, bits of rusted chain, an old rusted hand scythe.

"Are you all right?" Ben asked.

She thought. Weighed the question. Weighed the answer.

"Yes. Just thinking of what must it must have been like here in 1943. I guess there are no answers. Hard to imagine. Quiet maybe. I am not sure why here. What it meant. Did they live in fear? Afraid of discovery? Were they hungry? Alone? I do not know. It is hard to explain."

Aga sat down on a fallen wooden support beam by the collapsed staircase, staring into the emptiness of it all, listening to the wind and grass blow and forest talking to her but revealing nothing.

Ben walked away from the ruin, looking at small things fallen on the ground. A nail here. A broken spoon. Bits of wire. After a few moments Aga stood to follow him. Her shirt caught on the splintered wood support as she stood. When she leaned over to free it something caught her eye. She leaned over further then wiped some moss and dirt from the side of the wood beam.

"Ben?"

He looked back at her and wandered over.

She stared at him. She did not smile. She barely moved. She looked away from him.

"What?"

She did not answer, not at first. When she looked back at him, he realized that a tear or two now quietly ran down her face.

"Aga? What?...Aga?"

She turned and knelt beside the beam, staring.

He bent down, gently wiping away dirt and moss and dust, the time, the truth. He saw.

Crudely carved into the wood, weathered and blackened with age and silence and memory but clearly readable, were two still distinct letters.

H S

*

It took about an hour to drive from the property to Kobierzyn, now within the environs of Krakow. Once a village, it had gradually become a suburb of the larger city. Beniamin drove onto the grounds of the State Neurological Hospital and parked. He explained that he had written to the administration but, as expected, they would not release any records of a patient, even one from sixty years ago, without a court order. They did confirm that records showed a Dr. Kazimierz Palinsky had practiced as a psychotherapist at the Babinsky Institute Hospital for a short time in the mid 1940s.

"You could always put in a request to the courts," Beniamin suggested, "but I am not certain much would be gained by doing so. From the papers your Grandmother had, he must have kept some if not all copies of his case notes but there is no way of knowing. What she did find and kept tell a great deal about the Hannah Kielar she had become, but about him as well I think. I am not certain she ever told your Grandfather the truth of her past or what had happened in her life to push her for a time into silence. I am also not certain it matters."

"I do not think she did," Aga answered after considering it. "I think she kept her secrets to herself until after her death."

"The doctors here thought she was schizophrenic. Your Grandfather did not agree. In those days it was very possible they would have performed surgery on her, a lobotomy. From his notes that she kept, he stopped that from happening. If it had..."

"If it had I likely would not be here."

"No. You would not. Fate—life--sometimes does not move in a straight line. Does not move in a way one might expect or imagine. You are the product of chaos."

"Chaos?," Aga asked, looking at him.

"Yes. Chaos. Randomness. Had Palinsky not studied where he did, been asked to come here, had he been a less forceful man of opinions, who can say. We live--no, survive--by randomness. Some think it is chaos."

"Do you?"

He thought for a moment.

"That is not the word I would choose, perhaps."

"What is?"

"Human."

He had driven them both to Kobierzyn so they could walk through the grounds; so they walked. Many of the older buildings that had been the hospital in the 1930s and 40s had long been abandoned and fallen into disrepair. He told her what he knew of the hospital from the War period.

"It was the Babinski Institute even then. There were hundreds of Jewish mental patients confined here when the Nazis came to power. Perhaps one thousand in all. The Nazis put a man named Kroll in charge. He systematically starved the patients. Half died that way. In 1941 ninety patients were sent to Otwock, then Treblinka. The remaining Jewish patients, more than 500 people, were transported to Auschwitz in 1942, except those unable to walk. They were murdered by lethal injection. Nazi euthanasia. Many of the staff who had not left here were murdered then as well. Only one woman survived by hiding in a closet."

They walked amongst some of the older buildings largely in silence, imagining what must have gone on there. They found some old, abandoned cottages and farm-like buildings. They sat on a porch with its railing collapsed where once patients perhaps sat with staff staring over the town beyond, now staring across a mud filled damp field, lonely, empty but for dark crows flying across. They wandered into a couple buildings. Nothing but mildew, a few broken chairs. An old wooden chest of some sort that had once been papered over with blue or green flowered paper. A few people had written their initials on it, memories of tourist visits without memory. If there were ghosts, those ghosts were silent.

"It is now a national heritage site as well as a hospital. Sometimes they use it as a film set, apparently." Ben shook his head. "This I have trouble understanding."

They walked quietly across the grounds, thoughtfully. It was so different when her Grandmother was here, when her Grandfather who she never knew had been here as well: a place of ghosts and Hania, Hannah, almost a ghost herself. Had it not been for a Psychotherapist who fell in love with her she might have died here. Or remained forever silent. As it was she remained largely silent for almost the next sixty years. So a place of ghosts haunting the buildings, haunting Aga also.

"I think she needed to tell her story," Aga said finally. "I think she needed to--to exorcise her ghosts. Her devils. Fears. But she only told it in fragments. Names here and there. Short reminisces. Bits of diary. Like a puzzle with pieces missing or that she could not quite remember how to make fit together. But the pieces need to fit together to make the image. To make the past understood."

"She was old. She was dying, Aga."

"Yes. And she waited. I just wonder…"

"What?"

"…The puzzle of it. Different pieces that do not seem to fit, until you can find just the right angle, direction. She did not have enough time to put them all together for me. Enough time to…to talk. Remember."

"I think…I think she did not expect to put them together", Beniamin told her after carefully considering his words, her words. "I think she gave these pieces of her puzzle as you call it to you for reasons that had to do more than with you simply being a beloved granddaughter. I did not know her, of course, but…as I said earlier, in my work I research and observe and come to understand the chaos of life, the chance that life brings, unexpectedly. Harshly sometimes. What overcomes that chaos perhaps are the choices we make. I think your grandmother Hannah made a choice. That choice was you. She wanted you to put the pieces in order, to turn them just so. She wanted you to complete this journey for her."

Aga glanced at him. He seemed so serious, thoughtful now. She smiled at him, slightly. Nodded, just a little.

"Thank you, Beniamin."

"Ben," he smiled in return, then shrugged. "It is what I think."

It was too late to drive back to Warsaw, so they took two rooms at a small guest house in Krakow old town. They found a small Italian restaurant nearby with a garden where they sat quietly, speaking little as they sipped on glasses of Chianti with their pasta. Aga told him some stories of her Grandmother she remembered, how Hannah as she knew her had seemed so strict yet still played hide and seek in her garden, took her to a zoo to see giraffes, read stories to her at night taking on voices of the characters, never missed coming to a performance when Aga acted at drama school and later professionally.

"She told me I should write to Hollywood and ask to work with Paul Newman."

"She must have realized you were that good, so."

"No, she just thought he was the most handsome man she could think of. And that he should marry me--if not her. That was my Grandmother."

"You were lucky."

"Yes..."

They were both exhausted, so they had a quick cognac at a bar nearby then headed back to the guesthouse.

"Thank you for allowing me to come with you today."

"It has not been easy."

"No. But...Hania came here. All those many years ago. In such pain. Lost. Hania Stern, my Grandmother. She went to Nowy Wiśnicz from the hell of the Ghetto. And when she eventually left Nowy, she left as Hannah Kielar. I think Helena Kielar's daughter must have died somewhere, somehow. I feel it. So my Grandmother, Hania Stern, became Hannah Kielar in this young woman's place. And committed Hania Stern to the world of shadows and ghosts. She did, didn't she?"

He looked at her for a long moment, then nodded.

"Yes. Yes she did. That is her story."

"Part of it. Only part. The mystery remains, the most confusing piece of the puzzle that you need in order to see the picture. To make sense of it."

"I do not understand," he said.

"Josef Schipper said he saw Hania at Umschlagplatz."

342

"He did."

"I think he did see her there. I think she watched as her mother was pulled into that cattle car. I think perhaps her friend Alicja had managed to take Hania's place. And I think Hania watched as the door to that cattle car was shut, locked. Closed to life itself."

"Yes."

"Then she herself was pulled away. Behind the train Schipper said, by an SS officer. But she did not die there. How was that possible? How did she live? Why did she live?"

He said nothing at first, shaking his head.

"I do not know an answer to that. If we did, it may be difficult to hear. Such terrible things happened. But I doubt we will ever know the answer."

"That is why Hania's story will never be complete."

She smiled at him.

"Goodnight, Ben" she said and walked up the stairs to her own room.

She sat there in darkness for a long while, thinking about Hania, about Hannah, about her Grandmother. She could not get the images of the farmhouse near Nowy Wiśnicz, the broken wooden beam with initials carved into it, or indeed the empty, rather haunted buildings of the Kobierzyn hospital from her head. She felt broken yet alive. She walked in the forest with her Grandmother, took that journey, sat on the now broken porch of the hospital building, perhaps wryly, silently observed the doctor who one day would become her husband. And as she sat there, staring into darkness, Aga felt Hania's hand in her own and heard her whispers telling her it would be all right, that she need not fear, that she need reach for life because life was there to take. Aga missed her. And loved her. And saw her. And understood then that indeed there was a life that was there to take.

Aga thought about something her Grandmother had written about her friend Alicja. Alicja, Hania wrote, had promised she would protect her. She had lived to that promise. Died to it…And now Aga sensed her Grandmother making the same promise to her. To her Granddaughter Aga.

And she heard her Grandmother whisper: "Agnieszka. Not Aga. Agnieszka." It made Aga smile. That was enough.

343

Beniamin Zuckerman sat up in his bed reading through paperwork that he had brought with him, although he had trouble focusing. He too thought about the day, about the woman Aga who, for reasons he was not clear, had allowed him to share in this journey of her Grandmother's. Of Aga's as well. He too thought about the farm and the derelict cottages of the Babinsky Institute. He too thought about Hania. He too now believed without doubt that Hania and Hannah were one and the same although he did not understand the details. He too believed that these voices from the past now spoke both to him and to Aga with purpose, not simply to bear witness, to keep the flame of memory alive, to remind what had gone before so as not to relive it in the future. Rather the voices spoke in whispers both to remind who they were, but also who they would be. Past and present and future. Not just Hania, and Hannah, but Aga as well. All was within her and within him. Not simply the deaths of millions. Not simply the cries of the Ghetto still echoing in memory. Not this is who I was, but rather, this is who you are. Do not forget that you are a part of a greater whole, with all its fear and hope, all its hate and love. Yours is the journey we all must take, from the confines behind the walls of our fears to the freedom we can find in our hearts and our minds, in our imaginations and in the possibility of our basic humanity.

He did not know Hania, yet he knew her nonetheless. And although he never met her, he understood that she was beside him too, now, on the journey, showing him the direction, helping him to find himself. The journey was not simply a journey of discovery for the granddaughter Aga; it was a journey of his own self-discovery as well. He knew this. And knew this to be true.

He heard a quiet knock at his room door.

"Aga?" he said as he put the papers aside, got down from the bed and opened the door. She stood there looking at him. "Are you all right?"

She stared at him, at his face so serious. And she knew that Hania had whispered to him, as she had whispered to her. And she knew that he understood.

"I prefer Beniamin," Aga said, as she walked into his room and closed the door behind her.

*

12 June 2007

From: David Weinstein
To: Beniamin Zuckerman
RE: Hania Stern / Agnieszka Janiec

David
Just to confirm, I have removed the question mark from the name of Hania Stern in the database and added her details and those of her parentage from the documents provided by her granddaughter, Agnieszka Janiec.

As we discussed, I will follow up with Ms. Janiec, as well as carefully reviewing all the names, memories and indeed included paperwork in the file that Hania Stern (aka Hannah Kielar) left at her death, to cross check for other names and information for our database and files. I will continue to keep you informed as and if other details come to light, particularly in relation to the names mentioned in Kielar(Stern) papers who we might add to the registry database when appropriate.

Thank you for your help in clarifying some of this for me. A fascinating discovery and, from what I have been able to surmise from Hania Stern's limited diary and reminisces, a painful but unique story in many ways.

I will leave it to you to drop a note to Mrs. Sellin at JHI, as requested.
Ben

*

14 June 2007

Professor Dorothy Sellin
Jewish Historical Institute of Poland
Ohel/Polin Public Private Partnership

Dear Dorothy
Wanted to drop you a note re: Agnieszka Janiec, who you kindly introduced to JRA back in February. One of our analyst/researchers, Beniamin Zuckerman, has worked with her and has indeed found evidence of her Grandmother's life in the Warsaw Ghetto. Hers seems to have been a most interesting story, in certain respects quite unique I suppose. But then every story is unique.

It would be lovely to see you and Walter and to tell you about it. Why don't we fix a date for dinner in the next few weeks? It would give Wendy and myself great pleasure.

I look forward to it.

As always,

David Weinstein

*

27 June 2007

Hi Mother
Many thanks for the socks. Needed and appreciated.

The weather has been beautiful here, although it is starting to get very hot. Feels almost like Tel Aviv, but sadly no beach.

Yes I know I have more to tell you about the story of the actress Aga Janiec's family. It is perhaps a story best told in person. Perhaps in the autumn I will be back in Israel and we can talk then. You will find it quite interesting, with many unusual twists unlike so many of the sad stories of those from the Ghetto who lost their lives in Treblinka. So I look forward to filling you in soon.

Your loving son,

Ben

*

Aga knew she now had to talk to her mother and her aunt. She knew that the story belonged to them as much if not more than it belonged to her. Her mother had never asked her about the contents of the folder that she had found in Hannah's box at the bank following her Grandmother's death, but she would have wondered. Aga knew they would not be upset at discovering their Jewish heritage, but the story that had come to light, the details, were hard to take in. Not shocking, but painful.

Aga decided to ask Beniamin to meet her parents and aunt as well, perhaps for support, but also to help her explain Hania's story as well as the story of the Warsaw Ghetto that he understood far better than she did. He did not hesitate in accepting.

So on a Sunday afternoon at the beginning of July, as her mother brought out tea and cakes, they sat down together in the large family room to hear a story of a life, a story of their lives that they had not ever imagined. Lives lived, lives lost.

Aga brought out the bound folder of her Grandmother's documents she had collated. She explained that she felt she now needed to discuss what was in the manila envelope addressed to her found in her Grandmother's bank box.

Her parents, her aunt looked perplexed, as Aga removed the letter addressed to her and read it to them all. They listened politely at first, then with deep concentration. When she had finished, both her parents and her Aunt Maja sat silently, trying to take in what she had read.

"Over the last months I felt I needed to understand who Hania Stern was, who Grandmother Hannah was, what her life had been, why she had kept this secret all her life. A woman I know suggested I speak to an organization here in Warsaw, the JRA, which is where I met Beniamin, who is a historical researcher there. He has helped me put the pieces of her story together as best we can. All of the papers Grandmother left are here. I have tried to put them in some sort of order and to make as much sense of who she was, really was, and why. Sometimes as you will see she just leaves notes, or names, or tells a few stories. But it is not the entire picture."

Aga proceeded to tell the story as she knew it: of Hania Stern's parents Marek and Zivia and her brother Shaul. Of the Aunt and Uncle, Lea and Michael, and their infant child Jakub. Aga related how they had to leave their apartment in a Zoliborz after the Germans invaded and went to live in what became the Ghetto. How they had survived. How Hania met a girl, Alicja, and loved her, and lost her, then found her again. How the Ghetto became ever more dangerous and of some of the things she saw there. She told her parents how Hania's father was shot, and of the family then moving from Twarda Street to Dzielna Street. She told them of a Polish policeman called the Magician and a German policeman called Frankenstein, of the horrible things that they had done. She talked then of The German who Hania had encountered before the war, who came to frighten her, and haunt her, and who killed the boy Jakub.

Both Aga's mother and Aunt listened quietly, with pain in their faces. Her father said nothing. At times she saw they were quietly weeping but she knew they needed to know what she had to tell them. They needed to see in their minds and their hearts what she saw. She knew that they had not known the story and indeed had known little of the Warsaw Ghetto, just as so many never really knew nor asked what had happened. Many, indeed most, knew of the Warsaw Uprising and the Jewish defense of the Ghetto that was always doomed. They had known statistics of loss and death. But they had not known, not really. Aga and Beniamin spoke until late in the afternoon, explaining how things daily became worse for the Warsaw Jews, until the Nazis began their first 'Aktion' in July, 1942. Aga showed her parents and Aunt a diary note about Hania's Aunt Lea and Uncle Michael leaving for resettlement after the death of their only son, unable to accept life without him. Hania had written how she would watch her Uncle washing the stones of the courtyard below their apartment in moonlight when it was safe to go out, and Aga read them the diary fragment. Her Aunt Maja had become quite upset at this point; Aga's mother took Maja's hands in hers, holding them tight. She told Aga that she must continue. They needed to hear. Needed to know.

Aga told them how Hania and her mother had lived in the attic with others, but that Hania's mother had been rounded up and taken to the Umschlagplatz for deportation, that Hania had tried to find her mother and joined the march towards the cattle trains that waited.

She then explained that so much of this seemed hard to believe; the very fact that her Grandmother had survived left a question mark. She told them how Beniamin particularly felt there were doubts in the story, doubts about its veracity, but that he had come upon the testimony of one Ghetto survivor that they needed to hear.

It was not easy for Beniamin to relate Josef Schipper's story, but he did so gently, with compassion and empathy. He tried to explain what the Ghetto itself was like, then what the Umschlagplatz was like and what happened to the Three Hundred Thousand Jews who started their final journeys to the Treblinka death camp from there. He talked about his own background and his Polish parents, about his work and his various research at Yad Vashem and elsewhere. He explained that he had doubts about Hannah's story when so few had either escaped or survived the razing of the Ghetto, but then he had come upon the testimony of Josef Schipper. As he had with Aga, he quietly, gently read the passages from Schipper's testimony about the Stern girl who he mistakenly called Stein, and what Schipper had seen.

Finally both Aga and Beniamin related how they had together visited the Kielar farm, what remained of it, had seen the initials carved in the fallen wooden beam. How for reasons they would never know Hania became Hannah and was taken from there to Kobierzyn, mute, presumed schizophrenic, but had been treated, and saved, and loved by Kazimierz Palinsky, Hannah's husband, Katarzyna and Maja's father.

Unsurprisingly, Aga's Mother and Aunt were deeply upset by all that they heard, saddened and moved. When Aga and Beniamin had finished saying what they now knew, Aga's Mother and Aunt sat quietly, thoughtfully taking in the story of their own mother, holding one another's hands. Her father Witold turned the pages of the notebook, looking at names, descriptions, diary pages, saying nothing at first. Aga said she had made a copy of everything for both her parents and her aunt, so they could go through the material when they were ready. Finally her father addressed her and Beniamin, indeed them all.

"You will understand, Aga, Mr. Zuckerman, this information…it is difficult, painful for us to take in. For your Mother, your Aunt. Not because Hannah, or rather Hania, had this secret, this—life--that she carried with her all those years, the burden of it, the pain and horror of it, and not because in fact she was Jewish, her family, your Mother, Aunt, you. But because now we must understand, and face and indeed live with the events of long ago as our own. It will take time to understand this. To take it into our hearts...It will take time for us to grieve, not just for your Grandmother Hannah, your Grandmother Hania, but for ourselves: for what we have lost and what we have gained, for who we are and who we must be. I want you both to know, Mr. Zuckerman firstly that we are—grateful, for your kindness to our daughter, to ourselves, for your dignity, your sincerity. I suspect over time we will have questions and there will be many more things we need to know, to learn. I am sure we will be able to turn to you for this. It is a journey I suppose we are all taking together, difficult although this is."

"Of course," said Beniamin quietly.

"And to you my Aga, my Agnieszka," continued her father then, "do know we are terribly proud of you. I know this has not been easy. I know too, as does your Mother, why your Grandmother came to you, why she loved you as she did. She was right to do so, myszka. She was wise. And truth be told she was not alone at the end. She was not alone."

*

Over the coming weeks Aga and Beniamin saw each other often when they could. They both were wrapped up in work, Beniamin with various research projects at JRA, Aga with two commercials and a small part in a television series episode that she took only to keep her mind free when she most needed it free. It was of course inevitable, given her emotional rollercoaster over many months, that she should want to turn to someone, that the someone was inevitably Beniamin. She needed him in order to come to terms with the grief and the pain of what she had learned, let alone the emotional turbulence of the two plays that had so taken over her life for a time. And he needed her because of a shared experience, because at times he realized he too found himself alone, in need of companionship, in need of the bond that she had forged with him. And he with her.

Aga found him to be a good lover, gentle and caring. So different to Stefan. She knew he also had needs, but he listened to her and listened even when she did not speak. He could make her laugh and push her just when she needed that push. He understood in the way that others could not the turbulence of her experience, her story, her need to reach for it, cry for it and, hardest of all, live for it and in it.

Mostly, she found him generous: not just in his love making, or in the time he spent with her when he could, or in his listening. His heart was generous enough to leave her alone when she needed to be left alone, to hold her when she needed holding, to tease her when she needed teasing, to wipe her tears away, to let them fall.

She saw him little over the two weeks she was filming the series episode outside of Warsaw and was looking forward to sharing a meal with him when she returned, to sleeping with him. They had both known they had to be careful in what they felt, take it slow, but she was not so foolish that she could not recognize his need or hers. So Aga was slightly annoyed when he said he had to be in Berlin for a few days just when she returned to Warsaw. She knew she should not have been; he had his life just as she did. Still she could not keep disappointment at bay.

Three days after she'd been back in Warsaw he rang to say he was flying back that evening, but she put off seeing him. She could be stubborn when she wished. She could also be wrong.

She put him off the next day as well. She could be very wrong.

The following evening her buzzer rang a few times and she finally went to the building door. She suspected it had to be him. No one was at the entrance. But sitting on the ground, with a balloon floating above it, was a box that when opened held two pieces of cheesecake.

"All right, all right," she said and was hardly surprised when he peeked from around the corner. Very funny. For dessert, I assume."

He walked up to her. "No. For breakfast."

And he kissed her. And they went upstairs. And they made love with a need that made Aga stronger and weaker at the same time.

After, as she lay in his arms, she told him she was sorry she had not seen him at first, sorry she had been annoyed. Sometimes, she explained, the needs of her head took advantage of the needs of her heart. She had missed him.

"Don't worry," he said after listening. "I forgive you." And he smiled at her. "This time."

She rested her head against his chest. Quiet. And he let her be quiet. They lay this way for a long while, comfortable with one another.

"There are a couple of things I found out about your Grandmother's story," he told her after a while. "Do you want to hear now or shall we talk in the morning?"

She thought for a moment. Her need to know was almost as great as her need to be beside him.

"Now," she said.

"Firstly, I think I found the one she called the Sewer Rat, Simcha Gitler."

Aga looked at him. "Not alive?"

He shook his head.

"I was looking at a letter in our archives from a girl in the underground, Eva Baron. She survived, lived in the United States until the 1970s. Her daughter was looking for information about any family who might have survived. The letter was from her sister, Miriam, who remained in the Ghetto with her boyfriend, whose name was Simcha Gitler. Both Miriam and Simcha were killed in the building at Mila Street 9 towards the end of the Jewish Uprising. Eva Baron in her memoirs talks of some of those who Simcha helped to escape, including a girl at the beginning of the Second Aktion in January whose name she did not know, but who had escaped from Umschlagplatz. She was the last person he managed to get out."

Aga only nodded. She felt saddened but not surprised.

"There is something else," Beniamin continued. "It has to do in part with why I was in Berlin. It may not be what you want to hear."

"...Go on."

"In her comments, your Grandmother talked about a German wife she first met in Krasinski Park with her friend Alicja, and the German woman's husband who she refers to several times as 'The German'."

"Yes. She wrote that The German gave the order for Jakub to be shot in the courtyard."

"That's right. She mentions when she first met him his wife said he was a military attaché at the German Embassy before the War. Part of what I wanted to do in Berlin was to research the embassy…I think I found The German."

Aga felt a wave of coldness overcome her. She looked for a response. Found none. Beniamin waited, then continued.

"His name I believe was Sebastian Marcellus Radtke, a Reich Embassy attaché in Warsaw from 1936 until 1939. He returned to Berlin before the War started and was made a Sturmbannführer in the SS. Clearly connected and from a military family. He grew up in Lidzbark Warmiński in East Prussia. Because he spoke Polish fluently he was sent back to Warsaw once Germany occupied this city. There is a record of him there, with his wife Gizela. I am having his birth certificate sent to me. His marriage certificate. Documents of existence that explain…nothing."

"That do not explain a war criminal in the Warsaw Ghetto."

"Perhaps, although never charged. Before the Final Aktion in the Ghetto, in November 1942, he was ordered back to the Foreign Ministry in Berlin. Towards the end of the War he was captured by the Russians with many others. He spent seven years in a Russian prison. I found the details. He returned to Lidzbark in 1952 to retire there with his family. It had become a part of Poland again after the War. Because it had been his family home he was allowed to return. Apparently he lived quietly in the community."

Aga found it difficult to ask the next question.

"…Is he alive?"

"No. He died in 1995."

"Barely ten years ago."

"I cannot be certain. No one can. But I think he was the SS officer who Josef Schipper mentioned, the one who led Hania away from the Umschlagplatz behind the trains. Although I am not positive, but from her notes, from Schipper… somehow I think so."

Aga looked away. She needed silence. She needed to think. She lay back down against him, her back against his warm body.

"I need to sleep now."

He let her fall asleep, holding her.

When he woke in the morning, she was not in bed. He walked out to her small kitchen. She was sitting at the small table there, drinking coffee. He sat down across from her. She looked at him, set the cup down.

"Beniamin, I need to go there. To Lidzbark."

"What do you think you can find?"

"I do not know. Maybe the past. Maybe an answer."

"And if not?"

He stared at her, stared within. Looked down at her hand, stirring the coffee still although it did not need stirring. Around. Around. Around.

"I will go with you."

*

Lidzbark Warmiński was almost a four hour drive from Warsaw with traffic. It was already late afternoon when they set off and late when they arrived. The town was dominated by its 14th Century Castle of the Warmian Bishops and by tourist shops paying homage to its most famous citizen, Copernicus. They spent the night in a small hotel in the center of town. In the morning the tourist office gave them directions to the address that Beniamin had obtained from the Polish Civil Registration Office in Warsaw.

They followed the River Łyna to the eastern edge of the town then cut back just south from it. Beniamin found the long tree lined street filled with small two story houses. He checked the numbers and drove slowly down the street until its end where they discovered a large gated garden park—and no house. He went back over the address he had printed out. Shrugged and turned the car around.

"Must be one of the smaller house back there." He drove along the way they had come, looking at house numbers. Slowed, then stopped the car. Again stared at the address he had. Again turned the car around and drove to the end. No house.

"Something is not right. It should be here."

Aga looked at him, then at the gated garden. They got out of the car and walked through the small stone and wrought iron gate entrance. A path led through the large wild garden where wildflowers and small trees had been planted amidst more mature trees, pretty enough but unkempt. A sign inside gave the opening hours and said the walk was the Lidzbark Warmiński Memorial Park for The Fallen Martyrs of Poland, 1939-1945. There was something forlorn about the grounds, somehow overlooked, almost forgotten. In the middle were several benches overlooking a pond. An elderly couple sat watching the three swans on the water.

"Excuse us," said Beniamin. "We were looking for this address." He showed them the number he had written down.

They looked at the number.

"Forty-two? There is no forty-two on the road," said the man.

"Ah," said the woman. "It was here. Chrystian, it was the house that was here."

"There was a house here?," Aga asked.

"Oh yes," answered the woman. "Once a large house, but it had fallen into some decay."

"Do you know who lived there?" asked Aga.

"An elderly man, for years and years. He died, oh, maybe ten years ago. The house had to be destroyed. Such a pity as it had once been quite a lovely home, but time had taken against it. It was donated to the town on the condition they build a park here, as you see."

"You do not know anything about the man who lived in the house?"

"Not really. He was quite elderly, kept to himself. That is all I remember," said the woman. Her partner shrugged.

Beniamin and Aga thanked them, walked back to the car.

"Nothing," said Aga, sighing. "Perhaps there was meant to be nothing. We could check the City Hall. There may be records."

"Most likely but they will not reveal much…But I have an idea."

They got back into 'Golda', Beniamin's car, turned around, headed back down the road. At the first junction Beniamin turned left towards town, but turned again two streets along rather than driving back into the centre of Lidzbark. Just down the street was an old, large red brick church, The Parish Church of St. Peter and St. Paul Apostles.

"Sometimes the best ones for information are the priests. Rabbis too but not here," Beniamin said with a grin.

The church door was open. As soon as they entered they heard the gentle notes of an organ echoing through the large white nave and up towards the spire above them.

"Bach," whispered Beniamin. "So so Bach…"

They walked down through the church, their footsteps echoing off the walls beneath the quiet notes of the organ. Half way down the nave they sat down in a pew, staring at the rather nicely plain altar. The church had a simplicity about it, despite its largeness.

The organ music ceased and they heard footsteps descending the stairs off to one side. An aging priest appeared, red cheeks, a smile and small round glasses suggesting an inquisitive, kind face.

"Oh, I am sorry. I had not realized anyone was here."

Beniamin stood.

"No, sit, please."

"We enjoyed the music," said Aga.

"Ach, I need much practice. Our organ master died recently. We are in search of another. You do not perhaps play the organ?"

Aga and Beniamin both smiled and shook their heads no.

"That is a pity. Still…"

The priest sat down in a pew in front of them, turning to talk.

"You are not parishioners I should think. Tourists?"

"Not exactly," said Beniamin. "Academic researchers."

"I see."

"We had hoped to get some information about someone who lived near here, but discovered his house is gone. Now it is a garden. So, nothing," Aga added.

The Priest looked from one to the other, nodded and smiled just slightly.

"You are interested in the Major."

"The Major?"

"Major Radtke. It is what we called him. Am I correct?"

Aga and Beniamin looked at one another.

"Yes," said Beniamin.

"May I ask why?"

"We are doing some research into events in Warsaw during the War. His name appeared on some documents."

"I see."

The priest was thoughtful for a moment. His smile turned to an expression of quiet sadness perhaps and he sighed.

"You knew him?," asked Aga.

"Yes. And I buried him, perhaps ten, eleven years ago now. I can direct you to the grave should you wish. He was a difficult man. An unhappy man. His wife I did not know, not in my adult life anyway, but she had a special place in this church. The organ you heard, it was a gift from them. From her, to be perfectly honest."

"Did you know him well?"

"So: no, not really. I know he was in the War, fought with the Nazis. This part of East Prussia you probably know was heavily German, then made part of Poland after the First War. When the Nazis invaded it again became part of the Reich until 1945. Radtke had been imprisoned by the Soviets I know, but released. There were comments, rumors, but...little more. He was born in the house that used to be where the park of Fallen Martyrs is. His family had owned it for several generations. And then one day he dies and it is gone. A new world destroying the past, or perhaps not. You probably saw it."

Aga nodded that they had.

"The Major kept largely to himself, particularly the last years. We rarely saw him here. Perhaps never to be honest. My father...You see my father was the Parish priest here a long time ago. If you had asked me what I had wanted when I was a youngster, I would said to live my life in Paris, or New York, to leave Communist Poland far behind. But things happened. So I became ordained quietly, returned here as the Parish Priest in the mid 1970s. It was a different time then. Politics. The government. Poland...Hm..."

He looked away, thoughtfully, then back at them.

"So, Radtke: when I buried him, it was a sad affair. Two people only showed up for the funeral: his housekeeper, who lived in the Parish and who I knew. A decent woman. She passed away a few years ago. And then also an elderly man I did not know, I think one the Major's colleagues perhaps, but I do know not his son. His son did not come here. Never came here. Perhaps he was not alive. Or perhaps he chose not to come, I do not know."

"He had a son?"

"He did. Yes. I suspect it may have been his son who inherited the property and gave it to the town, but I am not certain of this. There had been rumors that the son was dead long ago, but no one knew that for certain. The son was everything to his mother. I remember that. But the father... I will tell you a story about the son, which is the story of the Major in many ways. I was a young boy; my father was the Parish Priest, as I said. Radtke returned to Lidzbark many years after the War to retire to his house with his wife and boy. His wife, she was lovely, even now I can remember. A very handsome woman. And so proud of her son. The Major...Well, he probably was a handsome man once but time had taken its toll and I remember his face was hard, without much life but with anger. I think he was a broken man. We were afraid of him as children, although rarely saw him. We understood at school that Radtke and his son fought, did not see eye to eye, although the son, Paul, was much older than me. The Major's wife, I cannot remember her name but it is on the gravestone, she on the other hand was very much a part of the congregation here. Sadly she was very ill already. She donated the organ that you heard. I was ten at the time, I think, so 1957. I remember because it was my birthday, a special day even in Communist Poland and for me certainly. There was to be a wonderful concert here in the Church to celebrate the new organ. Radtke's son, I remember him still. A wonderful organist. His mother asked him to play for the inaugural concert and he agreed. I will never forget it. Our church was very full. Mrs. Radtke was already ill and had to be wheeled in in a chair. The look on her face: so much pride. Expectation. Love even. The Major—not quite the same. They closed the doors of the church. A hush. The music began. Bach. I do love Bach. And even then, as young as I was. 'Ebarme dich mein O Herre Gott'. Funny I remember that now, half a century later. 'Have Mercy on me, God...'"

The Priest was quiet for a moment. His eyes filled with sadness, thinking about that day so long ago, about the music, about the sound filling his church, about his own father perhaps.

"It was to be the first piece of three. The room here, the acoustics: I had never heard anything like it in my ten years on this earth. Heartbreakingly beautiful. Such emotion. Like each note asking, no begging even for Mercy. But then, half way through the music, it stopped. People looked at one another, confused. I remember the sound of footsteps coming slowly down the steps from the choir. Right there…Their son appeared, this quiet, sad young man of 17, 18, I do not know. He walked down the aisle to where his mother sat, his father sat. His father looked so angry. His mother stared at her son, trying to understand. He took her hand and kissed it. Then he turned, walked back down the aisle to the back, opened the doors and walked out, closing the doors behind him. And do you know that young man, Paul Radtke, was never seen here in Lidzbark Warmiński again. Ever. There were rumors: that he had committed suicide. That he was in France, England. That he was in America. There was an older woman involved. An illegitimate child. People gossip, make up things. But no, in truth nothing. I asked my father, but he did not know. Two weeks after he disappeared, his mother died. Even then, nothing."

The priest shook his head.

"That says as much about the Major as it does about his son I think. I do not know what the Major did in the War. He never came to confession. He kept to himself. I think he lived with guilt. He died an old, unhappy man. Unmourned. Forgotten."

Aga and Beniamin sat in silence, uncertain what to say.

"I do not think that is probably what you came to hear, but it is what little I know of him. His house, everything is gone. As if he was never here. Forgotten now. No one left to remember and now no one really left to forget. I tried to see him just before he died but he would not see me and my father never spoke of him. I know simply that he was an unhappy man without a wife, a son, alone. I pray for him, for whatever it was that caused such unhappiness in a man, and perhaps such unhappiness that he may have caused in his life to leave him with no one. He was a ghost and a forgotten ghost at that. When I play Bach here, I hope that the notes reach to Heaven to comfort his poor wife, to those who suffered and if to the

Major, to grant forgiveness for the sins that so ate at his heart and his soul. Because I have to believe in forgiveness. If I do not, there is hope for no one."

They walked back to the car, saying nothing. Got in. Sat there. Beniamin looked at her.

"Aga?"

"Drive. Just drive. I don't care. Just drive."

So he did, away from Lidzbark into the country, past fields of grain, and empty fields, past nothing, saying nothing. Finally Aga told Beniamin to pull over. She sat for a moment, got out, started to walk over an open field, the river beyond flowing, but no one. Emptiness. Beniamin got out and followed but held back several paces behind and did not call to her. She walked. She kicked at the dirt. Her anger, her hurt, her frustration, all written on her face. She finally stopped. She did not turn around. She looked at nothing, looked into the distance.

And she screamed, as loud as she could. And screamed again. Her scream echoed over the river, across the valley. And beyond. Far beyond. Scream of anger. Of loss. Of hate. Of unknowing. Then Aga seemed to wilt into tears, her anger and frustration spent. She kicked the dirt. Sat. Slammed her fists into the ground. And again. Then her shoulders hunched. Defeated. Weakened. Isolated.

Beniamin sat down beside her. He put his arms around her, held her tight. She let her head rest on his shoulder, spent.

"I wanted him to pay. I wanted to scream and tear it down and curse him and curse the dead. I wanted someone to explain how this man could kill a child and yet let my Grandmother go, to say this is what he had done to my family, to my Grandmother, that he made her live with her guilt and her pain and her haunting memories all these years, all these years and he did not pay for it. I know he never paid. But maybe he did. I do not know and will never know. I hate him. I hate the memory of him. I hate him and his wife and their son and Bach and the Priest and I hate, I hate, I hate."

Beniamin held her tighter still.

"You have to let it go now, Aga. You have to or it will eat you. You have to let it go."

"I can't. I do not know how. I am Aga and I am Hania, like being Elektra and Iphigenia, one and the same and neither and needing one needing the other needing…Needing…I do not know how to let go, Beniamin. I do not know how to escape. She escaped. But I do not know how…Just hold me tight. I think I am falling. Don't let me go."

*

She had not seen her mother in several weeks. Following the difficult journey to Lidzbark Aga had felt she needed distance, simply to think things through, think all of it through. Try to forget. Need to remember. Let go and never let go. She could never let go. When Aga's mother rang to see if she could meet, she could hardly refuse. Her mother asked if Aga would join her for a walk and suggested meeting first at the Saxon Gardens, then walking up to the Krasinski Palace and Park, an unusual request to say the least. Aga had a sense of why her mother wanted to go there, but agreed.

They met early on a warm Thursday morning when the gardens were not crowded. At that hour mostly strolling through the manicured pathways and lawns were tourists, dog walkers and any number of joggers. They admired the flowers and quietly walked around the small lake and fountain. They walked and spoke quietly about nothing in particular. Her mother put her arm through her daughter's as they walked.

"You are looking a bit tired, I think, Aga."

"I am perhaps."

"Working?"

"Reading scripts, some plays. Nothing excites me, really."

"Stefan?"

"He is in St. Petersburg on a television project. He said there would be a role for me but to be honest I am not interested."

"And your friend, Beniamin: you are seeing him?"

"Yes, Mother."

"I think that is a good thing."

"Then you approve?"

"I neither approve nor disapprove. You are too old for me to do so. Grown women do not need to seek parental approval. Although approval helps if you are getting married. Are you getting married?"

"No, Mother, I am not getting married."

"Okay. Just checking."

Aga looked at her mother and noted the amusement in her face, forcing her too to smile.

"Seriously: I only want to see you happy. I know these last months have not been easy for you, Aga. And Beniamin seems like a good man."

"I think maybe he is."

They left the Saxon Gardens, walking for the few minutes to nearby Krasinski Park. They found a place to sit not far from the entrance.

"I have struggled with what you told us," her mother finally said. "It has been a lot to take in."

"I know."

"For your Aunt as well. It has brought back memories of when we very small, of course. Of my father too for me, although my memories are so vague. Your aunt would have been too young but some things I do recall. And his doctor notes from that Institute, about Hannah. I read them carefully. I can only begin to imagine what my mother must have thought when she walked into his office and found him standing on his head. I wish I could have been there. I do. I wish."

Katarzyna smiled at the thought, shook her head in amusement tinged with sadness. Then her smile faded.

"Mostly I think of your Grandmother though, of course. All she went through, lived through. She was not a bitter woman, Aga. Distant perhaps. And she could be strict. But never bitter although she had every right to be. I think she must have been incredibly lonely in her way. Or alone. Yes, alone. I feel...I do not know. I feel that I should have tried better to be a good daughter. Spent more time with her those last years. Maybe a better mother too. Tried to listen or...I do not know."

"I think Grandmother Hannah needed to find Hania again. I think she tried so hard to forget all, perhaps to forgive all, but deep down inside she must have felt she had lost something. Or run away from it. Or suffered with it."

362

"Being Jewish?"

"No. Not at all. No, I think more than looking for a way to tell me, and through me telling you and Aunt Maja about all she had witnessed, felt, she was trying to tell her story to herself. Needing to remember."

"It is funny: at times I struggle to forgive her for such silence. And you know, Aga, at the same time I find it hard to forgive myself for… for not being there. Or maybe we were. I do not know. I will never know."

"You have nothing to forgive yourself for, I think."

Her mother shrugged. Looked at her. Smiled gently. Smiled within.

"We all struggle with who we are, Aga. I see it with my patients. Families. Your father. Me. And now I see it in ways I had never seen before. I see it in you too."

Aga looked at her, nodded, slowly. There was a time she might have been angry with her mother's observations. Certainly rebelled against them. Now she realized her mother was right. She, Aga, was still searching.

"There was a reason I wanted to see you. And a reason I wanted to come here. I have in fact taken to walking in this park several times over these last few weeks. That probably will not surprise you. I have tried to picture my mother here as a young girl, taking that baby for a walk, completely—ignorant—of what would happen. I have tried to imagine what it was like. What she was like. I know from what little she left we have created a picture. Still it seems somehow far away. Out of focus. I am connected to it, but I remain disconnected. She was terribly brave. I do not think I could have ever been so. I find it difficult to understand, almost difficult to believe. I suppose in time it will sink in. Will move more clearly into focus."

"I know."

"When we opened her bank box after she died, besides the large envelope she had left for you, the story that she needed you to read and make sense of, as I told you there were some papers, some financial information. There were also a few photographs. These were not part of the envelope. Maja and I stared at them for a short time, without thinking about them much I suppose. Without wondering, asking. They meant very little to us, so Maja chose to keep a wedding photograph that my mother had placed within. I do not think you have seen it before."

"No."

"There was also a small photograph that at the time meant nothing. I thought it sweet, my mother as a young girl, with another. Now I understand it better."

Her mother opened her bag and took out a small photograph, handed it to Aga.

"I want you to have this now. It should rightfully be yours I think."

Aga stared at it for a very long time. She knew immediately why her mother had brought it.

"Out of focus, you see. Just slightly. Just enough…I had thought I could find the very spot this was taken, here in this park. I have not been able to. Perhaps it does not matter, not really. When I first saw this, sitting with the lawyer, I thought it interesting. No more. A curiosity. But it is more than that."

"Yes. It is. I can have a copy made, Mother. I think we should both have a copy. I think we both need a copy of this."

"…I had not thought of this idea, my Aga. But I would like that. Something we can share. Something we need to share."

They both stared down at the photograph Aga now held in her hand. Said nothing. Even slightly out of focus, Aga knew what it was, who it was, exactly. It showed two young girls, one with her head on the shoulder of the other, sitting on a bench in the park. Beside that girl was the raised hood of a baby's carriage. Aga knew the photograph was of her Grandmother, her friend Alicja and in the carriage, Hania's aunt's only child, Jakub. She turned the photograph over and saw in deeply faded lettering: In KP, with the beautiful H.

"They must have loved one another," Aga said quietly. "Alicja. Her friend. Yes. It must be so. Hania told the story of her friend in some of her pages. You remember? Alicja said to her 'I will always protect you' when they encountered those cruel boys in the cemetery. 'I will always protect you.' And she did. As we know. She did."

Neither Katarzyna nor Aga said anything further. They sat quietly on the bench, two women drawn together by a Mother, a Grandmother, drawn together by two women from such a long time ago. Now, seventy years later, neither this present day mother nor her daughter needed to speak. Now was a moment to sit beside one another quietly in this garden, as it was now, as it possibly would have been then. They both understood the need for words and the need for silence. And in truth they understood too Hania's need for words and for silence.

Her mother again put her arm through Aga's. Aga turned, smiled at her gently. They sat back. They sat.

*

JRA (Warsaw Office)
VIA FACSIMILE

From: Beniamin Zuckerman
To: Fraulein Ingrid Schneider
  Das Bundesarchiv
  Serviceteam Abteilung Militarchiv
  Freiberg
Date: 16.7.07

Ingrid:
Many thanks for all your assistance the other day. Do you have the contact name for the Berlin office?

Thanks
Ben

*

JRA (Warsaw Office)
VIA FACSIMILE

From: Beniamin Zuckerman
To: Herr Dieter Meyer
  Das Bundesarchiv
  Serviceteam Berlin-Licterfelde
  Berlin
Date: 19.7.07

Dear Herr Meyer
I understand from Ingrid Schneider of the Freiberg office that you are on holiday. If you could give me a ring when you return, I would appreciate it.

Yours,
Beniamin Zuckerman

*

JRA (Warsaw Office)
VIA FACSIMILE

From: Beniamin Zuckerman
To: Frau A. Becker
  Deutsche Rentenverischerung
  Karlsruhe
Date: 1.8.07
Dear Frau Becker
Thank you again. I have let Herr Meyer at DB know how helpful you have been. Particularly let me thank you for agreeing to check into the pension records as we

discussed. I know this is not a normal request. If you need further information from me please do not hesitate to contact my office in Warsaw. I look forward to your earliest response.

Yours
Beniamin Zuckerman

*

<u>*JRA Internal Memo*</u>
7.8.07

From: David Weinstein
To: Beniamin Zuckerman

RE: Hania Stern / Agnieszka Janiec

David
I need to speak to you once again about the Stern matter, and Aga, when you're back.

Thanks
Ben

*

"Hi. It's me. Do you have time to drop by?"

"What, to your office?" she answered. She was supposed to have dinner that night with him and it seemed a rather strange request seeing that she would see him in a few hours.

"Is everything all right?"

"Yes. I thought perhaps we could talk."

Aga sat quietly in her car in traffic. She and Beniamin had been discussing perhaps moving in together. Both still wanted to be careful: less because one or the other was afraid to make a mistake, but rather because one or the other would think it was a mistake. Perhaps each wanted to make certain that the foundations of the relationship were built not on the past, or memories of the past, but on the desire and needs of the present. Aga knew she was in love with him. She was quite certain he was in love with her. She wanted to be certain that it would be only for the right reasons.

"All right. Sure."

She did a U-turn, ignoring the honking cars and headed off to his office.

When she got there he had a serious expression on his face.

"What it is Beniamin? You seem…Did something happen?"

He sat back in his chair. She watched him from across the desk as his gaze turned inwards while he sought the words he needed.

"You know I…" He sighed, trying to continue.

"We could reconsider. Finding another apartment or…But I do not want to reconsider us. That is not what I want."

"No, Aga, no it is not that. No…This search, this journey, Hania…it has taken over your life."

She looked at him. She could tell he struggled.

"Yes. Perhaps it has. But it is not my life."

"I know."

"You are my life right now, Beniamin. I think so. I know so. But…but this matters too. Deep within me, this journey as you call it. I think it is more than perhaps my Grandmother's hope for me, or request, or fear even. I have this need to… understand. Something. Everything. But it is not about us."

"I know."

"So tell me: what is it? What are you afraid of?"

He shrugged.

"An obsession. Your obsession. It has to come to a conclusion."

"Yes."

"And it may not be the conclusion you want."

"I do not understand."

He hesitated. Then looked at her, her blue green eyes, in them her past and her present and he hoped, really hoped, that he could see in them a future as well.

"I spoke to David Weinstein. I explained my concerns. He said something interesting. He talked about my research work, about your Grandmother as well. He said he, I, JRA, we are simply gatekeepers. Facilitators. We can neither judge, nor be judged. But the world here we open for others, as painful as that is, we must not keep our thoughts, our knowledge, to ourselves. It is not our right. Our responsibility, either professional or personal. I suppose he is correct. This journey of yours, this need: it is not mine, Aga. What we have right now matters. But Hania, she and her story belong to you. To your Mother, your Aunt. For a time I thought she was mine too. But she cannot be so, any more than the others I learn about in this work I do. He said rightly that we are the witnesses. Bearing witness for others, of others. We are like those actors who played the chorus in your plays. But what I do, it takes its toll. I do not think I could survive with all that knowledge, that…that realization and discovery of others' memories and lives and experience within me forever. It can be soul destroying as well as a gift. You see?"

"Yes. Perhaps, yes."

"David said I must speak to you. I was reluctant, but he said I must speak and you alone must choose what you want to do."

She shook her head, confused.

"I told you once I believe that sometimes to understand the story you must come to know those you do not want to know, hear their words, find them to find those who matter."

"As with The German, Radtke."

"Yes. But then it was with the foreknowledge before driving up to Lidzbark that

Radtke was dead… I went through the documents again. Looking at names, events Hania mentions, trying to get a picture. I thought you needed this picture. I suppose you do, but it worries me. Yet David is right."

Beniamin hesitated, then continued. "Herbert Kolbe."

She looked at him, thought, shook her head.

"I do not…"

"No. No, you don't. I went back through my notes from my trip to Berlin. Through the names I got from the archives of those in that embassy in Warsaw in the 1930s, how I found Radtke ultimately. There was another name but it did not register. Not really. Herbert Kolbe. Your Grandmother mentioned him, several times. Only that is not what she called him. She called him a teddy bear. Misio."

"The driver."

Beniamin sighed. "His name is Herbert Kolbe. He too grew up in Lidzbark as best I can tell. I was able to find some details. Perhaps he was a school friend of Radtke's. I am not certain. But it does not matter. Kolbe's family moved to Prenzlau near Berlin in the 1920s. He joined the Auswärtiges Amt, the Foreign Service, as a clerk. At some point he must have met Radtke again. Radtke had also applied to join the AA service and had been a high flyer from a military family so was posted to the embassy as a military attaché. He requested to take Kolbe as his adjutant. His request was granted."

"He was more than just a driver," Aga said quietly. "Kolbe."

"Most likely. A confidante. Assistant. Friend for all I know. When Radtke was imprisoned by the Russians he was not alone."

"Kolbe."

"Yes. I work with German Federal Archives. I have contacts there. Good contacts. They are helpful. Through them I was given the name of a woman who deals with German pensions. Even from the War time, Wehrmacht soldiers who survived and retired were granted pension rights. Kolbe was one…The thing is, Aga, Herbert Kolbe is still alive."

Aga felt a painful pounding in her chest. For a small moment she stopped breathing. She felt numb.

"He lives in a nursing home near Leipzig. I telephoned there. I spoke to a nurse.

I said he was a distant relative but that I had lost contact. She told me he was ill, the illness of age, but that if I ever wished to visit she was sure he would be happy to see me."

Aga said nothing. She thought about Josef Schipper, about his description of that day at the Umschlagplatz. She thought about what she imagined, what Beniamin said he too imagined: that Radtke, 'The German', had been the one to pull Hania away from there. Had let her escape, helped her escape, had… had also been the one to order Hania's young cousin who Hania so loved be shot in the courtyard at the back of their apartment building on Dzielna Street. And the one who had carried the little boy away, who had been in that apartment and grabbed the boy and followed orders was Misio. Kolbe. Had followed orders. Orders.

"Aga…I cannot go there. No more. David was adamant that you have the right to know. This part of your journey, this final piece of your puzzle perhaps…But I do not think I can finish this with you. It must be your decision and yours alone. I cannot go there with you."

She stared at him, deeply looking into his eyes, his face so direct, so honest. She understood. She nodded.

"No," Aga said. "I do not think you can. Not this time. But Beniamin I have to. I have no choice. Not for Hania. I need to go for me."

Beniamin thought for a moment. "Yes. I know. Perhaps I always knew this once I found his name. The only thing is I need to warn you because I care, because you are someone I have come to respect, to want to be with…Do you know the writer Hannah Arendt?"

Aga knew the name, but only vaguely.

"Hannah Arendt was a writer, a philosopher. She attended the trial of Adolf Eichmann in Jerusalem in 1963, wrote about it. She said of Eichmann that he was 'neither perverted nor sadistic' but almost simply, 'terrifyingly normal'. How I remember those words. She coined the phrase 'the banality of evil' not just about Eichmann, but about the Reich, Nazism, about those who saw everything and saw nothing. I have learned to keep the warning always in front of my eyes: evil, real evil, and events that have happened but are honestly beyond understanding, beyond comprehension, many of those who perpetrated these acts without conscience, sometimes they turn out to be banal. And that perhaps is what is most frightening of all."

*

Aga took an early morning flight to Leipzig and rented a car. She stopped on the way to pick up a small bouquet of flowers. She knew she had to act a part. It took another forty minutes to get to the nursing home with the address that Beniamin had given her. She sat in the car for five minutes, breathing, nervous. But this was something she had to do. She was determined to do it.

At the reception desk inside Aga explained that she was hoping to see an old neighbor and family friend, Herbert Kolbe, that she was only in town for the day and had come last minute. The receptionist asked her to wait while she contacted Herr Kolbe's carer. She asked Aga to fill out an information contact sheet. Policy.

After twenty minutes or so a middle aged woman appeared from a closed door at the side.

"Fraulein Janiec? I am Sister Theresa. I am Herr Kolbe's primary carer. Would you like to come back?"

Aga followed her into the building.

"I apologize it took so long to come for you. Herr Kolbe does not normally get visitors. He has no family to speak of you see. One of our long term residents. He has been here longer than I have and that is some time. So we are surprised by your visit as you can imagine. But he is most pleased I think. It took some time to get him up and he insisted on putting on a tie, bless him. You will find him to be rather weak. He is not terribly well. But his memory is very much intact for a man his age. It will do him good because he grows weary of my face, or so he tells me."

She stopped at a bright room in the back of the complex, knocked and opened the door. Aga followed her in. The room was a small bedroom and sitting room with some medical monitors against one wall. There was no décor other than a small cross on the wall at one side of the bed and some small cupboards across from it. A window at the back overlooked large gardens planted with trees and flowers. Just in front of it was a small table where Herbert Kolbe sat in a wheelchair. He had once been a large man, but Aga saw an old man now,

372

somewhat hunched over, the folds of his skin loose on his quiet, easy face. He had a thin oxygen tube over his head, clipped below his nose and attached to a tank hanging from his electric wheelchair. He looked tired but smiled when Aga entered.

"Herr Kolbe, Agnieszka Janiec has come for a visit."

"Lovely. Lovely," he said.

"You see, she even brought you some flowers. You are a lucky man. Here Fraulein, I will put those flowers in a vase. Sit, please."

Sister Theresa found a small vase for the flowers, left them near the bedside.

"I will leave you both to talk. If you need anything Herr Kolbe press the button there."

"Yes, yes, I know."

Aga stared at the old man, taking him in, taking everything in, past and present, unsure how to start. She wanted to hate this man. She felt pity. She felt nothing. She saw an old man staring at her, a smile on his face and she felt nothing at all.

"She takes care of me, Sister Theresa. I call her Mother Theresa. She would be the perfect saint if she did not drive me so mad sometimes. But that is her job and she keeps me going so far."

"She seems nice."

"Yes. So: Janiec. A Polish name. Did you come far?"

"From Poland. Today."

"Ah, good!," said Kolbe. "I can speak Polish then with you. I get so little opportunity here yet my Polish is as good as this blasted German! So, excellent! I was born there you know. In Poland. A long time ago now, but I still have my memories. In Lidzbark Warmiński. Do you know it?"

"Yes. In fact I was there recently."

"Were you? A lovely place. Of course it has changed so much since I was a boy. And we moved away when I was a teenager. Those days it was barely more than a village. It has been a very long time since I was there. I am certain I would not recognize it. Mother Theresa said you were a neighbor of mine. You must forgive me, my memory is not always what it was. This was not in Lidzbark, surely?"

"No."

"No. Where is it you came from?"

"From Warsaw."

"Warsaw? Warsaw. I have been there, you know. A long time ago. But not for too much time. I have little memory of that city. I am certain I would not recognize it. But we would not have been neighbors there. Was it here in Germany?"

"No."

"No. I must be a bit confused. But no matter. That happens. You said you were in Lidzbark recently. It has been years since I visited."

"For a funeral perhaps."

Kolbe stared at her. Cocked his head just slightly.

"For the Major's funeral. Radtke."

"You were there?," he asked hesitantly, confused.

"No. My Grandmother, in a way...you might say she was there. In a way. Observing."

"Funny, I do not..."

"Hania. Hania Stern. That was her name."

"Stern...No, I do not recall any...Stern. She was not the...but no that woman was a distant relative of mine. Housekeeper for him. She is dead now too. No, I do not remember anyone else..."

"It is why I went to Lidzbark recently. Because of Radtke. His house is gone. It is a park now. A park for those who died in the War. For the Polish who suffered. Who died."

Kolbe stared at her. His smile had been replaced by an expression of confusion, of pain.

"The War."

"That is when my Grandmother knew Radtke. And I think knew you as well."

"The War."

"In Warsaw. Do you remember Warsaw?"

"No, I..."

"Hania Stern. Her name was Hania Stern."

Kolbe shook his head.

"Hania Stern. No, I…"

"She is dead now. Last year. I am her Granddaughter. Here…"

Hania reached down to her bag. She took from it a photograph of two young girls sitting on a bench in Krasinski Park, a long time ago. Such a long time ago. She put the photograph in front of Kolbe. His hands shook as he picked it up. Stared at the girls. Hania could feel anger rising in her.

"The girl there, with her head on the other's shoulder, that was my grandmother. Perhaps you may recall her face. Only thirteen or so at the time I think. Hania Stern. She sits beside a baby's carriage. Her aunt's son was in that carriage. His name was Jakub. Jakub Elster. He died. Killed in Warsaw. Perhaps you remember."

"No, I…"

"Hania Stern. My grandmother. Later, she went by Hannah Kielar. A different name. So she could forget. She had much to try to forget. But when you knew her she was Hania Stern. She was marched up to Umschlagplatz. Trying to get to her mother. The other girl in the photograph. Her name was Alicja. Alicja Leder. Alicja was at Hania's mother's side when they were put on the transports in the Umschlagplatz. The transports to Treblinki. Hania Stern was looking for her mother but The German, your Radtke, he stopped her from getting on the train. He took her away. You were there too. His driver. His…adjutant. That was you, wasn't it? Look at the picture, Herr Kolbe. Look. Please. Alicja Leder, she was gassed. Treblinki. Hania Stern. My grandmother. She lived. Why did she live? I do not know. Radtke let her live. He did not kill her. But she died there anyway in her way. A living death. Why? Why, Herr Kolbe? This is what I flew here to ask you. Why?"

Herbert Kolbe did not take his eyes from this angry young woman, speaking loudly to him now, speaking to him of things he did not remember, did not want to remember, had thought he would not have to remember, demanding that he did remember. His face hardened in pain and with that memory. With grief. The grief of time, of guilt. No escape. He could never escape. Never. He looked at her, at the photograph, at the young girl Hania Stern and the young girl Alicja Leder. He shook his head. He did not remember. He wished he would not remember. But he had never escaped memory.

"I think you should go, Fraulein. I think you should not be here. I do not know what it is you are saying."

Kolbe pressed the button attached to his chair.

Aga stared at him. Stood. Hated. Pitied.

The carer, Sister Theresa came in.

"Fraulein Janiec forgot she has an appointment. She has to leave now."

Sister Theresa, confused, looked from one to the other.

Aga, standing, stared deeply into the face of this once big man, his broken face, old, tired, dying probably. Stared with no real emotion. She picked up the photograph, put it back into her bag.

"They had a name they knew you by. Misio. Teddy Bear. I tried to imagine. They were afraid. Terrified. And yet they called you Misio."

Aga turned, nodded to Sister Theresa and walked from the room. She marched quickly down the corridors and found the exit through the reception area. Only outside did she feel herself crumbling, breaking. She ran to the parking lot. Fumbled looking for the keys to the rental car. Dropped them. Picked them up. Swore. Her hands shook. She climbed in. And sat. And banged her fists against the steering wheel once, twice. Again. And sat. And wept. And closed her eyes. Shook and closed her eyes.

At first she did not notice the knocking on her car door window. She opened her eyes, staring in front of her out of the windscreen. Shaking still. The knocking. It registered and she turned her head. Sister Theresa. Urgent. Pleading. Aga took a breath, put the key into the ignition so she could lower the car window.

She stared at the woman whose own expression seemed filled with sadness and some pain.

"I am sorry, Fraulein Janiec. I am sorry, he… Herr Kolbe would like you to return. He asked me to try to stop you. He said please, find you, tell her to come back in. The shock, I…Please. Please…"

Aga stared, sitting stone still. Found her breath. Calmed herself. Closed her eyes and found calm. She climbed out of the car and followed the nun back into the care home.

Herbert Kolbe sat quietly in his chair, his face drawn, tired. When Aga entered the room behind Theresa he stared at this Polish girl, this Granddaughter, this memory of a ghost who had haunted him for more than sixty years. Stared at this young woman now who looked so like the other who he had tried to forget but had never managed to forget.

"My good Mother Theresa," he said without emotion. A voice resigned. Tired. Tired of this life. "The lovely Fraulein Janiec I am sure will be happy to push me out into the garden. It is a such a peaceful day. We will sit and talk. There is much to say. Would you mind bringing us tea and perhaps some of those lovely cakes that you tell me I am not allowed. Today I will be allowed. We have no pond so Fraulein Janiec will be unlikely to push me into what does not exist. Or perhaps she will. We will see. I will give her directions to the garden exit, but let her drive me in this chair. Yes?"

Aga stared at him, and nodded.

They found a place in the grounds outside in the shade of a large elm tree, with flower beds beyond, full of color. They had the garden to themselves. Sister Theresa appeared with a tray shortly after them, with tea and teacups and some cakes on a plate. Aga carried over a small garden table and a chair for herself. Sister Theresa smiled gently, sadly, at the Polish girl.

"Please, Mother Theresa" said Kolbe, "if you would be so kind to leave us now. Old men are never safe from pretty young women, but I think in this case I am safe. We will call you when we need you."

Sister Theresa smiled again, quietly, nodded at them both and withdrew.

Aga poured Kolbe a cup of tea and put it beside him.

"Pour yourself a cup as well, Agnieszka Janiec. I think you could use it. I think we both could."

Aga nodded quietly and did so.

"Agnieszka. It is a beautiful name. Yes. Without knowing, I would say your Grandmother must have been proud of you. What is your work?"

"I am an actress."

"Um. In Warsaw?"

Aga nodded. Kolbe was quiet for a moment.

"I knew…one day…someone would come. You would come. Or another like you. Perhaps I hoped it would be so, I do not know. I have waited. In fear. But somehow I thought this day would come, yes. Even now, when I am… as you see. I still thought, every day thought, one will come. Today. Tomorrow. My days are now shorter. Time itself is shorter. I did not stop thinking this however."

Kolbe looked at her, then away. Far away. He sipped his tea. Aga did not speak.

"He always hated it when they called him the Major. He said it sounded like the Americans. He never liked the Americans much. But I think perhaps he began to accept the name. They could not exactly call him Sturmbannführer. Not after the War. Those who knew. Most did not."

Kolbe chuckled, just slightly, but there was no humor in his expression.

"Radtke died I think eleven or twelve years ago. Did you not know that when you visited Lidzbark?"

"I knew."

"Then what did you hope to find?"

"Answers. Understanding. My Grandmother left some diary notes. We figured out that the man she called 'The German' was Radtke."

"The German. Hm. And did you find your answers?"

"No. We found a garden; that was all."

"I did not know that his house was no more. That they tore it down. It was a big house. Nice. We were classmates so long ago. But I was never invited there when I was a boy. I came from a different world."

"The land was given to the town on the condition that they created a garden in memory of the Poles who were killed. The martyrs. Not the Jews. The Poles. The Jews remain…forgotten mostly. His son gave it perhaps?"

"His son? His son disappeared so long ago. I doubt he lives still. He hated the Sturmbannführer. It could have been him but those who knew, even Radtke, imagined the boy hanging from a tree somewhere. Maybe that was true. Maybe not."

"Why?"

"Sebastian Radtke was a complicated man. At the end of the War we were together, in Berlin. The Russians arrested us and we were both sent to a camp.

378

When we were finally released, Radtke returned to Lidzbark, to his beautiful wife who already had the disease that killed her. His son had grown but they did not know one another. Not really. And I think perhaps the boy learned about his father, from the War. From Warsaw. After…They barely spoke. When they did I believe they argued. His mother, that was different. Gizela. A woman so full of life once. I believe he adored his mother. The son left them. Sebastian turned his back on the boy. And Gizela, it broke her heart I suppose. Killed her in a way although she was already dying, yes. Radtke had turned bitter when he returned from the camp. And turned even more so after the death of Gizela. He shut himself away from most. Not from me. Too much—knowledge. Memory. Not from me."

He took deep breaths. The oxygen pump worked hard; Aga could hear it. After a moment: "You should know that this, here, for me, this home, the lovely Mother Theresa: it was Radtke's money. He did not let me slip away. I had almost nothing, but he made sure I would have this. I owe him that you see."

"He was your friend."

"No. Not like that. He arranged for me to join him in Warsaw as his Adjutant when the War started. I was never going to be what he was but for some reason he said he would take care of things. He did I suppose."

Kolbe again sipped his tea. Again took time to remember. So much painful memory in his face. He looked at Aga. Shook his head.

"When you showed me the photograph… You look like her. I should have realized. I remember the girl."

"Radtke could have killed her."

"He was a man of many faces. Moods. You cannot know, he…You want to understand. Answers…We were ordered to participate in the Aktion. To go into the Ghetto, round up the Jews for transport. It had gone on for several weeks. Marching them to Umschlagplatz. The transports. What happened. Different times. I do not say this to excuse. I do not excuse. But if you were not there, it is difficult to understand. We followed orders. In doing so we became--inhuman. We were told what streets to seal off, search. Which Jews we were to…which Jews had to be resettled. We did not know about Treblinki. Not then."

"Would it have made a difference?"

Kolbe looked at her, this young, attractive girl, this Granddaughter, angry yes, but reaching out to see, to know. To understand. She would never understand, but she had to seek answers. She had to journey.

"No."

He hesitated, closed his eyes, remembered.

"I think it was September. A warm, sunny day. We were told which buildings to empty. The girl, your Grandmother—we knew she lived in this street. Which apartment. The Sturmbannführer, he had known this girl, seen her several times, even before the War. That photo, I remember. Gizela Radtke, she…"

Kolbe shook his head. Sadly. Remembered. Wished perhaps that he did not.

"So the Sturmbannführer said to me that we must go to the girl, her family. I do not know what he thought. Warn them? Move them? I did not understand. So many different faces, intentions, this man. We went there but they had gone. Taken. Hundreds of people, lined up, marching. Guards everywhere. German. Ukrainian. Polish. Jewish Police, too. You cannot know. You can never really know. Radtke said we will go to Umschlagplatz. Drive me to Umschlagplatz, Kolbe. Take me there, Kolbe… Yes, Sturmbannführer. As you command, Sturmbannführer."

Kolbe spoke. But as he spoke he was not there, in this garden with this Granddaughter, this young woman. He was in Warsaw in 1942. A different life that he had not wanted to remember but that now he had to remember. He had to live and relive forever.

He saw the Umschlagplatz as it was then, with thousands waiting like cattle, Jews who were less than people, less than human. He and Radtke pushed their way through this mass of humanity, subhumanity as they had been told, as they had come to believe, these Jews, waiting, silent, afraid. They looked everywhere for one face, one young girl. Radtke would only say that they had to try to find her. Not desperation, not a need. Rather an order. It had to be done.

Then he, Kolbe, saw that Radtke had seen this girl. Almost amazingly perhaps, he saw her. She was walking towards a train car, shouting out to someone just climbing in. Kolbe looked at the train and saw an older woman being pulled inside, turning to the girl calling out to her. And another girl too, a cripple, helping the older woman inside. Holding her. Protecting her. But she could not protect her. He saw them turn and look at the girl that he and Radtke had come to find, then disappear into the transport, its door slammed shut behind them. He could still hear it, even now. Sixty-five years later. He could hear that train door slam shut.

He was there, again, that time, that place. Although here in the safety and comfort of this nursing home where he lived but he did not deserve to live, he knew he did not deserve to live, he still saw the Ukrainian grab the girl they had come to find, take his gun out to shoot. And he saw his Sturmbannführer, his Sebastian Radtke, hurry over and push the Ukrainian away. He saw Radtke then grab the girl, she staring at him with hate and fear and disgust, saw him drag her towards the train, but not to the train, not there. Rather he, Herbert Kolbe, watched as the man he knew but could never understand pulled the girl to the back of the train, and around it, behind, disappearing.

This and more he told the girl's Granddaughter now. But he did not see her, this Granddaughter, Agnieszka Janiec, because once again it was 1942 and he was at the Umschlagplatz in the Ghetto and there were the Jews and the death and the hate and he did not understand, did not really understand, did not hate but was told he had to hate, had to despise and so he did hate, did despise then, because he did what he was told. Always did what he was told.

He followed the Sturmbannführer around the back of the train, to await his orders, to make certain his superior would be safe. Kolbe did what was required.

And he saw this man, this Sturmbannführer, this Radtke push the girl down along the back side of the train, towards the edge of the Umschlagplatz. Pushing her, dragging. Pushing. And he stood, Kolbe, he stood there and watched. And he saw the girl fall. The Jewess. He had helped the Sturmbannführer find her because he was good at finding people, he, Kolbe, who had learned to hunt as a boy and could hunt and now hunted people because this was the order, this was the instruction. And he had found the girl. She had not been hard to find. Never hard to find.

And he saw her now. And he saw her fall down. And the Sturmbannführer, Radtke, standing over her. And ordering her to stand up. And she did stand up. And she stared at him, at Radtke, Sturmbannführer, without fear but with hate in her eyes. Waiting to die. Indifferent at death. Stared at his commanding officer, this Radtke, who he had known since a boy and yet did not know.

And he watched as Radtke took out his gun, pointed it at the girl, hesitated, and shot. And shot again. But shot not at the girl, rather at a place far away, above her head, one side, another. And she did not fall. And did not die. She looked at him, confused, at Radtke, at the SS Sturmbannführer in his black uniform. And he said something to her and she turned, took a few steps, a few more, and began to run. And she ran. And he watched her go. And she ran still and disappeared into the collapsed buildings of the Ghetto. And she did not die.

And this he told the girl. The Granddaughter. And this he remembered. Then Kolbe looked at Aga. Aga said nothing, just stared at him, her face now without a readable expression, trying to take in his words.

"Radtke started back towards me. There was a body lying on the ground, a Jew, lying by the tracks. Shot. Radtke walked over to that body, loosened his own tunic, bent down and wiped his hand in the Jew's blood, then his hand to his shirt, as if the blood was from the girl. Then he walked over to me. He pulled one suspender of his trousers down. I knew he wanted anyone who might have seen him disappear with the girl to think he had taken his pleasure with a Jewess. His revenge with a Jewess. And he looked at me, then away, then back at me. And he said: 'She should not die here, Kolbe. She deserves to breathe the air, not this stench. She should think she is free. But there is no freedom in this Ghetto, is there, Kolbe?' That is what he said."

Kolbe sighed deeply. Shook his head.

"And then he said to me: 'Tomorrow, find her. You are good at finding people, Kolbe. You know where she will likely be. If not you will search, find her. And when you do—shoot her.'…I was not surprised. I should have been, but I was not surprised. Radtke: you think he was pure evil. Perhaps he was. But nothing is pure. Nothing is absolute, Fraulein Janiec. Nothing."

Aga looked down at the tea still sitting in her cup, reflecting the sun behind her. She looked far away, into shadows. The tea, into shadows. She tried to be there. With her Grandmother. With Hania. But could not be there.

"The next day I went back to the apartment. I knew she would be there. Up three floors, four maybe. I walked in. It was a large room, but I knew there was a secret room behind a sink. I stood there and I could sense her, hiding, waiting. I was sure. I stood there. Did not move. I had my rifle. My orders. But I did not push open the space behind the sink, so well hidden, although yes I knew she was there. And I heard others beginning to search the building. Looking for Jews. Any Jews. Jews to die. And I could have said: she is in there. She must die. But when the other soldiers appeared, I said no. No one. No one here. In the building. I had looked. There was no one. No one…"

Kolbe looked at her, then away.

"It was the only order ever I did not carry out. I could not do this. Not to this girl who suddenly seemed to me… human. I told the Sturmbannführer that I had found her. That I had done as ordered. I knew she would not likely survive the Ghetto but I would not be the one to take her life. Not then. Not ever. I always thought she must have died. They were bad days. So very bad."

Aga stared at him. Looked for words. She could find none. Then found what was inside, what she wished to say.

"She did not die. My Grandmother. Hania. Others died. Everyone died. She did not. Why did he not just kill her at the Umschlagplatz? I think there were times that she wished he had. I think there were times that he had killed her, then, before, when he ordered her little cousin murdered. He made her watch."

"No."

"You did that. She watched. He made her watch. He was guilty. And you too. Do not look for forgiveness. I will not absolve you of guilt. I will not."

She grew angry. She was crying now. He stared at her and his eyes, although dry with age and tired and old, his eyes too wanted to weep, to cry, but he could not cry. Could not. Old man. Without forgiveness. Without absolution.

"No."

Aga started to stand. She had to leave.

"Sit," he said. He asked her. Almost ordered. Begged. She looked at him and he asked. Then he asked again, with a cry from his heart, pleading: "Please. Sit."

She stared at him. And sat.

"You said you wanted to understand. You cannot understand him. You were not there. You do not know."

"I do not want to know. No more. I do not want to hear."

Kolbe took a deep breath through his breathing tube. Closed his eyes. Opened them again and looked at her.

"We were attached to the Embassy in 1936. Things were already difficult. The Nazis were in control. We knew what would happen. It was inevitable. Sebastian had a good apartment in Warsaw. He brought his bride with him. Gizela. So beautiful. Perhaps I loved her too. She was sunny. Good. He would do anything for her. But the War was coming. He knew, and knew he would have to serve. Maybe he wanted to serve. Gizela, she became pregnant. She was so happy. And he was happy for her. He wanted her to return to Germany. He wanted to return with her, but he could not do so. And then she lost the baby. She lost it with an illness that she had, that one day would kill her. She changed. Her happiness, her joy disappeared. She lost—everything. And he could not understand. He did not know what to do. You see?"

Aga did not respond. She stared at him and said nothing.

"Gizela had met a girl in the park. A girl with a small child she took care of. A Jewess. Your grandmother. That child. After Gizela lost her own child they were ordered back to Berlin, as we all were before the German invasion although we did not know. Knew and did not know. Before they left, Gizela wanted to see the girl, the child one more time. She had something she wanted to return, she said. And that child, he was the most beautiful child she had ever seen. She wanted to see him, wanted to see that which a Jewish girl had that she could not have. She made Radtke take her to look for the girl. For the child. I drove them. I was ordered to help. They went to the park, many days. On the last day before they had to leave she found that girl. Your grandmother. And the small child. There, sitting in the park. Like the photo you showed me. I remember even now. Yes…"

"Then after Poland fell, we were part of the army then. Radtke had joined the SS. A Sturmbannführer. He was to return to Poland, to Warsaw, because he spoke the language. Gizela went with him. I went with him as his Adjutant."

"There were times I had to go into the Ghetto. Usually to drive him. He had orders. Things he was told he must do. To observe. One night I crossed into the

Ghetto through a checkpoint. He was not with me. But when I came through, I saw a face. I saw the girl. Your Grandmother. I recognized her. I am good with faces. I do not forget. I followed her to her street then. I knew where she was living. And I told him. And he told Gizela."

"After we saw the girl several times. He spoke to her. He needed to know her house, her life. Because his wife needed to know. Needed to know. She wanted to see the girl, the child, but Radtke refused. He tried not to listen but sometimes he had to listen. Gizela was everything to him and he loved her deeply. Would do anything for her."

"Your Grandmother, she left where she was living with her family. I did not know where. But then we saw her again. The Sturmbannführer was given an order. A Jew, others, had to be arrested. We knew he would be at this concert that the Jewish leaders arranged. So we went to arrest him. And when we were the, the girl was there. Radtke told me to follow her, learn where she was living then. Orders. I had no choice you see. And I followed her. I followed her."

"Gizela, all she ever talked about was the girl, your Grandmother, and the beautiful infant she cared for. Gizela loved that child because he was the child she had lost. She was half mad thinking about him. Radtke did not know what to do. He hated that child because it was not his, hated the girl because he could not make Gizela happy, could never make Gizela happy, yet this girl, this Jewess, had what Radtke could never have. Gizela could never have."

"No," said Aga.

"You need to hear," he said.

"No. No."

But he continued.

"There was a Polish policeman I knew. Chimczak. A bastard. He used to do magic tricks for children. But he…he was a sadist. I went to him to help us. I told him what the Sturmbannführer wanted to do but did not know how to do. Chimczak said he could help. Early in the morning Chimczak went with some others to a Jewish orphanage. The children there were starving. Dying. He took a small boy who was dying, maybe dead, I do not know. Typhus I think. This boy had no more life in him. He was waiting to die. Chimczak took him, wrapped a blanket around him. Carried him. Property. Not human. Property. We drove to the girl's building. Your Grandmother's building. I went up the stairs with the Sturmbannführer. It was an order. I was ordered. You need to hear. To understand. I went up the stairs, leading him. I knew where she lived. I pushed open the door. The girl was there. Your grandmother. She was there. And she said she did not know where the child was. And all the Sturmbannführer could think of was his wife who had nothing. Nothing...Then the small boy's mother ran in. She was screaming. Radtke hit her and she fell. She went quiet. And he ordered the girl, your Grandmother, to show him the child. She would not do this. She refused. Then we heard the cry of a little boy. And we found the room hidden behind the sink. And Radtke forced the girl your Grandmother inside. He called to me. Take the child, he said. Take this boy. An order. You understand? An order."

Aga shook her head back and forth. "No," she said. "No."

"I did what I was told. I wrapped the child in a blanket. I carried him downstairs. He was so quiet. So frightened. And at the bottom of the stairs Chimczak stood with the other boy wrapped in a similar blanket. Magic he had told me. A sleight of hand. He told me to stand back in the shadows. He went out into the courtyard with the child from the orphanage, the silent boy dying or dead, already dead, silent and not breathing and I did not know. I did not know. And Chimczak lay this boy wrapped in the blanket on the ground and looked up, looked up to the room above, where the Sturmbannführer still held the girl, wanted the girl to see things that were not real so she would not know, not realize. And Radtke had said if he signaled Chimczak was to kill the boy from the orphanage and if he did not signal both children would be shot and it would be your Grandmother who would decide without deciding, who would kill without killing, who would know without knowing. But it was not your Grandmother. It was Radtke. It was him."

"No!" cried Aga. And still Kolbe did not stop.

"And the Sturmbannführer was at the window with the girl, staring down, staring down to that courtyard behind the building. And the Sturmbannführer was shouting. Shouting louder. At her. At God. At his wife. At himself. And the Sturmbannführer shouted then to Chimczak. Do it. Do it! And Chimczak shot.

And shot. And shot…"

Kolbe took a deep breath. Tears were streaming down his face.

"It was as the Pole had said. Anyone who was watching saw only what they were meant to see: a boy wrapped in a blanket in a courtyard, shot there, dying there. And with no eyes around, I took the other boy, the boy that Gizela so loved, a beautiful boy with green eyes, who she had begged her husband to bring to her, her child she said, hers, I took him, silent child, wrapped in that similar blanket, I lay him quietly in the car. And we drove away…Chimczak expected to be paid for his work. And he was paid. Sturmbannführer Radtke himself paid him with a bullet in his heart and his body dumped into the sewer, the same as Chimczak did to the boy from the orphanage. There could be no witnesses. Radtke knew if his superior officers ever found out he would be executed and he warned me that if he died, I would die. So I never left his side. And never spoke. Several months later when we returned to Berlin I helped him get a false birth certificate for his son who did not die. His son with green eyes. I could not forget. His son Paul Radtke."

Aga was crying hard now. She understood and the understanding had broken her spirit in ways she would never be able to explain.

"Radtke, he knew your Grandmother, her family, could not know the boy did not die. Never know this. Never know this truth. It would have meant the Sturmbannführer's life, Gizela's life. He told me he had done this so the boy could live and had done this so the Jews would not have to carry the thought of the boy living as a German. And he hated that boy. And loved that boy. But he would have done anything for his wife. Anything. And he did. He gave her a son when she thought she would never have a son. He gave life even as he took life. And I have never forgotten it. And I have lived with the guilt of that day all the rest of my days, in Warsaw, in prison, here…I have lived and I have never lived since. Never."

*

Aga did not catch the return flight to Warsaw as planned. She drove to the countryside beyond Leipzig and found a cheap run down hotel in a very small town. She stayed in her room there for the next four days. She ate nothing, drank only water, remained within. She told the housekeeper to leave the room as was while she stayed there. She saw no one for those days. She turned off her phone. She did not shower until the final day. She lay on the bed and did not move.

And on the fifth day after meeting Herbert Kolbe for the first and only time she flew back to Warsaw. She did not choose to tell Beniamin or anyone else what she now knew, not yet. Just not yet. She had too much to process and understood she would need to process. Like her Grandmother, very much like her Grandmother, like Hania, she no longer had words.

And did not speak.

Not yet.

*

Five weeks after that day in Leipzig, she received an envelope from the nursing home, sent by the carer, Sister Theresa. In it were two letters and a photograph. Sister Theresa's letter read:

Dear Fraulein Janiec

You will recall our meeting at the care home here in Leipzig. I am sorry to inform you that Herr Herbert Kolbe passed away into the arms of our Lord Jesus Christ two weeks ago. It is with great sadness that I inform you of this.

Herr Kolbe had no family of which we are aware and, as he had requested, all of his belongings were removed to a charity shop in Leipzig with the exception of the Cross that had always been above his bed and which was buried with his remains in our local cemetery.

He did request, however, that the attached photograph and letter be forwarded to you. As the note he wrote shortly before his death was not sealed I hope you will forgive me for taking the liberty of reading his words to you, thinking these might refer to family unknown. I do not feel in a position to comment on these in any way, other than to say that I daily whisper a prayer for him, asking that he may be forgiven for his sins; if you will allow me, I will light a candle for you as well. I remain your sister in Christ,

Sister Theresa Lange

Aga removed the other letter from the unsealed envelope. She struggled to read it. In a shaky hand, Kolbe had written:

My Dear Miss Janiec

As I said to you when you came to see me, I thought, even hoped, that one day you or someone like you would do so. I suppose I hoped that such a visit would bring forgiveness, even redemption. But I now know that such will never be possible. I must take my sins with me to my grave. My sins are many and great.

I attach with this note a photograph taken when I was still a boy to show you that once, long ago, I was as any boy then or indeed now, with the hopes and dreams and humanity of boys everywhere. I understand now that on 1 September 1939 I relinquished that humanity forever. I would ask for your forgiveness but know such is unlikely as I cannot grant forgiveness to myself. I take this realization with me for these final days.

May God find a way to grant you peace, Miss Janiec, peace that I have never known and never deserved.

I remain your servant
Herbert Kolbe

Aga picked up the photograph, a picture of a group of small boys in sporting outfits in front of a school, probably in Lidzbark. A pen had circled two faces. One round face she was sure was Kolbe, around eight years or so of age. The other boy she did not know, but had no doubt that this was Sebastian Marcellus Radtke. She stared at their faces. All their faces. Just boys, as boys anywhere. Boys who grew up to become monsters. Yet not monsters. Just men who took orders. Who became something she could not really fathom. Who became ordinary. Who became banal.

She knew, and knew that she knew nothing. She needed time. Time to understand. Time to process. Time to reach and grasp. So it was meant to be.

Aga sat quietly in the small apartment room. She began to think about Kolbe, and Radtke, and Warsaw, and the boy Jakub, and so much else. But she decided to push these thoughts away. She did not want them, not right then. Not there.

She went to the shelf and took down the photograph of her Grandmother Hania sitting with her friend, Alicja. And for a moment, Agnieszka smiled, as they smiled. For a moment, there was peace. Only for a moment, but a moment was a lifetime.

Aga went to the fireplace and lit a small fire. She watched the small pieces of wood catch. Burn.

Then she placed Kolbe's photograph and letter on the low flames. Watched them smoke, then turn to flame. Watched them disappear.

This was Hania's journey, she thought. And mine. Not theirs. Ours. We have found where we were meant to be. And we are here. That is enough.

That is all.

Fourth Movement

Yeshu'a:
The Journey of Loss and Light

Warsaw / New York

2007 – 2008

The Juilliard School
Samuel Adler Memorial Lecture Series
March 26, 2014

"Pawel Weisz: A Life, A Composition, a Reflection"
Arthur Schamus
Guest Lecturer

I would like to thank you all for attending on this lovely spring day. I know many of you would far prefer to be out with your friends enjoying the cherry blossoms or no doubt practicing your various musical talents to the birds in Central Park. Mind you, the birds can be harsh critics. You're better off with me. Although their jokes are probably funnier.

Your first question—and there will be time for a second and third as I don't intend to speak forever—is no doubt: Arthur who?

A fair question, I grant you. Because I am not a musician, not a composer. Given the talent I know will be in this audience today, I stand in awe. And given the illustrious alumni from the Juilliard School I can honestly say unlike some from this wonderful institution neither am I a famous actor, dancer, performer. I will confide in you, even my circus skills could not have passed muster here at Juilliard. Although I have been known to juggle rather well. In fact my career has been that of a juggler in the arts, but juggling on behalf of artists, at their command, rather than on command, as in command performance.

So: who am I? What matter of man? Alas, most illustrious students, I am one of those lowest of the low, a manager of artists rather than an artist myself. In fact, let me clarify that. Critics are the lowest of the low. Management comes second. Ask any artist.

Now, much of my later career has been as manager, agent, confidante and friend to several artists, but in particular and for the sake of this lecture I was the manager of one artist who meant far more to me than, well, your normal client, shall we say. The composer Pawel Weisz. Composer of wonderful musical suites, sonatas, three operas, four symphonies, avant garde compositions and pathways early on. Also composer for some wonderful films in Europe and, dare I say, later in Hollywood, many of which you will know. And no doubt many of which you will have looked up in the library or on your computers before attending my reminisces today. But then some of these works you may have performed yourself. Or will one day.

So: Pawel Weisz. Polish composer. My client. My friend. And yes, my civil partner for many, many years.

Now, as I said, I am not a musician. And if you want analysis of his works, a technical understanding of the pathways he took, musical specificity, well you have the best teachers in the world to discuss and argue that. I am broadly ignorant of so very much and I admit it.

Rather I am here to tell you a different story. A story of what makes an artist. A man. A dreamer and his or her dreams. What makes the music, not just in notes, and sounds and commissions or visual reflection. And not just given the times in which one lives. But a more—fundamental—reflection. As a manger I have come to understand a far more important story that does not get put onto the sleeve of a recording or that can be downloaded from a website or found in concert notes, or indeed will be discovered by reading Wikipedia—as I am sure you all probably did.

A story. About one man, one artist, one composer, but as such a story in a way about us all. Who we are. Why we are. So bear with me and I will try to direct you on his journey. Many of you will know the basics. Pawel Weisz composed his first works in Warsaw where he studied in the late 1950s and 1960s. You will know he experimented in so-called Modern, or Avant-garde, or New Wave composition, often in canons, repetitive figures, processes, atonal and twelve tone techniques, at least at first. And you can read about his influences, from Bach to Stravinsky, Schoenberg, yes, but also jazz and even certain writers: Beckett, Brecht, Camus.

Lists. Just lists. But not who he was.

Pawel left Poland in 1968 and went to study in Paris with Nadia Boulanger. It was in fact in Paris that he had his first break out success in 1969 with the Virginia Woolf Suites, in particular the fourth of these works, inspired by Woolf's 'The Waves' that crossed over into his first film soundtrack with Poulez's rather haunting "Memory of You".

It's all there in the textbooks, on Wikipedia. But what is not there is the story.

Remember. The story. Stories give us context. Emotion. Pain. Love. Hate. Hope. Dreams. A future...and a past.

Pawel lived in Paris until 1974, then in London, until 1977. It was in that year that he moved to New York. His reputation had grown. Slightly. He hardly arrived here a penniless artist. But he was also not well known in this country. Appreciated only by the few.

So it was in 1977 that I first met Pawel. His licensing agency in England had contacted the management agency where I then worked to ask if we might help him become established here and perhaps represent him. At that time I was young, enthusiastic, hungry. And I loved 'Memory of You.' Who could not? So I was the perfect sucker to ask the agency to represent this rather quiet, talented, uncertain Polish artist who after all his years in France still spoke lousy French and whose English was--well, enough said.

My first problem was to find Pawel a place to live. Not easy, when he had enough money to eat, but New York rent in those days...Yes, even in those days. And he was an immigrant. A stateless one at that. Again, a story. So I needed to help this rather good looking Polish composer who could and would do film work but whose compositional 'Classical' work was at the time not a huge money maker find a place to sleep. And the most obvious place for that, certainly at first, was on my 1940s partially collapsing sofa.

That became his bed. My living room in my rather dark, edge of Harlem on the bad side of Morningside Heights in those days then became his home. That was to last for a couple weeks. It turned out to last a lifetime.

Pawel became my client. Then my friend. Then, yes, after some time in fact, my lover. And over time my partner, my companion, my mentor, my hope, my life. Mostly, I think though, always my friend.

That was his beginning here. But it was not the beginning, and that is what I want to bring to you today, the reason I agreed to speak in this very fine lecture series. Pawel's story and mine became entwined. But this is the story of many, so many. Not just Pawel but others unknown then. And in ways it becomes the story of all of you...

*

Beniamin helped her to pack the remainder of her Grandmother's personal belongings. The movers would be at the house the following morning to take the last of the furniture and boxes. The house in Otwock had finally been sold.

Aga had told her mother that she would take care of closing it up. Her mother had been grateful. Katarzyna had been strangely silent when the sale had been agreed, or perhaps not so strangely silent after all. She had of course grown up in this house, with all its memories, some of which Aga shared, others that remained strictly her mother's. She had wanted it that way, something Aga completely understood.

Beniamin had volunteered to drive down with Aga for the weekend. He wanted to see the house in Otwock, both because of Hannah and indeed Kazimierz, but also because so much of Aga's heart and sweetest memories could be found there as well.

They spent the morning and much of the afternoon labeling things of her Grandmother's, taking some final few items to a charity shop, organizing what would go into storage, what would go to Aga's mother, to her Aunt Maja, to her cousins and the very few things that she herself would keep.

When they finally finished Aga made them each a cup of tea. The two cups and the kettle she said would be the last things they would pack. Her Grandmother would have wanted it that way.

A cool early September wind blew that afternoon so they sat inside quietly, sipping at their cups, both in their own way remembering the woman they had known and the woman they had come to know—one and the same and yet not one and the same.

"You remember you told me what your Grandmother said to you shortly before she died, about waiting for someone here?," Beniamin asked Aga after a while.

Aga took a moment before answering.

"Her words I think were that maybe she will come. One day maybe she will come. I remember. I thought she was confused, was thinking about the postman, or my mother."

"She was not thinking about them."

"No."

"I think she waited for Alicja. I think all those years she hoped, dreamed, I don't know, that Alicja would one day knock on the door."

"I have thought so too," Aga mused. "She told me she waited for her. She said there were ghosts. She said she could hear them playing; sometimes she said she held their hands. I remember her saying that. I did not understand."

"During the War there was a ghetto here in Otwock and a sanatorium for Jews. Some of those from the Babinski Institute were in fact sent here first, before Treblinka. After the War, there was a well known children's home here, a home for orphaned Jewish children. I imagine it was probably both a sad place and a place of hope. It only existed until probably 1949, 1950 or so. Most of the children eventually went to Israel."

"You think Hannah knew that?"

"…I think she knew. The home had closed by the time she left Kobierzyn with your Grandfather. And he would not have come here because of the home. But I think she may have known. Perhaps quietly. Perhaps there, inside, a thought, something she carried with her. And waited."

"Maybe that is why she never wanted to leave here."

"In part. She may have—hoped, or dreamed, or imagined that Alicja her friend had not died. Alicja was an orphan; perhaps had she lived she would have come to Otwock."

"But she did not."

"No. And by then Hania had--disappeared into Hannah. But inside of your Grandmother, however deep, the hope within did not disappear. Alicja did not disappear I think. And I think she would never disappear."

"She may have been waiting for Alicja all of her adult life."

"Perhaps, Aga, by remaining here…she found her."

Aga looked at him, and away. She sipped her tea and wondered if Hannah had indeed finally found Hania and had finally found her friend Alicja. She hoped perhaps she had.

Later, before they returned to Warsaw, they looked for a tourist office, but there was none in Otwock. They instead found a visitor centre. The woman who worked there knew nothing of a Jewish Children's Home, long ago disappeared or where it may have been located. She was however able to direct them to the Jewish Cemetery.

They finally found it at the edge of Otwock, an area of pine forest overlooked by huge electricity pylons, filled with broken and toppled tombstones. A forgotten, unvisited place. They spent just a few minutes walking amongst the fallen stones before Aga said she had to leave. She could not remain there. She hoped her Grandmother had never visited.

"She would not have found Alicja here," Aga said.

"No. Not here. In her heart only. But not here."

"In her heart. Where Alicja belonged. Lived. Died. Was."

*

After Aga told Beniamin about her encounter with Herbert Kolbe, about what the former adjutant had told her, Beniamin spent several weeks trying to find Paul Radtke, first in Poland, then further afield. He made phone calls, wrote letters, used all the tools at his disposal through the JRA and approached any and all the contacts he could think of. He wrote and telephoned civil registration offices, public records offices, genealogical societies, made tax and pension enquiries. He found nothing of Paul Radtke in Poland other than the school records he was able to uncover in Lidzbark Warmiński. After 1957, nothing. Records of Polish births and deaths proved largely fruitless. He exchanged correspondence with the Vice President of the Lidzbark Warmiński City Council, learning that the former Radtke property had been donated to the city by Radtke's sister-in-law who had become beneficial owner when Radtke died. She had gifted the land to the city on the condition that a Memorial Park was built there when the house was torn down. Beniamin tried to contact her only to discover she had died three years after Radtke himself.

Beniamin turned to places Paul Radtke might have gone if alive. Over many weeks he searched German archives, tax offices, pension information. Nothing. He looked in Austria, in France. No success. He found Radtkes living in the United Kingdom, but no Paul. He wrote letters to anyone he could think of but all came back negative. He went through genealogical information, databases, even online phone books in the United States. He found quite a few Radtkes and in fact three

Paul Radtkes. But none of these led to a Paul Radtke who had grown up in Lidzbark Warmiński.

He had simply disappeared. He either wanted it to remain that way or had long since died. Beniamin promised Aga he would keep looking but the truth was obvious to her: the likelihood of finding Paul Radtke, whoever he might be, was remote. If alive, he might have changed his name. If not, finding a record of his death would likely prove daunting. And if he chose to keep his past invisible it would not have been difficult for him. The road had for all practical purposes come to an end and with it her own journey.

Beniamin had warned her that the obsession to know must one day come to the conclusion that she had learned all that she possibly could, that her search would need to cease. That she would need to move on with her life. The knowledge she had gained, the pain and indeed wonder needed to be stored away inside her. Her life had changed and had not changed. It perhaps would never quite be the same. But it must now continue on the path that she had chosen for herself, long before. Hannah, Hania would remain a part of her, but it seemed it was now time to put the past to rest. To find peace for her Grandmother. And for herself.

Aga and Beniamin had decided they would move in together and began looking for an appropriate apartment they could share and could afford. However they had to delay their plans slightly when Aga was offered a minor role in an American film shooting in Warsaw about the Polish educator, children's book writer and ultimately director of the Chłodna/Sienna Street Ghetto orphanage, Dr. Janusz Korczak.

She had been wary of accepting the part but Beniamin encouraged her. As it was but a minor role it meant only three weeks of filming and he argued it would be cathartic. Aga had real doubts but ultimately agreed it would be best to confront the stories in her head, the memories she had inherited, rather than to run from them.

Most of her scenes were to be shot in studio, in a mock-up set of the orphanage as imagined by the designer and director. The shivers that ran through her on the first day soon dissipated into a sort of calm, an understanding at what had happened there, of those who had lived it and indeed died it as well. Although always wary of making comments to a director, Aga did proffer one remark that took the American director aback.

"The children called him Dr. Janusz," she told him in passing.

"How do you know that?"

Aga had to look away for a moment, then turned back to him.

"A girl lived here. A girl who had her leg crushed when the German bombs fell on the Ghetto. And a boy who smuggled in apples. I know; that's all."

The director looked at her for a long moment, asked nothing further. Changes to the script appeared in its pages the following morning.

On the final day on this particular set, while waiting for her call, Aga wandered into a side room used for other scenes in the film, a room dressed to look like one of the children's dormitory rooms. She sat down on the makeshift bed and looked around at the false, cracked walls that made up the set. She could almost see there the ghost of Alicja sitting on a bed staring at her and smiling, the ghost of Simcha Gitler walking in through a door with an apple in his coat pocket.

"I am your man," she heard him say. "I am your man..."

She knew the final scene in which she had to appear would be the most difficult. Her character was to join the Korczak character and others as they led the two hundred or so children from the orphanage to Umschlagplatz and on to Treblinka on that warm August day in 1942. Many child extras had been brought in for the scenes and several streets of Warsaw old town had been closed off for some of the shots. The children in the scene were dressed up in their 'best' 1940s clothes. Each carried a blue knapsack and a book or a toy. As the filming progressed so too did Aga's emotional composure crumble until she could no longer stop the tears from falling. Another actor she walked beside had to support her by the arm as she struggled with her thoughts and emotions.

Beniamin had intended to visit the set on Aga's final day of shooting but several days prior to that he had had a call from his mother in Israel. His father had had a stroke and was in hospital. Beniamin took the next flight to Tel Aviv.

He spoke to Aga several times over the coming days. His father slowly improved although exhibited some speech and memory loss. He was expected to improve with time. Beniamin could not be certain how long he would remain in

Israel; he warned Aga it could be several weeks. She asked if he would like her to come there once the filming was over, but Beniamin thought it best for her to wait at least for the time being.

This put their search for an apartment to share on temporary hold, although Aga was not particularly bothered. The filming had taken more out of her than she had at first realized. The quiet and empty space would do her good.

A week after she had completed her scenes in the film, Aga went to Beniamin's apartment to collect his post and to water his rather sad collection of plants. Letting herself in, she found herself enjoying a space not hers but his: his few pictures on the walls, his mess, his still dirty dishes in the sink, his books and cd's. She found even his smell, his sense of being, a comfort. She realized she was in love with him, something passionate yet more than that: a love that was gentle, warm, a shared time and sense of support. He made her smile by not being there, with his post-its everywhere, his crosswords in Polish never completed with more than four or five words, his few plants half dead and without personality, the photographs of his family scattered around.

Aga made herself a cup of coffee, sat down at his tiny kitchen table with enough space for two when two was a crowd. Moving in with him would be the right thing to do. For the first time in a relationship she saw a future.

She sipped the coffee and thumbed through his few letters as he had asked her to do, looking for any unexpected charges that she could help him sort, looking also for any lingering letters to his enquiries (there were four, all negative.) She had a sense of him sitting beside her, laughing easily, keeping her safe. Although she knew he might be away for some time she knew too he would return and that the return would be a homecoming.

Aga placed the letters seeking information about Paul Radtke into the file box that he had created concerning Hania and all the information he could garner. Largely full, she knew there would be little else he would find to put in there. The search for a woman named Hania who became Hannah had largely found its conclusion, or what conclusion they had reached. This was the messiness of life: life did not always provide answers. If anything it provided more questions. More mysteries. As Beniamin liked to say, the chaos of humanity: gift and curse.

Although he had warned her that she must begin to let go of the obsession that her Grandmother had become she could not yet let go. Not just yet. She decided that even if Ben might not approve she would take the box home and go through everything that he had put away: the questions he had asked, the search, the research that he had recorded. Perhaps there would be something he missed, or even just something further allowing her to put her Grandmother's journey into context and make her own journey settled and complete.

Aga spent the next few days going through the documents Beniamin had collected, rereading also the notes she herself had made, the fragments, diaries and papers that her Grandmother had left, many of which still saddened her or sometimes made her smile. She read through her Grandfather's case notes again and spent some time looking in various psychology texts and histories to try to get a sense of this man not only as psychologist, but as humanist as well. And a Grandfather. It helped Aga draw a picture of a relationship that her Grandmother rarely referred to, but which clearly had helped Hannah reconcile Hania, had helped Hannah find a sense of inner peace.

Over the following days she went through every note, letter, reference in Beniamin's file box, reliving the discoveries she had made. She closed her eyes and saw the first visit she made to Beniamin's office. His doubts. She listened in her memory to his reading the transcription of Josef Schipper and witnessed again the resulting regret in Beniamin's expression. She relived their journey together to Nowy Wiśnicz. Relived the Kielar farm hidden beneath undergrowth and a difficult past. The barn with its secrets. So many secrets. Radtke. Kolbe. Still Kolbe. Secrets, memories, disassembled, assembled, lived, discovered, cried over, obsession.

She understood finally, despite her unquenchable desire, Beniamin was right. The story had reached its end. It gnawed at her, tore at her heart. But it gave no more answers.

She sat in her sitting room drinking a glass of wine, looking through the last of the documents. She wondered, when all was said and done, if there was truly meaning: in her Grandmother's story, in the sublimation of Hania Stern, in Hania's resurfacing. In Hannah's desire to make the story known to her Granddaughter.

After all, what had her Grandmother hoped to achieve? Was she too looking for some sort of redemption? An explanation? A cry that she had lived a life unjust by her living? She had survived. Perhaps there was no answer to that. To seek meaning, cause and effect, definition, perhaps that was Hannah's mistake, as it was perhaps now Aga's.

She put on some music, in honor of her Grandmother. The last thing her Grandmother had heard, perhaps. Gentle cacophony. She listened while raising a glass to Hannah and to Hania. The 'Warsaw Suite'. But her Grandmother said she hated Warsaw and now Aga understood why. Understood loss. Understood so much, yet not enough.

She thought about that last afternoon in the garden, sitting with her Grandmother. Waiting perhaps for Alicja, or perhaps just for Hannah to find a voice. To find some sort of explanation. Indeed some sort of meaning.

"Here's to you, Grandma. Na zdrowie. To health!" Hannah, Hania, had lost so much, sacrificed so much and yet despite them she had survived. Despite 'the Magician.' Despite Kolbe. Despite the unfathomable evil that men showed themselves capable of. Despite 'The German'. The monster Radtke who had let her live and killed her in the process. Lost, yet alive, she had been both. A wonderful woman, Aga thought. Remarkable…

Aga pulled out a few of the files at random from the box. Stared at them. There the file of letters. There the file on Schipper. On Simcha Gitler. On Nowy Wiśnicz. She opened Radtke's file. What sort of monster was he really? Or was he, as Beniamin tried to explain to her, just a man, a mediocre, weak man who kept his eyes closed like so many others, who pretended he did not see when he saw? Banal.

"You deserved the death that came to you," Aga said to herself. "You deserved all the loneliness, all the abandonment. You deserved emptiness. That is what you deserved. It is what you found at the end. Emptiness, loneliness, alone. God damn you…"

She shook her head. Sipped on the last half glass of wine. Looked at Radtke's file. Thought about his wife. Her son. Was she any better? The pretense of a child, not hers? She too deserved no memory. Nothing. Paul Radtke must have hated his father. Not his mother. Gizela. He should have hated her too. Should have walked out on both of them. Must have known.

The wine began to affect her thoughts, just slightly.

Must have known.

Aga looked at Beniamin's ordered, carefully collated work. There Paul's birth certificate, 1939, a year after Jakub's birth. Were they one and the same? She would never know. Suspected, but never sure. Never certain. Uncertainty was the only certainty in life.

There Radtke's military record under the Nazis. Bastard.

There his arrest record by the Russians.

Better he died lonely and alone.

The lies. So many lies. She hated them, hated them both. Hated them for what they had done to Hania, for the grief she always felt, for her need of redemption. Hated that she did not know. Hated them both.

She remembered what the priest had said. Paul Radtke had played Bach in the church. Aga hated Bach. Hated Paul Radtke. Hated the lie. Hated that she could do nothing. 'Have Mercy on Me, God', she remembered. 'Have Mercy on Me' he had played, and walked out. Never seen again. Was there ever really mercy for any of them? And for Hania? For Hannah?

Died or did not die death or not death hidden or not hidden never to be found never will be found. She stared at their marriage certificate. She hoped that in the end theirs was an unhappy marriage together. She hoped both Radtke and Gizela lived tormented. Died tormented. An unhappy life. An unforgiving life. May they never have found redemption. May their ignorance condemn them forever. Aga raised her glass.

"To Sebastian and Gizela Radtke, in your deaths may you find no redemption for what you did. May there be no mercy for you in death or in life. Let us listen to Bach, will we?"

Tired, tears on her face, Aga stood to change the music. To enjoy what Sebastian and Gizela Radtke would never enjoy, the Bach that would always torment them. She stood, turned. Picked up the CD cover to return the 'Warsaw Suite' and replace it with Bach. Picked up the CD cover and…

Dead in her tracks. Stopped.

She turned back, sat down slowly. Motionless. Sat, did not move. Sat and stared. Finally picked up the paper still on the table in front of her, her hands shaking. No. Trouble breathing. No. Pain in her chest… No. Trouble thinking. No. She… no.

She shook her head, back and forth, back and forth.

She stared at the documents spread out on the table. At a life shared and lives destroyed. She stared at that file and thought of Bach. She stared and heard the music playing through the speakers, heard and did not hear.

Shook her head again.

And stared.

And felt ill.

And did not move, but stared down at the papers on the table. And could barely breathe. And could barely…breathe.

Aga spent the next two days in the library. Reading. Listening. Around her only chaos. She listened to the chaos. She learned all she could. Read all she could. Tried to understand all she could. She bought music, all she could. And listened all she could.

She tried to believe, but could not believe.

She tried to think she had drunk too much, but knew she had not.

She tried to think that things were not possible, that her imagination was too great, that the obsession had taken command of her senses. She did not believe the thought. Her thought. Would not believe. Not possible.

A foolish obsession.

She tried to be rational. She tried to be realistic.

She was none of these.

She slept badly. And she tried to dream when she did sleep. But finally she realized she did not dream. She woke and saw what she saw and who she saw. And she knew.

She sat quietly in her apartment and rationally, quietly, over a cup of tea and in a moment of clarity, with a quiet whisper she said only 'yes.'

She rang Stefan Marcin's mobile phone several times, each time leaving a message. She knew he was in St. Petersburg, but she needed to speak to him. Desperately needed to speak to him. He rang back once, but her phone did not pick up the call and he left a recorded message.

"How are you, darling?," he said. "St. Petersburg is cold and empty without you. I miss you."

She tried him yet again. Missed him yet again. Shooting. Damn film. Shooting.

She said nothing to Beniamin, who remained in Israel, who said he would need to remain there for the next month or six weeks to help his father, his mother, his family. She understood and said nothing. Not yet.

She knew what she had to do. Had to.

She left a final message for Stefan.

"I need to see you," she said. "It is important Stefan. If you are not filming this weekend, can we meet?"

She left the message and did not wait for a response, but caught the mid afternoon flight to St. Petersburg.

She could think of only one thing. And one name.

Pawel Weisz.

She was certain.

*

Stefan's new assistant, Nina, left Aga a message that Stefan would meet her for lunch on Saturday at the Severyanin Restaurant, a short distance from her hotel. Her concierge told her she could walk there as it was only ten minutes away. When she arrived Stefan had already been seated at a quiet table off to the side in a room purposely meant to resemble a private apartment.

"For you my Aga, champagne and caviar. Welcome to Russia."

"Oh Stefan, you never change. How are you?"

"At my ripe age I no longer need to change. To answer your question, I am tired. The shooting days are too long here. The actors have no sense of humor and no imagination and I miss autumn in Warsaw. And the food...except for the caviar."

She laughed.

"I have missed you, Aga. Clearly you have missed me too."

"Enormously."

"As I thought. Have you come seeking a role in this series? I can have the writer write you a part. Something 19th Century sexy I think."

"No, Stefan. But thank you."

"Then you came purely for my company. I knew it."

"Purely."

The waiter appeared with a bottle of champagne and caviar, as promised. They ordered a light lunch. Stefan raised his glass.

"So," Stefan said, "I cannot tell you how happy I am to see you, Aga. Have you come to ask my forgiveness and tell me you want to move back in with me?"

"No, Stefan. In fact I am seeing someone."

"What? A duel. Tragedy. Do I know him?"

"No."

"That is something. An actor?"

"No. Not an actor or director. And I am moving in with him."

"Hm," he grunted, sitting back. "I am jealous already. Are you in love?"

"Yes, Stefan. I think I am."

He sighed. Shrugged.

"In fact you should be happy. I wish that for you. It is the least you deserve."

"And what of Mariana? You seem to have a new assistant."

"Alas, things change. Mariana…she wanted more than I could offer. And after losing you…I was never in love with her, Aga. Not as I was with you. But as you get older, so little time."

"Is there someone else?"

Stefan smiled.

"Of course," Aga laughed. "There is always someone else."

"I suspect, Aga, you did not fly all the way to St. Petersburg to discuss our future together or apart after all. Let alone my sex life."

"No. I need your help."

"For you, my muse, anything. On condition that we find another production to do together. I want to direct you once more while I still have the energy. After your Elektra, your Iphigenia: you were magnificent. Truly."

"I would like that."

"So, tell me, what is it you need?"

"Pawel Weisz."

"Pawel Weisz? You need Pawel Weisz?"

"Yes. Yes I think I do. I have a story to tell you, Stefan. A long story."

Over lunch Stefan listened for the next hour, and hours that followed, as Aga told him all that had happened over the last many months. She told him about the letter Hannah had left for her, about the papers and documents found in the file kept at the bank. She told him about piecing together a story, a story not of Hannah but of Hania. About Warsaw in the late 1930s. About the events of September 1939. About an apartment in Zoliborz where a happy Jewish family lived, and an Aunt and Uncle on Twarda Street who took that family in when the Ghetto was created. She told him so much she now knew about the Ghetto, so much that even now it frightened her, upset her, tore her insides.

She told him about the young girl Hania and her brother Shaul, about the infant child Jakub. She talked of a girl named Alicja and walks in Powązki Cemetery and Krasinski Park, stories of boys who threw stones and a girl who promised always to protect Hania, always to be there for her. She told Stefan about the death of Marek Stern, the subsequent move to Dzielna Street in the Large Ghetto. She told him about a secret room, about the death of the boy Shaul to typhus, about the death of an infant child with green eyes. She talked of the Umschlagplatz, and the marches and the Aunt who played Chopin on the piano bringing tears to people's eyes and the Uncle who scrubbed a courtyard but could never remove the blood of his tiny son.

She talked of life, and death, a story woven that had been in the past but had become her present.

Stefan listened quietly. His playful expression disappeared. He heard of a world he had known and not known, stories he recognized and did not recognize. He asked few questions. There were few he needed to ask.

Aga went on, talking of a Polish policeman called The Magician who killed for sport and an SS German Officer who had ordered the death of a boy, an infant, out of hate or not she never knew. How that same German Officer had allowed Hania to escape Umschlagplatz, even as Hania's mother had boarded the cattle car and the door slammed shut removing the sunshine forever. How a girl with only one good leg had helped her into the car so she would not fall. And how the girl Alicja had kept her promise as best she could to protect Hania, always protect her.

And she had.

Aga told Stefan of what she knew of Hania's eventual departure from the Ghetto, helped by a boy named Simcha Gitler, a sewer rat, but not a boy then, not a child, rather a brave young man who brought her back from death. And led her away. But then who returned to Warsaw and his own death, knowing as he must have known that he would not survive. He would die fighting. Die standing next to a girl he loved. And so he had. And so she had, beside him.

She told him further about her own need to understand what had happened, all that had happened, so much needing to understand; thus turning to Beniamin who had become her friend and, yes, her lover. About a mechanic named Schipper who survived but who suffered every day for the remainder of his life. Who could never forget. And she told him about Nowy Wiśnicz, about a woman there who hid Hania and gave her a new life as her own daughter, her own Hannah, and who died for it. And about her Grandfather Kazimierz, then a young psychotherapist. About the hospital. The silence. And the voice.

Then she told him about Otwock. And waiting. A life time of waiting for the girl who did not come and for the ghosts who did.

So much to tell. So much to explain. Kolbe and Radtke. Pain and sorrow. Loss. A search.

Hania. Hannah. Hannah. Hania.

So much to remember.

And told. A story told again and again. Needing to be heard and understood and witnessed. Again, and again.

Lunch had long passed but the restaurant staff kindly let them remain in the quiet of the restaurant. Aga spoke. Stefan listened.

She continued to talk about Hania who disappeared and Hannah she became. And she explained how Beniamin had said to understand that journey you needed to try to find not only those you loved and sought but those you did not want to know, did not want to understand. So she told Stefan how Beniamin's search had led to Sebastian Radtke. How together she and Beniamin visited Lidzbark Warmiński and found the house where Radtke had lived with his wife and son torn down, made into a garden of remembrance. She told him about the encounter with the priest who had remembered Paul Radtke as a young man who played Bach in a church but half way through a recital had walked out and was never seen again. How the young man's mother Gizela died shortly after and how the young man's father, the one-time SS Sturmbannführer, lived alone with only his hate and anger and, hopefully, despair that saw him to the end of his days, if not beyond.

She told Stefan how Beniamin then came upon Herbert Kolbe, the Adjutant, but said visiting him was a journey he could not make, was likely a final journey that Aga needed to make alone.

And so she had. She had visited this old, dying man in a nursing home. And heard his confession. And refused to allow him the absolution he sought because absolution was not hers to give. Was no one's to give. Forgiveness, simply, could not exist from her. The forgiveness of mediocrity was not hers to offer.

And she heard too, there, from this Kolbe who she could not forgive, heard too another story of an infant boy in the Warsaw Ghetto who was shot but not shot, of another put in his place, of a child stolen away, stolen from mother and father and leaving only despair and loss and death. But death in life because the child had not died but had lived, likely believing his parents were others. His father a man he would reject. His life a lie but a lie he probably never knew.

He had lived, just as Hannah had lived.

And Hannah had died unknowing.

But the boy could not be found. Until one moment, a moment of drunken revelation when all had suddenly seemed clear. And the possibility, the very possibility, that that boy had lived. And lived still. And had a story to hear. A story that needed to cry out now for him to hear. Because of Aga's Grandmother. Because it was time.

Aga finally stopped talking. She looked at Stefan. He said nothing, but looked away. Troubled. Engrossed. Lost himself. Lost in the past. Lost in memory, memories perhaps not his own but part of his world too, his experience and not his

410

experience. So much loss.

He too understood the need now to forgive not those who had done the unspeakable, but those who had survived. Who had lived and then had to live with the living.

To self-forgive as well. He knew that what Aga sought, really sought, was not only a final resolution for her Grandmother, the resolution of a life and a death, but also the resolution for herself, for Agnieszka who he in his own way had loved and would always love, for the journey she had been on that had taken her into the dark heart of despair and from which she needed a final, confirming release.

Stefan sighed and looked up at her.

"And you think Pawel Weisz is the end of the this search? You think he was the infant your Grandmother looked after in the Warsaw Ghetto, a survivor like her?"

"Paul Radtke disappeared in 1957. He hated his father, whatever he thought of his mother. Did he know about Michael and Lea Elster? About their son Jakub? I suspect not. But he probably knew what Radtke was, some of the things he had done."

"Possibly. Yes."

"Paul," she said with half a laugh; "the Apostle. The name in English. It is the same in German. In Polish however the name is Pawel."

Stefan nodded slightly. He understood.

"Beniamin searched everywhere he could for Paul Radtke. But Paul Radtke hated his father. Despised him for whatever reason. So much so that he disappeared. He did not die like many thought. He simply ceased to exist. He wanted a new life. For a new life, he needed a new name. Perhaps he despaired at what the Germans had done to Poland. Nazis like his father. So he kept his name but took the Polish equivalent Pawel. It should have been obvious. It was there all the time on a marriage certificate. We just had not seen it but it was there amongst those papers. Sebastian Radtke perhaps wanted a son. Or wanted none. I do not know. But his wife so wanted a child, a child as beautiful as a Jewish infant with green eyes she saw by chance one day in Krasinski Park. An infant she fell in love with in Krasinski Park. And who she knew would probably die soon. They would all probably die. Perhaps she urged her husband to bring that child to her if he ever saw the infant again. Or perhaps it was this German SS Officer's decision, his alone. Questions that will never be answered. Only Sebastian Radtke and his wife knew the answers and only God will have heard their confession. But whatever or whoever drove them, they did this thing. An act of salvation and an act of condemnation. Life and death. They took that child and raised it as their own."

"Sebastian Radtke and his wife," she continued, "married in 1934 in Silesian Voivodeship city of Częstochowa but returned to the Radtke family home in Lidzbark Warmiński. Radtke and his bride Gizela. Gizela Weisz, Stefan. Her family name was Weisz."

Stefan stared at her, feeling only sadness at the story and the heaviness of the day. Still she could not stop.

"And the boy, Paul Radtke, who so hated his father and so loved his mother, retook his Polish name, and his mother's name, That boy who played the organ so beautifully on that final day in Lidzbark Warmiński, a place he must have hated, a place to where he never returned, that boy Paul Radtke played his Bach but stopped midway through his recital and walked out, on that day became Pawel Weisz, a composer of difficult music. Music he must have played like his real mother. And like my Grandmother Hannah, who hid a truth so painful within her for her life, so that boy hid who he was. But he cannot die with it, Stefan. Not like Hannah. He cannot die without knowing the truth. Who he is. Who he was born as. Those who loved him and died for him and dreamed for him and even as they turned to ash in Nazi ovens or pushed him in a stroller in Krasinski Park or thought he died on the cobblestones of a Warsaw Ghetto courtyard, they lived for him. They lived for Jakub Elster. Not for Paul Radtke. Not for Pawel Weisz. For Jakub Elster. He needs to know."

She looked out the window at the day now ending and could say no more. She was near collapse with emotion. Stefan stared at her for a long time. Finally he took her hands in his.

"You could be wrong, you know. You cannot be certain."

"I cannot be certain until I have met him. Have spoken to him. Until he tells me I am wrong. Or I am not. This is why I have turned to you, Stefan. This is what I need from you."

He sighed. He looked for words, but found none. Finally, still holding her hands in his, he said quietly:

"I will walk you back to your hotel now. We will have a quiet drink there, you and I. We will say nothing more of this for the moment. Then I think you should go to your room and sleep. I know this is what I need to do. Tomorrow I will come to your hotel in the morning. We will walk quietly along the banks of the Neva, as we once did along the Vistula. You remember? We will walk together as friends, because we are. I am happy for you and your Beniamin, and our own friendship will last and help one another as it should. As it must. Tomorrow we will decide what must be done. We will breathe the fresh autumn air as we walk along the river. We will think of your Hannah, of Hania, of a little infant boy whose life was taken, but not. We will talk then. And move forward."

Hannah nodded gratefully.

Stefan paid the bill even as the dinner guests were arriving.

They walked quietly to Aga's hotel, had a quiet last drink there, then Stefan left as he said he would.

It had been the longest of long days.

*

They met mid-morning and walked the streets along the Neva River saying little. Stefan looked weary Aga thought. They took in the view of the Winter Palace, the Hermitage, St. Isaac's Cathedral. All beautiful in their way, iconic. Aga looked at the picturesque images but found she did not engage, did not care. They bought coffees and took them to the Summer Garden where they found a bench and sat quietly near the Crown Fountain.

"I have thought about all you told me yesterday." Stefan finally said. "So much to take in. Not easy."

"No."

"You do realize it is possible that Pawel Weisz is not the son Jakub, the son of Hania's Aunt Lea, Uncle Michael. It is possible still that the infant did not survive. Your Adjutant, your German officer Radtke—shadows. Evil men who did evil things. Who lived lies, told lies."

"Beniamin told me about the writer Hannah Arendt, what she said about

Germans like them."

"The banality of evil. Yes I know. I wish I could say I do not agree. What frightens me, Aga, frightens me even now, is that she was correct."

They sipped the coffees. Sat quietly, huddled together in their heavy coats against the cold air. Stefan smiled just slightly, almost laughed.

"I was just thinking: Elektra and Iphigenia. Both victims, brought about by a war. Who really suffered? You explored it so well, playing both roles. Now, you are playing them again perhaps...So, Weisz: you want to see him. I understand that need. I hope wherever it leads you it brings you some peace."

"...So do I."

"Do you remember a year ago, you put on music, his 'Warsaw Suite' I believe."

"Of course. The music that connected the dots for me."

"It got me thinking about him at the time. As I told you then, I had known him when I was a student. He left Warsaw in 1968. Disappeared at first. Those too were difficult times. A different story. Or perhaps part of the same. Yes, perhaps. Weisz resurfaced in France first, I believe. And over time became a composer of note. Not famous then, but known. Over the years his fame increased."

"I know. I read."

"Our paths crossed two, maybe three times over the years. I never saw him again after 1968, but he dropped me a note after my first film was released to say it was very good. Once in London we exchanged letters about a project. I cannot even remember what it was. We tried to meet but it did not happen. I had not been in contact with him for many years, however, until you brought up his name when listening to his music. The thought rather stuck with me last year. When I decided to do this series here I contacted him through my US agency. He lives in New York. I did not speak to him but I spoke to the man who manages him, also his live-in partner I understand. A man named Schamus. He told me to send the script. I did, but Weisz said no. He wrote to me himself, said he was unsure if he would do further film work. I think he has been ill. He invited me to call on him when I might next find myself in New York. He left the door open to collaborating one day. Perhaps even still we will."

"I see."

"Weisz was always rather introverted. I understand he is slightly reclusive, except when it comes to his music I suppose. Still, I will do what I can to introduce you, arrange for you to meet him. I know you need to."

"I would be grateful, Stefan."

"You need to know he is not an easy man. I know that much about him. I remember. He needs to hear what you want to say, but from what I know he may not greet you with open arms. After all, if what you say is even partially correct he has spent a lifetime running from his own ghosts. Some of those ghosts I knew. Clearly some I did not. I need to think how best to approach this. I cannot say that you want to find out if he is a long lost relative, or that his father was not his father and you come with words of joy and blessing. It will not be that easy, Aga."

"There is no joy. Just loss. And maybe need."

"Just so. The nature of truth. I will need a little time but I will do what I can. You have made me feel my age, Aga. Funny, but this has brought back my own memories, experiences. It has made me realize that I have been lucky. Life sometimes has been hard, but mostly, yes, I have been lucky. If you are right, and I cannot be certain you are, then yes he has to know. Our paths take twists and turns. Something unexpected always there. We do what we do. But inside, deep within us…" Stefan shook his head, weighing every word. Hesitated. Finally: "We need that truth I think. He will also, if there is another truth."

"Yes."

"But so do you, my lovely Agnieszka. I want to tell you something else. I am very happy for you with your Beniamin. I look forward to meeting him. May your love bring you the blessings of life and strength to weather its storms. But I want you to know in my own way I did love you and I do love you. And while your story has made me very—sad—I want to say I am grateful that you came to me. Told me. That I might play a small role in your own drama."

She took his arm, leaned against him.

"Funny," he said, "it would make a good film. Or television. Maybe one day. But perhaps there are stories that must not be told that way. Stories of the heart. We will see."

*

Aga returned to Warsaw that night. By the time she reached her apartment, it was too late to telephone Beniamin. She needed time to think anyway so waited until the following evening when she knew he would be free to talk.

He listened quietly as Aga told him of her connecting Jakub Elster to Pawel Weisz, a connection of names, of music, of certain commonalties. Of need. What references there were to his childhood only said that his parents had died in the War, that he had been born in Germanic Polish Silesia, which Aga reminded Beniamin was where Gizela Weisz Radtke had come from. But beyond that, there was nothing. She told him that she had contacted Stefan to ask for his help in trying to meet Weisz; she did not add that in fact she had flown to St. Petersburg for the weekend. Some things were best left unsaid.

Beniamin listened quietly to all she told him. She could not know how he would react so she went through as much detail as she could. After she had spoken he said nothing at first. Silence sat heavily over the telephone line.

"Beniamin?"

"I am thinking."

She waited.

"You know Aga, much of what you say, it is circumstantial," he finally said. "That does not mean you are wrong. There are at the very least coincidences. But no guarantees. It is all very tenuous, full of hopeful thoughts. And hope may be a risk."

"Stefan said much the same. I could be wrong."

"It is not simply wrong or right. You are opening yourself to the possibility that you will get hurt. Badly hurt perhaps, because your need here is very strong. Weisz is not an uncommon name. I could talk to contacts, go through channels as I did before. See if I can find something concrete."

"I cannot do that again, Beniamin. I cannot wait for weeks on end. I have this feeling inside of me. I have to act on it. If I am wrong then I have to accept the consequences but I have to see this through. If I am to be hurt then I get hurt in the process. So it will be. But this is what I have to do."

"You need to understand however that you are not the only one, Aga. If you are wrong, if you can meet this man and discover that you made a mistake, he will probably simply shake his head, say no. But if you should be right, even should he not be who you so desperately want him to be he may in fact still be Radtke's son. That too is possible. And if so you may bring great hurt to him. Paul Radtke, whatever the truth of his birth, walked away from his family before his eighteenth birthday. He never looked back as far as we know, and that assumes he is alive. Not a certainty. But if he is, why did he go? Why did he run as he did? If you should stumble onto his truth you may find some answers for yourself but you may cause this man great distress, or hurt, or anger. Despair is a dangerous thing. You must be very careful."

It was Aga's turn to be silent. She thought for a few moments. Then she answered.

"This is something I have to do. And it is something I think Hannah would want me to do. For her memory. And for my need, yes. I know I could be wrong. But if I am not, even if it causes distress for Pawel Weisz I think he needs to know. I think so with all my heart. I do."

Beniamin sighed. "Then you must do this because closure too matters."

Aga spent a week waiting for her phone to ring. It didn't. She believed Stefan would try to help. She understood too that he had his production, that her need was secondary to that. But still she hoped he could open a door for her. She tried to second guess what may have happened. Perhaps he had been unable to contact Weisz. Or perhaps Stefan had done as promised but Weisz shunned any contact. Several times she picked up the phone to ring him only to place it down again.

Her fretting and anxiety finally came to an end about some ten days after she had returned from St. Petersburg.

On a crackly phone line Stefan apologized. He had been caught up in work. He sent word to Pawel Weisz and at first got no response. It seemed that Weisz had been in a recording studio and not got the messages Stefan left.

"I contacted him through his partner, Schamus. I said I was working on a project that I wanted to discuss with Pawel. Pawel then sent me a message. He said he was trying to finish a recording session he had promised to do then had a concert to prepare for next year so would not be able to take on anything else just now."

Aga sat, deflated.

"Well," she started to say, when Stefan interrupted her.

"Wait. My US agent, it took him a few days to coax out a home number for Pawel Weisz but he finally succeeded. I spoke directly to Schamus there instead of simply sending messages back and forth. He listened. I told him I was working with a young actress on this project and we simply needed only some background from Pawel. We thought he could help. I said we are doing a play based on a musician named Robert Mandeltort. A young man both Pawel and I knew in 1968. I sent word that you were related to Mandeltort. A little lie for a bigger purpose. I just had a message back today. Pawel will find some time for you if you are in New York. So it will be up to you, Aga."

"Thank you, Stefan. I...Thank you."

"Let me know what happens. Remember. Robert Mandeltort. He..."

The crackly line from St. Petersburg went dead before he could finish. Aga would remember.

She looked for the number for LOT airlines, then picked up the phone and dialed.

*

"Pawel Weisz: Life, A Composition, a Reflection"
Arthur Schamus
Guest Lecturer

Now in Pawel's early works he liked to experiment, shall we say, with musical form. As he put it, he wanted to explode what was and put it back together as it might be, or should be, or could be. He once explained to me that in his early works he was in fact most influenced by Picasso. Who isn't? But in Pawel's case, the Picasso of the artist's Cubist phase.

Pawel explained that he liked to take composition that existed as regional, country, folk tradition, call this what you will, and break it apart. Examine it like an artist with Picasso's eye, each element, each note and theme and sound, then reassemble these as was and is and might be using modern technique and a cutting edge composer's box of tools and tricks. Perception is of course all. A cubist portrait of a world. The world he had come from. The world he knew. He was trying to define not only that world he saw, Poland in the 1950s, but the world he felt within him, needing definition and redefinition. His particular self.

Reassemblage to reveal, he called it. And indeed this became his hallmark calling card for much of his earliest work.

But there is another influence here that I need to bring up now, an influence throughout his life in a way, but that has particular relevance to this lecture.

Pawel was a great admirer of Wordsworth. Yes, William Wordsworth, the poet. Now Pawel did not compose any Odes to Daffodils and he was not a pastoralist composer by any means. Romantic, I would suggest, but not pastoral. Still, Pawel did quietly enjoy Wordsworth's words when he needed to clear his head.

This matters. Let me explain why. One of Pawel's favorite poems, or rather ideas, came from Wordsworth's 'The Prelude', where the poet writes: 'There are in our existence spots of time'.

Spots of time.

Pawel often remarked such to me. And what he meant were those keystone moments that define a life, dictate it, that make us choose to take one road rather *than another, unexpectedly. Unintentionally. Chance. Chaos. Possibility. The artist's journey? Yes. But a human journey and a human experience. And this is at the heart of the story I want to tell. For those 'Spots of Time' that Pawel Weisz referred to often do not appear in your history books or on Wikepedia. They do not always appear chronologically, some playlist in which you can hear how he wrote this, and this became that, and he went here then there then...*

What Pawel discovered, what he was, was not orderly, not chronological. A life is not always chronological. And that matters in an artist's journey.

In my case it matters in how I want to reflect on this artist's life. I could begin, as I almost did—almost—with the early years of the 1950s and 1960s, then Prague, Paris, London, then a falling apart 1940s sofa in a small 1970s New York City Morningside Park apartment.

But that is not the story of a life.

Rather the story of this life begins months before. Before the 'then.' Begins in certain ways in 1968 before he left Warsaw, where he had lived, studied and worked for a decade or so. But you need in fact to venture even earlier, to a Warsaw we now barely know, barely remember, a Warsaw that he did not know but that was very much a part of who he was. He came to find a side of this city in his quite wonderful 'Warsaw Suite' of 2004. Yet in many ways that was just a façade, indeed arguably a façade of contrivance—a façade that is but artifice. The artifice of something deeper. Something more fundamental. Something older. Alive. Painful.

A Spot of Time that came to haunt. A Spot of Time that came from far away, because someone chose no longer to forget, and someone else sought answers.

So if you will allow me a few minutes, I will explore a life that, like a cubist painting, was reassembled from elements hidden deep within. I begin not at the beginning, not at the ending so to look backwards. Indeed I begin not with my friend and companion and artist and the wonderful, wonderful composer you know as Pawel Weisz, or those whose influence weighed heavily on his artistic gift and the exploration that was unique to him. Rather I begin with a young Polish woman who knocked on the door. And changed a life...

Forever.

It had not gone at all well.

She sat at the desk in her small hotel room, staring at her laptop computer screen. After seeing him two days ago, she could have left. Perhaps she should have left. But she was not prepared to do that.

Yesterday she had walked. All day in this mammoth city, not her own, walked. Feeling small. Looking for light, finding little in the canyons they called streets. Feeling empty. Walked and thought. In the cacophony of noise and honks and voices and sirens around her she heard nothing. Only silence. A silence of anger. And of despair.

She knew she had to start again. She had to make him listen. To know. Where then to begin?

Sitting at this desk now she remembered the meeting. The short talk. She remembered and felt the stabbing pain of that memory.

*

The taxi ride from Aga's small hotel off Washington Square to Brooklyn Heights had taken about half an hour. She sat nervously in the back of the yellow cab, going over and over in her head what she would say to Pawel Weisz when she finally met him. Stefan had given her Weisz's phone number. She had had to leave several phone messages on an answer machine before she heard back, finding a note at her hotel reception that he would be available early on the Tuesday afternoon at his residence, with an address on Willow Street in Brooklyn Heights.

The address turned out to be a small building of brown stone in a quiet residential area not far from the Brooklyn Bridge. Aga took a deep breath, walked up the steps to the front door and rang the bell. After a moment the door was opened by a middle aged woman.

"Yes?"

"I am looking for Pawel Weisz? Is this…"

A voice behind the woman interrupted.

"It's all right, Pina. She's expected. Ms. Janiec?"

Aga nodded at the well dressed man appearing behind the woman. Not Pawel Weisz. She had seen his photograph in articles and on covers of CDs and records.

Not Weisz. The man held out his hand.

"Arthur Schamus. Pawel's partner. Come in, come in."

He showed her into the entry hall, took her coat.

"I apologize for taking so long to respond to your messages. Pawel is recording at the Island just now. That's the studio we use. It's a few blocks from here and he likes to walk back. He should be here in the next few minutes. Come."

He led her through a room past a baby grand piano to a small study at its side in the back, filled with books and papers, where he showed her to a small sofa.

"You've come a long way. Have you been to New York before?"

"Yes. A few times now. I have friends here. It is a nice city."

"Ah, good. And you found us easily enough. When did you arrive?"

"Three days ago."

"Well, I'm certain Pawel will be pleased to meet you. He'll have another session later this afternoon. He's recording a compilation of his early work. He says it is what you do when you run out of important things to do, but I think he is enjoying it. Juilliard Chamber Orchestra. Very good in fact. I know Stefan Marcin was eager for him to meet you and Pawel insisted we put some time aside. He should be here shortly. Would you like some coffee, tea?"

"Tea, please."

"I'll have Pina make a pot. Pawel should not be long. I've got a contract call on behalf of a client I'm supposed to make just about now. I hope you will forgive me for a few minutes. Please, make yourself comfortable. Pina will sort you out in the meantime."

Aga nodded, smiled. Arthur Schamus disappeared. Aga sat quietly. A few moments later the woman, Pina, brought in a tray with tea and some sweet biscuits. Smiling, she put the tray down and left Aga alone.

She sat quietly looking around the room. Beyond the room, into the larger room, the baby grand piano. Sound of music. Sound of the 'Warsaw Suite', Chopin, Bach, Stravinsky, there but not there. Instead she heard only silence. No music. No Pawel Weisz. Silence surrounding. Aga stood, looked around his study. Many books, in English, French, Polish. Polish but not home. This home, but whose? Who was he?

Some photographs. Famous faces. His face. No family. Who does this man look like? Who does he really look like? Sheet music all around. A past but limited. And again, who does he look like? She did not know. She could not say. Aga looked at the rows of books again. Pulled one down. Virginia Woolf. Many annotations. Had he used this in writing the music for his 'Virginia Woolf Suites'? She remembered: his breakout success. She had listened to it by herself in her apartment in Warsaw. The Fourth and final suite, 'The Waves', had moved her greatly. He had used recordings of waves in the music, then the music itself became like waves, growing more distant, more alone. She had heard the sadness. Why had he chosen Woolf? Had he used his thoughts in here to find voice, the notes, the sounds, the music itself?

She put the book back. Picked out another. Poetry. The Polish poet, Wisława Szymborska. She had won the Nobel Prize for Literature. Aga had read her in school. She remembered a line from a poem called 'The End and the Beginning' that she had had to recite in her literature class: "After every war someone has to clean up. Things won't straighten themselves up, after all." Perhaps that was why Aga had come: to clean up a lie. Chaos. Another line hit her memory, hard: "Those who knew what was going on here must make way for those who know little." Aga shook her head. A lesson learned now, lived now, almost too late. She noticed in the front of the book an inscription written by Szymborska herself: 'For Pawel, In the small moments, we must breathe and remember.' Aga wondered.

"Are you fond of Szymborska?" a voice behind her asked. Aga turned quickly around, startled.

There he stood.

"I am sorry. I startled you."

"No, I…I should not have…"

"But you should have, Miss Janiec. Words are for reading as music is for listening. Pawel Weisz."

He took a few steps towards her, took her hand. Stared into her eyes and smiled. He was thin, looked tired. Rather frail. His head was full of thick grey hair. His face was kindly, but his gaze sharp. He must have been handsome once, Aga thought. Time had hurt him. No, pained him, she also thought. Not the pain of age.

The pain of experience. Of something else too.

"I'm sorry. I meant to be here when you arrived. Please…"

He pointed to the sofa where she had been sitting, then pulled around a chair opposite. He put the walking stick he used behind it and sat.

"I hope Arthur and Pina have looked after you. I see you have tea. Would you like fresh?"

"No, it is still hot. Thank you."

He nodded. "You have only recently arrived in New York?"

"Yes. Three days ago."

"Holiday?"

"…Family. And some friends. And…"

"And business. Research. So Stefan suggested in his message."

He smiled. His smile was warm, but cautious.

"I apologize again for running later than expected. We are recording some works with a chamber orchestra. Old pieces. I am not certain of much value."

"Mr. Schamus told me. I am sure they have great value."

"He probably said they were brilliant and wonderful and you should go out and buy the CD as soon as you can. He is a manager, after all. But he means well."

"No. He only said they were early works."

"Then I shall have to find a new manager who does a better job at selling my work. Not so easily done alas."

"No. I suspect not."

She smiled.

"So first tell me about Warsaw. I was there several years ago. The first time then in many years. The city had changed much."

Aga shrugged. "It is a city. Not New York. The weather now is turning cold. The river still runs through."

"Yes it does," Weisz smiled. "Indeed. The Vistula carried me away and will bring me home. I never had a huge love of Warsaw I suppose. The Russian pierogi at U Fukiera, perhaps. Otherwise…"

Aga laughed slightly. "My boyfriend Beniamin would argue with you that the only place for pierogi is Zapiecek. Except for his mother's."

"Then he is a lucky man to have such a mother and I suspect as well to have one such as yourself. As for my Arthur, he would argue that Beijing steamed dumplings in New York's Chinatown outdo pierogi by far. He is a peasant," he said with a grin. "So Warsaw has changed and not changed, just as its people. Hard to leave. Hard to return."

"Yet you found its music in your Warsaw Suite."

Weisz nodded, thoughtfully, shrugged. "Do you know the Irish writer James Joyce? Joyce wrote 'Do you know what Ireland is? Ireland is the old sow that eats her farrow.' I suppose I felt somewhat like that towards Warsaw. I had to leave there to find it in my head and my heart, just as Joyce had to leave his Dublin to be able to find it again. Now they tell me I am a true New Yorker after all these years. But my music is a true Pole's music I think. Without Poland, Warsaw, no music. No sound. And, I still prefer pierogi to the pretenders."

He smiled, again. His smile disarmed her. And searched her. Read her.

"Your given name is?," he asked.

"Aga. Agnieszka."

"Agnieszka. A lovely name. May I?"

She nodded.

"So, Agnieszka. I understand you are an actress of some talent. Stefan had suggested as much."

"I am not so certain."

"Hm. From what I read…I in fact take note of what happens in Warsaw. It is often not terribly far from my thoughts and memories, despite myself. I read your reviews, Stefan's reviews, of the two *Elektra* plays. *Elektra* and *Iphigenia*, I believe."

"Yes."

"And you played both roles?"

"Yes. Alternate nights, except on Saturdays when both plays performed."

"That must have been difficult."

"Yes. Emotional. Trying. Difficult."

"Your reviews were very good. Congratulations. They are interesting stories, interesting characters. A lot of passion. Soul searching."

"Stefan purposely pushed the politics of both plays. His way."

Weisz laughed at that.

"Of course he did. I have not seen Stefan Marcin in many, many years, alas, but even back in the day long before you were born he was like that I think. And his film work often explores such political themes. Interestingly. I admire his work."

"He said he had hoped to work with you one day."

"We tried. Without success. And he contacted me about this work he is making now in Russia, but it was not something I could do."

"Perhaps one day."

"Perhaps."

"Which leads to why you are here, Agnieszka, so I believe?"

She said nothing. Held his gaze.

"You are working on something new with the director. Political, I do not know. Something to do with music. You should know, if you do not already, that I told Stefan this was not something I could be a part of. These days, my age, my health, it is hard to plan too far in advance. So I said no."

"Yes, he told me."

"Then he sent another message that you wish to use Robert Mandeltort in your research. A relative he told me. That is a name I have not heard in many years. A name buried deep within I suppose. There are things I remember about Robert, much of which I choose to keep in memory. So I decided to see you, but I need to explain that I am very opposed to using Robert's memory, even as research."

"I understand what he may have told you. And what he did not explain."

"Is there something that needs explanation?"

"Much, perhaps."

He stared at her, then looked away. Looked out the window for a moment. Then back at her.

"Robert was a wonderful violinist. Second to none. I took his loss personally, for many reasons. But it was all so long ago. So much has changed. I am happy to speak to you about music, Agnieszka, but not Robert Mandeltort. If he is your relation, somehow, you can discuss him with his family. But his memory with me must stay with me. I want you to know that. I want Stefan to know that as well. I could have chosen not to speak to you at all but I wanted to say this one thing in person."

Aga stared at him, nodding slightly. She could sense something more than anger. Something verging on despair, perhaps. She could not put her finger on it. She too turned to look out the window at a small garden beyond, its golden leaves falling in a slight breeze.

"My Grandmother Hannah, she was the only one who called me Agnieszka, rather than Aga. Insisted on this. I can hear her voice in yours," she said as much to herself as to the composer, looking back at him. "I suppose she is the reason I am here."

Pawel Weisz looked at her, slight confusion in his expression. He sat back in his chair.

"She played your 'Warsaw Suite' the first time just before she died. And then the day I found her, her heart extinguished, I think she had been listening to it again. I wonder if it gave her comfort? I wonder what she would say to me now if she knew I was here before you like this, knowing what I know? And I know."

Aga felt a tear slide down her face, even as she tried to smile.

"Miss Janiec, Agnieszka, I'm sorry if I…"

"I am not related to Robert Mandeltort. I do not know him as a person. A musician. He did not bring me here."

Pawel's expression froze. Greater confusion. He stared at her. She shook her head, wiping her tear away.

"I do not understand. The message from Stefan…"

"A fabrication," she said, interrupting again. "He said it would be difficult to see you, but he knew I had to, I had to know, to understand. For my Grandmother's sake."

He continued to stare at her for a long moment, saying nothing. Looked at this young woman, obviously touched by something, obviously needing something. And he did not know what he could give her. In truth he did not know what she really wanted of him. Or why.

"Go on," he said then.

"I listened to so much, your music. I did not always understand, but I made

427

myself listen. Some of it, so beautiful. I read all I could. Your life, your past. What is revealed. What is hidden. Everything I found seemed to start mostly in 1968 when you left Poland. But that is not the beginning. It never was the beginning."

"I do not know where this is leading."

"Almost nothing is said of you before, of your life. Just minor detail. The biographies say you were born in Silesia. They say your parents died in the War. That is all. That is all that is ever said."

"Agnieszka…"

"You need to hear. My Grandmother's name, Hannah Kielar, you did not know her. Or Hania Stern. Did you know her?"

"I don't see where…"

"Then perhaps the name Herbert Kolbe. That is a name you must know I think."

Pawel's face froze. He stared at her.

"Herbert Kolbe, Adjutant to the German Officer. The Officer: you know that name because it is your name. Radtke. Sturmbannführer Sebastian Radtke. Your father."

He stared at her, his face set. She met his gaze and held it.

"Miss Janiec, I am afraid you are mistaking me for someone else."

"Pawel Weisz. Weisz was your mother's name. You took it. Why? Did you hate him that much? Did you know what he was, what he did? What he did to my family. But not just my family. So many, so…

"Miss Janiec, as I said…"

"I was there. I went Lidzbark Warmiński. The house is gone. Your house. Torn down as it if it never was. As if you never were, your father, mother…"

"Why are you here, Miss Janiec? I must insist."

"Do you know, I met a priest who remembered you from when he was a boy. He told me about that final concert when you played Bach on the organ but could not finish, how you walked down the stairs, your steps echoing in the church, walked down and kissed your mother's hand, then walked out. They all thought you were dead, but you were not dead. Not dead."

Pawel stands, staring at her, his face hardening. Tears slipping down her face. Unexplained tears. He does not understand. He does not wish to listen.

428

"Miss Janiec, please, you are confusing me with someone else."

"I found Kolbe. I talked to him. You need to know. You need to know about Radtke. About Lea and Michael Elster. About my Grandmother. You need to understand."

"Miss Janiec. Agnieska. My parents came from Silesia. I grew up there. That was my home."

"You were Paul Radtke. But you chose the Polish name Pawel. Paul became Pawel. And you took your mother's name because you knew what Radtke was, what he had done, didn't you. But you did not know. You did not know at all because of the lies and the secrets and you need to know now. He lied to you. They both lied."

"I'm sorry," he almost cried out, his voice raised. "I am sorry for whatever has happened to you but you are wrong. You have mistaken me for someone else. Or someone in your imagination perhaps. You are…"

"You need to hear. You need to understand."

"No!"

The door opened and Arthur Schamus looked in, surprised.

"Pawel?"

Pawel Weisz, composer, old man now, in pain, old man, stared at Aga, stared with anger, with fear. He did not want to hear more. He did not want to know more. He was depleted and exhausted and broken and he would not listen. He could not listen.

"You have mistaken me for another, Miss Janiec. I grew up in Silesia. My parents died during the War. That is the only truth I know. None other."

His shoulders hunched, he stared at her for only an instant longer, this woman with tears in her eyes, on her face. He looked somehow broken. Torn asunder and adrift. He glanced at his partner, his friend of so many years, confidante and lover and guardian. Turned his back on her, on all, and glanced only at his friend, one he had trusted with much, but not all.

"Arthur, I have explained to Miss Janiec that I cannot be involved in her project. That is my final decision I am afraid. I am due back at the studio now. If you will arrange a taxi for her, I'm certain she would appreciate it. Miss Janiec, good day."

Pawel took his cane from behind his chair and left the room. As he walked past the piano, he stopped, stared at it. His shoulders hunched, his demeanor far more of pain than anger, he reached out and touched a single white key, a single note. He kept his finger pressing down on the key for a moment, holding the sound, the music that was not, staring, thinking. Thinking forward, past, secrets and lies. Finally he removed his finger and the sound ended.

He did not turn back. He walked on. Schamus stared at him, shocked, confused. They could hear the door close behind him as Pawel left the house. Schamus looked at Aga, wounded, tearful, silently staring out the window, her head shaking back and forth, just slightly. For the first time in many years Arthur Schamus felt at a loss and unsure what he should think. Or do.

*

She now sat before her laptop in the hotel room, staring at it. She had let herself down. She had let the past get the better of her. A combination of anger, hurt, fear, need, all had got the better of her that day. She had been unable to stop, but it was not what she had wanted to say. She needed to reach him, needed to reach out to him. He needed to hear, to believe. But did she believe herself? What if she had been wrong? What if all along she had wanted something so badly that she had no longer been able to distinguish truth from fantasy, hope from need misplaced?

There was something…Something. What was it? Clawing at her. Nagging in her brain. How to reach out? What was it? What path?

She closed her eyes. She felt the confusion. She felt too the pain. She saw his own confusion. And heard his denials. But she could not stop herself, could not find calm, could not explain.

She stared at him, even in memory, her remembrance of events from two days before, she stared at him and knew why her heart felt so broken, her pain so overwhelming.

She stared at his face, then, now, and felt so alone. She saw the age in his expression, the lines deepening in his face, the shoulders slump, then the questioning turn to anger. But none of this she saw as she stared at him and spoke, and needed to explain, so needed to explain.

Instead she felt the pain within her. And the pain growing within him. Heard his protests. Felt the tears on her face. And saw one thing that kept eating at her and tearing at her heart then, staring at him and seeing him but not him, rather staring and feeling her Grandmother Hannah and the young Hania whispering in her ear, begging in her ear. So she, Aga, staring at him, trying to explain and to cry out and to tell him who he was, who he really was, all that had happened and that he was a part of without knowing he was a part of, staring at him, staring still, then and now, with her eyes closed in this hotel room still seeing him and staring at him. Him. Staring into his eyes. The revelation of past. Of present. And of story. The revelation of human touch that reached for him and called out to him. That is what she saw then, remembering, staring into his face, staring into his eyes.

His eyes.

Into his green eyes laced with hazel through age, but green still. His green eyes. And she knew.

She opened her own eyes, looked at the computer screen waiting to hear, listen and record. Looked at the computer screen, considered, then she began to type.

It was him.

She knew.

She had a story she needed to tell.

*

The taxi left her once again in front of the house on Willow Street in Brooklyn Heights. Determined, unsure, she walked up to the front door, rang the bell. Waited. Heard footsteps. Closed her eyes. Opened. Steeling herself. But it was the woman Pina who opened the door. Not Weisz. Not Schamus. Not there, the woman Pina explained. Neither of them there. Aga said she had something she needed to give to them.

"Are they at the Island still? Recording?"

The woman Pina hesitated, then nodded.

Aga thanked her and set out walking. She had made a point of remembering the studio name, easy to keep in her head. She had looked up the address at the hotel before she left. Drawn herself a map. It was not far. Not hard to find. Ten minute walk. Ten very long minutes.

She found the building. Felt her heart beating. A security guard at the entrance. She said she had some papers for Mr. Pawel Weisz. Papers she needed to give him. She showed the guard the thick leather file case she had bought for the purpose.

"Studio C," he told her. "They're recording. It will be lunch break soon. There is a studio waiting room just down the hallway."

And he let her in.

She found the room. Sat down. Alone. Sat upright. Straight back. Heart beating hard against her chest. Sat and waited. A monitor hanging from the ceiling in a corner. She could see the small orchestra of perhaps twenty people. She could see his back, standing before them, looking through some notes. Weisz. Radtke. Pawel. Paul. She watched him as he studied a score then worked with the orchestra. Pages of score. Conducting. Stopping. Giving instruction to a musician, to the studio engineer. Starting again. Stopping. Looking at the score. Starting again. No sound on the monitor, just images. Aga turned away. Sitting upright. Still. Waiting.

She tried to keep her mind blank. Think of things far away. Think of Hannah. Hear her Grandmother whispering in her ear. I am waiting, she heard. Waiting for ghosts. She held the file case tightly against her. Closed her eyes. Breathe. Just breathe.

After a while she noticed people, some holding musical instruments, walking past in the corridor. She looked up at the monitor. Musicians filed out. Had she missed him? No, he was there still. Sitting at the piano looking at the musical score.

Aga quietly stood, left the room and walked over to the doorway of the large studio where musicians emerged, heading for their break. She waited, but Weisz did not appear. When the last of the musicians had left, she took a breath and walked in.

The seats of the orchestra musicians were all empty. She quickly took in the room, the recording engineering room off to one side, its door open. She blinked once or twice, then saw at the far side Pawel sitting at the piano, talking quietly to Arthur Schamus who stood beside him. Again she took a deep breath then walked towards them. Schamus was first to hear her footsteps and looked up in mid-conversation, clearly surprised to see her. Pawel Weisz then looked around his friend as well. Saw her. He did not stand. Aga walked purposely up to them. They stared at her, saying nothing. She looked for her words.

"Miss Janiec," Schamus began. "I don't think you…"

"I know," she interrupted. "I understand."

Neither man responded. She looked from one to the other, then focused her gaze on the Composer.

"I know what you are thinking," she said to him in Polish, "but you are wrong. I do not care about Sebastian Radtke, or Gizela. I am not here for them. That is not who you are. Your name is not Radtke. Not Weisz. You are Jakub Elster, son of Michael Elster and Lea Elster. My Grandmother Hannah pushed you in a push chair in Krasinski Gardens when you were an infant. She loved you. She always loved you even as she died. Even when you had died. She needed me to find you in her heart but did not live to know you as a man, as a composer. She did not know of your life. She did not know…anything."

Aga placed the leather file folder on the piano, then continued in English.

"You are in my blood. My dreams. My journey's end. I have copied everything here for you and now written all I could remember, all I knew, so you would know. Every detail of these days. This search. This is my gift to you. I hope you will read. I am at my hotel for two more days then I fly back to Warsaw. If you wish to speak to me, you can speak. If you wish silence, I will be silent. You need to know as I needed to know. To understand. I am not here to hurt your life. I only came here to give it meaning."

She nodded at both men, who still stared at her, confused stares, without vitriol but without comprehension either.

She turned and walked out of the studio. She held her composure, even on the journey back to her hotel. She would not let her emotions enter her heart. She chose not to think. She did not know where to focus. She closed her eyes on the ride back and instead let her mind's eye focus only on a fallen rotting beam in half collapsed barn on a farm in Nowy Wiśnicz. It was the only image in her head and it would not depart. She thought she heard music in her head as well but if she did she could not remember the composer. She chose not to try.

*

The phone did not ring.

Aga spent much of the next two days in her hotel room, hoping Pawel Weisz might telephone her but he did not. She cancelled the dinner she had arranged with friends, decided to leave the seat empty at the theatre she had arranged for the matinee performance on the Saturday afternoon. She went out to do some shopping but came back with nothing. Nothing interested her. Later she walked again all the way up to Central Park. She found a bench on which to sit. She sat for a long time, thinking about her Grandmother, about all that had happened over the last many months. She felt somehow empty and a bit lost.

Beniamin rang her early that Saturday evening. He sensed something was wrong and knew it had been hard on her. She said she would explain everything when she returned, that she would still catch the flight the next day. She said little else. She would call him then. He hoped he would return from Israel in the next week or two. She told him she hoped so as well. She knew he was needed by his family. But her need clawed at her and he could sense it. He told her he would not remain away any longer than he absolutely had to.

She put down the phone.

She refused to cry. She waited. She refused to be hurt so, but was hurt so. She refused.

Later that night she took herself out for a quiet meal at a nearby small restaurant. She ate little. She needed to leave New York. She needed to go. Empty.

Again at the hotel, no message.

This is how it ends, she thought quietly. The poet Szymborska was right: things indeed do not straighten themselves up. And she could not help. She had tried but could not. Chaos. She sat on the bed. No longer waiting. Just sat.

"I am sorry, Grandma," she said quietly to no one. To ghosts. "I tried. But you were right: the Nazis they took everything, until there was nothing left to take. They took who you were. Maybe who I am too. I am sorry." She sat longer, staring at emptiness, then added in a whisper: "Uncle Michael, he knew. You can scrub the stones in the courtyard forever, but the blood is always there. Staining the

434

stones. It never goes away. Never."

Later Aga slept, still dressed, deeply, without dreams.

She woke in the morning, took off her clothes, went and took a shower. She let the water run down her for a long time before washing. She wanted to wash it all away. She did not feel cleansed regardless. Blood on stone. She felt only empty. She had not known she wanted this so much, wanted him so much. Wanted what?

Acknowledgement, she thought to herself. Acknowledgement of self. She wondered too if she even existed. She was no longer certain she did.

Aga sighed, feeling the water running down. Sighed, feeling nothing. She had reached her end. The end. This had led only to pain. She would move on. Time.

Later, she packed her small bag. Took one last glance at the phone that did not ring. Looked around the room. She had no regret. She would not leave with regret. She would not allow herself that. She closed the door behind her.

At the reception desk she waited to pay her hotel bill. A car was due in a few minutes. The receptionist smiled.

"Oh, Ms. Janiec, your guest is in the front reception waiting for you."

Aga stared at the woman, then turned and slowly made her way to the front room. Arthur Schamus sat in a chair near the windows, staring out, his expression thoughtful, his chin resting in his hand, his eyes tired. He turned as she approached, stood.

"Ms. Janiec, I'm sorry. I rang early but there was no answer in your room. I knew you were checking out today so on the off chance I would still catch you..."

"I must have been in the shower."

"Please?," he said quietly, pointing to a chair opposite. She hesitated, then sat down, as did he.

"When is your flight?"

"In a few hours. I have a car picking me up shortly."

"I see."

He said nothing at first. Then he reached beside his chair and picked up the leather file folder sitting there, the file folder unopened.

"I came to apologize. On behalf of Pawel. And myself. Pawel is not normally rude. Nor am I."

"You were not rude."

"Then remiss."

Again she said nothing.

"I have brought this back to you. Pawel has not looked at it. He has refused to do so. And I have also not reviewed what you brought for him. I felt somehow it was not my place, my right. Pawel wanted this returned. Insisted. Perhaps he is right. Perhaps not. I cannot say. It is thus returned not in anger but because whatever it is you brought here from Warsaw is somehow a part of you and should remain so."

He handed her the folder. She looked at it for a moment, placing it then in her lap. And looked back at him. Looking down, he continued.

"I met Pawel many years ago now. I think I probably loved him from the first day he walked into my office. Ours has not always been an easy relationship. Like any close couple we each make demands on the other. Returning this was one of his. I do not agree with that demand but as his friend, his manager too I suppose, I must accede to his request."

"I understand," she said quietly.

"I have never talked to Pawel much about his past, at least most of it. When Stefan Marcin mentioned Robert Mandeltort, I did not know who that was. Pawel has not said more than it was someone he knew a very long time ago. He must have been someone very important to Pawel, important enough to want to see you. I have not enquired further. And Pawel has never spoken of his childhood. Not once. He has talked of the Warsaw Music School. His teachers there. He has talked a little of the experiences of his departure from Poland. His regrets too. But he has never once mentioned his early years before that, never mentioned his parents. I did ask him once but saw only pain. He answered that it was of no importance and I decided that this is how he wished to leave it. If he had wanted to talk he would have talked. He did not. Unless he ever does, I cannot take him down that road. I hope you understand."

She stared at him, then away, out the window. She thought for a moment. Looked back at him.

"Mr. Schamus, I am very tired. I have been on a long journey. Longer than I can explain to you. A journey that has taken me so very far. Far from Warsaw. My Grandmother, whose name was Hannah Kielar, I think she hoped I might take this journey and I have done so. To honor her you could say, but more than that because I had to seek myself and find myself. Perhaps I have done so. Perhaps not. My Grandmother left me a letter when she died. It was the start of that journey, although not its beginning. A copy of that letter is one of the documents copied in here. In it she wrote that she often thought of destroying the fragments and stories that she left for me in her papers, but could never do so. She said I was free to destroy them myself or to bear witness. I chose to bear witness. She said also that she hoped what remained of her memories might help her to find some sort of redemption. Some sort of peace. In what she had to tell me here some sort of truth, if I chose to take this journey along the path that she left for me to discover. I have done so now. I have reached the end of that journey. If Pawel Weisz chooses as well to bear witness his truth is here. If not these can be destroyed. It is the same choice my Grandmother left me. Our lives are about such choices. Only we can find the peace we each seek. Need. Dream of. I can say no more, Mr. Schamus. I have come to the end of that journey. Nothing else remains."

Aga stood and smiled, sadly. She put the leather file case on the chair she had sat upon, allowing it to remain there. She held out her hand towards him. He hesitated, then took it and held it for a long moment.

"My car will be waiting."

He nodded.

"I wish you well, Ms. Janiec."

"And I you."

She turned and walked away, out of the hotel. Arthur Schamus did not watch her go. He sat quietly in his chair, his chin again resting on his hands. Finally he stood and left the hotel, alone.

A few hours later Aga was on her flight back to Warsaw. She looked out of the plane window at the city below her receding. Turned away and closed her eyes. She was very tired. She quickly fell asleep and did not awaken during the entire journey back.

*

The Juilliard School
Samuel Adler Memorial Lecture Series
March 26, 2014

"Pawel Weisz: Life, A Composition, a Reflection"
Arthur Schamus
Guest Lecturer

Pawel and I spent many years together. Many happy years. Like any couple there were disagreements, patched up, never festering for long. The foundation of our relationship I would like to think was truth. We worked together. Planned together. Discussed together. But to be honest with you now this was the only time I remember going behind Pawel's back and telling him a lie. I would like to think a small lie. But even small lies can have great consequences.

So at the end of this particular week in October, Pawel had completed recording his last in-studio project, a collected works project of those compositions he wrote and performed in his early years as a composer, including 'With Memory for Twelve Musicians' first performed in 1968, 'Silence, Krakow' first performed in 1969 and his seven part experimental work 'Remembrance of All Things Past' from 1971.

As was often the case, Pawel and I would spend weekends or holidays at a small cottage we have long enjoyed on Lake Huntington in the Catskills. Pawel often retreated here when composing. He enjoyed the solitude and quiet. Some of his finest works were in fact composed at the property. When he was working I was asked to disappear and largely left him to his own devices. Silence, I discovered was quickly filled with the most wondrous music.

As soon as Pawel had completed the last recording session he arranged for our driver to take him up to the property. I remained in New York City with work to tend to and because I had determined that Pawel needed time to himself. He was tired and clearly needed space.

It was while he was away at our cottage that I sat down to look at some documents I was able to translate and that would prove to have a dramatic effect on me, on our relationship and ultimately on Pawel himself. Without saying anything on the matter. Without admitting that I had not returned these as

438

requested. In fact I told him the opposite. Thus: the lie.

Those documents ultimately told a story. A story that was, in truth, a Spot of Time I would now say. Essential. Quintessential. Touchstone. Also something—heartbreaking. Transformative. Urgent. They told Pawel's story as I did not know it and indeed as he did not know it. They told the story of a family. Of the past. Of history. Of loss and survival. Of pain and longing, of a journey that a young woman had taken finally to our door, but also the difficult, tragic journey of a young woman before her. In truth, they told of the journey of this Composer as well. And arguably one that we all have taken ourselves in ways sometimes not seen, not understood, not known. Each one of us.

At the end of that week alone, I drove up to join Pawel at our cottage. I carried with me a leather file case of those documents. I carried with me the past. And the future.

There were times we fought, Pawel and I, as I said. Normal times. We learned to accommodate. To accept. To scream annoyance, then move on.

But this time, this was different.

We fought. Anger and emotion. I stayed in that cottage only one night before returning to New York. And as I said to Pawel, he could look at what I left behind, or burn it all. Sometimes one needs to hear other voices. And turn to one's heart. One needs to know. And seek truth.

I did not hear from Pawel for a week. Eight days. Nine. I have to admit to you, lovely students, I grew concerned. Okay, he was angry, but who else would he find to play chess with, or read with, or freeze his bottom off with in the lake below the cottage? Yes, swimming there even in October. Pawel always was a bit mad. I reveled in sharing that madness. Frozen bottom madness.

I did hear from him finally, some ten days or so after I had left. He rang. Sounded tired. And he asked that I give him space to work. He wanted to turn to something new. He did not mention the documents. He did not mention the anger. He said nothing further about my small lie or omission. He promised he would telephone again soon but needed now to think and compose.

Again: Spot of Time.

As in so many of his finest works, the beginning is not the end, the end not the beginning, rather we commence a story, a musical idea, we hear the sound and need to reach for it mid stream while looking both forward and back.

Life, my friends, is never straight forward. My friend Pawel Weisz was not straight. In many ways.

He also was not forward. Well, not always.

No, life is not static nor orderly, not always expected. It is chaotic. Pawel's music was sometimes explained as such. But in fact, chaos too is an exploration of meaning in all its confusion and its richness. Like Pawel's music. Like all music, drawn from the imagination, from the silence into the world of color with all its glory.

So then: we fell into November as the weeks passed by. Even into December. Occasional chats. Nothing substantial. I did not return to the cottage we shared and knew I had to wait until he was ready. He would tell me. And he did. We agreed to have Christmas at the lake.

It was then that he played for me what had been driving him for several weeks, even when he was tired, and not really well, and confused I think it is fair to say. That Christmas of 2007, I listened as Pawel sat down at the piano in our cottage by the lake. Although only partially complete he began then, simply, Opus.

As I listened, I think I finally understood the true meaning of the journey, his musical journey and more. I understood then that music, like life itself, does not stand alone, that it speaks to all that went before and all that will come after. A Spot of Time, ladies and gentlemen, not just for Pawel but for me, and I will say in our shared human experience, for all of us.

Ultimately, this story, this lecture, is about the birth of music. And what music can do. In particular it is about the birth of one composition. It is perhaps the story of his last great work. Even now I hear its notes, its harmonies, its melodies, its tonal challenges sometimes, not always associated with Pawel Weisz. And even now I travel on such journey.

That was what happened in the cold days of 2007 as the year drew to a close.

In this way I learned to hear the music. Not just the notes. Not just the emotion. But the story. There is somewhere, sometimes quietly in the background but always there, the story. And I have learned, after so many years of missing this, that there is a time to listen. Now is such a time. We all need to listen, to hear the music, to hear the story that music relates.

So this lecture is about the story as it is about the music. It is about a time and place long ago, when the world forgot the tears that were shed, the pain and the sorrow. That story was Pawel's story, a dream hidden within him, deep inside, that finally found its voice in his music.

That music was his gift to us. To you. If we listen hard enough, we can hear it when we rise each morning and sleep each night. It is a gift that says this is what it means to be human. This is what it means to suffer, to survive, to live. This is one of those Spots of Time in which the world changes forever.

This is a story. Pawel's story. The story of a woman whose own spirit refused to break. The story of a city that did not die.

Listen now and you will hear. I promise: you will hear.

*

Aga and Beniamin moved into their new apartment in mid January. Aga had found a tenant for her own apartment easily enough. Beniamin had given up his small studio before the holidays. They had discussed his remaining in Warsaw over Christmas. Aga's parents said he would be welcome. Indeed they had developed quite a fondness for him. But Beniamin chose to return to Israel again to be with his family. His father had improved but he knew they wanted him there. As the new apartment was not free until two weeks after the New Year, Aga had agreed it was probably a good time for him to return to his home. He had suggested she might like to join him in Israel, but she decided to remain in Warsaw over the holidays, to be near her own Mother and Father. It seemed the right thing to do after such a tumultuous year, right for all of them.

When Aga had returned from New York, she had had a long talk with Beniamin about all that had happened and not happened. He listened quietly, saying little at first, taking in both her hurt and her disappointment. He told her that, regardless of her conclusion, regardless of the truth of Pawel Weisz's parentage, his background, Weisz had made his decision. Ultimately it simply did not matter if she had been correct about Radtke and indeed correct about him being the once assumed murdered son of Michael and Lea Elster. Pawel Weisz had chosen what road he wished to take. Aga had done the best she could. What mattered truly were the choices she made now for herself.

Aga had also had a long telephone conversation with Stefan, who said much the same as Beniamin. He too felt that Aga had done the right thing in approaching Weisz, no matter how painful for either the Composer or for her. But now the story had reached its end. It was indeed time to move forward and to take the gift of knowledge that had been handed to her into her own heart, her own memory and ultimately her own experience.

Admittedly with difficulty Aga began to let go. She enjoyed the quiet holiday she had with her parents and the special time she also spent with her Aunt Maja. She spent Christmas Eve as always with just her parents, enjoying a gentle but stomach filling Wigilia feast. On Christmas Day her Aunt and Uncle and rather unusually both their sons and their daughter came to the house where gifts were exchanged and stories were told.

Katarzyna and Maja both wondered if they should do something a bit differently, given the revelations they had received about Hannah. Suddenly theirs was a Jewish household after all. This did make Aga laugh a bit, as it did Aga's father. After all, Hannah had never celebrated any holiday but Christmas, which for her had been a time of gathering, a time of family.

Aga suggested simply that they carry on with their family traditions as usual. If in time any or all wished to learn more about the traditions and celebrations that may have been a part of their family for generations but about which none of them had any clue, especially without Beniamin around to explain such to them, perhaps they might learn over time. What was important, whatever their beliefs, whoever they in fact were, was that they were all together. That they had memory. That they were able to hold one another and carry love for one another within.

This of course brought out the bottles of vodka, which quickly eased uncertainty and any troubled consciences.

Aga spent the New Year packing her apartment. Beniamin returned from Israel shortly after and they moved together into the new apartment they had found on Długa Street, indeed a rare find in the old town. It particularly pleased Aga as it was hardly more than a five minute walk to the Krasinski Gardens. Beniamin warned her there might be ghosts there. She laughed and said there were more likely to be children there than ghosts; thus he should be more worried than she.

"I see your point," he muttered and scuttled away. This only made Aga laugh all the more.

They spent the first couple of weeks in the apartment decorating, buying things they knew they did not need and did not care, keeping warm against the cold Warsaw winter wind and snow. They found warmth together in so many ways: in humor, in gentleness, in companionship, in love making. They found strength.

Aga also understood that she had passed through a mourning stage, mourning not only for Hannah but for something deeper, harder to take in. She was healing; healing was necessary. She knew she would not let go of all she had learned and indeed become. But she could move on now and grow. Beniamin had told her it was time, and it was. More to the point she felt it within herself.

She had hoped for weeks still that Pawel might contact her, might indicate that he wished to share that journey, that knowledge, but this never happened. At first she admitted she had been angry, but finally she came to accept the advice and indeed wisdom that both Beniamin and Stefan tried to proffer. She knew she would never let go, but neither would she cling to the hope. She held no remorse. Sadness, yes, and a quiet unshakeable belief that she had been right in who she was, really was. But she knew too that the gift that had been handed to her ultimately was hers alone. Others would take what they wished, what they needed. Her own understandings, needs and indeed love within her, love for the story, pain at the story, would remain hers that no one would ever really understand in full, no one would ever share in full. Not even Beniamin. As he had said to her months before he had gone as far as he could and she would have to finish the journey alone.

And so she had finished.

Aga had been offered another film, a bigger role to play, but she decided to turn it down. It was to shoot in Romania. For the time being she wanted to remain in Warsaw, to be near to Beniamin. The previous weeks had been filled with upheaval. She did not want to travel far.

So when another offer came to do a series of new short one-act plays about women at the National Theatre in the summer, Aga jumped at it. The pay may not have been that of a film project, but she was indeed looking forward to acting in front of a live audience.

The plays had been forwarded to her at the end of January and she said yes almost immediately. Readings were planned for the end of April, with rehearsals in early May. The plays would run through June, which suited her.

Stefan too let her know he would be returning to Warsaw by May and wanted to discuss his newest idea with her. Again theatre. Again he wanted to search for a pop-up location where he could create his 'vision', with her acting making that vision come alive. She had to love Stefan. Always a schemer but often his schemes were rich with possibility and potential.

So all in all things were looking up for later in the year. For the moment she simply enjoyed domestic life, enjoyed settling in with Beniamin and finding a direction together.

In early March Aga was asked if she would give a lecture and reading from the *Elektra* plays for a drama class at the University, something she both dreaded and looked forward to. She had spent a week reviewing the work and remembering how she had approached the plays before spending the morning with a class. She found it proved to be terribly enjoyable working with young, enthusiastic students. But it also rather exhausted her.

She had lunch with the professor, an old friend, then started to walk home as the early spring day felt glorious, when Beniamin rang her mobile phone.

"Hi. I am just on my way back home."

"How did it go?"

"Well. Enjoyable. I am tired though."

"Are you too tired to meet me at To Lubie for coffee?"

"Beniamin. Now? I am going to see you in a few hours."

"I know. But I miss you. Say yes. Aga?"

He always was hard to refuse. She sighed and agreed.

He was waiting when she arrived, on the second floor at his favorite table overlooking the street below. Coffee was already on the table and a piece of cheesecake for each of them.

"Oh no. That is not good," Aga said.

"What? You like their cheesecake."

"I like their cheesecake."

"So?"

"So, whenever we come here and you order cheesecake and coffee, it means you have something to tell me and that usually is not good."

"Ridiculous."

"Especially when you sit at this table."

"The table was free."

"Fine. So you had a need for cheesecake and the table was free. And no doubt you have something to tell me."

"Ridiculous, like I said. I simply missed you."

"Uh huh. You are not pregnant are you?"

"What?," he exclaimed. "Very funny."

"Just checking." She took a small bite, sat back in her chair, stared at him. He smiled. Ate. Looked up, then down. Then up again.

"Okay, there is something."

"I knew it."

"You are not going to like it."

"Probably not. What is it, Beniamin?"

"I had a phone call in the office. Out of the blue. You are not going to like it."

"Beniamin?"

"Yes, well. From New York. From Arthur Schamus."

Aga's grin quickly disappeared. She stared at him. He looked at her. Shrugged. Took another bite of his cheesecake. Tried to look elsewhere.

"Beniamin…"

"I knew you would not like it," he said, putting down his fork. He smiled. She did not. "I think perhaps he was afraid to ring you directly. He said he got my work number from when he met you."

"I never gave him your number. I did not even give him your name."

"It is what he said."

"But I did not…Oh. Yes. I did. When I typed up everything, all of it, in New York…It means he read the file."

"Perhaps."

"And Pawel Weisz?"

"He did not say. He said nothing of your Grandmother, all the documents, memories… Nothing."

"Then what did he want?"

"There is to be a concert next month, a gala benefit of Pawel Weisz's work in New York. For his seventieth birthday, apparently. They wish to invite you."

"No."

"He was quite insistent. He said Pawel has been ill but would really be pleased if you would try to make it."

"No."

"More than that, they are sending two tickets and two plane tickets for you and for me."

"No."

Beniamin sat back in his chair.

"Aga…"

"No. I cannot do this, Beniamin. Not after my last trip there. He did not even mention the file, did he? I can't."

"It is a free trip to New York at the beginning of April."

"I am busy."

"Not then."

"You have said over and over it is time to move on. I have moved on, Beniamin. I can't do…"

"Aga," he interrupted. "I have always listened to you, to your wishes and desires. You have always been right. Well, almost. But this time, you are not right. The invitation came from Weisz, whatever his motivation. Schamus said they feel badly at how you were treated when you were there to see them. Whatever Weisz thinks, knows, read, did not read… He wants you there. Badly, Schamus said. He said you would probably say no and he could understand this. But he said to say to you that you were right, our lives are about choices and only we can make them. That if we need to find the peace we each seek it is perhaps time for you to find yours and for Pawel to find his. He said you said this to him and now he returns this comment as a gift. He said Pawel would like to see you. And would like you to consider. And to be their guest. I think this is important."

"No, Beniamin. No…No."

She stared at him, sitting back in her soft chair in this café, stared at him as he smiled, sadly. Shrugged.

"Eat your cheesecake," he said.

*

She barely uttered a word in the taxi on the way to the Brooklyn Academy of Music. Aga could see Beniamin was looking forward to the concert. She on the other hand felt a mix of dread, indifference, fear and curiosity. Truthfully, mostly indifference. She wished she had said no more forcefully. Beniamin had been insistent, however, and she was never going to say no. She knew inside she would have to make an appearance, even if the voice in her head said otherwise.

The tickets and the program for the evening suggested that the first half of the gala concert would include a performance of Weisz's 'Virginia Woolf Suite", the second half the 'Warsaw Suite' as well as an earlier work, 'The Bridge' and themes from various well-known movies. Aga had heard them all before from the collection of cd's she had bought. The tickets included an invitation to a reception after the concert. She had told Beniamin she was not sure she wished to attend. They had not heard from either Schamus or Pawel Weisz. In fact there had been no contact from either since Beniamin had received the tickets and hotel information, excepting the flowers in the hotel room when they arrived, with a note that only said 'Thank You'. She was not certain she wished to see either of them.

The Music Academy was much larger than she had imagined. Many in the audience had dressed in their finest. Beniamin had refused to rent black tie but he still looked handsome in his dark suit, as Aga took his arm to go inside. She was not really surprised at how well attended the concert was. Weisz had made a name for himself. She was surprised however to realize when they arrived how little she now felt about anything that evening. Where once there had been a connection that connection now seemed tenuous and unemotional. A night out but little more. If New York's famous and finest had come out for the evening to listen and celebrate she did not know and did not really care. She felt that even while her Grandmother might have had initial doubts about Weisz's 'Warsaw Suite', she would have enjoyed the evening in whatever circumstances. So Aga told herself that she would listen with generosity and fondness on behalf of her Grandmother. It would suffice.

They took their seats several rows from the front of the stage in the centre. Aga noticed a few faces she recognized from film and television, but then she sat back, looking more within herself than around her. She really just wanted the evening to be over. She wanted to return to Warsaw. She wanted, as she had told Beniamin after he had pressed her for so long, to move on. Let the evening provide closure. Let it provide an end point for such a long journey over generations and so many lives.

The concert hall filled up entirely. The air was expectant. The charity cause apparently was a good one and the audience supportive. Aga and Beniamin sat quietly without talking to one another, waiting as the large venue filled and as the symphony orchestra musicians found their seats on stage.

Finally the house lights dimmed. The orchestra waited patiently on stage. After a few quiet moments, the conductor, Avram Neverly-Baron, made his way to his podium to applause. He nodded to his orchestra. Put some music onto a stand in front of him then turned to the audience, silent now.

"Well, let me welcome all of you to this gala concert for the Seventieth Birthday of composer Pawel Weisz. It promises to be a very special evening I think. And rather different. We first began to plan this concert last year. It was a wish close to my own heart, having worked with Pawel so often over the years. And I can say honestly a wish close to his own, to see performed some of his best appreciated compositions for an audience of friends and supporters of the medical foundation so dear to him."

"As most of you will know, Pawel himself had hoped to conduct tonight's concert. Unfortunately, his health has meant this is not possible. He begs your forgiveness and hopes that his far inferior replacement will not disappoint."

"I am also afraid I have some other information to impart. Unfortunately, I am sorry to tell you that the program we had planned for tonight's performance has been abandoned."

A murmur in the audience as this was unexpected.

"That is the bad news," Neverly-Baron said. "Now for the good news. And I think you will agree it to be such. The symphony orchestra and I began initial rehearsals for this concert many weeks ago. Pawel himself had originally decided on the works he wished to see performed. However, only a month or so ago Pawel rang to tell me he wished to change the program. Unbeknownst to me he had been working on a new composition, quite a major work. And he desires that this new opus be performed for you this evening."

"Now, the first thing to say, on behalf of our Composer, is that the Opus is a work in progress. Hot off the press as they say. Pawel has asked me to beg your forgiveness if it still seems a little raw. I will let you be the judge of that. He felt very strongly that it be performed for his birthday gala concert. And although the

449

orchestra before you had very little time to prepare this concert—a month is not a great deal of time to rehearse an unknown work such as this--we agreed together that it was appropriate to perform it without normal fanfare or announcement. This has been difficult as Pawel had hoped to work with us these last few weeks, but unfortunately illness has meant this has not always been possible. Still, we are very pleased to premier this new major piece for you here tonight in this beautiful concert hall, whatever the flaws in performance remain."

"Pawel explained to me that this Opus has been a journey for him. A difficult journey over many months. And he has made an unusual request to help you the audience understand some of the meaning of that journey. The work consists of a prelude and four movements. Pawel has requested that each of these musical sections be preceded by certain images projected on the three screens behind us, and by the name signifying each movement. Unusual, but illuminating perhaps. And all arguably a part of what he seeks to tell in music, from his head, from his heart."

"We are very lucky tonight to have two soloists joining us in the performance. Yin Zi Huang studied with Pawel Weisz at the Juilliard School and is now a fine composer in his own right as well as a piano soloist with the Philadelphia Symphony Orchestra. Violinist Anna Bednarz first studied at the Warsaw School in the late 1960s where she performed some of Pawel's earliest works under his tutelage. Anna tells me that Pawel has barely changed since she first performed with him in 1968. I take it to mean that he was as grumpy then as he is today..."

The audience laughed at this remark.

"Anna is presently a soloist with the Birmingham Chamber Orchestra in England, and also performs with the Warsaw Symphony Orchestra. Pawel and we are particularly pleased that both these wonderful musicians could join us for this very special occasion."

The audience applauded, then Neverly-Baron continued.

"The work you will hear this evening is the culmination of a difficult journey. The culmination of a life's work. The culmination of a life in music in so very many ways. Perhaps with some raw edges but with a great deal of heart and I think it fair to say, much soul searching. For Pawel this has been a journey of meaning. I think that you will find in this new work not something removed from all that has gone before but rather the answer to a career in music, a great love for that music. It is also, I would like to suggest to you my friends the demonstration of a great love for something deeper: for our common humanity. An understanding of such. An understanding of loss. And an understanding of all that is gained. A discovery. Music touches something deep within all of us. It takes us on a common journey. A journey that comforts the soul. I think tonight's performance of this new work will be no different."

The conductor was quiet for a moment, as if thinking through his own thoughts. Then he continued.

"Ladies and gentlemen, it gives me great pleasure on behalf of the orchestra and myself, and indeed our Composer, to welcome you here tonight, to lead you now on the journey that is this new Opus, and in doing so, in celebration of the Seventieth Birthday and indeed the life and work of Pawel Weisz."

As the audience again applauded, Neverly-Baron turned and looked at his orchestra. Aga was trying to understand what had changed, and not just in the program for the performance. She looked at Beniamin, who glanced at her and shrugged. He too realized that they had been brought here for a reason and that the heart contained within the music about to begin was that reason. What it meant exactly neither of them could be certain. What was clear to them was that, in many ways, in speaking to the audience through his music, Weisz was speaking to them. What was also clear was that lives had changed. His. Perhaps theirs too.

In the darkness they sat back and looked up at the many musicians sitting expectantly on the bright stage. The Conductor looked at his score, then back up at his musicians, from one section of instruments to another. He smiled at them, waiting, holding the moment. The lights over the orchestra dimmed. And on the three screens at either side and at the back of the stage a single photograph was projected to the audience, moving unsequentially between each screen, slowly at first, repeating several times, speeding up. A photograph in black and white from decades ago. A photograph of Warsaw early in the 20th Century. The photograph then disappeared from each of the screens and a white title over a black background was projected on each simultaneously. *'Prelude',* it read, the single word. The word disappeared and on each of the screens the following appeared: *Trisagion: Hymn of Prayer and Remembrance'*. The words held for a moment, then also disappeared. Avram Neverly-Baron raised his baton. Looked at his orchestra. Nodded.

And the music began.

Aga sat forward in her chair. She stretched to listen. She almost reached out and in so doing her emotions were pulled towards the notes and quiet, repeating melody. Pulled by something calling to her. Listening, she began to understand. She knew she had to see the music as well as hear it. Feel it. In the music she saw pictures in her head. A story she recognized. And a story she realized was not hers alone, but one she shared. Had always shared.

The Prelude began with four notes played on an organ. Several times played, in repetition, but each repetition with slight variation. Soon the organ was joined by two women sopranos at one side of the orchestra, singing together two notes also in repetition, led by the organ. Over and over, two notes, repeating, with expectation, dream like, following the organ, complimenting it but not copying it. The sopranos faded as the orchestra itself began, working sometimes with, sometimes against, the organ continuing to play its four notes, deviating in the note at the end of each phrase from the phrase that came before. Finally the violin soloist picked up the music for just a few bars, leading the orchestra now, simple notes that sounded almost church-like, certainly haunting. It was as if the music was asking questions and leading the audience into a story. Into something deep and uncertain.

Here in her thoughts Aga found her Grandmother. She had heard something within, searching. She felt pain inside, the pain of longing. And now she knew that the reason she had come here, to this place, that the reason Pawel Weisz had so wanted her to come here was to reveal to all, in music, the story of her journey. It had become his as well.

The two sopranos repeated their notes, several times, a question asked, a desire reaching out in music, then stopped. The orchestra went silent. Neverly-Baron put his arms down, nodded at them.

On the screens at the side, the screen behind, several photographs then appeared, a different photograph on each screen, each one from a bygone era. On one screen, a photograph of Warsaw again. On another, in black and white, several children playing in a street. On another, a horse and cart pulling a family. Soon other photographs took their place, alternating between screens, sometimes repeating what had been projected before. An Old Jewish Man, a huge bag over his shoulder. A crowd of people staring at the camera. Collapsed sepulchers in a graveyard, most with Stars of David. Images now of the Ghetto. The Warsaw Ghetto. Women working at sewing machines. Laborers building the wall. Food lines. A body lying in the street. More food lines. A sick child in agony lying on the ground, dying. A family together. Another family, and another. People marching, some with suitcases, looking terrified, some with their hands in the air. People climbing into a train's cattle car. Finally a small girl, sitting on a bed, staring into the camera, thin, a question in her face, an expression of unknowing. On one screen. On the screen opposite. The screen in the middle. The same photograph. The young girl on the bed staring in fear. In uncertainty, almost as if asking all who looked at her a single question: why? Then the screens went black. And after a moment, in tandem on each screen, the title *'First Movement'*, followed then by *'Lachrymosa: Lament'*.

The screens went black again. Darkness again in the theatre with the orchestra in shadow. And the music began once more.

The first movement of the work was long, largely in two contrasting parts. It began with the soloist at the piano, playing a light tune of four notes over and over, gently, warmly. He was joined then by the solo violinist and the rest of the orchestra, repeating, diverting, music with a hint of summer, a sense of air and lightness. The lightness of being. The lightness of youth. The Conductor led them forward, directing, feeling, getting the most from the wonderful orchestra.

Aga was not experienced enough to define the music itself, to understand what was being created technically. She could not define the terms. But what she understood was that being relayed to her, as to the rest of the audience, was not simply a wonderful piece of music. It was a voice, speaking to them in musical notation, speaking to them without words, a story, images, a portrait of a time long before, of lives lived, ultimately of lives lost.

She closed her eyes. The music of the first part of this movement transported her to Warsaw in 1938, where a young girl, not yet woman, sits on the back of her mother's bicycle, her mother in front peddling furiously, the girl laughing and waving at shopkeepers and pedestrians as they ride through the streets of Warsaw. And there now the girl picking strawberries in the woods to the north of the city on a warm summer's day. Aga saw the same girl walking with her father hand in hand over a bridge crossing the Vistula, looking at the early morning lights of the city beyond. She saw her with another girl with red hair, playing hide and seek amongst the monuments and tombs in the Powązki Cemetery, laughing, falling onto the ground together as one; then later walking beside one another, beautiful with their blushing youth, pushing a pushchair in front of them. Aga felt as if she herself was in that park with them, running along the streets with them, free, the joy of being young. The joy of hope and possibility. The orchestra carried her away into a world generous, at ease with itself. As if it was her. And it was. Then, at that moment, it was.

The orchestra slowed. Changed tempo. Changed key slightly. The piano faded over its notes, playing them once more, slowly, one time further then hesitating so that the strings of the orchestra picked up a different sound, a different direction. The music repeated its four notes, but these became somber with the cellos playing, slower now, slower still. Somber. In pain. Suddenly lost. Suddenly broken.

Aga felt that pain. She felt the streets darken. She saw buildings collapse. She saw fear. She saw uncertainty. She felt as if she was walking through the streets of the city, now in shadows of grey. The Ghetto in shadows and shades of grey, only grey. She saw faces she thought she must know. Faces of a world she knew she had to embrace. Faces that expressed in their eyes pain, and hunger, and loss, and sickness, and fear. She knew them. She was at one with them.

In her mind's eye she turned even as the music turned, then moved forward, slowly. She saw faces and knew them. There her Grandmother's mother, Zivia, sewing with her hands, her fingers bleeding, no longer smiling. There her Grandmother's father, Marek, reaching out at a table, grasping the hands of wife and daughter, bowing heads, praying with eyes closed. There the aunt, Lea, cradling her only child, cradling the infant boy against her breast, her only infant boy against her breast. There the uncle, Michael, on his knees in a courtyard, scrubbing at stone, scrubbing, pushing harder and harder on that cobblestone, harder still at that stain, looking up then, higher, higher, higher towards the sun with tears streaming from his face. There the boy, Shaul, staring with wide, confused eyes at his older sister, trying to smile through the haze of fever and sickness. There the young woman Hania, child no longer, childhood stolen, lying on a mattress in ruins, eyes closed, her mouth muttering words no one would hear, no one until a young man barely a man, almost a boy, Simcha Gitler, sewer rat, leans over her and gently wipes the damp hair from her brow.

It was not her Grandmother, not Hania; it was Aga lying there. And looking up she now stared at the one she recognized as Beniamin, sitting beside her, there, holding her hand, keeping her warm, keeping her alive.

And it was Beniamin, beside her now in this theatre, holding her hand, keeping her warm, keeping her alive. Reminding her she was thus even as before her she saw that life ebb away and disappear. The fear of it disappearing.

The music continued, sorrowful music, transporting Aga then to the woods above a farmhouse where a woman named Helena pumps water into a bucket, turns and carries it into a farmhouse. And there a stream with water running through, there her Grandmother now Hannah steps into a pool of water, naked, beautiful woman, quiet, strong in her way, stepping into the cold water, sitting, closing her eyes, sitting back in the cold. Sitting back with eyes closed. Cold water. To emerge with the music and walk through the woods with the music still and coming to a quiet mound overshadowed by a small wooden cross, two rough sticks held together by a piece of rusted wire. The woman, Hannah now, her Grandmother, there kneeling and bowing her head. And beating her chest with pain. And grasping dirt from that mound in her fingers, her fists, then beating those fists on the ground, beating and crying and screaming out only in silence, always in silence, the pain, the music, the memory.

The unquenchable sadness of the strings leading the orchestra, asking not questions but simply asking where are you, asking need, asking names lost forever. Asking how did this happen?

The orchestra now in full flow, repeating melody notes harmonies majors and minors, repeating faces dreams hopes disappearing beneath the weight of that music the sheer pain of that music. All instruments playing the pain of the moment, the cries of the lost and forgotten, the city destroyed, the lives destroyed. The tears. The tears of the many, taken away, carried away. Forever carried away. Lives lost. Love lost. So much there in that music, growing louder, urgent, in pain…lost.

And coming to sharp stop. A question left hanging. Like a hand reaching towards another, reaching out, seeking salvation. Salvation, but none found. The tears. Lachrymosa.

Aga looked at Beniamin, and he at her. Their eyes wide with emotion, their expressions speaking so many silent words to one another, each one understanding the other. The music was for them. The photographs, the words, for them. And for everyone. In the theatre. Outside the theatre. For all. For Pawel as well. They understood the images on the stage as in their heads. They had walked down that road together. They knew what was being said to them. Each realized the same thing: he has composed us. He has composed who we are, what we are. He has brought us together at such great cost. They both knew. They both saw.

Silence in the concert hall. An overwhelming, emotional silence. And in the near darkness of that theatre again photographs on the screens.

Warsaw once more, but years after the previous photographs. Warsaw in the 1960s. New cars. A city rebuilt. Facades. Artifice. A piano. A conductor young and demanding from a time decades before. On the right screen, then the left, then the middle, the photographs become images of marching students. Of people with tears in their eyes, hugging loved ones. Departures. Leaving forever. Uncertain. While on right, on left, images of hand-held placards lying now in the road. A girl with blood streaming down her head supported by two others. Military style police. Politicians. Photographs from a different time, but a not dissimilar story. Hate and despair.

The photographs alternated and overlapped on the screens, then disappeared.

Once again, the titles echoing on each of the screens, echoing three times. *'Second Movement'*, followed a moment later by *'Furorem: Awakening'*. The words then disappeared. The Conductor, Neverly-Baron, thrust out his arms and the second movement began.

Difficult music, very different than what had come before. Again the same four notes, but crashing down in percussion this time, crashing through. The movement of music now hard to define. The romantic melody now replaced by structures of sound as if harsh words, notes suddenly in conflict one with the other. Where before the music had carried the listeners into need and pain, now it challenged and felt angry, demanding, like words without vowels. Harsh, with different sections of the orchestra working against rather than in tandem with one another. Here now too the voices of the two sopranos rang out often challenging the instruments themselves. Tones became complex yet simple, simple yet complex. A sense of chaos and confusion throughout. A sense that demands have been made not only suddenly on the orchestra but on the audience as well. Modern sounds, angry rather than pained. The strings in the orchestra took over, faster and faster still, anxious, pushing. Four notes over and over but played at a different pace, with different accents, moving up a scale, then down a scale. Pushing, harder, harder. Uncomfortable. Severe structure. Severe sound.

Until the strings stop. A breath. And the piano takes command. Slows the confusion down. No longer argues with the strings but compliments them. Moves in a different direction but by a different direction the same direction. Hypnotic sounds. And the drums crash. And the orchestra reaches out to the piano, when all join together. Quieter now. Transfixing.

Aga sees pictures again in her own head, pictures she struggles to define. Struggles to understand. Motion passing by quickly. Motion in light. And some images she recognizes. The gardens of the Babinski Institute. The building on its grounds, once dormitory, now derelict, its door banging in the wind. She hears that banging in the music but sees it in her head. The music becomes saxophone led, jazz-like. Aga sees a city of lies. Her city. Sees people running. Why are they running she thinks? What do they fear? A face turns towards her. He laughs and pulls a handkerchief from his coat. A magic trick? She flinches. Is this the Magician?

Sitting in this chair, this concert, she freezes. But not him, another. Confused images. A sense of confusion, meant to be. A policeman raising a baton. A woman lying on the ground in a pool of blood. Shouts of anger. Of desire. See me, see me. Voices demanding. The clock ticking. Uncomfortable sounds. Uncomfortable music. The story, chaotic, broken into many elements, confused, confusing. The music confused, confusing.

Once again the strings taking over.

Burning. She sees burning. The flames taking over.

Once again wavering back and forth their notes and sound. Growing quieter. The flames now becoming embers. Smoldering.

Now she sees, in a garden somewhere in wasteland, a wall where a building once stood, and a single flower, a single small flower growing, weak, but growing. And amidst the chaos and the anger and the confusion the orchestra too slows and finally a voice takes over, a woman's voice crying out as if in pain, as if uncertain, as if questioning. The soprano asks a question with a single musical note. The piano answers. She asks again with four notes and the piano seems to answer. Four notes. At first in conflict, then in harmony, then taking over. Four notes. Then fading. Fading as the notes grow quiet. Fading. And silencing. And silent.

Avram Neverly-Baron stops his arms in mid air. Hesitates. And drops them to his side.

The audience seems to sigh collectively. An uncomfortable movement of music. Trauma. Demands made on them, demands that have raised questions, proffered no answers, brought out anger, brought out fear, brought out motion. No conclusions were drawn. And they were left with the loss. They were left needing more.

A gap of silence. Catching breath. Until the next movement of the work began.

On the screens, different photographs. A house in a garden. A cemetery below pylons. A disused asylum house. A photograph of a forest in snowfall, finally repeated on each of the screens together. A message sent. A photograph of a man with anger and indeed hate in his eyes. Another photograph of a child, afraid, hiding behind the door of a wardrobe. Film footage of a fire burning, funeral pyre burning, on one screen, the second, the third. Simultaneous footage, the images end. Disappear.

Black screens, and the next movement in titles. '*Third Movement*' the words read. *'Sacrificium: Supplication'*.

This time the music slower, gentler. But music that questions rather than leads. Reaches out. Brings them back. Raises them up. Puts them down. Strings and piano up the scale, then back down. The journey. The search. The constant search.

Aga saw herself then. Closed her eyes and saw herself driving down a country highway, sitting beside Beniamin. Saw a farmhouse. A fallen wooden beam. Saw the violence and the pain. Saw her Grandmother silently standing before the window of her house. The flowers planted on the sill are dying. All dying. Silence. So much silence. The seasons changing. The flowers bursting forth then dying. And dying still. She saw Beniamin taking her into his arms. Making love. She saw him smiling and frowning and needing and afraid. She felt him take her arm and walk in a garden of remembrance. She saw her screaming into an empty field, screaming in anger and loss and frustration and hate. So much hate.

Searching. Searching still.

She saw an old, broken man racked with guilt in a room looking quizzically at her. Saw him with tears in his eyes and bowing his head.

She saw redemption but refused to acknowledge it. She saw papers on a fire. She saw again the fire burning outside.

She saw herself.

And them. And the road she had taken.

She saw the need, here, saw it with her eyes closed and the music carrying her still. She needed. She needed so very much.

And the image in her head grew dark. She turned in her mind to the side and saw a light. And the light was her Grandmother. And the light was Hania. And it said do not stop. Search. Find. You will find. You will find so do not stop.

The music, repeating, the four notes softening, the theme, the music, still the music.

I am here, she thought. I am here, Hannah, Hania. I am here…for you.

As the music came to an end, Aga opened her eyes. She felt her breath, shallow. She felt the pain. Beniamin squeezed her hand. He understood. He was there for her.

Silence, with the music stopped. The dim light on the stage dimmed further and extinguished. In the darkness that was the theatre the sound of shuffling and the audience could tell that the musicians were standing and leaving the stage. All leaving.

Avram Neverly-Baron, the conductor, was the last to go.

A sense of uncertainty from the audience. A slight sense of confusion.

And once Neverly-Baron had disappeared, from the shadows two stage hands carried a high seat and music stand onto the stage then disappeared. After a moment, just at the wing, Aga and others made out a wheelchair being pushed to the edge of the stage. From it a person stood. Turned to say something to the person pushing, then started forward towards the bench. Slowly. Step by step, led by a walking stick. Step by step. Tap. Tap. Tap…

Aga knew. They all knew.

The man with the walking stick that led him with a tap, then another, along the stage, tapping until he came to the bench and sat down, putting some papers onto the music stand before him. A spotlight illuminated the very tired, pale, drawn face of composer Pawel Weisz. He looked at the audience, one and all. He seemed to hesitate then seemed to look directly towards Aga. Perhaps he did. He nodded, just slightly. And then he spoke.

"The poet T.S. Eliot wrote that April is the cruelest month. After many cruel months, I have come to the conclusion that he may have been right. My doctor said: not tonight. I said: I will go and offer up two free tickets to you if I should win the next game of chess. I won. I cheat."

Pawel smiled, gently, and there was quiet laughter in the audience, both pleased that he was there and saddened at his illness.

"It pleases me to have you all here this evening. I thank you all from the bottom of my heart. I have been on a difficult journey, as Avram said. My eyes I thought were open. But they were not. They were closed. I realized then I did not want them to open. I was afraid to see. Afraid to know. But there were things I had to know, just as this road I have had to take has been necessary. And painful. So: I now I am an old man. Not so old, yet older than I realized. So much not realized. But now understood."

460

He hesitated. Continued. "I heard in my head the music. I heard the story. And I knew that once more, perhaps one last time, this time, I had to tell that story in the only way I knew how. I had to speak. For me, that speech is in musical notation. In every note. Cadence. Arpeggio. In the phrases, the themes, the instruments playing words that I cannot say with my voice. I can say this only with my heart so that you too may hear, may listen. The music for me has been all. The love. The pain. The loss and the tears. The sadness and the joy. They come together as one, hand in hand."

Pawel hesitated here again, gathered his thoughts. Stared at his pages on the stand. Absolute silence in the auditorium. Every word, every breath, seemed like balm, like the whispers of a lover, a friend, a teacher. The words, like the music, spoke from the heart and to the heart.

He took a deep breath, and read again. "I sat down and wrote my prelude. Trisagion. It is a hymn. A beginning. It was there, inside of me. Then the first movement. I cried. The tears spoke to me. Lachrymosa. The tears. The music spoke my name, before I knew. Before I understood. A lament. So much lost. So much unknown. So much learned. I needed also to say what I had felt, once, early on. That I had given up. I had run away. The anger. The fury. And thus the second movement. Movement of fury. Who I had been, then. And why. This too I found within me. The music. I needed here to create afresh. To struggle against confusion. To imagine chaos. I too needed to hear. I too needed to listen."

Pawel rested a moment. So tired. So very tired. Catch his breath. Find his words. Difficult words said to all. Said to one.

"I did not want to go on," he said then. "But I saw that I had to. I saw because you came to tell me that I had to go on. I had to bear witness. I had to know. It had been a search. And so a third movement, sacrifice. A movement that spoke of so much sacrificed in the desire for understanding. The need for that understanding. You had come to know when truth came knocking at your door. As in time you would come to find me. And knock as well. The journey for all of us was not simply a journey of the past. It was of the present. A journey that was, if I can say, a love story. A story of lovers desperately reaching for one another. The world can be so hard, so cruel. The pain so real. Such a sacrifice made. But the sacrifice was

461

a gift, my friends. A gift to me. And to you. I was once wrong. So now I beg forgiveness. Understanding. My music is my supplication."

"I had my three movements, but I needed a fourth. An ending. A conclusion. Where I might go. Where I had been. Reflection. I knew there was something else I needed to say. Something tied within me. My soul. I did not know where to look. I could not hear the notes in my head, my heart. I found myself lost. How to find myself? How to come to the end of this story that has so badly needed to be told, this story tonight. I heard nothing. I did not know where to start. Or where to finish."

Pawel sighed. Aga was close enough to the stage to see the real hurt in his expression, the real pain. He looked at the audience, away for a moment, then back. The entire large auditorium was silent. He stopped reading his notes, and spoke to them, to each and every one of them.

"You have come to celebrate the birthday of an old man, even now older. I wanted to present you with this work, this work that is my life that I had so missed, and then found. But I was unsure of how to bring this to a close. That had never happened to me before. And then... and then. I knew how the work needed to end. It had in fact ended a long time ago. Eliot also wrote 'In my beginning is my end...In my end is my beginning.' My own ending tonight is therefore also my beginning. A movement of love that I first began to compose some forty years ago and to which I needed to now revisit, having never done so before in all the music I wrote. Remembered. Felt. I once thought it was written for one—boy--alone, never heard. But it was not. It belongs to the many. To you. To this greater composition you hear tonight. I returned to that composition, made some changes, some additions and in doing so I found my fourth movement. That has been my journey. It has been a long, difficult journey. My journey of loss. And light...Thank you all for coming. From the bottom of my heart, thank you."

Pawel pushed himself off the stool. He tapped his way with his walking stick to the edge of the stage, where his wheelchair waited to be pushed away. The applause was loud and real. The spotlight faded out. The stool was left before the audience. The dim stage lights came up, casting shadows. The solo pianist appeared and sat down at the piano on one side of the stage. On the other the guest violinist. The only musicians, with an empty stool between them. All that remained.

On the screens behind, two photographs were projected onto the side screens, one on each: on one a photograph of a small child, a young boy, staring at the camera, with such a serious expression. A small child with green eyes. At the other side, that child now a young man, sitting at a piano, still with the same serious expression. Then on the middle screen a third photograph projected. A photograph that meant almost nothing to the audience there, save two. The photograph was of a young girl, smiling, her head resting on the shoulder of the slightly older girl beside her and between them a push buggy for a small child. A photograph from a summer's day in the Krasinski Gardens, so long ago, many lifetimes ago. A photograph lost and rediscovered.

Aga winced not with pain or anger, but with longing. She glanced at Beniamin, but he did not look at her. She lowered her eyes, then looked back at the screens. Even before the music began she could hear it. She understood that music, that song. The song sang to her from the past. Silent. Haunting. It was the music they all heard that evening.

The photographs disappeared and a title appeared simultaneously on all three screens: *Fourth Movement* it read, then disappeared. After a moment, *'Yeshu'a: The Journey of Loss and Light'*.

The titles disappeared.

There was absolute silence in the large auditorium.

And after a moment the pianist began the final movement of the work. He played a short introduction, gently playing a few notes that spoke from the heart. Leading. Beckoning. Calling. Then after a moment the young woman put her violin just below her chin, breathed, and played.

She played for Pawel. She played for Robert. She played for all those who came before, and who came after. She played such music, such sadness but with such generosity of spirit that all were moved. All humbled.

Aga felt Beniamin's hand holding her own. But she did not look at him. She looked up at the stage but did not see the musicians. She looked up, and beyond, into the faces of all who were, of all she was as well. And she knew herself now.

463

She knew who she was. Not who she had become. Who she was.

Within that final movement came notes that spoke words, spoke the story, the story of loss and pain, the words that spoke of the soul and of humanity. Part lullaby, part love song to the many, part lamentation for those lost. Painful, emotional, unlike anything Weisz had written, the movement took the four notes and transposed them into a cry from the heart, speaking to the one and to the many.

The music spoke to the audience and beyond, reminding each person of the story within each person's heart. The story of what it meant to suffer and to survive. The story of what it meant to be alive. The centre of the movement was the sound of the violin, aching, crying, reaching to every single heart in that room with a spiritual ache and loneliness that most had known but few had known how to articulate. In its language were the faces and tears and laughter and undiminished hopes of those from the past calling out, reaching out, remembered, whispers of the heart. In this work, this musical gift, Weisz spoke to each of those now in the audience. His music spoke of longing. It spoke of love. It spoke of loss. And it spoke of grace.

Aga sat and listened and did not try to stop the tears from falling. The music touched her as nothing had touched her before. Aga understood and knew that Pawel Weisz too understood the same. In that moment, in that music, she knew that Hania, that Hannah, that those who came before, the Mother and Father, the Aunt and Uncle, the Brother and Friend had finally found peace. That Pawel too had found peace.

As had she.

They had come to the end of their story. They had found one another. They had found themselves.

When the movement came to its end, the violin played alone, playing finally first one high note, then rising to another, holding that note as triumph: triumph of the human heart, of life over death. Of love. And with that note, the music stopped. The lights went down and the following title appeared on the middle screen only. *Opus* it said. Then: *A Requiem For Hania.*

White letters on a black screen. *A Requiem For Hania.*

464

A prayer for a life lost. And for many, lives found.

*

The applause had finally stopped and the audience made its way out of the auditorium, many whispering in hushed admiration and deep emotion at the evening's concert. Aga and Beniamin, however, remained frozen in their seats. Sitting quietly. The concert had clearly been a success and Aga knew that all around her had been terribly moved, often to tears. But for her that emotion went far deeper than the music and the story it tried to tell but could never really tell. Not really. For Aga the notes resonated within, that journey shared, that journey that had eaten at her for so many months. And on reflection had done so for a lifetime.

She could breathe now. She could reflect. And she could cry.

Beniamin felt it as well. He saw the pain in Aga's face and knew it reflected both loss and joy. He sat quietly beside her, holding her hand, saying nothing. Even as the rows emptied he did not suggest they go. It was right to let the overwhelming emotion of all that had passed now settle and calm.

"Schamus telephoned not long before we left Warsaw," he said. "He asked for one thing if possible. He said Pawel would like to see a photograph. He asked me to help, quietly. I did not want you to say no."

Aga nodded. He knew she was not angry. Grateful, perhaps. Enough.

Aga finally turned to him and said she would like to sit a bit longer, alone, to reflect. She needed just a bit more space. A bit more time. He nodded, understanding.

"As long as you need," he said. "I will wait out front."

He squeezed her hand, then slowly and quietly joined the last of the audience at the back and left the theatre auditorium.

Aga did not look around. She sat quietly, emptying her thoughts. She heard the final movement of the *Requiem* playing over and over again in her head. Requiem: the music of a death. Of loss. Music to remember, to guide one's soul to heaven. To rejoice at a life. To seek atonement. To find through music the words of love and forgiveness. And mostly, mostly, an act of remembrance.

Aga remembered now. Her Grandmother. Those who came before. Those lost.

She had heard their cries in that music. Had felt their tears. Shared them. Walked with them. She would hold her head high for them, a belief not in God but a belief in the possibility and hope of life itself. The gift.

Now, more than ever, she truly understood the gift. The gift that Hannah had bestowed. The gift of Hania. Of a past. An understanding of self. She knew who she was, now as then, who she would be.

She closed her eyes and saw Hania on the park bench with Alicja beside her. And an infant child, Jakub, asleep perhaps, in the carriage beside. She saw them. She was them.

She became aware of someone approaching and looked up. Arthur Schamus walked towards her, now in this empty auditorium, walked up to her and sat beside her. At first he said nothing but just sat. After a moment, without turning to him, Aga smiled with great sadness.

"Thank you," she whispered.

He simply nodded. Waited.

"He read through the file," Aga said.

"Yes. Yes, he read through the file. What you had written. Your Grandmother's letter to you. All the stories and fragments and documents. It has been very difficult, for him. A hard road to travel. He has spoken to others whenever he had time. Made enquiries. Looked for help to explain. To understand. Yes a very hard road to travel. And he could not tell you until now. Until he was ready."

"Yes," she nodded in a whisper.

"I will speak to Ms. Janiec, I said to him. I will explain what I can. In that grumbling way that he can do so well, with his accent thickening as he spoke, as if he had only arrived in America, he said to me: 'Not Ms. Janiec. Her name is Agnieszka. But only I can call her that. Only Hannah and now I will use this name. When you see her, it is Aga.' So may I?"

Aga smiled. "I would like that," she said simply.

"Aga. This has been difficult for him. He had never spoken of Radtke, Gizela. I told you, I believe: he never mentioned them to me. Then all that you left in your file, this made him remember, return to it I suppose. To face things. Understand. He was not eighteen yet when he left that home. He told me his school friends used to whisper about the man he thought of as his father, so he went to the library, learned what he could. He did not know about Warsaw, the Ghetto, but he knew this man had been a Nazi in the SS. Pawel despised him for that. He could not stay, as much as he loved Gizela. And he did love her, whatever she had done. He could not help but love her."

Aga nodded, listening, saying nothing.

"He went first to an aunt he loved very much, Gizela's sister. She gave him some money. He made her promise she would never say anything to Radtke or Gizela as to his whereabouts. After Gizela then died, her sister felt only antipathy for Radtke and wanted no contact with him anyway. So Paul became Pawel as you surmised. He took his mother's name, went to Warsaw. Was able to study. Compose. Grow. Love…He left Poland and could not return. Those were hard times for him. And he sent word to his aunt when he learned of his father's death that the house Paul had grown up in be torn down. He wanted nothing to remain. I knew none of this. He never said a word. He carried such—guilt. Such pain. He excised Radtke from his memory. From his life. That was the end of it. Only it was not the end of it. Because one day you sat in his study and tried to tell him a different story, a painful, tragic story. He is still learning, Aga. Still coming to terms with so much and it is difficult for him. He will need some time."

"Will I see him?"

"No. No, he would have liked to, but he has been ill. The doctors did not want him to come tonight but he felt he had to be here. I think he did bribe them with free tickets as he said. He left just after he spoke with a nurse who looks after him. They are driving tonight to a house we have in upstate New York so he can rest there and be looked after."

"I am sorry."

"He has carried this illness for many years. He sometimes falters but he is improving. Right now he needs a great deal of rest, space. He hopes you understand. He has promised he will come see you in Warsaw later this year if he can, or next year, depending on his health, his schedule. I will keep him to this."

Aga nodded.

"He said to tell you he owes you something he can never repay, a debt that has no words. He said to tell you he has Hania in his heart, Lea and Michael. Hannah. He sees them beside him now and they hold his hand. That is what he said to say. He also asked me to give you this."

Arthur Schamus reached into his pocket and pulled out a small book, handed it to Aga. It was the small volume of poet Wisława Szymborska's poems that Aga had looked at months before in Pawel's study. She opened the book and found a note from Pawel inside, written with a shaky hand. He wrote: 'For you, Agnieszka. I am one of those who knew little. I am learning that things will not straighten themselves up. I have much work to do. Thank you for helping me to see this. Pawel.'

Aga closed the book, held it tightly in her lap.

"There is the reception now and Avram, the conductor, has arranged a small dinner at which he would like you and Beniamin to be guests as well. There is of course much that Avram knows but he has so many questions."

"I do not know that I can. I..."

Her words faltered.

"I understand your hesitation. Pawel said you would likely want space. But what I said to Pawel I will now say you as well, dear Aga, if I may. I think you should join us because I think it is now time to reenter the world. This world. I think it is now time."

She looked at him. Hesitated. Stared into his serious face, kind now, gentle. She held his gaze, then nodded.

He smiled, gently, quietly.

He took her hand. She followed him down the row of seats in the now quiet theatre. He then took her arm and they walked up the aisle to the back, where Beniamin stood waiting. All disappeared together.

It was time.

Coda

Tacet:
Kaddish

Warsaw / New York
2009 - 2010

Pawel kept his promise. By the following March his health had improved and his schedule allowed him to visit Warsaw, to coincide with some workshops he had agreed to give at the Chopin University of Music, renamed from his old State School of Music many years before. Arthur Schamus had business in London, so he would arrive a week later. He knew that Pawel would want a week to himself, to spend with his family, family he had never met, indeed had not known existed for most of his life.

Pawel sent word to Aga that a car had been arranged to take him from the airport but that he would be happy to see her again at his hotel. She decided at this first meeting it would be best if she went alone. She was surprised at how nervous she felt. She could not be certain exactly how he might react or exactly what she should say to him now.

She arrived at the hotel purposely early and sat waiting in a quiet corner of the lobby. She watched without getting up when he finally arrived, his walking stick once again leading the way. He seemed to have a serenity about him she had not seen on the first encounter. She wanted to give him time to check in but once he had registered at the desk she approached, standing behind him and to the side while he finished.

Only after he had turned away from the receptionist did he realize she was there. He smiled just slightly, reading her uncertainty. He too had not known quite how to greet her.

Neither of them should have worried. The answer to the question posed by this first re-encounter was there, always there. She walked up to him. He looked at her, nodded, reached up and ran his hand gently over her cheek, like an old lover, a friend, like a parent. His hand of need, warm and now reaching out in so very many ways. Aga put her arms around this thin, gentle old man and he held her. Tightly. And they stayed this way for a very long time. It felt like an eternity. In some ways, it was.

*

The scene was replicated several times over the coming days. Many tears were shed when Pawel met Katarzyna and Maja at the Janiec house. Other family members came by to pay respect, to make Pawel feel welcome. He and Aga's father, Witold, particularly got on well, discovering a mutual love of chess. Several afternoons were taken up with long serious games over a chess board. Witold grumbled a great deal and swore in mock annoyance that his older opponent had to be cheating. This only made Pawel giggle like a young boy, shrug and whistle much to the annoyance, and indeed appreciation, of Aga's father.

Most of all Pawel liked nothing better than to sit quietly with Katarzyna and Maja, talking of nothing and everything. He asked question upon question about Hannah and Kazimierz, about the sisters' childhoods, simple things about their growing up: the games they played, the meals Hannah cooked, what she was like as a mother and a teacher, the songs they sang, the walks they took. It was as if he had been starved for so long for those little things that now gave his life meaning, that he could not now get enough of them.

They also talked of his music, about what it had been like for him in Paris and London and New York. He told them too about his days in Warsaw, about the confusion and tragedy he felt in 1968. He told them about Robert Mandeltort, a young violinist he had loved and lost. And he told them about leaving Poland, about emptiness and grief. He told them how at the time he knew he would not be able to return once he left in the manner he had, but that he had to go when he did. He explained it was not simply about the music, although music had been everything to him. He had gone in search of himself, in search of something he did not understand, for forty years did not really understand. It had taken that long to find it. Now he had come home.

They talked as well about the dark past, of what they each in different ways, had taken away from the stories gathered about Hania and Hannah; more than just those experiences, they talked about others who had been a part of that story: not just Hania, Marek, Zivia and Shaul, not just Michael and Lea, but the many others as well. Alicja. Gitler. The school friends. Helena Kielar. Schipper and Yitzhak. Henryk Pilichowski. Names slipped off their tongues and took refuge in their hearts: those who lived in the Ghetto, from a certain time that felt distant, untouchable, had found their way into the pantheon of the story that they all shared. Their story. Such names now gave their own lives meaning and place and shape, more than sixty years later. Together they looked at old photographs and books of what life had been like then, a life particularly once hidden deep within Pawel, now released.

There were also times they just sat, sometimes quietly holding hands. Joining their thoughts and memories together. Closing their eyes and seeing the past but held together in the present. They were as one and separate. Each could feel the others' needs. Each held them close.

For several nights they ate together at the Janiec house, simply, as a family. Katarzyna was a decent cook; Pawel liked nothing more than to sit around the family table, laughing and telling stories, sipping glasses of wine and the odd glass of vodka. For him, this notion of simple family evenings held more value than anything he had known in his life. He wanted to hold onto those feelings forever.

Beniamin too was welcomed into the house as family. Indeed he had been so for a long time. Pawel clearly enjoyed teasing the young man and arguing about the best pierogi in Warsaw. Beniamin brought them stories he had learned in his research of what Warsaw had been like in the days of the Ghetto and from some of the searches he had done in his work.

He and Aga took Pawel 'sightseeing' one day, to look at Twarda Street, Nowolipki, Dzielna Street, other landmarks from Hania's fragments and recollections, but none of these places really remained. Names only with the Ghetto buildings long since disappeared, replaced with tall ugly apartment buildings and Holiday Inns, cheap fast food restaurants, all night markets. The past had disappeared from the physical landscape. From the emotional landscape, however, it remained vibrant with memory and necessity.

"I remember," said Pawel, "my friend Robert and I walked from the university one day and I told him how I found Warsaw full of life and creative energy. We were in the old town. He laughed at me, said it was nothing but artifice, that the city was gone because the world that architects had tried to replicate was not real, the life itself from the past was not there, was merely a recreation of something that no longer existed. He was right in some ways of course. Then. More so now when even that artifice of the 1950s recreated Warsaw has disappeared. But I think we still hold inside the city as it was when I was an infant pushed around by

473

Hania, by Alicja. It is a part of us. Yes. I think it is here."

Pawel put his hand over his heart.

"I think it is," he continued saying to Aga and Beniamin, "and here it will remain. It will always remain."

One afternoon Aga joined Pawel for a quiet stroll in Krasinski Park, much as she had done with her mother nearly a year before. They found a bench in the spring sunshine and sat quietly, watching the people pass by: children playing, mothers with strollers, young lovers.

"So, some things are not artifice after all," Pawel said.

"Perhaps not."

"Hania and Alicja, pushing me here, sitting on a bench just like this one, I can almost see it."

"The view from a baby carriage," Aga grinned.

"I have no doubt that I would have been the perfect baby."

"That is what Hania swore—often," Aga laughed. "The most beautiful baby in all the world."

"Wise woman," Pawel said with a grin, "Unquestionably."

They were quiet for a few minutes.

"You know, Agnieszka, you have given me something for which I can never repay you. It took courage. I do not mean coming to see me in New York, although that did take courage. And I do not mean your visit to Lidzbark Warmiński or to see Kolbe. All that you did, searching, discovering, needing to know, this had an emotional price, but still you did not give up. Courage."

"No. I needed to--know. My Grandmother's need handed to me, I suppose."

"Um... She must indeed have been a wonderful woman."

"She was."

"You know, I am an old man now. Really. And all this... a gift, but a gift of questions. I think perhaps the answers, so many of them anyway, are not in our grasp. Perhaps they should not be...You have not asked me about Radtke. Never asked me about him. About Gizela."

"No."

"Perhaps that is right. My memories of them are distant. And I feel I have released them, I have been released from them. But still, that period of my life too is within me. As the past was in Hannah. Unlike her, or you, I do not wish to go in search of those days, those memories that remain. I have buried those within; so they will stay. But had things been different, I would not be here now and I cannot deny that. I do not know if this is a blessing or a curse or a perhaps a bit of both. I think both. So no answers, just questions."

Aga nodded, understanding.

"Music has been my life, my lovely Agnieszka. It has brought color and warmth and a feeling of humanity when I thought I might not feel these things as a young man. It has not always been easy, you know. But I have found in my music a language to say what is in my heart as well as my head. Sometimes to speak to others, but mostly to speak to myself. To explain. To find resonance. I remember my mentor here in Warsaw, he once talked to me about finding my voice. Music has been my voice when I could not find the words to use. A bit like now I suppose. I lived in the Ghetto. I died in the Ghetto and was somehow reborn as someone I should not have been. Now I suppose I am reborn again. Human again. That was your gift to me. Music is my gift to you, to others. Some will like this music. Some will not. But all will find a voice within, my voice. That voice is our common humanity I hope. Does that make sense?"

"Yes."

"We have relived the past. Now we embrace the future."

Aga smiled at him. Nodded.

Pawel looked away. He stood and carefully walked over to a nearby grove of trees, looked around. He bent down here with some difficulty and picked up a large, rounded stone from the base of a tree. He stared at it in his hand, then put it in his pocket. Aga watched him.

"Souvenir", he said to her. "The verb in French means to remember."

"Yes," Aga nodded with a quiet smile. "It does."

"Um… I have a favor to ask of you, my Agnieszka. Something I would like you to do with me tomorrow."

She listened, nodded. Understood the need.

*

The road north to Treblinka took Aga ninety minutes to drive. Ninety minutes and a lifetime. For much of the early morning drive she and Pawel sat in silence, staring out the window but staring far further than that. Both knew this would be a difficult journey, one Aga had as yet refused to take.

Unlike perhaps the camps of Auschwitz, which served largely as a dark, painful museum to what had happened in the Holocaust, Treblinka revealed little of its terrible past to its visitors. It had been raised to the ground by the Nazis in 1943 in an attempt to hide all the evidence of the hundreds of thousands of deaths that took place there. The ground, sacred ground of loss and death, the Nazis plowed over before retreating, leaving only a farmhouse for a watchman to live in and to keep the curious away. The Soviets too had not wanted to preserve evidence of the camp. It was only in the 1960s that the site was declared a national monument. Over time a memorial was built, with its tall granite tower wall, surrounded by rough standing stones engraved with the names of towns and cities from which Jews and Romany had been transported to the death camp, stones standing in silence as a memorial to all those who had died.

Aga and Pawel walked amongst these stones, keeping their thoughts close. Thoughts in pain. Memories in pain. In front of the stone with 'Warsaw' carved into it, Pawel stopped. He bowed his head just slightly. He thought of his mother Lea, his father Michael, his parents as they were. The city of his birth that now cried out even louder in his thoughts. The pain of it. The emptiness. His heart was broken at the silence. Aga walked up beside him and took his arm. They did not speak.

They spent a long time there, mostly just the two of them amongst the stones before any tourist buses arrived. Although a few other visitors joined them to wander around the monument and stones, the only sound was the sound of the slight breeze blowing through nearby trees. These were the ghosts that would walk beside them forever.

"There is no music here," Pawel said to Aga. "This is the only place I have ever visited where I do not hear music."

Later they slowly walked together from the monument towards the edge of the forest nearby where a path inlaid with flat stones led to a ramp where the train cattle cars unloaded their human cargo to be marched to the gas chambers. Concrete blocks here were laid in a long parallel file, a silent memorial to the train track that ended here at Treblinka. Along the sides of it, further standing stones had the names of countries from where many of those transported took their final journey.

Aga stood with Pawel, quietly staring at what had once been the end of the track that would have brought Michael and Lea Elster to the end of their own journey, just as it brought Zivia and Alicja here. Aga closed her eyes and saw Alicja carefully climbing down from the cattle car when its door was thrown open by harsh, shouting guards, her wooden limb making it harder to move than it was for others. Alicja then turned, reached up and helped Zivia climb down as well. Aga saw it still, staring down the path leading away and imagined seeing these two women forever in her memory and in her heart slowly, resignedly, walk to the gas chamber that brought an end to all the pain, all the suffering. Aga knew she was crying and felt Pawel hold her arm, even tighter. They stood in silence, stood as one, until they finally turned to leave. The emotion was too difficult for both of them to take in completely.

"Wait," said Pawel.

Near the ramp, he knelt down and picked up two stones, white stones streaked with lines of grey. Aga helped him stand. He put the stones in his coat pocket. She did not need to ask why he wanted them.

"Come, Agnieszka," Pawel said, quietly. "Now we can go."

*

The following day Arthur Schamus flew into Warsaw and clearly took great pleasure in seeing Aga and Beniamin again, as well as meeting Aga's family. Pawel had agreed to three days of workshops at the music school, so Arthur spent much time on his own with the Janiecs. He enjoyed telling them about Pawel's arrival in the United States back in the 1970s and how difficult it had been at first. He spoke kindly, indeed lovingly of those early years, regaling them with stories of concerts, film work, monster directors and mishaps that seemed to follow them wherever they went. Arthur was good at laughing at himself, and it has to be said at Pawel. Humor and a touch of the absurd had been one of the cornerstones of their relationship.

Aga and Beniamin joined him for lunch with Stefan Marcin one day. They heard stories of the days of protest in 1968 and of Stefan's encounters with Pawel, as well stories of others from those turbulent times. Stefan still hoped that Pawel might one day compose a score for one of Stefan's film projects. Arthur promised he would discuss it with Pawel and promised that if Pawel would consider such, Arthur would do his utmost to convince him.

Aga did not see Pawel during the days he led the workshops, but on the last evening a concert had been arranged for the entire Chopin School, as well as for invited guests. Pawel was guest of honor. Aga's parents, her aunt and uncle and cousins all came to the concert, as well as others, including Beniamin's boss David Weinstein and his wife, and Dorothy Sellin who had introduced Aga to the JRA. Many were familiar with Pawel's story and how that story had come to light. Indeed many people came up to Aga and Beniamin to tell them how moved and indeed astounded they were by all that had happened over that two years. Most found it remarkable.

Pawel sat between Katarzyna and Maja, all looking hugely pleased to be there. Sitting with Beniamin and Aga was the violinist Anna Bednarz who had been a soloist at Pawel's Brooklyn concert and who had attended the State Music School when Pawel taught there in the 1960s. Aga was incredibly touched when she leaned over and whispered to Aga that her life and career had changed completely when studying and performing with Pawel.

"Is it not funny how these things can happen," Bednarz whispered; "how chance can take us in directions we might never have imagined?"

"Beniamin calls it chaos," smiled Aga.

"From Pawel, definitely chaos," Bednarz grinned.

Several of Pawel Weisz's compositions were performed that evening by students from the music school, all rapturously received. The final work was the movement called 'Spring' part of an early work by Pawel, 'With Memory for Twelve Musicians', composed when he was still in residence at the school. Aga found the work difficult to understand. Anna Bednarz leaned over to her and whispered:

"You see, chaotic," she grinned.

As an encore, however, the orchestra's Conductor enticed Anna herself to come to the stage and perform the fourth movement from this work, the 'Winter' movement, with the other musicians on stage. Before beginning, Anna herself explained to the audience that this was the last thing of Pawel's played in concert before Pawel decided to take a 'rather extended' sojourn from his life in Poland. She said he had given her the opportunity of a lifetime to play it with him and ten others in Prague in that early August of 1968.

"So much history from that moment, in Poland, in Czechoslovakia, for Pawel, for so many of us. But for me this always is something special in my heart," she said.

With that, she performed the movement beautifully with the other musicians on stage. Pawel was clearly moved by this. And while the music itself was quite in keeping with the other movement performed earlier, the work was clearly deeply appreciated.

At the end of this encore the audience stood to applaud the musicians, but in particular to applaud Pawel sitting in the front with Aga's mother and Aunt. He was gracious in the receipt of this and clearly moved by the entire evening. At that point the Conductor walked down from the stage to the seats and took Pawel's hands in his own, acknowledging him. He then bent to whisper in Pawel's ear, as the audience continued its applause. Pawel looked up at him, at those standing for him, hesitated, then nodded.

The conductor, with Arthur, helped Pawel stand. Pawel acknowledged the applause, then with the Conductor walked up onto the stage. The piano from the previous movement was pushed forward. Pawel sat down at it, nodded to the audience and gestured for them all to sit.

Once the hall was quiet, Pawel smiled at all.

"You know, it is a long time since I did this myself. And with the students I have listened to these last few days, I have to tell you this could be an embarrassment. Especially as my hands, they are a bit slower than they once had been. Like the rest of me. So… So. You have all touched me very much. I thank you from my heart. And I thank my family in ways that only they can know. You are… here."

He placed his hand on his chest.

Pawel Weisz turned to the piano, his hands at his side. He closed his eyes in thought. After a moment, he placed his hands over the keys. He hesitated again. Closed his eyes again for just a moment, then began.

It was possible that most in the audience had heard better renditions of Chopin's Nocturne No. 20 in C Sharp minor. However none had heard any rendition that could have meant more, or held within that music greater emotional need.

Aga knew. For her the music meant more than to most anyone there. It meant the past. It meant Jakub Elster, on the eve before his death. His death until now. It mean Hania's journey, and Hannah's, just as it meant her own.

About half way through the short performance, Pawel came to a natural rest but held it longer than most would tend to hold it, almost as if he was lost. Pawel removed his hands from the keys. He stopped, took a deep breath and looked up as if searching for something. He looked up, above him, staring towards the ceiling. But it was not the ceiling he stared at. Aga knew he was looking beyond that to a time long ago, to a face he thought he could see, she thought she could see.

Pawel waited another moment, then looked back at the keys and took up the Nocturne where he had left off, finishing the piece because now it was time to finish it. As he played Aga imagined a large hall in the Ghetto, a room that had once been a synagogue, filled to the edges of the room on that May evening of 1942, where Lea Elster placed her hands on the perhaps slightly out of tune piano and began to play for an audience, played like none before or none after. On that night, on this night too, music brought tears to so many, tears of sadness, but tears too of emotions that warmed hearts, because these were tears that confirmed that their humanity and spirit would last beyond the body, that life had value, even as the music spoke to them. Nothing could take the music away from their hearts.

Later, after the audience had stood around to offer their congratulations and good wishes, after the students had come to say thank you, after the music was finished, Aga went and sat beside Pawel Weisz. He looked at her, smiled sadly.

"You finished it," she said

He stared at her, nodded slowly. Smiled with a yearning, pained smile.

"My mother was unable to finish that Nocturne on that night. She would have played beautifully. But I think…I think she wanted me to finish it for her. I hope so."

"Yes. Yes I think she would have."

He smiled with his loss reflected in his eyes and hers. He took Aga's hand. They sat quietly. They both remembered.

*

His flight from Warsaw was due to leave late in the afternoon, so Pawel asked Aga, Katarzyna and Maja if the three women would take him to visit Hannah's grave in Otwock before taking him to the airport to meet Arthur, which they were more than happy to do. The weather on that spring morning was crystal clear as they drove from the old town towards Otwock, following the Vistula for some of the time, then crossing over the Swider River into town. They drove past Hannah's house before proceeding to the cemetery. Aga knew this was not easy for her Mother or her Aunt, but like them she knew Pawel would be interested to see the world they had grown up in. He nodded as they looked at the house only from the gateway. All that remained was the building; the life, the story had been removed. But the memory they would hold onto.

They then drove to the cemetery. Pawel walked beside each of the sisters. Aga led towards her Grandmother's simple headstone at one side of the cemetery, beneath a large willow just beginning to come into leaf. They stood in front of the gravestone with its simple engraved names: Hannah Kielar Palinsky and Kazimierz Palinsky, Mother and Father. They stood quietly, their thoughts taking them each down different paths.

"I am not sure my Grandmother would have liked Palinsky being added to her name after all those years," Aga said with a quiet smile. "She could be quite insistent on this."

"She could be quite insistent on many things," said Katarzyna.

"That she could," added Maja also with the hint of a smile.

"Well…maybe that was a good thing," Pawel said after a moment. "After all…she insisted taking me outside to walk on all those Warsaw days, whatever the weather. I remember."

All three women smiled at that.

"Yes, maybe that was a good thing," he continued. "Thank you all for bringing me here. And for being here. And thank you too to Hania… You know, a name…it is simply a name. Who we are, who we really are, is here, inside," he said, putting his hand over his heart. "And maybe who we will be. I am Jakub. I am Pawel. And I have come home."

He looked at each woman in turn, nodding, with warmth in his eyes. He then walked up to the gravestone and placed a stone on top of the gravestone, a stone that Aga recognized as one taken from their time at Treblinka. She knew what he meant in doing so. He was telling Hannah, telling Hania, that he had come back to her.

Later, at the airport, Aga saw that her mother and her aunt were in tears as Pawel said goodbye. He promised he would see them in a year's time. He had made a deal with Beniamin: Pawel would return to Warsaw first, but then Agnieszka and Beniamin would have to accompany him to Tel Aviv. Pawel had a concert he would attend and he wanted to meet Beniamin's mother to find out if she really did make the best pierogi anywhere. He told Beniamin to let his mother know he would be there and to start planning.

Aga smiled later when Beniamin telephoned his mother to tell her. And to warn her she had better start preparing.

Pawel turned to Aga last to say goodbye.

"My Agnieszka," he said. "You have given me such a gift. An old man doubts, questions, but your journey and mine, they are one. You, all your family are in my heart. You wrote in your reminisces that your Grandmother called you angel, aniołkuy. You have been my aniołkuy too. May you, may all of you be blessed."

He held her tight in her embrace. Stepped away. Nodded at Aga, at her mother, her aunt, then turned and disappeared into the airport.

Three days later, a package arrived for Aga, which she opened with Beniamin. In it was a note from Arthur: '*Pawel asked me to arrange for this to be framed for you in Warsaw. I join him in sending love, Aga. Arthur.*' In the simple box frame was a copy of the photograph of Hania with Alicja and the baby carriage in front of them. The glass frame had been specially made so that mounted beside the

482

photograph was the stone Aga remembered Pawel taking when they sat on the bench together in Krasinski Gardens.

Even then, she almost heard his voice: "It means I have come back to you. It means we remember."

He did. As did Aga, his Agnieszka.

*

Pawel did not keep his promise.

In January of 2010, before his return visit to Poland could be finalized, Arthur rang Aga to say that Pawel had fallen ill. He would not improve. Not this time.

Aga and Beniamin together flew to New York. They spent three days or so with Pawel, sitting at his hospital bedside, talking, telling stories, sometimes simply sitting. On that third day Pawel turned to them. He no longer had strength to talk. He reached out towards Aga and she took his hand. Then he looked at her, his eyes wide, and gave the slightest nod as if to say it would be all right, that he was grateful she had come, that he was grateful she had found him. And rescued him. Although with difficulty, in pain, the lines in his face grown deeper, sadder, he managed to smile. Just slightly. A quiet smile. A nod of his head.

Then he turned away, closed his eyes, slept.

Late that night, Pawel Weisz fell into a coma. The following morning he died. Arthur was at his side, holding his hand when Pawel took his last breath. The HIV virus that had been in his system since the early 1990s had finally exploded into disease. His immune system gone, Pawel could no longer protect himself. But he seemed ready. His life had been full of music and story. It was all he could ever ask for he had once said. He had lived his life and now it was time.

Aga and Beniamin took a walk in Central Park and found a quiet bench to spend an hour, sitting quietly, remembering. Both knew Pawel's life had been a gift. Both felt a mixture of emotions at his loss. So much had now gone. A lifetime now gone. With it so much history, so much memory. But so much too had been given. And so much Aga particularly would forever hold inside.

"When I was sitting with him, that last time," Aga finally said, "and he took my hand. The strangest thing…"

"I know," Beniamin said quietly. "I saw."

They had both seen. They had no need to elaborate further, one to the other.

Before he closed his eyes, Pawel had looked up at Aga, holding her hand, trying to smile. She embraced that gaze and would always hold it as a memory of him. She held his stare as long as he allowed, as long as she could, and she saw that his eyes had grown clear, had become a deeper green than they had been in a long time.

A very long time.

*

Aga's mother and father flew in for the funeral. Her Aunt Maja could not join them. She had had a resurgence of her own cancer and was once again undergoing chemotherapy.

There were easily three hundred or so people at the funeral, filled with friends and colleagues. Arthur asked Aga and Beniamin, Katarzyna and Witold to sit with him in the front seats of the Brooklyn Mount Sinai Synagogue where Arthur had arranged for the funeral to be held. Aga sat beside Arthur. He held her hand much of the time.

Three works of music were played during the service, works that Arthur knew held much meaning for Pawel and that through music spoke of different facets of Pawel's life. At the start of the service an organist played Bach's prelude *Ebarme dich mein O Herre Gott.* Have Mercy on Me, God. Aga and Beniamin almost alone understood the reference of the hymn, what it had meant. They both could see within themselves a young man perform the work in a the Lidzbark Warmiński church, but stop half way through the recital, kiss his mother's hand and disappear forever.

Later, the organist played an excerpt from Pawel's 'Warsaw Suite'. Near the end of the funeral service finally a violinist played from the fourth *'Yeshu'a'* movement from Pawel's *A Requiem For Hania.* In these works, Aga heard Pawel's voice, his words, his heart, just as he had explained to her. And in each of these she saw him as boy turning man, as an older man longing for something lost, as an old man having found himself.

In the music Aga saw Pawel. And felt him beside her.

Three people gave generous eulogies as well. A young woman, a student of

484

Pawel's, spoke how Pawel had been more than a teacher, he had instilled in his students the language of self, the possibility of the human through music. The conductor Avram Neverly-Baron then spoke of the many years he had worked with Pawel, of all that had meant to him. He talked to of Pawel's final composition that he had conducted for the first time almost two years earlier.

"Some will know the story of this work. Some will not. It is not mine to tell; that will be for other times, from those whose story it is. But suffice it to say, 'A Requiem For Hania' remains a final tribute to Pawel himself. In it he put all the humanity, all the generosity that was his to give. And that had been given. It will always, always have been my greatest privilege to work with Pawel on this final great work and to be a part of its performance. It is a work that not only speaks to Pawel, that speaks of Pawel, it speaks to each and every one of us, reminding us of who we are, of who we can be," he said.

Finally, Arthur himself gave a short eulogy. He spoke of his friendship over many years. Of their love. He spoke of what the music meant in Pawel's life and to so many who listened. And he spoke of family that had come only near the end of Pawel's life but that had become a blessing that the Composer held in his heart and thoughts, even as he had died. It was not easy for Arthur. The words he spoke touched all there.

It was, however, the words of Pawel's friend, the Rabbi of the synagogue where the service was held, that touched Aga the most. David Stone had taken time to meet Aga, Beniamin and Aga's parents before the funeral, to talk quietly with them, to hear their story. Aga would always remember what he then said at the funeral.

"I have listened to all the beautiful words, and to the beautiful music here today," he said. "I think we were all very lucky to have had Pawel Weisz in our lives. I know he felt he was lucky to have had us in his. After such heartfelt eulogies there is little I feel I can add. I was fortunate enough to spend many hours with Pawel over this last year or two. We had been friends through music. I had always been a fan. But he came to me with troubles, seeking an understanding of things, events that cannot always be understood, explained. Sometimes, there are no answers. There is only life and the living. And our need to go on. Only the questions asked. Sometimes, these matter more than the answers. Several of Pawel's family from Poland are here today and yes, as Arthur said, Pawel was eternally grateful to have found them. His own journey, as theirs, has been painful. And loving. Full of loss. Full too of hope. Full of questions and not always with answers forthcoming. Lives lived. Lives living."

"In the last days of Pawel's own life, I sat with him one afternoon. He had two requests of me. The first was that I consider holding this funeral here, in our lovely synagogue. It was easy to say yes to this. Pawel was not a congregant here. His beliefs he kept largely to himself. His Jewish background came late to him as most of you will know. But I think perhaps he found his God through his humanity and his humanity through music. That is a lot. He was always welcome here. And I welcome him now."

"And there was a second request. Pawel, like so many of us, had been to so many funerals over the years, particularly these last years. Thus, the nature of growing old. That is never easy. He said his other request was that we today say Kaddish for him, the Mourner's Kaddish at his passing. Kaddish in the Jewish liturgy has been said for a thousand years. It is a prayer that praises God. But it also is a prayer to honor the deceased. It reflects on life itself. On tradition. And most of all I think for Pawel it reflects on family. To say Kaddish is an act of kindness. An act of remembrance."

"Pawel's lovely Warsaw family told me how they had visited their mother's grave with Pawel, an act of remembrance. Of thanksgiving for them and for him. Agnieszka told me quietly how touched she was when Pawel left a stone he had picked up at Treblinka days earlier, how he placed this stone on her Grandmother's headstone. I explained to her, as Pawel would have known, that this is part of our tradition. For us, we do not leave flowers, as flowers are temporal. Rather we leave small stones at a grave. Those stones that we place on a headstone or nearby suggest that we are all of the earth, where life is short and long at the same time. The stones say we remember all our lives and beyond. That we were there and that the loss of a loved one will be part of our memories forever. An act too of remembrance. Kaddish."

"Pawel asked me if I could say Kaddish here for him at his funeral. But he

486

asked too that I include in this Kaddish the remembrance of those so deeply a part of him, within, a very great part of him, those who may not have had this prayer of remembrance uttered for them. He asked, as we remember him, that we remember from the Ghetto his mother Lea Elster, his father Michael Elster. He asked me to say Kaddish for his Aunt Zivia Stern and Uncle Marek Stern. For Hania Stern. For her young brother Shaul. He said he had in his heart a girl named Alicja Leder and asked that she be included. There were other names too; some he remembered, some he did not. He said, instead, remember the lost ones of the Ghetto of Warsaw. I was a part of them he whispered to me. I am of that place. That time. Remember them as you will remember me. Finally, he said, say Kaddish for the infant Jakub Elster. For the boy who took his place. For the boy he became. Remember those lost, and those found."

"The Kaddish we will all say now together, it is a mourner's prayer in which we remember them, we honor them, we do not forget. In our lives, our loves, we reach to them as a gift and touch them as mothers and fathers, brothers, as sisters, as family."

All stood then to recite this ancient prayer, as had been Pawel's wish.

And Kaddish was said.

Warsaw

2014

Aga woke early to make the sandwiches and a thermos of coffee before waking Kuba and dressing him. Kuba was her very active and oft smiling two and a half year old, the joy of her life. The exhausting joy of her life. Beniamin and she had both decided on the name Jakub even before his birth, and even before the encouraging suggestion of her parents and Beniamin's. So Jakub he was, and Jakub he would be, although they used the diminutive Kuba.

Aga smiled as she made the sandwiches. She could hear her Grandmother Hannah scolding her even now.

"Kuba? What name is Kuba? He is Jakub," her Grandmother whispered in her ear.

"Yes, Grandma. But we like Kuba. He is Jakub but we like Kuba."

"Well I will not call him Kuba. Ridiculous. Jakub he was born and Jakub he will be."

"Yes, Grandma."

"Jakub is a beautiful name, Agnieszka."

"Yes, Grandma."

"So I will call him Jakub."

"Yes, Grandma."

"What color are his eyes again?"

"They are blue, Grandma. Like mine."

"Hmph. Still, I will call him Jakub."

"Yes Grandma," Aga said to herself, to no one but herself. She had lost the argument with a ghost. She always did. Perhaps she enjoyed losing that particular argument, especially when she heard it through her Grandmother Hannah's scolding voice.

"Hmph," she heard again. And she smiled. She missed her still and smiled at the thought to keep it alive.

Soon there would be the rush to leave. It had been Beniamin's idea for the picnic. Aga had been resistant at first, but it was indeed a lovely summer's day, too lovely to pass up. So she agreed they would pack the car for the short drive up to the Kampinos National Park for their walk and picnic. Beniamin had always wanted to go there and it seemed like the perfect day for it. He had also insisted they stop first at To Lubie to get a couple pieces of cheesecake to go. Him and his cheesecake, she thought. He will get fat. She laughed at that picture that entered her head. Some arguments she would never win, whether with her Grandmother Hannah or with Beniamin.

After breakfast they dressed Kuba and made the mad rush to put things into the car. Aga had to bark at Beniamin twice to quit picking small bits off the pieces of cheesecake with this fingers. He then gave her *that* look that he knew would melt her heart. He always made it so very difficult to yell at him, giggling when she tried, that he made it impossible even to feign annoyance.

Things were good between them both. Aga had been afraid that happiness might be a curse, always ready to disappear. But it did not disappear, not in all this time, so that now she embraced it.

Beniamin found the route to Kampinos easily enough, but they decided they would first stop in Żelazowa Wola, at the small dworek, the so-called manor house annex that was the birthplace of Chopin just at the edge of the Forest. It was early enough to stroll in the house, now a museum; other tourists had not yet arrived, but it was clear they would not be able to stay for long as Kuba wanted to run and play. Still, Aga was able to linger over the lovely baby grand piano and the walnut grandfather clock. She wondered if this was the room that her Grandfather Kazimierz had taken her Grandmother to so very long ago: to listen to a small concert, intending that evening to propose, only to see the woman he loved rush from the room rather than listen to a performance of Chopin's works. And then to throw up outside.

Beniamin saw Aga smiling. When she explained why he grinned.

"I guess Hannah was not always right."

"Oh I don't know; she married him in the end."

"At least you did not throw up when I proposed."

"Are you sure?," Aga said with a smile on her face and walked out of the museum house with Kuba holding her hand. Beniamin followed behind, a somewhat perplexed expression on his face.

They strolled around the gardens and stared at the Chopin Monument. Kuba pointed at it and said it was his Grandfather Witold.

"When he is playing chess," Beniamin laughed. "That is what he looks like."

They explored the grounds for a while longer then continued on their journey. Further on the way, Aga saw a sign posted for Palmiry.

"I think I would like to go there," Aga said.

"What, now?"

"Yes."

"Are you sure?"

"Yes. I think I would"

Beniamin looked at her, then turned to head to the town of Palmiry, with its memorial in the forest nearby.

During the War from 1939 to 1943, the Germans had marched Warsaw Poles—intellectuals, leaders, teachers, Jews and non-Jews alike to Palmiry where they were executed in the forest. The German officers told the prisoners to take their personal belongings with them for reassurance, marched them to pits dug days before in forest glades, forced the prisoners to stand before the pits and machine gunned them in. The Germans then filled in the pits and planted pine trees over them. They tried to keep these executions of more than two thousand people secret but the Polish underground knew what had taken place there and secretly marked the trees below which the graves had been hidden.

The memorial at Palmiry was now a national monument. Beniamin parked in the small museum's parking lot. Aga decided that they should not wander in the museum. Instead they quietly strolled amongst the hundreds of marked and unmarked memorial crosses placed in long lines, some with names of the Polish Warsaw elite murdered in the nearby woods.

Kuba began to run amongst the crosses, playing, laughing. Aga went to grab him but Beniamin stopped her.

"It is all right, Aga. Places like this, sometimes I think the dead yearn for the laughter of children. I think maybe it is right to let him run."

And so he did, this little child whose name signified one from Warsaw who died and who did not die, whose testament was in itself a memorial to the power of a child's laughter, a testament to life that could not be extinguished. Beniamin was likely right, Aga, thought. The ghosts here, the forest itself yearns for such laughter, such life, reaches for it and embraces it. So Kuba ran, laughed, was a child as children can and should be. Finally he reached up to his father, who swept the two year old into his arms and kissed him with unmatched love.

A little later they found a parking place for a walking trail into Kampinos and left the car behind. Beniamin put Kuba into a child backpack carrier. Aga took sandwiches and coffee in her own backpack, as well as the waiting cheesecake and other goodies.

They walked for a good hour deep into the forest. The warm day was a blessing. They were kept cool and shaded by the high forest trees along the path. They found glades of flowers, admired the birds chirping loudly all around. On the far side of one large glade they saw a moose grazing. A little later, walking along a quiet road through forest a herd of deer suddenly burst across their path, jumping with freedom and almost indescribable abandon, disappearing through trees on the other side of the road. Even Kuba said nothing, watching the majestic animals, some of the stags sporting their magnificent antlers, the envy of all who witnessed them.

They walked through another small meadow and found the ground covered with clumps of wild strawberries that all three picked with abandon, enough not only for the waiting cheesecake, but to take home with them later. Aga told Beniamin her Grandmother had once given her a recipe for Warsaw 'Babka cake' so she would put strawberries and cheese in one that she would make the following day. Beniamin looked a bit skeptical; he was rather familiar with Aga's cooking, but Aga insisted this would be the best cake he had ever tasted, handed down for generations in her family.

"Really?," he asked.

"Yes. Really. Better than your mother's pierogi. You will see."

Beniamin gave her the evil eye, then proceeded to pick even more strawberries at the thought of what might appear in his kitchen in the coming day or two.

At the far side of the meadow and forest they put out a blanket Aga had carried in her backpack and sat down to eat their sandwiches, cheesecake, drink their coffee, to talk quietly and listen to the birds, the insects. They felt at ease here. At peace.

"My mother would love it here. And Aunt Maja. She would have loved it."

Aga's Aunt Maja had succumbed to her cancer almost a year to the day after Pawel had passed away. Only after she too was gone did Aga realize how much she missed her Aunt. How much she missed all of them. Only with Kuba's birth did the pain of her own loss, following on from Pawel's, from Hannah's, really ease.

After they ate, Aga stretched out on the blanket beneath the canopy of trees, still feeling the warmth of the day. Kuba ran and played, and Beniamin played with him.

"I might close my eyes for a bit," Aga said. "You will look after him?"

"Of course. Sleep if you like. We will be fine."

Aga watched them for a while, running, laughing, father and son. Their simple happiness brought her joy. She thought about her own life and knew she had always been blessed. Not only because of Beniamin and Kuba, but because of all of her family, her dreams, her journey into the past, now her journey towards the future. She thought now of Hannah and her Aunt, of Pawel, of Hania, of those who came before. What they had gone through. What they had lived. Life had been rich, even if difficult. She thought too of the story, of all that it meant. Ultimately it meant everything and nothing. Everything because it told her who she was, who she perhaps had to be, but also because the story told her of the underlying belief that was the true fabric of her life. Not only the story of herself, of Hannah's self, her mother's and her relatives, it told her of the faith in one another that was instilled deep within her, the hope and the fear, hand in hand. It had taught her about life and all that was human. About need and about survival. Now more than ever she understood what her Grandmother Hannah had wanted to leave to her in the papers and fragments of a life, the gift that she would one day pass on to Kuba. And she knew she could do so, with Beniamin at her side, Beniamin who she loved, deeply loved.

As she lay there, she felt a shadow cross above her. And she heard her Grandmother Hannah speaking to her.

"You know, Agnieszka, aniołkuy, my angel, it has not always been easy. There are many I miss, so badly I miss. But we have choices and we must make our choices. I chose to live. It is not whether I am Hania or Hannah. It is not the tragedy of fate that came my way. It is that life itself is a blessing. Has meaning. It is not my name you should remember. It is what is in my heart. For you. For your Jakub. For my children. For those who came before and who come after."

Aga looked up and saw her Grandmother, looking at her, smiling quietly, nodding her head.

"Memory is life. It cannot be taken away, no matter how hard some try. That is the blessing. Now, Aniołkuy, you are a little tired. Close your eyes if you like. Your Beniamin will look after your lovely Jakub. He will protect the child. They are safe. Close your eyes, just a little, if you like. Sleep."

Aga closed her eyes, and in the warmth of the day, she slept.

*

In the silence that was this forest, she now hears the music that before she thought lost, music that comes not just from the birds surrounding her, from the wind blowing gently through the trees, but the music that talks to her of all that had passed, that will pass still.

She knows where she is. She recognizes the path she is on. She finds her way through. She hears the music play, gently, as if beckoning, and it leads her forward from the darkness behind. Light, ever more present, peeks out from the leaves whispering above, grows brighter and warming.

She feels at ease now. She feels safe where once she felt fear. She is no longer afraid. Perhaps this is because there is no longer need for fear. Perhaps this is because the sun now warms her to her very core. Perhaps this is because she has managed to leave so much behind, while finding before her so much to hold. She holds all tight.

She emerges once again into open ground. High grasses stretch and bend around her. Whispering in this sound, this music that is life. Golden brown and beckoning, the blades of grass brush against her thighs like velvet against a child's face. Gentle, without pain.

She walks on through the meadow with the wind blowing quietly around her. She has left the dark mosses over the great rocks, the ivy climbing the pines, even the primroses behind her now. She is in open ground and here she feels warmth. Here she belongs. Here she has always belonged.

She does not pretend that she does not know all that has happened. Here. Around her. This sacred ground. She does not pretend she has not bent like the grasses now bend. That her tears do not fall.

But neither is she consumed nor destroyed. The forest does not destroy. The forest does not threaten. It has given her nourishment and that nourishment is hope. She is here because she is home. It is what she had looked for and found. It is the music around her.

She comes to the other side of the clearing she has crossed as she has many times before. She turns and looks behind her, looks at the grasses blowing, canvas that they are still, with patterns shifting sometimes in chaos, right and left, shifting because it is their nature to bend in different patterns, in different directions, like life itself. The patterns, she thinks, are everything. Not simply life affirming and life destroying as she once thought. Rather these are the patterns of life itself, creating on this canvas the various movements that determine one direction or another, by chance perhaps, by necessity, by variety. And that is their beauty. She sees them as beautiful. This canvas. This movement, like the movements of a great symphony that speaks words in notes and gives meaning.

Oh yes, she thinks, I am indeed home.

And she turns back, here, at the far side of this clearing, this meadow, she turns back to walk forward, to come once again to the quiet lake she can see below, this lake where once there was a pit, a pit of souls where many fell in silence.

Only now there is not silence.

Now there is the music that is the wind, the music that is the song of birds and insects. Now there is life.

She stands there, meters above this lake, and once again stares to the far shore. And she sees emerge one such as she, one now she knows as Hania, also Hannah. And beyond, further beyond, another emerges, one she also knows as Composer, as Jakub who is Pawel. She knows their names now, just as they know hers. Know she is Agnieszka, no longer of sorrow but of joy.

She begins now to see others emerge from the forest, to meet around this lake in the sunshine and the warmth, to greet one another in joy, in memory, in life. They are the chorus that have come to greet the day, the singers of the song that she has heard when not listening, has imagined when she had forgotten. They are the past and the present. They are faces she knows and has always known. There Zivia and Marek, Michael and Lea. There Katarzyna and Maja, and Kazimierz beside them. Her own Beniamin and her lovely Kuba. Others emerge. Shaul and Alicja she sees. Edzia and Noemi. Fanny Pozner and Mrs. Garfinkel walking with Dr. Korczak. There the lovely Arie, alone but no longer lost. And Simcha Gitler with Miriam and her sister Eva. Josef Schipper, Henryk Pilichowski with his sons. There Helena Kielar, looking up and nodding. Knowing. There Robert Mandeltort, standing with the others, linking his arms with others, held up and holding up. So many others, from Warsaw, from beyond, gathering now to celebrate and remember, gathering here, in this place. Without fear they have all come. Agnieszka sees them all and knows them all. She is of them. She acknowledges them and she remembers. And she is at peace with them, just as they are at peace. They wave to one another, embrace and cry. Tears not of pain but tears of joy. Tears of life itself.

They are quiet then. They are quiet and all turn in the direction of he who they now recognize, he who is Jakub with green eyes, who is Pawel with a broken heart, broken no more. He looks from one to the other, looks at each of them, all of them. They are all one, here, in this place. They all belong. They are all indeed at peace.

Then he is who Jakub Elster, who is Pawel Weisz, he who has finally found where he belongs and why he belongs, who has looked from one to the other and greeted all who stand before him silently, he now looks across the short distance over this water, up at she who is Hania, she who is Hannah, and finally at Agnieszka. He looks at her, smiles gently and nods. He has finally come home.

Then as all watch, as he who is Jakub who is Pawel raises his hands with a small baton in one. He looks around at all, his musicians, his chorus. He holds them, catches their eyes, his hands high in the air. They watch him, waiting for the moment, they watch, wait. He takes one last glance towards Agnieszka, his Agnieszka, even as one who is Hania takes her hand, one who is Hannah takes her hand. The Conductor waits, his hands held in the air.

They rise just a little. And they fall. And all know those hands call out to them: let the music begin, because it is time. And it is…time.

And so the music thus begins.

Warsaw

July, 2006

Hannah Kielar feels so tired. So very tired. She should take herself off to bed, but she is not quite ready. Not yet.

She walks into her kitchen, turns on a light. Puts the kettle on the stove. Waits until the water boils, then pours herself a cup of tea.

Hannah carries her cup into the sitting room. She does not turn on the lights. She prefers to sit in darkness. Time to think and reflect. Lights are a disturbance. She puts on some music, music she has come to enjoy. Music that makes her remember. That touches her.

She sits down in her 'favorite chair' with the cup of tea on her lap. She removes the teabag and stirs the tea around and around, staring at the hot liquid reflecting the moonlight coming through.

She thinks: I forgot to lock the door again. I must do it when I get up, before I go to bed.

She thinks: Tomorrow Katarzyna is coming. She looks forward to that. She enjoys her daughter's visits. And Wednesday, God willing, Agnieszka will visit. Agnieszka, aniołkuy, her angel. She worries about the girl sometimes. She knows Agnieszka is searching, in her way. Hannah understands. She loves the girl very much. She sees in her Granddaughter's face hope perhaps. Love certainly. A gentleness. Hannah smiles. She has always loved this girl.

She stirs the tea, round and round.

She listens to the orchestra on her music player, quietly playing out the city.

She stares towards the window. Again smiles.

"I wonder if she will come tomorrow?" she thinks. "I wonder if she is sleeping tonight up at the orphanage and will come tomorrow to visit?" she asks herself aloud and does not expect an answer.

She sighs. So very tired tonight. Yes.

Hannah hears something behind her, coming from the kitchen.

"Mama," she says, "is that you? Is it time to take Babka's cake from the oven? When it is done I will help put on the strawberries." She smiles, looking forward to the delicious cake. The Babka cake.

"Mama," she says, "we will not tell Papa. We will make it a surprise. He does love that cake. And we will cut an extra piece for Alicja. One piece for you, one for Papa, one for Shaul, one for Aunt Lea and one for Uncle Michael. A small piece for my sweet Jakub. But save a piece for Alicja. She is coming today. Coming from the orphanage. I am waiting for her."

Again she smiles. She looks forward to Alicja coming today. They will take Jakub to Krasinski Park. They will sit and gossip and laugh and enjoy the hot summer sunshine Alicja loves Jakub almost as much as she does. What a lovely day they will have.

Hannah stirs her tea, over and over, the cup of tea sitting on her lap. And she smiles. What a lovely day it will be. A lovely day in the sunshine.

She hears, just beyond, a knock, very quiet, but she hears it. She knows Alicja has arrived. Finally arrived. Hannah smiles. She has so looked forward to her visit.

That will be her, Hania thinks. Stirring the tea sitting on her lap. Alicja. That will be her.

"Time to go, Mama, Papa. We will have Babka's cake later. Alicja is here."

Hannah smiles, again, and closes her eyes.

Time to go.

Acknowledgments

'A Requiem for Hania' is inspired by several true stories, but one in particular that came to light in the spring and summer of 2014 and triggered a long personal journey. This and others told became an obsession that deeply affected and finally inspired this book.

I owe a great deal to many friends in Poland, Israel and the United States for confidences and long chats over meals or beers or vodka and, thanks to a pandemic that came from nowhere and changed the world for two years, to zoom and skype and the world of the internet. Many of these stories found their way into the book; all became obsessions and a journey that is as much about me and my own family as it is about others. 'A Requiem for Hania' has given me the opportunity to learn, to reflect and I think to grow.

Karolina Dryzner from Warsaw became a friend at a workshop in Berlin and it was through her that a door into the past, and into my heart, first opened. It is hard to say how grateful I am for setting me on a certain path that became this book. Mostly thank you for now many years of a friendship and a commonality discovered: we are kindred spirits. That our paths have crossed will be with me all my days.

To Rachela Gelerner as you were, who once disappeared but who discovered that one never disappears, not entirely, and whose self-rediscovery in the autumn days directed me to my own odyssey and my own discoveries into self and self-knowledge, I offer my deep respect and gratitude. Your secrets will remain such, but those self-same secrets helped unleash within me a desperate need to know, and understand, and journey. Thus in the penetrating, clouding glance of Helena Chylińska I was able to bear witness to memory and hear the notes on the piano played, notes of remembrance, and loss, and in that loss a heart found. You too are within me as well and I offer my deepest thanks.

To Pawel, Rafał, the Zasks from Minks and Lvov to Israel and further afield. I recognized your own roads taken, and in yours, mine. And to Louis and Ida, whose journey across a continent and sea, and thus to a new world far away, guiding lights both, as indeed Israel and Rose, Samuel and Yvette, this book is yours too. And yes, to Arnold. I have heard. Learned. Learning still.

My grateful thanks to Victor Gwiazda in Munich, who helped guide me through Warsaw of 1968: the images, the feelings, the anger and the hopes of many.

Thank you also to Professor Max Sternberg of Cambridge University who helped further illustrate a 1947 and 1968 Poland world that was entirely new to me, but so integral to the story I needed to tell.

To Feena Kavanagh, for her design work and patience, to David Blake Knox and Susan Chernus for comments, I'm grateful.

And to Marianne Sweeny who took time to read, reflect, comment and suggest and help immeasurably, you're a star.

'A Requiem for Hania' is the result of many long months of reading, research, finding a voice in the voices of others. Although the research net was wide spread, the following particularly deserve acknowledgement. Many of these resources, testimonies, photographs, music compositions have touched me deeply and have weighed heavily in the telling of this story.

About the Ghetto, Emmanuel Ringleblum's 'Notes from the Warsaw Ghetto' are an essential and unforgettable record, often painful to read, but an historical reference second to none. The fact that these notes survived, hidden, buried and then discovered in the ruins of the leveled Ghetto is nothing short of a miracle. 'The Diary of Mary Berg' too is a remarkable document. Mary Berg survived her Ghetto years in America and later chose to close the door on her past and experience of those dark days. Such is understandable given her experiences. But as a window onto Warsaw and the experiences of the denizens of the Ghetto, it is a document second only perhaps to Anne Frank's work. Dan Kurzman's 'The Bravest Battle' about the days of the Warsaw Ghetto Uprising is a fine bit of research and scholarship. Leon Uris's 'Mila 18' too is a moving read and a true portrait of the Warsaw Ghetto Uprising. While not about the Jewish experience of the Ghetto, Jack Fairweather's 'The Volunteer', a true story of non-Jew Witold Pilecki who spent time in the Auschwitz prisoner's camp to escape and bring out much needed information is a fine resource and a fine read. As for Holocaust literature in general, Elie Weisel's 'Night' and Primo Levi's 'The Periodic Table' are must reads for any reader not only in the study of the Holocaust, but for their quiet humanity both enlightening and troubling. Such a list could go on and on, but if nothing more is read, these cry out to any reader. Although about neither the Ghetto nor the Holocaust war years, Dr. Stephen Grosz's case studies in 'The Examined Life' proved invaluable in thinking about the very human relationship between psychotherapist and patient well beyond the analyst's sofa, which helped me flesh out the Kazimierz Palinsky character that I sought to find as a man who is not just a doctor, he is a humanist.

Photographs played a huge part in the development of story. They gave me faces, expressions, place in ways that words often could not. There are too many resources to give thanks to here, but I would mention with appreciation 'Warsaw Ghetto' edited by Grupińska, Jagielski and Szapiro, the many photos and archived testimonies found through Yad Veshem, which is truly a remarkable resource, the Jewish virtual library, and for stories and testimony, the online resource from sztetl.org.pl (Virtual Sztetl). There were many more pictorial and testimony resources that I read through, more than I can remember. I also mention the incredibly remarkable photographs of Russian born Roman Vishniac, whose book of collected photographs from between the wars were given to me many years ago and stuck in my memory and thoughts for years that followed, coloring my view of a black and white Jewish world in Poland and Eastern Europe.

I also must mention and acknowledge the poetry of Wisława Szymborska, whose wonderful poem 'The End and the Beginning' is quoted within. Her poetry and essays are understated, deeply touching, thoughtful and worth exploration.

Music is integral to the story and structure in 'A Requiem For Hania', and my musical knowledge is marginal at best. My apologies for those who understand much better than I do for the mistakes in intent and language. Although aural references, the work of Steve Reich, of Philip Glass were of great use—and great comfort. But particularly I extend heartfelt thanks to the wonderful contemporary composer Max Richter. Once upon a time I spent many all night hours at my father's bedside in hospital and home as he lay dying. Richter's music was my constant comfort, companion and friend. It was only much later that I learned our paths had crossed in very different contexts. His music was ever-present in my thoughts as I developed and thought about the Pawel Weisz character, about the music he composed, the music he too heard in his thoughts in the dead of night, as he fell in love, as he was lost, and as he found. Without some of Max Richter's compositions in particular, I would never have found Pawel or 'lived with' Hania and Aga.

Finally, I pay homage to John Williams' wonderful theme for 'Schindler's List' performed by Itzhak Perlman, which serves as the final movement of Pawel Weisz's 'Requiem', described in words by a layman. It may seem obvious, but for this novel that piece of music was essential not only in finding the 'song for Robert' and the final movement for Pawel's composition, but in speaking from my own heart to the very real pain I felt when writing this story.

Although not directly about the material in 'A Requiem for Hania', I also wish to acknowledge two very fine works by Professor Phillipe Sands, 'East West Street' and his follow up 'Ratline'. It has been a great pleasure reading Phillipe's work and stories, quietly following his fine work in Human Rights in its many facets since I was fortunate to meet him a very long time ago. Particularly through the above two books I was given much to think about not only in terms of his theme of genocide and crimes against humanity, but about the ethics and morality, or lack thereof, in a particular time in history. Our families have similarities of geography but far more in the lessons he sheds light on, taught to me as well from grandparents who shared a time and place and lessons taught about the meaning of a just life.

'A Requiem for Hania' could not have been written without the emotional and financial assistance of family, and I remain incredibly grateful for that. Particularly in my head and my heart rests memories and the testament of my parents and grandparents. I never thought this book would be one I would need to write. Through the lessons they handed down, I came to realize that Hania's story was in fact my own story, my own journey. It has at times been brutal, at times been eye opening, always necessary. And always moving. To the many, I say thank you. To Annie, Samuel and Jacob in particular, you are always a part of me and I hold you tight, hold you forever and a day.

George Santayana wrote the oft quoted 'Those who cannot remember the past are condemned to repeat it.' I have seen in my lifetime the sorrowful past sometimes denied and repeated. But I can also say it is important, no, imperative, that the past be remembered, taught, held onto for the lessons to try to better ourselves and those who come after. So to the relatives lost, to those not related but so many taken, to the memory, I say finally, I do not forget.

1. There are numerous themes explored in the novel. What do you think some of these are? What are the different ways they are explored?

2. There are three primary characters in the novel: Hania, Pawel, Agnieszka. Each of these characters has her or his own journey. Yet how are these journeys the same? Different? Look at these in both such lights and discuss.

3. Music is a critical part of the book. The author speaks of repetition, variation, musical notation, exploration. Why else is music important in the story, and indeed of the story? How has the author used to music to structure the book? What are the many reasons he might have done so?

4. Identity and what that means is central to the movement of story and character. Names constantly shift. Characters constantly evolve. Hannah says in her revelation letter to Agnieska that Hania disappeared. In what ways did she disappear, or did she? Discuss this in relation to theme, journey and the critical reasoning for such. 'The German' and 'The German's Wife' too have no identity until deep into the book, yet their shadow runs throughout. This is intentional. What are various explanations for why this was done? Discuss too, as with Hania: what does it mean to disappear?

5. In discussing the journey of his characters, the author delineates three different movements defined in the structure of the material. But he has also said there is a fourth journey in the story as important as that of the primary characters. At other times he has said in fact there is only one journey in the book. What does he mean?

6. In the 'Prelude' section of the book, Aga performs in dual productions of *Elektra* and of *Iphigenia*, stories translated for the theatre by her then lover Stefan. Greek tragedy is alluded to often in the novel. In what ways has the author utilized ideas from Greek drama—not just tragedy, but also comedy? Why has he done so? In this same context, Aga was purposely written as an actor, done so not only because of the genesis of the story on which the novel was based, but for specific reasons. What do you think those reasons are? In what ways is Aga an actress? What about Hania, and indeed Jacob? How is the art of acting important in these characters as well, both in what they do, and who they are?

7. Images of the woods are also used throughout the novel. What are the author's intentions in doing so? How are the woods as metaphor used? What is at the heart of this particular metaphor?

8. A very key relationship in the novel is the friendship between Hania and Alicja. The author has said that in truth theirs is not only a love story, in one another they find themselves. Discuss this. Discuss it in relation to the book's ending.

9. When Aga meets Pawel for the first time, he refuses to listen to her story, turns away then departs. The author has suggested this has religious significance, and that indeed Judeo-Christian imagery runs throughout the book and underlies much of story. Where else is the case? What do you think the author means by this? How does this relate to shifting identities throughout the novel?

10. Another undercurrent that runs throughout the book in the conflict between artifice and the real, like between the modern and traditional romantic. The nature of Truth, indeed of history and storytelling, is a theme in the book the writer is interested in: in psychology, music, drama, but also in architecture. This Hegelian conflict has Freudian undertone as well for the author. How is this reflected in story? Why? Again, how is it tied into theme?

11. What are the central dramatic points in the story? What are they in each movement? How is one reflected by another?

12. Each movement not only has a Latinate to describe it, it has a thematic description. Why was this important to the writer? To Pawel? How do the Latinates and movement key words play off one another? Describe one another? Particularly look at the final Coda movement, and discuss.

13. Perhaps one of the most famous quotes from Holocaust survivor, writer and commentator Elie Wiesel in his book *Night*: "Never shall I forget that night, the first night in camp, which has turned my life into one long night, seven times cursed and seven times sealed. . . . Never shall I forget those flames which consumed my faith forever. Never shall I forget that nocturnal silence which deprived me, for all eternity, of the desire to live." Central to Wiesel's writings, indeed to the Jewish understanding and teaching of the Holocaust, is the notion of Bearing Witness. Bearing witness, and indeed witnesses, are an essential aspect of *A Requiem For Hania*. Discuss what this means generally in the book, but also in relation to the narrative voices of each movement. Who and what are the witnesses here? Why are they more important in this story beyond just literary devices? Discuss too in recent history why bearing witness has become more important than ever, and where you might proffer a cri de coeur that each of us still needs to bear witness...

14. Read the very opening sequence of the 'Prelude' section in italics aloud. As in question 7 above, this short opening section is set in woods. Why? What is in fact going on in this short opening sequence? Why is it here? Some readers have commented that these are dream sequences; however

the author insists they are not. But if not, what are they? The section echoes again just before the final few pages of the novel, but with obvious significant differences. Discuss those differences. Whose point of view do you think proffers these two opening/closing sequences? Why are they set where they are? Refer too to the question 13 just above. How are these pages about bearing witness? If they do, who is bearing witness here? Read these last italicized pages aloud as well. What are the pages meant to evoke? How are you meant to feel after reading such? The opening sequence? The closing sequence? What are the pictures in your head? .... What is the music you hear? Can you hear it? Can you hear the wind as well? What do you feel reading these pages at the opening? At the closing? What do you feel?

CPSIA information can be obtained
at www.ICGtesting.com
Printed in the USA
JSHW050824250222
23323JS00003B/9